THE PROPHET OF THE
DRAGON

MARK DOUGLAS, JR.

Kingdom of the Four Winds

Winterhall

Graywinds

Castle Rominas

Whitewinds

Fortress of the Moon

Mt. Shade

Shade Town

Church of Lucidus

Lorenta

Castle Wyndsor

Castle Lombard

Lake Blackwater

Wyndsor

Maelstrom Island

Forest of Ardenia

Highwinds

Parliament

Derbent

N

The Forgotten Forest

Isle of the Winds

W   E

Port Coalcliff

Voss Town

S

The Orphanage

Summerhall

PROLOGUE

Samuel Ryker stomped to attention beside the Duke's chamber doors, his sharpened longspear gleaming in the torchlight. "How is our lord this evening?" he asked, and he blinked the weariness from his eyes.

"Hmm? Oh, same as this morning," said Morley, the bags beneath his eyes dark from a lack of sleep. "Same as last night. Same as a fortnight ago. Bloody hell, he's like to be the same 'til he takes his last breath—unwell."

Samuel sighed.

"What did they serve in the kitchens?" Morley sheathed his longsword.

Samuel twisted his lips in a mocking half-smile. "Same as last night."

Morley chuckled. "Well, that's where you'll find me. Belike that foul pig-feed is what I'll eat 'til I take *my* last breath." He strode down the hall and descended the winding tower steps. Morley's clinking armor grew fainter and fainter. The oaken door at the foot of the steps shut with a *click*.

Samuel was alone to guard the Duke.

He stood beside the door, occasionally shifting his weight from foot to foot. He listened as Duke Lombard drew sucking, heaving breaths from within his sleeping quarters. Curtains fluttered as wind wafted into open windows. Across from Samuel, a large map painting of the Four Winds hung in an elegant, gilded frame with silver scrollwork. Torches sat in their iron sconces the length of the hall and flickered red and orange. They filled the corridor with a smoky haze and the smell of burning pitch. Samuel lost himself in the map, and in the sounds, but mostly in the Duke's breathing.

The torchlights dwindled, and the hours passed.

Then Samuel heard the faint *clink* and *clank* of steel-plate boots on stone.

Darrion, the Captain of the Guard? He knew his stride well; long and smooth, yet hard, like the heavy sauntering of a king's elephant. But these footsteps were different. *The hour's too early,* he reminded himself. *And my shift is not finished.*

When the figure appeared at the top of the steps, Samuel saw he was no guard, nor any servant. Golden steel covered the man from head to foot. On his hip, he wore a shortsword sheathed in plain, black casing. Across his back, a round-shield and crossbow. *A knight of the Kingsguard,* Samuel knew at once, though his weapons were unusual for a knight. *At this hour?*

The knight marched toward Samuel and to the Duke's chamber doors. He gave a curt nod, then reached for the handle. Samuel swung his longspear sideways to block the way.

"Sir, no farther." Samuel's voice was hard with intent. "Duke Lombard is resting. He seeks no audience at this hour."

The knight lifted his visor. "I'm here on King's business." He had a scar across his right brow—a jagged white line that cut from eyebrow to cheek.

"I manage the Duke's affairs. He seeks no audience."

"Is Duke Lombard aware that Wyndsor was attacked?" The knight focused on the doors.

"He is," Samuel said. "A messenger bird was sent."

The knight cleared his throat. "I must see the Duke." His voice was impatient. "It regards a matter of utmost importance."

"He seeks no audience. The Duke is not to be disturbed."

"Step aside, *guard.*" The knight moved a hand to his shortsword and thumbed an empty notch along its hilt where a gem had once been. "Or I shall take that spear and—"

"—Samuel," a frail and hoarse command came from within Duke Lombard's chambers. "Let the knight pass. I will take his audience."

Samuel Ryker jerked his longspear upright and slapped its butt against the stones at his feet. He opened the door, then stepped aside. A grin stretched across the knight's face as he strode past and into the room. Samuel turned to follow.

"Samuel," Duke Lombard was abed with feather pillows fluffed behind his back so he could sit up, "wait without. If you will."

"M'lord?" said Samuel. "I'd rather stay." He locked eyes with the knight.

Duke Lombard waved a hand in the air. "He's a knight of the Kingsguard. Fear not for my safety."

"Y-yes, m'lord." Before taking his leave, Samuel scanned the room. A chill breeze stirred the drapes framing the balcony window. The fireplace crackled with the embers of a dying flame. Shadows stirred in the corners, but he knew there was no other entrance but the one he guarded.

"Shut the door behind you."

"Yes, m'lord."

The chamber doors clicked shut. Samuel took his place, resumed his guard.

Muffled words slipped through the cracks of the door, too unclear, too quiet to discern. Then, just after he had once more lost himself in the map of the Four Winds, he heard the cry.

He turned toward the door. "What in the Four Hells was that?"

Another desperate shout sounded, and Samuel's heart sank. It was the cry of Duke Lombard.

He burst into the room …

… and saw Duke Lombard lying lifeless atop his bed, unblinking. The golden knight held a jewel-encrusted dagger in his hands and stared at the Duke.

"You!" Samuel shouted. "What have you done?!"

The knight looked up at Samuel. He had removed his helm, giving Samuel full sight of the white scar.

"You murdering thief!" He gripped his longspear in both hands and charged toward the knight.

But the knight dashed for the balcony.

Samuel threw his spear at the fleeing knight's backside. It spiraled through the air, then soared over the knight's head as he jumped from the balcony. Samuel rushed onto the balcony to see him hit the cobblestones one hundred feet below.

He leaned out over the railing. "Impossible!"

The knight was gone.

A commotion stirred from behind. Samuel turned to see Darrion, the Captain of the Guard, along with six others sprinting into the room with swords drawn.

"Check on the Duke," Darrion commanded, and two men

approached the bed. The captain joined Samuel on the balcony. "We found Morley dead in the kitchens. We rushed here at once."

"You are too late." Samuel's stomach was tight as chains. "He was dressed as one of our own, Darrion. A knight of the Kingsguard. But I think he is the windstriker the kingdom searches for, the one responsible for the attack on Wyndsor."

"The rogue agent, Gabriel Lost?" asked Darrion.

Samuel nodded.

"How do you know?"

"The scar, Darrion. He had a scar."

"Where'd he go?" the captain pressed. "He cannot have gotten far."

"He jumped." Samuel gripped the balcony railing, squeezing so tight his knuckles whitened.

"To his death?"

Samuel motioned to the empty courtyard.

"Impossible." Darrion looked over the railing and squinted. "By the gods." The two men who checked on the Duke came out to the balcony.

"Well?"

They shook their heads.

Darrion sighed. "Wake the castle," he ordered. "Send word to king and parliament." He turned to Samuel and removed a pair of iron shackles from his waist. "And arrest this liar."

1

HIGHWINDS HOSTAGE CRISIS

~One week earlier~

Gabriel Lost pulled himself atop the castle wall after the guard passed. He was dutiful, the guard, predictable. He took his fifty-six steps along each rampart, stopped at each corner and planted his halberd, checked in all directions, and then marched on.

Gabriel counted the guard's steps as he slipped out of the shadows. He crossed the rampart toward the other side, and eased over the edge of the wall. He held on by his fingertips.

Fifty-four. Fifty-five.

Now. Gabriel dropped and hit the grass just as the guard thumped his halberd against the stone walkway. It would have been a soft landing anyway, but a windstriker survives on paranoia.

The yard was large, with a dead oak tree towering over it, and the castle as big as a mountain of bricks and flags. It was a typical Highwinds castle built in the ashlar style. Silver-grey stones were worked until square, and its towers machicolated for dropping objects on attackers. Battlements stood indomitable at each of its four corners. A second floor walkway encircled the keep.

Gabriel watched the guard continue his patrol from the wall's shadows.

He ran his hands carefully over his equipment and clothing, checking for the hundredth time that night to make sure he had everything he needed to carry out his mission. A dark grey cloak with a hood, grey gloves, black trousers and boots. A slim dagger, firmly secured to his ankle beneath the trousers with two leather straps. Hanging behind his shoulder was a miniature crossbow, and across his other shoulder, a round-shield. A sheathed shortsword hung from a belt fastened around his waist. Red gemstones were attached to each weapon, so if he wished, he could even risk a fight with a score of knights in their cowardly armor or an assassin with his poisonous darts. The small calfskin bag hanging from his belt contained the crossbow's bolt, thin wire, flint, and a folded hook for scaling walls.

That was all. No more time for delay.

The guard had completed his patrol of the eastern wall and disappeared around the bend of the next rampart.

Gabriel dashed for the castle, all the while keeping as close as possible to the wall's grey stones and its shadows. He ran fast, until he closed in on the left side of the castle. Its crenellated wall flashed before him and rose up into darkness. He fingered the grooves between each stone. The shade of a smile appeared on his lips as he realized the grooves were deep enough to grip.

He climbed to the second floor walkway.

Damn. Another guard stood sentry before an open window. Gabriel pressed himself against the wall and peered around the corner. The guard fiddled with a pipe in one hand and a bottle of shabu in the other. Gabriel knelt and drew his crossbow. He took the dark bolt from his bag, loosened the shortsword in its scabbard, and stole another glance.

The guard was gone. But Gabriel caught sight of his boots dragging—kicking—inside the window.

Strange. Gabriel took a steady breath, swallowed. Whoever removed that guard had talent. Parliament would not send two windstrikers, would they?

He loaded the bolt into the crossbow and locked the taut twine into the catch. Then he rushed to the window and peeked inside.

A long hall stretched before him, flanked on both sides with hollow knights of gilded armor inside niches recessed into the walls. Torches sputtered in iron sconces between the statues, all the way toward a set of doors thirty paces away. The doors were cracked open, and shadows stirred from within.

But there was no guard, and no one else for that matter.

He inhaled another breath to calm his nerves, then he slid inside the window, into the hall.

"Show them who they're dealing with. Torture the hostages and make them talk!"

Whoever had spoken was on the other side of those cracked doors. Gabriel crept closer. He had a perfect view of the Great Hall within.

Captain Lukas Steele, a blond giant of a man who wore a fine nimble coat of bronze chainmail over layers of grey wool and black leather, paced the Great Hall floor. He had a black greatsword strapped to his back, the hilt rising above his head. Gabriel did not know the man, but he knew his reputation. The captain, at the behest of the Knight's Order, was known to torture men into service.

As Steele paced in front of the doors, Gabriel noticed the hostages behind him. Men, women, children—old and young—herded into a dark corner, all on their knees with rope binding their hands.

"And why haven't you found Vincent?" the captain demanded.

"We've searched all the hostages, sir," another said, "of those alive and dead, and none be him."

"Well, keep searching."

Footsteps pounded from within the Great Hall. They grew louder as they approached the doors Gabriel eavesdropped behind.

Gabriel swore beneath his breath and looked for somewhere to hide. No other doors, just the long hall and the hollow knights in their recesses. But there! To the right and above the doors, a stone air duct led into the Great Hall. He hurried to it. The doors opened, but Gabriel climbed inside just as fifteen knights darted through the corridor.

Wooden rafters spanned the distance across the Hall, twenty feet high. Gabriel brushed away spiderwebs and crawled atop a dust-covered beam. He scooted across on his belly. Below, two men-at-arms pulled a hostage to her feet. She ran trembling fingers through her straw-colored hair.

"No, please," she pleaded. "I know nothin'. Please, I'll do anything you ask."

One of the men slapped her, and she fell to her knees. He drew a dagger and put it to her neck. "Where's the cult leader, Vincent?" he asked. "Where's the Duke and his family?"

"I don't know. Please! I don't know!"

Draw blood, and I kill you. Gabriel neared the area where the hostages were being kept. He held the crossbow in his hand, the bolt still loaded. He took aim and recalled the description of Alivia: long dark hair, slender figure, and eye color—purple.

A most unusual touch.

There she was. Alivia kept her eyes downcast, but even though Gabriel could not see her eye color, he knew it was her. She was the only one calm, more of an observer than a victim. And she was in the corner amongst the darkest shadows.

Perfect.

"This is your last chance. Say their whereabouts or say your peace!"

"I–I don't know!" the woman cried. Blood began to trickle down her neck. She screamed.

Damn you! Gabriel got to his feet, kept his balance on the rafter while he stepped toward the wall, aimed, and fired. He dropped behind the hostages as the bolt released. It cut through the air, becoming invisible in its flight, and cast only a shadow across the Great Hall's floor. The bolt struck the man's neck and sent a spray of blood onto the woman's face and hair. She screamed louder than before, as did the hostages, masking Gabriel's landing as he hit the ground.

He darted for Alivia behind the hostages' shadows.

"Fredrick!" the other man-at-arms shouted. "Fredrick?!" He knelt and inspected his comrade, who sputtered blood as he suffocated in it.

"What's going on?" Captain Steele demanded.

Gabriel crouched behind Alivia. "Don't be alarmed," he whispered. "Parliament sent me."

"It's Fredrick, sir! He's got a hole in his neck! He's got a feckin' hole in his neck, sir!"

Alivia whispered: "Tis about time parliament sent one of you in."

"Has someone already made contact with you? I believe another windstriker may have been sent."

Alivia glanced over her shoulder at Gabriel. "No," she said.

The man-at-arms was still yelling. "Who did this? What did this?!" He looked at the woman, who racked with sobs. "You! You did this, didn't ya? You did this, witch!"

"Where is the Lombard family?" Gabriel asked.

"They are with the leader of Dräkenkamp, Vincent Black," she said. "He somehow knows the castle. He has hidden inside its walls."

The man-at-arms drew his longsword. The woman shrieked, and the hostages cowered back.

"He is going to kill her," Alivia said.

Gabriel reloaded the bloody bolt—which had reappeared in the crossbow's barrel when he thumbed the gun's gemstone—and took aim over Alivia's shoulder. "Don't move."

The man raised his longsword overhead, the woman raised her hands in defense. Gabriel squeezed pressure on the trigger …

… but Captain Steele caught the soldier by the wrist. "Don't be a fool, Hackott! Parliament has presently sent us a windstriker." He thrust the man's blade aside. "Go find Sir Ellard and tell him we have more problems."

Hackott hesitated, shot a glance toward Fredrick's corpse.

"Go!"

"Y-yes, sir." Hackott dashed for the doors, leaving the captain alone to guard the hostages.

Gabriel eased the crossbow away from Alivia's shoulder. Despite the situation, he could not kill Lukas Steele—he was a knight of the Church, revered throughout the kingdom. He should not have even killed Fredrick, he knew.

"What happened here?" he asked Alivia. "I expected the religious cult Dräkenkamp to be in charge. Instead I find the Church's knights wreaking havoc."

"Shortly after the cult's takeover," she whispered, "the Knight's Order arrived, in greater numbers. They seized control from Dräkenkamp and sent Vincent running with the family."

"How do I get inside the walls?"

Alivia shrugged. "I have spied on the Lombard family for six months and never once seen a hidden door. I overhead Vincent mention it. I do not understand how he found it."

Gabriel rubbed his chin.

"Knights did pound wooden mallets against the floors earlier. Like they were searching for a loose tile. They searched the floors here in the Great Hall and in the servants quarters."

Gabriel grunted and glanced at a side door.

Captain Steele began pacing again, striding toward the hostages, away from them, toward the hostages, away from them.

"When Steele turns around I am exiting through the servant's entrance," Gabriel said. He unsheathed a dagger from a belt on his ankle, and pressed the blade into Alivia's hands. "Thank you for the information. Good luck."

"What? Wait."

He was gone. Slipped into the servant's quarters and down another hallway. This one dark and dusty, but similar to the one with the hollow suits of armor. Three sets of gilded knight armor flanked both sides in niches recessed into the walls. One was not as dusty as the others, Gabriel noticed. He moved closer to it and ran a hand lightly across the plate and mail.

A rumbling overhead.

Hard rain.

Great.

But he had other problems. A pair of footsteps pounded from the Great Hall, armor clinking as they came closer. Gabriel cursed. With quiet footfalls, he slid behind the suit of armor he was inspecting.

The servant's door opened.

Captain Steele and an older knight walked out.

Gabriel felt something tingle on the back of his neck. He ignored the sensation and focused on shallow breathing.

"Sir Ellard," Captain Steele said. "You and your unit stay here and guard the hostages. Question them again and report to me if any so much as speak Vincent's name."

"Aye, sir."

His neck started to itch. *It's not my imagination.* Something was crawling up his neck and into his hair. Whatever it was, it was big—bigger than a spider. The tingling prickles confirmed his fear—eight heavy legs: a white-tail scorpion. A killer of its own fame. One sting would mean death in minutes. Gabriel reached up to brush the scorpion from his hair, but froze.

Captain Steele stopped marching down the dark corridor. He cocked his head to look at the hollow knight Gabriel was hiding behind. "Strange," he said aloud.

Gabriel didn't move. If he brushed the scorpion away now, the captain would hear and know he was there.

Steele stepped closer. He looked the suit of armor up and down, ran a finger across its breastplate. He rubbed the dust between his fingers.

Gabriel eased his hand to his face, hoping the scorpion would crawl for it. The scorpion crawled across his hand, then into his palm. He was right. It was a white-tail scorpion, its white tail stark against its black body. He flung it to the ground, and it crawled on his boot.

"Captain Steele, sir!" A voice called from the direction of the Great Hall. "Our guards on patrol. It appears they've disappeared, sir."

Steele snorted. "May Lucidus have mercy upon their souls." He brushed the dust from his fingers and marched down the hall. The echo of his footsteps dimmed with each step.

Gabriel shook his boot, then squashed the scorpion. *Damnable, vile scorpions.* The stone beneath the crunched arachnid depressed into the floor. The recess behind the gilded knight rumbled—sand and dust falling from cracks of rock and plaster—and the stone wall behind him eased into the floor.

The fates shine on me. Gabriel grinned. He inspected the hall to make certain the rumbling was not overheard by any knights of the Order. Within the Great Hall, figures moved back and forth and voices rose and fell, more knights and men-at-arms questioning the hostages. No one heard. The downpour rumbled above it all.

He examined the passageway. Stone steps spiraled up into darkness within a narrow stairwell.

The windstriker entered.

2
DRÄKENKAMP

Light seeped from the stairwell's exit. Gabriel took several minutes to climb to the top. He groped the rough and uneven stone walls to guide his way and listened to an argument taking place in the distance ahead.

"Why have the two of you come?" The voice was forceful. "I hope it's to tell me you have found them."

"It is hopeless," a second voice responded nervously. "We've found nothing that fits your description. We've searched the castle inside and out, and there's nothing here. Anywhere."

"Stay the course," the first voice demanded. "Keep searching!"

"No, Vincent," a third said, more confident than his counterpart. "The Knight's Order is slaughtering us! We'll not find them."

"Oh," Vincent said.

A green flickering spark shifted shadows throughout the stairwell.

"Do you still want to give up?" Silence. "I thought so. Now end your complaints and search!" The green light vanished.

Gabriel reached the stairwell's exit and moved into the shadows behind a similar statue from the long hall—a hollow knight of gilded armor.

Lightning flashed. It illuminated the room through a circular ceiling window of stained glass. A thousand different colors splashed across the floor. Gabriel knew the mosaic well: four knights, each representing a realm of the Four Winds, slaying a dying dragon.

The Dragon Wars.

But this stained glass mosaic was different, the story reversed. The ruby dragon had slain the four knights—two under black talons, one struck with the beast's mighty tail, and the last gnawed in the creature's razor-sharp jaws.

Thunder shook the castle's walls.

Gabriel's eyes readjusted to the low light. He found himself in a candlelit cathedral. Empty wooden pews filled the space, separated by a thread-bare carpet running down the center. The pews were directed toward seven steps climbing to a central dais, the room's focal point. Atop the dais was a plain wooden altar, with golden cups, plates, and water-filled basins. The place smelled of incense, wine, and the yellow beeswax candles burning throughout gave off the summer scent of honey. An arched window behind the altar reflected the cathedral like a mirror.

"Curse the gods." Vincent spat. "Where has the Duke hidden them?"

"What if the Duke has led us into a trap?" another voice asked. "Hell, Vincent, are the damned things even real?"

"Do you doubt me, Stone? Do you doubt my power?"

"Vincent, please," Stone shuffled across the nave, "it's just your vision—did you foresee the Order's strength? I fear we've no escape if we do not flee now!"

"All right," he said. "Retrieve the boy."

"And the others?"

"Leave them," Vincent said. "My visions tell me the Knight's Order will not harm them. But worry not, Stone. It is all going as I foresaw."

"You—you've had another vision? Another prophecy?"

"Yes. Now go and retrieve the boy."

"Aye." Stone's footsteps pounded. He walked past Gabriel's view. The man, aged with grey streaks in his dark hair and beard, appeared sturdy and strong, with arms chiseled like a hammer. A heavy door scraped against the stone floor off to the side, then clanked shut.

Vincent was alone.

The cult leader walked toward the altar. His gait sounded strange. *Clink* and scrape, *clink* and scrape, *clink* and scrape. The thud and lug of his stride sounded like a chain striking the stone floor, and then dragging across the rough surface. Gabriel studied him for injuries.

"He's a cripple," Gabriel whispered in astonishment.

Few with such maladies survived in the Kingdom of the Four Winds. Unholy in the Church of Lucidus, the gods would not allow such abominations to exist. The Church excommunicated any family that harbored a child with deformity. Yet Vincent was a person of authority within the cult of Dräkenkamp.

Vincent knelt and placed his elbows on the surface of the altar. He clasped his hands together and chanted a prayer in low whispers.

Gabriel eased to the shadow's edge for a better glimpse. Vincent's left hand had an unusual mark—a tattoo?—no, a scar. The disfigurement made a shape of some kind: a fire-breathing dragon, wings outstretched?

His slender black armor looked almost like obsidian. *Dragonglass?* It glimmered as though alive. It drank in the candlelight. On Vincent's feet were sharp-tipped boots, and at his waist, a slim rapier. Yet the dark, mournful dragonglass armor starkly contrasted against Vincent's long, blond hair, which fell loosely onto his narrow shoulders.

The windstriker moved between the flanked pews. With his crossbow at the ready, he took aim at Vincent's back. "Don't move, Vincent," he said. "I have a bowgun aimed at your heart."

Vincent continued praying.

"Stand. Slowly. And turn toward me."

Vincent lifted his head toward the reflection in the arched window. "You don strange attire for a knight of the Order," he said. "Pray tell, who sent you to this evening's gathering?"

"Are you deaf as well as crippled? Arise, heretic, and face me slowly, hands in sight."

Vincent hobbled to his feet. He turned around, hands at eye level with palms outwardly open. He wore a silver necklace with a dark red stone dangling from its chain.

"Please don't shoot," Vincent said. "I ... I want to help."

Gabriel repositioned the crossbow in his hand. He rolled his fingers around its tiller and tightened his touch on the trigger.

Vincent limped forward a step. "I'm here for the Lombard family," he went on. "The Duke is dying. I'd be surprised if he's got a week left."

"Remove your sword and place it on the ground," Gabriel instructed, "then slide it over."

After a pause, Vincent did as commanded. "You are making a grave mistake." He laid the sword at his feet, but he hesitated to slide the rapier ... something caught his eye.

The red gemstone attached to Gabriel's crossbow began to dimly glow. Gabriel raised an eyebrow. *What in the Four Hells?!*

"Those gems." Vincent narrowed his eyes. "Most peculiar. You're no knight."

"Slide the sword!"

"Ah, let me guess. A windstriker? You have the stink of one of parliament's attack dogs."

Gabriel advanced slowly toward Vincent, keeping his aim steady.

A *click* sounded from behind. Gabriel stopped his approach, turned toward the noise. Stone entered the cathedral carrying an unconscious boy over his shoulder.

Vincent seized his rapier and dashed toward Gabriel with alarming agility. The windstriker redirected his focus to the charging threat. He leaped rearward, narrowly evading a downward slash, and fired the crossbow in mid-air. The invisible bolt hurtled forward like a deathly wraith.

"Vincent!" Stone yelled.

The bolt drew near Vincent's throat …

… but passed *through* him like wind stirring leaves of a tree.

Gabriel landed, unsure of what he had just witnessed. He quickly set the crossbow to his back and unsheathed the shortsword from his waist. Finely honed steel rasped against the blade's casing as he prepared for close-quarters combat. "What foul trickery is going on here? You should be dead!"

"I've died once before, Windstriker." Vincent addressed Stone, "Take the boy and go to the Fortress of the Moon."

Stone did as commanded. He turned to leave.

"You! Halt!" Gabriel shifted his stance toward Stone and the boy. The heavy door clanked shut.

"Pay them no heed, Windstriker." Vincent touched fingers to his chest, just above the dangling stone, and traced them to his neck. He glanced up to the stained glass ceiling window and shouted: "Des'tok, to me!"

Glass shattered into a thousand pieces as a blur of red fell from the ceiling into the cathedral. The colorful mosaic became a shower of swords, unaffecting Vincent, but sending Gabriel to the floor with arms overhead. The floor shook hard and pews splintered. Gabriel fell onto his back. His shortsword bounced, clanged, then landed in front of the hidden passage, at the base of the gilded knight.

15

Gabriel froze. A red dragon raised its long neck from the destroyed pews.

The dragon's jade-colored eyes were slit like a cat's and its triangular maw filled with blades of ivory. Its deep bloodred scales glowed and sparkled in the ambiance of the candlelit cathedral. Extending down its spine, from the base of its neck to the tip of its tail, were sharp black spikes.

"My apologies, Windstriker." Vincent retreated from the dragon's range. "I'm afraid our game has come to an end. But please, continue enjoying the night's festivities."

Des'tok arose to the summit of its height and unfolded its crimson, leathery wings. The dragon raised its neck upward toward the hole where the stained glass ceiling window had been—the storm outside now raining down into the circular tower—and shrieked a deafening roar.

Gabriel cursed and scrambled back. He slipped on a shard of glass and cut his hand.

The beast lunged.

Des'tok's mighty tail spun round. It crashed into the remaining pews and whipped over to the downed windstriker. Gabriel sprang to his feet, narrowly avoiding the heavy blow, and rolled toward his sword. The tail struck the rough stone with the impact of a meteor.

Gabriel reached his sword, grabbed its hilt, and stood to face the ferocious beast. But the dragon slashed at the windstriker with its razor-sharp talons. Gabriel ducked, yet the beast seemed to anticipate his movement. As the dragon struck with its talons, it swung its tail low to the ground, hitting Gabriel square in the chest. The windstriker's breath left him in a *whoosh*, and he was thrown off his feet. The tip of Des'tok's tail smashed into the hollow knight, shattering it, sending bits of armor clanging against the stone.

The altar broke Gabriel's fall. He hit the dais with a fierce intensity that slung him and the platform into disarray. Gabriel slumped to the floor, his back throbbing. As the windstriker tried to stand, the dragon's tail hit his chest again and hurtled him and the altar into the arched window. The glass pane smashed into shards as the altar, then Gabriel, flew into the raging storm.

Gabriel grasped and clawed for something—anything—to stop his slippery descent from the cathedral tower. He slid past the arched opening, felt the weightlessness of flight take hold, and made an urgent last-effort grab for safety. He seized a protruding ledge three feet below the shattered window in his right hand and swung into the rigid tower wall. He grunted in pain as the force of the impact pulled his arm like a team of driving horses.

A hundred feet below, the altar struck the ground of the stone courtyard. It exploded into a hundred pieces.

Chill rain and wind hammered Gabriel. His fingers holding the ledge throbbed. Above, he could hear the *clink* and scrape of Vincent's approach. The cult leader reached the opening and stood over the dangling windstriker. The bloodred dragon followed close behind as a sentinel. It sat. Breath steamed through its nostrils like smoke.

Vincent squinted at Gabriel. Then his eyes suddenly glossed over and he began chanting in strange whispers. "The horses of war," he mumbled.

Gabriel grunted and struggled to get a better grip.

Vincent turned toward Des'tok. He placed a hand on a dark spike and lifted himself onto the small hollow at the base of the dragon's neck. "If you want to save the boy," Vincent ran a hand over the dragon's scales, "give chase."

Then the beast unfurled its leathery wings and flapped. Each beat of its wings like a crack of thunder. Along the ground, broken glass tumbled back into the cathedral tower from the airstream's force. Gabriel felt as though he had grown heavier from the wind's downward push. Des'tok leaped through the arched window and took to the air. It beat its wings three times before soaring into a glide, and carried the cult leader away into the morning's gloom.

Gabriel reached with his left hand and slowly pulled himself up. He stood on the ledge and clutched his side, the pain from the dragon's attacks almost unbearable. He clenched his fist, blood streaming through his fingers. The dragon and Vincent grew smaller in the distance as the byrd continued to flap its enormous wings.

The Fortress of the Moon. Gabriel turned and marched away. As he descended the spiraling steps within the hidden passage, blood dripped from his wounds. He may have broken a rib, his left hand might be useless, but one thing was for certain.

He must save the child.

17

3

FORTRESS OF THE MOON

Alivia Corwyn was cutting the hostages' ropes when Gabriel stumbled into the Great Hall, bruised and bloody. *He is hurt*, she realized. He was bent and pale and cradled his chest with a bloody left hand. "Did you save the family?" she asked.

Gabriel grimaced and bit his lip. "What happened to the Knight's Order?"

"Twas unbelievable." She helped a mother and child to their feet and asked if they were okay. Then she motioned toward one of the Great Hall's towering windows. "A red dragon flew west with a rider on its back. Captain Steele and his knights fled in pursuit."

"They took the Duke's son."

Alivia's mouth fell open. "Little Patrick—"

"Tell me, how long have you been a parliament spy?"

Alivia squinted. She couldn't reveal that kind of information.

"Have you have been informed about Dräkenkamp and their residence?"

Alivia nodded.

"Then come with me." Gabriel started for the courtyard. Once outside he went straight for the stables. "Who drives the Duke's coach?" he asked as they walked.

"A man named Wilmont. Why?"

"I'm going to borrow it. Find Wilmont. Tell him to ready the Duke's horse and carriage."

"You mean to give chase," Alivia said. "You should take a horse. 'Twould be faster."

Gabriel shook his head. "I need your help along the way. Go find Wilmont."

Alivia hesitated, but then she darted back inside the castle. She found Wilmont tending to the scared and wounded. When she told him Patrick Lombard had been kidnapped and his help was needed, he came at once. Together they readied the coach while Gabriel found a muscled courser, spotted in bronze and chocolate. They hooked her to the coach. Alivia clambered inside. She heard Gabriel mumble something to the driver before he climbed in to join her.

"What did you tell him?"

Gabriel sat across from her. "We're going to make a stop on the way." Then he laid his head back and closed his eyes and said no more.

A few hours later the coach jerked to a stop.

"Wait here," Gabriel told her. He opened the door and stepped down from the coach.

Despite his command, Alivia stepped outside. She saw Gabriel approach a building on wooden stilts—its walls made of translucent rice paper and its roof of bamboo. He tugged on a sliding door and entered.

The Burrows, she thought. This was no place to be caught alone and unawares so late at night. The narrow, twisting alleys were dark and treacherous; the gangs who ruled them even more so. She glanced at the Duke's carriage, with its dark wood and gold trim, unlit lanterns lined in silver. *We are going to draw attention.*

She waited several minutes.

Then Gabriel returned with a slim, three-foot wide case tucked under an arm and a bag slung across his shoulder. He made eye contact with Wilmont. "Do you know how to get to Mt. Shade?"

The driver spat. "Aye. 'Tis a three hour trip from here. Might be sunrise fore we arrive."

"Then let us begone." Gabriel set the case atop the coach and strapped it down. Then he took off his sword belt, removed the crossbow and round-shield from his shoulders, and tossed them inside the open door and onto a seat. He looked at Alivia. "Have you been trained to mend wounds?"

"Of course," Alivia said. "Parliament trains us well. We not only know espionage and—"

Gabriel tossed her the bag. "Good." He took off his black cloak and undershirt and climbed inside the coach. Alivia caught a glimpse of numerous scars on his back. "We'll talk on the way."

Once inside, the soothing rumble of wheels on cobblestones filled Alivia's ears while the carriage rocked back and forth. She felt exhausted, and wanted nothing more than to lie back and rest a while longer. But Gabriel was loading the crossbow and pulling its string into the catch.

She quickly grabbed the slender blade she had tucked away, sprang forward and put it to his throat. "What is the idea?! You plan to kill me so you can return the Duke's coach and claim a reward?"

"Easy," Gabriel struggled to say. She didn't let up. "Look." He aimed the crossbow at the carriage wall, fired. The bolt shot forward, but became invisible when it left the barrel. An unseen force clunked into the wood. The impact sent splinters into the air.

"Where did it—" she started.

Gabriel thumbed a red stone attached to the crossbow's tiller. The bolt reappeared in its barrel. "Gemstones," he said. "They enchant my weapons. But they only work so many times." His eyes darted down to the blade at his throat. "Do you mind? I'm checking the crossbow for faults."

Alivia eased the blade away from his neck. She slumped back to her seat. "Why?"

"When I fought Vincent," he said, "I fired a shot at him that missed. But I did not miss. The bolt passed *through* him." He put the bolt into a calfskin bag and set the crossbow to his side. "I've seen mysteries, but none so strange. What do you know of Vincent and his cult?"

"Vincent claims to be a prophet, a Seer," she said. "He leads a cult of dragon worshipers known as Dräkenkamp. They believe the red dragon is a god."

Gabriel scoffed. "I thought the great byrds all went extinct?"

"'Tis what most the populace believes. Though there is a magister who has written accounts of their existence. He ruined his reputation but—"

"Why did a cult leader kidnap Duke Lombard's son?"

"Over the last few days, a strange man came and went from the Duke's residence. He wore a hood and it was late so I never saw his face, but he might have been Vincent."

"Are you saying the Duke is in league with Vincent?"

"Perhaps. They may have had a falling out. 'Twould explain why Vincent and his cult attacked the castle."

Gabriel grunted. He motioned to the bag he had tossed her. "Would you?" He held out his left hand, palm sliced open and still dripping blood.

Alivia picked up the bag. She dumped its contents onto the seat: a roll of white bandage, twine, a bottle of shabu. "Shabu?" she said.

Gabriel reached over and grabbed the bottle. "For the cut." He untwisted its lid and poured the alcohol across his wounded hand. He hissed. "And for the mind." He took a swig.

"Oh." Alivia began unrolling the bandage. With Gabriel's undershirt she dried his palm and wiped away the blood.

Gabriel gritted his teeth. "So why did the Knight's Order show up?"

Alivia wrapped a strip of bandage around his hand. "Throughout the Four Winds, Vincent and Dräkenkamp have garnered quite the following. Captain Lukas Steele is likely trying to capture Vincent so he might be brought in for an inquisition."

"An inquisition? More like a burning."

"In any case," she bit off a length of twine and tied it atop the bandage to keep it in place," the Knight's Order seeks to maintain control over the kingdom. Removal of Vincent will allow the Church to keep a firm grasp on the public."

It took the rest of bandage and twine to secure Gabriel's chest. He nodded his thanks and leaned back to rest. As the carriage continued to rock and rumble against the cobblestones, Alivia drifted off in thought. Before long she drifted off to sleep. She awoke when the coach jerked to a stop.

"I need you to travel to Wyndsor." Gabriel was putting on his undershirt and cloak. "Inform parliament of the kidnapping. Tell them I mean to return after I save the child." He thrust a handful of coins into her palm. He clambered out of the carriage and began unstrapping his case.

Like hell, Alivia thought. She scrambled out of the coach. "I must come with you. I know more about Dräkenkamp. I can help."

"Windstrikers work alone," he said, "you'd get in the way."

Alivia clenched her fist.

Gabriel finished unstrapping his case. He put on his sword belt, shouldered his round-shield and crossbow, and tucked the case under

21

an arm. "Thank you for bandaging me up," he told Alivia again. Then he turned and marched toward Mt. Shade—a solitary mountain peak capped with snow.

Alivia stood there, watching Gabriel walk away. She glanced up at Wilmont seated atop the coach. He held the horse's reigns and gave a helpless shrug. "Like hell," she snorted. She darted after the windstriker.

"I thought I told you to travel to Wyndsor," Gabriel said when she approached.

"No way. I'm coming with you."

Gabriel stopped and glared at her. Then he continued to hike up the mountainside. "Try to keep up."

She trailed behind him. After half an hour the sun crested the horizon, its rays at first purple and red, then orange, before they brightened to blue. The narrow trail grew steeper. It didn't take long for the air to thin. Alivia found herself wheezing the farther they climbed. Once her foot slipped on gravel and she stumbled, but Gabriel caught her by the wrist and pulled her forward. Not until they reached a wide plateau did the skies open with snow and sleet. Alivia shivered. She hugged herself for warmth.

"How long have you been a windstriker?" she asked to keep her mind off the cold.

Gabriel strode openly across the plateau. "A few years, longer than most."

Which meant he must have survived numerous assignments. A windstriker's mission was oft as not considered suicide—their tasks taking them into dangerous situations to thwart criminals and assassins alike. "Are you contracted by parliament?"

"Most of the time. Some missions are granted by nobles and lords ... sometimes kings." He neared the edge of the plateau—a cliff with a steep drop, mere paces away. He leaned the case against a white-capped boulder. Wind blew his dark hair and snapped his darker cloak like flags atop a battlement. "Parliament hired me after the takeover to save the Lombard family. But I won't get a coin unless I save the *whole* family."

"Oh." She understood now. *Save the child. He is worth a small fortune.*

"So," he pointed skyward, "what do you know of it?"

Alivia swept her gaze toward the clouds. Hazy in the grey morning horizon, high above the mountain and out across an emerald-blue sea, a floating island lingered amongst thin, white clouds. Atop it was a city, eerie and ominous and cloaked in menacing shadows. They shifted unnaturally as the sun climbed, making the city appear to be breathing, alive. A flock of grey gulls flew beneath the floating fortress and through a tangle of blackened roots extending from its foundation.

"The Fortress of the Moon," she said with a shudder. "A city cursed. Hundreds of years ago it was a thriving metropolis. But that was before the Great Catastrophe." She pointed toward the sea, where the flying fortress cast a shadow across the shore thousands of feet below. Scattered throughout the water, half-drowned buildings thrust above the surface.

"What happened?"

"No one knows for sure. All reports reveal the same account—the city tore itself from the earth and twenty thousand perished. The sky city has floated there since."

Gabriel pointed toward the tangle of roots. "Has anyone ever tried to climb?"

"Mostly thieves desiring to steal supposed treasures from the city's vaults and crypts. Few have succeeded, though. Those who managed to make it never returned." She shrugged. "Rumors abound that the cult of Dräkenkamp has claimed the fortress as their home."

Gabriel walked to his case leaning against the boulder. He laid it in the snow, knelt and unlatched three hinges.

"How are we to infiltrate the sky city? We clearly did not climb this mountain so we can climb those roots."

He opened the case and took out a strange contraption. It looked like the skeletal remains of a giant falcon's wings, but with the skin still attached. When Gabriel unfolded them, the wing-span extended twelve feet. "We shall fly. There's an updraft of air currents here, rising with the mountain."

You are mad, she almost told him. But rather, she said, "We will fly into a city of dragon-worshiping fanatics?"

"No." He shook his head. "Do you see that there?" He pointed toward the underside of the flying fortress.

Alivia squinted. Nothing stood out. Then a glimmer of light flashed into view, reflecting the sun's rays—a trickle of water falling into the ocean.

"That's an exposed pipe," he said. "The sewers." He fiddled with a series of belts and straps hanging from the glider's wooden frame. Then he made his way to the edge of the mountain's cliff. After fastening the belts around his waist and wrists, he glanced at Alivia.

"Will that support the two of us?" she asked.

Gabriel grinned. "Inform parliament of the situation." He jumped, the updraft of winds whisking him toward the Fortress of the Moon. The glider's wings filled with air, and he became smaller and smaller in the distance.

Bastard, Alivia thought. She brooded as she watched his swift ascent. Wilmont was probably gone, her provisions gone with him. Perhaps if she hurried she might find him waiting. She took one last look at the Fortress of the Moon. *You better save the boy, Windstriker.* Then she turned to leave, took three steps—and froze with fear.

The snow had bled.

Or so she thought.

Standing before her, nearly five times an elephant's height, stood the menacing red dragon. A dark rider straddled its back.

"Vincent." The name took her breath away.

"Greetings, m'lady," he said with a playful grin.

4

CAT & MOUSE

Water dripped in the round, brick sewer pipe, its echo chiming like a clock ticking seconds. The rancid stench of sewage mixed with a strong aroma of mold. Green slime caked the mortared brick in splotches, and a thin, grimy film floated atop a half-frozen stream at Gabriel's feet.

Next time, I climb those damned roots, he thought. The stench knocked his breath away.

He knelt in the cold, brown sludge and unlatched the last belt buckle from his wrist. He tossed the broken falcon glider aside, and stood, crouching in the low sewer pipe. Then he worked his wrist, squeezing it lightly to ease the sprain from his imperfect landing.

He stepped closer to where the pipe exposed itself to the outside world. The sun's intense glow was just as vivid here as from the mountainside. He leaned over the edge and glanced down toward the rippling ocean thousands of feet below. Even though the stream was partially frozen, a small waterfall of muck trickled from the uncovered pipe toward those emerald-blue waters.

By the Four Hells, this fortress possesses a strange power.

Gabriel began his slippery hike through the sludge and ice. He wasn't sixty paces in when a tremor shook the tunnel. Mortar and dust fell from the pipe's arched ceiling. Gabriel placed a hand on the rough wall, bracing himself. "No live burials today, thanks."

The violent quaking subsided.

"Perhaps I am not welcome here." He brushed gravel and dust from his hands and cloak. He glanced back at the sewer's opening. An intense glow shone inside the hole like a fiery eye. *I'll return to fix the glider if I can. Otherwise, I'll have to climb the roots to get back to the surface after*

I save the Duke's son. While carrying a boy? Details later.

After another ten minutes, he came across a broad cave, its vast expanse as immense as a small city. Rubies strewn along the ground twinkled from the cave's only light source—a wide hole in the ceiling.

One of the city's old treasure vaults? He knelt and picked up a ruby. It was hard, sharp, and glimmered when he moved it around in his fingers. *Where have I seen this before?*

Two wooden doors faced each other to Gabriel's left and right. Gabriel marched into the expanse, toward the door on the left.

He was thirty paces away when he heard the sound: *clink,* scrape, *clink,* scrape, *clink,* scrape. It grew louder.

Dread wrenched Gabriel's gut, and he stopped, dropping the ruby. He glanced at the rubies scattered throughout the cave, the wide hole in the ceiling. Then he looked at the door on the right. *This is not a cave,* he realized. *These are not rubies.*

The door opened.

Vincent Black limped out.

"Greetings, Windstriker." The prophet bent in a mock bow. "What do you think of Des'tok's lair?"

Gabriel took a step back and gripped the hilt of his sheathed sword. He stole a glimpse at the hole above, expecting the red dragon to come soaring through.

"It would do me honor, kind sir," said Vincent, "for you to divulge your name."

Gabriel snorted.

"No?" Vincent *tsk*ed. "Very well." He snapped his fingers. Behind him, a cult disciple emerged carrying a body over his right shoulder. The disciple stepped into the lair, grinning, and dropped the figure to the floor.

The woman let out a weak cry as she thumped against the stone. Her hands and feet were bound by rope, Gabriel saw, and her black hair covered her face.

"The kingdom will not tolerate this," Alivia yelled. "Untie me now!"

"Shall we try again," Vincent asked Gabriel. "May I have your name?"

Gabriel remained silent.

"Worry not for my safety," Alivia told Gabriel. "Take them, Windstriker!"

"Perhaps, you need a little more persuasion."

The left door clicked open. Stone pushed the Duke's son forward. The boy's hands and feet were unbound.

By all appearances, the ducal heir was the embodiment of nobility, with pant and shirt of burgundy, trimmed in gold and ivory. He held his head high, dignified, even for a boy of four summers. He seemed unafraid.

Gabriel swallowed. "Gabriel," he said, turning his gaze back toward the prophet. "My name is Gabriel Lost."

"I'm sorry, Windstriker," Vincent said. "I did not hear you."

Gabriel squeezed his shortsword's hilt in a white-knuckle grip. "Gabriel Lost," he said through gritted teeth.

"Ah." Vincent stroked his chin between thumb and forefinger. "Lost, you say?" He mulled over the word. "If you have been given *that* name, then you're either an orphan or a bastard. Which is it?"

Gabriel inhaled a deep, quivering breath.

"I have a fondness for names. They tell you so much about one's self: the future, the present—" Vincent smirked. "Even the past." He raised his left hand, exposing the strange scar. "'Tis time you showed me yours, Gabriel Lost."

Gabriel began feeling dizzy, then faint. His knees buckled. Darkness wove in and out, his vision blurring. He tried to focus on the prophet, but Vincent seemed miles away, like he was at the end of a very long tunnel, drifting farther and farther into the distance. He drew his sword, or maybe he only imagined it. He felt the cold stone smack his cheek. And the only thought that crossed his mind was: *The Duke's son is going to die.*

Darkness wrapped around him like a blanket, and he was falling—endlessly. Wind rushed past as he plummeted.

Was this death? Am I dead?! Or does death await at the bottom? Moments seemed to pass into hours. Hours into days. Time became non-existant, irrelevant.

Only the sound of wind.

Sleep overtook him. No dreams. He awoke. Still a consuming darkness, but the darkness was different.

Silence.

Whack! *The sound rippled through the silence like cannon fire.*

Whack! Whack! *The noise boomed in Gabriel's ears.*

Whack! ... Whack! Whack! *It blasted in unison.*

Light flared through the darkness, a hazy orange brightness. His eyes burned in pain. His vision blurred, then cleared. He was no longer in an all-consuming darkness. He could see. He could see stone. Stone walls. Stone towers. A stone courtyard.

An oak tree was centered in the yard, full of life. The courtyard reminded him of Castle Lombard, but bigger, more vibrant, more enlivened. Soldiers trained in the yard. Some practiced drills on hay-stuffed dummies, while others sparred.

Whack! *Gabriel turned toward the sound.*

Whack! *Boys were playing a game of Knights. Two exchanged blows while a third watched. They each appeared to be seven or eight years old.*

Whack! *Their wooden swords clacked against one another, the only sound Gabriel could hear.*

The boy watching began to speak. His lips moved, but without sound. The two boys stopped their skirmish, then turned to their observor. He wanted a turn. One of the boys shouted something back. Then he relinquished his wooden sword and marched away, kicking over a rack of wooden swords.

The newcomer grabbed the toy blade and readied his stance, ignoring the ill-tempered boy. He faced sideways to his opponent and aimed the sword with one hand toward his adversary. He rested his free hand behind his back, clenched in a fist.

A fencing stance? *Gabriel noticed.* 'Tis an unusual fighting style for a hopeful knight.

Whack! *The mock battle began.*

For their ages, they were fairly skilled. The newcomer parried a blow, then another, and another. But his opponent was aggressive. He raised his blade overhead and swung down with all his might. The newcomer sidestepped, dodged, and then started his own assault.

Whack! Whack! Whack! *He lunged sidelong with each strike. The opponent blocked the blows and then charged another attack of his own. The match went back and forth like this for several minutes, neither boy gaining ground.*

Meanwhile, the boy who had relinquished the toy sword returned, holding something behind his back. He spoke, but Gabriel could not hear. The two opponents stopped their game and looked at the boy. The three exchanged heated words, then the boy revealed what he was hiding: a sword, real and sharp.

The angry boy attacked. Steel struck wood and splinters flew. Blood splattered across the ground. Terror lined the boys' faces and soldiers' boots pounded against stone.

Soldiers finally reached the boys and tackled the attacker, disarming him, ending the brutal assault. One boy sobbed profusely, his face slashed and covered in blood and tears. While the other lay motionless in a pool of his own blood.

Gabriel's vision blurred. Darkness enveloped him once more. The wind lifted, and he was thrown into a swift upward flight. He felt the sensation of coolness on his cheek. The coolness of the cold, hard stone of the lair.

"You killed the boy." Vincent feigned shock.

"No." Gabriel was kneeling now, looking at the ground, one fist planted against the hard stone. "I did not."

"But I saw you."

"No. You are wrong!"

"My visions are never wrong, orphan. You killed the boy."

"Stop—stop saying that." Gabriel's breathing grew rapid and shallow.

"You were upset. *You* wanted to play. You felt mistreated, so you struck. Brutally. You *killed* the boy."

"I said stop saying that!" Gabriel charged at Vincent, screaming.

Vincent held up his scarred hand and flicked his wrist.

Gabriel was thrown backwards as though an invisible, giant hand smacked him. His shortsword flipped and bounced off the rocky terrain next to him. He curled over his stomach, gasping in pain.

"Pray tell," Vincent limped forward, "are you the black or white horse?"

Gabriel rolled onto his knees and grasped his fallen blade.

"The color black—the color of mourning, the color of sorrow. The color white—the color of nobility, the color of triumph. Which are you, orphan?"

Gabriel attempted to stand, but collapsed back to the ground.

"It is simple." Vincent moved closer. "The black horse brings a calamitous, sorrowful war. The white horse brings a glorious, triumphant war." He stood over Gabriel. "Which do you bring to the Fortress of the Moon?"

Gabriel stayed silent.

"We shall see." Vincent looked up into the hole looming overhead. White clouds darted across a bright blue sky at its peak. He brought his gaze back to Gabriel. "If you want a fight, orphan, I shall give you a fight. You shall be the cat, and I the mouse."

"What?"

"I want you to hunt me, Windstriker. I run and you pursue. I will be your prey, you my predator. It is time for your preparation." Vincent gave directions to his followers. Stone exited the lair and ushered the ducal heir through the wooden door. It slammed shut. The disciple lifted Alivia onto his shoulder and turned to leave.

"Gabriel!" she yelled.

"Alivia!" Gabriel tried to stand, but an unseen force held him to his knees.

"But your prey is cunning," Vincent said. "This mouse has laid a few traps of his own."

The prophet raised both hands overhead and tilted his head back. "Avronze rok," he chanted. The rock and stone around his feet began to rumble and shift. It lifted from the solid ground—raising Vincent along with it—creating an earthy, levitating platform.

Vincent slowly hovered around the immobile windstriker. He pointed his left hand at an area behind Gabriel, chanting. Rock and stone rumbled and shifted and raised from the ground. With his back to the noise, Gabriel could not see the rising mass, but he heard the grinding of gravel chipping away as it rose.

Something lumbered forward, each step causing small quakes to shake the lair.

A stone goliath loomed over him—twelve feet of chiseled rock, with a chest as broad as a round, drum tower. Its arms stretched to its ankles, and its fist gripped a huge stone club in its right hand. The goliath grimaced. But it had no eyes, mouth, or nose, only small facial indentions where its features should have been. The rock giant rolled its massive shoulders, knuckles cracking with sheer strength as it tightened its grip on the club.

"Your first obstacle," Vincent said. His levitating platform rose. He lifted higher and higher into the massive hole above and to the surface streets of the sky city. His voice echoed off the lair's walls as he spoke to Gabriel.

"Give chase, Gabriel Lost."

5

GABRIEL VS. GOLIATH

If Gabriel had never before encountered the immense and powerful dragon, Des'tok, he might have said he'd never viewed such colossal strength as he now witnessed in the massive rock giant. Viewing its grandeur now—its great size amplified by the huge stone club— Gabriel couldn't help but look upon the rock giant with overwhelming fear.

Gabriel was still kneeling, his hand grasped around his shortsword. Though he could now move—the restraining spell released upon Vincent's escape—he waited, patient, confident the goliath believed him to still be helplessly pinned by the prophet's sorcery. The killing blow would come, and the windstriker would die.

Unless he timed it right.

The rock giant swung the club down, fierce and powerful, yet slow-moving as though immersed in water. Gabriel waited. If he jumped too soon, the goliath would compensate its swing and crush him. If he jumped too late, well—

Gabriel rolled aside and dodged the felling strike. He got to his feet, but the club slammed into the ground and sent great chunks of rock flying. The impact threw him onto his back. He gasped and clutched his bandaged chest. His broken rib felt like a knife stabbed at his side.

The rock giant exploded in anger at the windstriker's trickery. It flexed its stone muscles in intimidation and lumbered forward. It swung the enormous stone club as it ran.

"Damn, oaf!" Gabriel wheezed, eyes darting left and right for an escape. He was too close to the rock giant to make a run for it, the wooden doors on both ends of the lair too far. He considered charging forward to meet the goliath head-on, but knew his blade couldn't possibly penetrate its hard, rock body. He stood and took a step back. He sheathed his sword.

Cool air gathered behind the goliath's club as it was lifted overhead.

Gabriel heard the swish of air, and waited for the sluggish attack. The wind changed direction suddenly, and he dove to the side. He avoided the blow, but not the blast of rock and stone that followed. The lair shook. Gabriel was thrown into a chaotic tumble. He regained his balance, and his feet, and ran. He might not be able to kill the thing with conventional methods, but maybe he could confuse the slow-moving giant.

The windstriker began to run circles around the goliath. He used the time to recover and study his opponent. The rock giant spun, slowly, trying to keep up. It swung another attack. But Gabriel's agility, combined with his speed, kept him alive. He dove forward into a roll and evaded the club's killing blow. He stumbled to his feet and continued to sprint.

I need to get closer, he told himself. The club smashed the ground behind him. He dove again, kept his swift pace. A moment later the club smashed down in front of him. He stopped, changed direction. *If I keep this up, he'll splatter me like a bug.* As the club was hoisted back into the air, Gabriel saw his chance.

Now! He dashed in toward the giant. He leaped between its legs, emerged on the other side. The rock giant reacted just as expected. It swung the club at Gabriel, dumbly disregarding its own well-being, and crushed its left leg. The force of the blow shattered the leg to gravel and dust. The goliath staggered forward and fell to its knees.

The windstriker dashed back in and leaped onto its shoulders. The goliath roared in fury. It shook its great weight left and right, trying to shake free of Gabriel's grasp.

Then the stone club circled overhead and cracked into the giant's back. The windstriker rolled to one hand, avoided the blow. The club rose up for another strike. Gabriel transferred his weight, shifting hands as the club split more rock on the goliath's back. Rock and gravel chipped away and crumbled toward the ground. He nearly lost his grip, the bandaged hand weak and searing from use.

Gabriel knew he needed to finish this slugfest soon if he were to survive the battle. He reached up, and clutched a jut of rough stone at the base of its neck. But as he began to pull himself up, the club smashed too close and he lost his grip. He staggered. He reached for the jut again, this time watching for the expected strike. It came. He dodged. And as the club was lifted back overhead, Gabriel scrambled onto the giant's shoulders.

The giant thrashed, but Gabriel kept his grip tight. He scaled onto its head. The goliath moved the massive club in front of itself. It took the club into both hands, and swung the club upward toward the windstriker …

… just as Gabriel somersaulted into a flip.

With his back to the giant while in mid-flip, Gabriel could not see the rock giant's devastating wallop. But he heard the earsplitting *crack* as rock and stone fractured.

Gabriel landed in a crouch, one hand on the ground, the other gripping his sheathed sword. A heavy thump sounded from behind and the ground shook. He stood to observe what was left of the giant's remains—an insignificant pile of rocks.

Suddenly, the red gemstone on his shortsword began to glow; the radiance basked the lair in a blinding, red light. Gabriel barely had time to look away, and despite his closed eyes, the light stung through like the force of a small sun.

A moment passed and the light diminished, but it did not go out. While the gems on Gabriel's shield and crossbow still held the appearance of common rocks, the gemstone on his shortsword now emitted a strange, swirling glow from within.

"What in the Four Hells is going on?" he said aloud. He searched for answers, but none came. Then he cut a strip of cloth from his cloak. He wrapped it around the sword's gemstone. *I can't sneak in the shadows with a glowing red light to give away my position.* He sheathed the blade, the steel's rasp echoing off the lair's walls.

Then he glanced up into the wide hole above. He took a heavy breath. "Is this your challenge as well, Vincent?"

No answer.

Only the passing white clouds and brilliant, blue sky beyond the hole's rim a hundred-fifty paces above.

6

CATACOMBS OF THE KINGS

Gabriel chose the left door from the lair. He planned to follow in the footsteps of the disciple, Stone, and the kidnapped ducal heir. He trusted in his decision to take the left. Both doors likely led to the surface and Alivia, he reasoned, was a trained spy of parliament. She could handle herself. But Patrick Lombard was a mere child and could not hope for protection.

Upon his entrance, Gabriel took one of the many lifeless torches lining the walls of the great passageway. The light coming from the huge hole in the lair's ceiling illuminated the entry, but the hall grew darker as its spiraling steps marched into the gloom. The torch's cloth still contained enough oil to ignite. So Gabriel pulled the flint from his bag and struck it against his steel sword to set the torch ablaze.

Shadows stirred and moved and lurked like monsters in the dark. Flickering lights graced the stone surface at his feet. They swept the long parade of stairs in a glimmer of red and orange. Along the walls, between the sconces of unlit torches, the dead slept in their stone beds, their mortal remains contained within.

It was a hall of tombs.

Every coffin was unique. Atop each bed, a stone sculpture was carved into the likeness of its resting corpse. On their chests they gripped rusty longswords, fingers curled about its hilt. But most impressive, each figure was graced by a brilliantly carved dragon statue. The dragons sat on haunches like loyal dogs, keeping watch against vengeful spirits.

The stone dragons reminded Gabriel of another dragon—one the color of blood. That one had loomed over him as he dangled from Duke Lombard's cathedral tower. "The horses of war," Vincent had said.

What does he mean?

Gabriel pressed forward, holding the torch high. The shadows shifted as he walked. The stone sculptures seem to rouse and breathe as he passed. Sounds of his footsteps rang off the walls and echoed deeper into the crypt. It smelled musty, mingled with a staleness that came from places unoccupied for a long time.

Moments passed whilst he walked among the dead, the deceased his only company.

"Well?" a gruff voice said from ahead, a grating whisper in the dark.

Gabriel stopped and held his breath, listening. He extinguished the torch. Then he crept closer. He kept to the blackest of shadows, and took cover in a small recess beside a coffin along the wall. From here he saw two figures: one with a beard carrying two torches, the other with thick sideburns carrying a sword. They both wore steel plate and mail over cloth layers of crimson on white and grey.

So the Knight's Order has infiltrated the sky city, Gabriel realized.

"Can ye open 'er?" the knight holding the torches said in the same gruff voice.

The knight with the sword was trying to open one of the coffins. He had managed to wedge the tip of his blade underneath a lid's seal. He strained and grunted as he pulled his weight down hard. The sword bent and bowed, threatening to snap.

"Blasts, I cannot," Sideburns said. He let up on the sword. He sheathed the blade and took one of the torches from his companion. "Shame, think of the riches lying within. If only—"

"Will ye look at this," Beard interrupted. He raised his torch up to the dragon statue sitting beside its sleeper. The flickering flame made the shadows dance as though the dragon was alive. He swept the torch's beam down the hall, toward Gabriel's direction. The light's outer edge was on the cusp of his hidden position. "There must be hundreds of 'em."

"If legend holds true, brother, this here is the catacombs of the old Dragon Kings."

"Kings, eh?" Beard moved his torch back to the dragon keeping guard over its dead king. "Riches indeed."

"The Dragon Kings ruled for centuries upon centuries over this land," Sideburns said. "Until our ancestors invaded nigh two hundred years ago."

"Save ye history lesson, brother." Beard held his gaze upon the sculpted dragon, its blind eyes tirelessly staring back.

Sideburns noticed him pondering over the statue. "A *byrd* was sighted at the Duke's castle last night, if you get my meaning."

"Aye, a dragon."

"Carrying a rider, no less."

"Ye think it was Vincent Black?" asked Beard. "Dräkenkamp's leader?"

"Tis just a rumor, but no doubt it was."

Beard brought his torch down. They began to descend the steps toward Gabriel's position, continuing their conversation.

"I heard tale Vincent's lot dabbles in magicks," Beard said.

"Or works miracles, as some might say."

"Bah, its magicks. They say Vincent can read your soul … if he knows ye name. Power like that be no miracle."

"Mayhaps."

Damn me to the Four Hells, Gabriel cursed himself. He had willingly given Vincent power over him when he gave him his name.

"How we s'posed to fight fire with swords anyhow?" Beard asked.

"Tis just another rumor, brother, but the boys claim our Captain Steele can use magicks as well."

"That's foolery," Beard said. "We be knights of the gods."

"Aye, but if Vincent can truly work magicks as many claim, then we need fire, too. Fight power *with* power, I say."

"And I say the gods guide ye."

"You ever were a minister of virtue."

They were getting closer. Only a matter of seconds and Gabriel's cover would be exposed.

He moved a hand to the hilt of his sword …

… but a transparent blue image blurred across his peripheral vision to the right. Gabriel turned to see what the distorted shape standing at his side was, and jumped back startled and spooked. His back banged into the coffin. The stone figure's rusty longsword rattled across the lid and clanged onto the floor. It skittered down the steps.

"Who goes there?!" the knights said in unison.

Gabriel heard them draw their swords.

The blue image began to glimmer and fade, but not before revealing a ghostly apparition of a boy—the slain boy—from Gabriel's dream in the lair. His clothes were slashed and bloodied, and he held a broken wooden sword in his hands. Blood streamed through his fingers and dripped onto the floor.

The boy looked into Gabriel's eyes—a pale, blue gaze. Gabriel felt a deep chill shudder down his spine. His skin prickled with gooseflesh. "Brother," the ghost said. "Why?" The blue light surrounding the boy-phantom pulsed. Then he disappeared. The ghost was gone.

"Show ye self!" Beard demanded. He spoke to Gabriel and not the ghost.

Did they not see the boy?

Gabriel didn't have time to ponder the vision, or its words. "Here we go," he said to himself as he slowly unsheathed his blade. He thumbed the shortsword's gemstone. He felt the blade's power surge. As the windstriker stepped out in front of the knights, he squared his shoulders and let a grin stretch across his lips.

"You boys looking for me?"

7

BUYING TIME

"They went this way!" a young, blond knight yelled to his companions. Alivia could see him through the dirty window pane of the antique medicine shop she and her captor hid inside.

In his haste to elude the pursuers, the cult disciple had darted down the street—still carrying Alivia over his shoulder—and stole into the nearest building. He slammed the door behind him, hastily set her down beside a stack of rotting crates to hide her from view, and hurried back toward the front door.

With her hands and feet still bound, Alivia managed to scoot forward to peer around the boxes. That's when she saw the knight. She thought about yelling for help, but then, whose side was the Knight's Order on anyway? They shouldn't have been at Castle Lombard last night without approval from king or parliament. They openly attacked the followers of Dräkenkamp, threatened hostages and put innocents' lives at risk. Now they are here in the Fortress of the Moon, and Alivia didn't think it was to save a Duke's son.

The knight turned toward the medicine shop window.

Alivia eased her face back, but kept her eyes peeled around the corner of boxes. The cult disciple, a man dressed in a brown, leather jerkin and rough-spun pants, crouched beneath the window. He was leaning back against the wall and his left hand gripped one of two arm-length daggers strapped crossways on his chest. He peered up at the knight on the other side of the window, unruly black hair falling into his eyes.

The knight cupped his hands onto the grimy window. He squinted into the old, dusty store.

The disciple tried not to move.

Seconds seemed to turn to moments, and then, finally, the knight lifted his face from the glass and darted away to the left. Alivia breathed a sigh of relief. The disciple's body noticeably relaxed, and he eased himself up toward the window's ledge to glance down the city streets.

But then another voice from outside shouted: "Are you sure?!"

The disciple wrenched his face from the glass just as six knights ran past. They chased after their companion. Alivia listened. Their footsteps pounded against the cobbles, chainmail clinking, labored breaths wheezing, and then ... *tap-tap-tap, tap-tap-tap.*

What? Alivia glanced up.

The cult disciple peered out the window, his long and bony fingers tapping at his leg. His head darted up and down like a man with a death threat, certain a group of archers took aim from an unseen position. He couldn't stop twitching, twitching, twitching.

He is full of fear.

"I ... I think they're gone." He slumped to the floor. "We'll wait here a while and buy some time before moving out. We need to let those choirboys get a little farther off our scent," he nodded toward where the knights ran past.

Alivia forced a yawn.

"How in the Four Hells did they get inside the sky city?"

"They must have climbed those roots," Alivia said. "Why, is there another way?"

Griff stopped tapping. A brief hesitation before he shook his head.

He is lying.

Alivia shrugged. "Well, I assure you we shall not escape." She moved so he could see her ropes. "Unless you cut me free."

The disciple eyed her suspiciously. "Not a chance."

"Suit yourself." She gazed toward a rack of unfamiliar medicine bottles behind the store's front counter. "It is not I they will kill."

"No, they'll have it worse for you." He spat.

"Then you have nothing to fear if you release me." She held out her hands. "For if what you say is true, I certainly would not desire their capture."

He scrutinized her ropes apprehensively. He snorted. "Fine. But you attempt to flee, I'll gut you. I don't care if you are bait for fish."

He took a quick last glance onto the city streets before sliding closer to Alivia. He knelt beside her. Alivia expected him to unsheathe one of those sizable daggers, but instead he reached for a slim blade looped through his belt.

The dagger Gabriel gave me.

She eyed the blade like a man who lusts for a maiden. She wanted to cut the disciple's throat and escape. But he only cut the ropes at her feet.

"That's all you get for now," he said. "Don't trust ya. You listen to me and do as I say and no harm will come to you. And maybe, just maybe, I'll consider untying your hands." He sat down with his back to the counter, rested an arm over a bent knee.

Alivia twisted her ankles. The rope's tight knot had chafed her skin. *'Tis a start,* she thought, *but I'll have that blade in your throat before day's end.*

She smiled at him. "You have my gratitude."

The disciple nodded.

Alivia studied the old store's contents. Wilted plants were strewn about the floor, on shelves and counters. Cobwebs, dry soil, and broken glass dotted the shop throughout. Strange bottles—dark blues, greens, and reds in varying sizes and shapes—lay scattered in medicine racks along the walls. The shop looked as though an earthquake hit long ago, like the store's owner and customers evacuated and never returned.

There was an aroma in the air. A hint of lavender and the mixed fragrances of potent flowers.

Garden smells.

Though staleness permeated the air; tainted it, really.

It reminded Alivia of a childhood garden she used to play in growing up on the Isle of the Winds. *Gods, I haven't thought of that place in ages.* Not since joining parliament as a spy.

As a student studying botany, she had to learn about plants and herbs. Many were used for drugs and hallucinogens, many more for poisons. One plant in particular was the exotic flower called the Redoulz—easy to pick out because of its bright, red bulb centered amongst thin, green pedals. When handling the plant, she had to be especially careful due to its poisonous characteristics. It was a flower popular among assassins.

The memory triggered her training in cult behaviors—a class detailing a psychological approach on how to interact with religious fanatics. Maybe she could get some answers.

"What's your name?" she asked politely.

The disciple gave her a suspicious glare.

"My name is Alivia," she ignored his annoyed reluctance. She looked around the store.

"Griffin," he said. "Most call me Griff."

She brought her focus back. "Tis nice to meet you, Griff."

He nodded, then glanced toward the store front. He appeared worried those knights might burst into the shop any minute. "Just a little longer before we move."

"Where are you taking me, Griff?" She used his name amiably, like they had been good friends all along.

"We make for higher ground. I plan to rendezvous with Gavin."

"Gavin?"

"Gavin Stone, the man you saw keeping watch over the Duke's son in the lair. He acts as Vincent's right-hand."

Gavin Stone, how could she have forgotten? She researched what little information there was on the man prior to the Castle Lombard takeover by the cult of Dräkenkamp. "He's your group's strategist."

"That's right." His tongue was beginning to loosen. "Vincent envisions and Gavin plans, according to what Vincent has *seen.*"

"Oh," Alivia arched an eyebrow. "So you do believe Vincent is a prophet?

"Aye." He took a deep breath. "His visions, they've never been wrong."

"But how do you know he speaks the truth?" she asked. "How do you know Vincent tells you all he *sees.*"

Griff's gaze turned to stone.

"I mean—" she was losing him. "Can you tell me what Vincent has *seen?*"

His face relaxed. "He has seen the glorious return of the Age of Dragons."

Alivia *hmm*ed. "Are the Fortress of the Moon and the Knight's Order among that vision?"

"You're awfully inquisitive for someone in your predicament." Griff sighed. "But I am impressed by your courage. I do not doubt Vincent's prophecies, but I'm uncertain as to what he *sees* in your boy."

Gabriel? "You mean the windstriker?"

"Aye, he's a bloody titan," Griff said. "That is ... if he can survive

Vincent's obstacles."

"What obstacles?"

"Vincent plans on challenging the windstriker, and each challenge will be different." He ran calloused fingers through his black hair. "And he will fail."

"Challenge him? How?"

"Vincent will call forth the fabled titans of old: the Goliaths."

A mere fairy tale, she began to say, but held her tongue. The Goliaths were legend, part of a child's tale called the Onion Knight meant to encourage boys' desires for knighthood. Alivia was incredulous. What illusions did Dräkenkamp hold?

"The Goliaths," she said slowly, making it a question.

"Aye." Griff stood. He brushed soil and dust from his pant leg. "And it has begun, in the lair."

Alivia found it hard to believe that Vincent possessed such power, or that such giants exist. Except, her cynicism was put into question upon seeing the flying dragon last night. "For what purpose?" she asked.

"I know not. Come, let's move." He hoisted her to her feet. "Like I said before, you attempt to escape," his look was grave. "I will hurt you."

If I get hold of one of those blades we shall see who gets hurt. "You have my word."

"Good."

They walked toward the medicine shop's entrance, Alivia's hands still bound behind her back. Griff eased opened the door. He peered out, onto the sky city's streets. He nodded. All clear. He opened the door further and they exited the shop. Then they ran in the opposite direction of the knights, to rendezvous with Gavin Stone and his captive, Patrick Lombard.

8

TWINS

It neared midday as Gabriel exited the catacombs and onto the surface streets of the sky city. The air was crisp and refreshing and the sun shone brightly overhead. The sun's warmth invigorated Gabriel. It reassured his senses after the lengthy morning spent underground.

He scanned the cobblestone street left and right. Deserted buildings with bone-white facades and brown roofs—crumbling from ages of neglect—flanked the city street. Two parallel ruts ran down the center of the cobbles, three feet apart, from cart and wagon use before the Great Catastrophe. Rotting signs hung loosely above shop doors, a strange writing scribed into the wood.

A business district, he realized upon peering into a dusty window. Dead plants scattered the counters and floors, and strange bottles were strewn about shelves and tables. Everything was covered in dust and cobwebs. He pulled his face from the glass.

Across the street from the catacomb's entrance was a small, round fountain set into the niche of a building. The white plaster on its walls was peeling and exposed a large slab of rough limestone beneath. A clear, clean trickle fell from the fountain's edge. Its sweet resonance parched Gabriel's lips. He hadn't noticed how dry his mouth was until now.

He glanced left and right again—no one in sight—then strode openly across the street.

He still gripped the shortsword in his right hand. Its sharp edges were covered in crimson, warm and wet. Though the battle in the catacombs with the knights had been short, one of them managed to slice open his arm. His wounds from last night had still yet to heal.

When Sideburns flanked him from the left, Gabriel tried to defend, but his bandaged left hand left him weak and slow. But he did repay the knight with a slash across the face—a wide red smile from sideburn to sideburn.

Gabriel knelt by the fountain. He set the sword down at his side. Then he cupped his hands and drank, feeling the water's freezing embrace go down like winter. When finished, he splashed water onto his cut arm. A minor scrape, he saw now. He picked up the shortsword and held its bloodied steel beneath the trickle to wash the blade clean. He dried the sword against the black woolen fabric of his pant leg, sheathed it, and stood.

All right, Gabriel, which way? He looked left and right, down both ends of the street. *And where in the hells do I start?*

The sky city was much larger than he first imagined when observing the Fortress of the Moon almost two miles away from atop a mountain.

"Did you find anything, brothers?" a voice rang out toward Gabriel's right, at the end of the street and around a corner.

Instinctively, Gabriel drew his sword and crouched against the wall. No shadows for him to take cover, but he'd sooner defend his back than be left vulnerable in the middle of a street. He cursed himself for his moment of respite. Both Dräkenkamp and the Knight's Order occupied the city, which meant hundreds of disciples and knights now warred for survival. And he, a sole windstriker in the mix of this religious warfare, was a third party either side would not hesitate to discard of.

"We've found naught but dirt and cobwebs this way, sir," another voice said.

The windstriker crept along the shops' walls, toward the voices. He halted short before the building's corner turned down the next street.

"All right," the first voice said. "We shall surrender our chase."

Gabriel stole a glance around the wall's edge. Five knights in heavy plate and mail stood mingled together. They wore the gods' badge of the Four Winds: a cross, its ends transfixed with the heads of four different beasts (wolf, griffin, chimera, and snake).

"The sinner undoubtedly carried the girl into one of the many stores," a young, blond knight said. "Mayhaps they exited through a rear outlet."

The girl, thought Gabriel. *Do they mean Alivia?*

A sixth knight approached from the south side, armor clinking as he marched. "Brother Clement," he addressed the blond knight. "Captain Steele is requesting our presence at the center of town."

"At what time?" Clement asked.

"Now, sir."

"We shall join him, then." Clement looked to his fellow knights, and ordered, "Make haste, brothers."

The knights did as commanded. They began proceeding toward the designated meeting place.

"Brother Brynden," Clement added. "A word, please."

The knight named Brynden halted his advance. "Aye, sir," he said.

Keeping his face and body pressed to the wall, Gabriel saw that Brynden was also young, probably the same age as Clement. His hair was the same blond as the other knight's, if not a little longer, and his six foot height and lean, but lithe, build the same as well. As Gabriel got a better look, the more he saw that the two knights might be brothers—*true* brothers—perhaps twins.

"I found something quite intriguing," said Clement. "I wanted to show you."

"What is it, sir?"

"Come on, Bryn. How many times must I tell you: don't address me 'sir' when it's just the two of us. Save the formalities for when we're around the men."

Brynden apologized, "Sorry, brother, habit 'n all. What is it you found?"

"Take a look at this." Clement knelt and scooped a handful of dirt and rocks into his palm. He stood. "What do you think will happen when I drop these rocks?"

Brynden shrugged. "Fall to the ground."

"As expected, right? But watch." Clement held his hand eye level and then opened his palm. He let the dirt and rocks fall to the ground.

Only they didn't drop.

They hovered in the air instead, spinning and rotating in place.

"By the gods," Brynden gasped. "What do you make of it?"

"I wish I knew."

Brynden reached out and plucked a floating rock out of the air with his thumb and forefinger. He scrutinized it. "Do you think this might

45

explain how the city flies?"

"Mayhaps," Clement shrugged, "but there is no way to know for certain." He collected the floating pile of dirt and rocks into his hands. "Put these in your pouch." He handed them to his brother.

"What for?" Brynden asked.

"I want to take them back home to Lorenta." Clement brushed the dirt from both hands. "See what happens if we do the same experiment there. Father Stefan might know what makes them fly."

"Lorenta," Brynden said longingly. "I wish we were home 'n not here." He glanced down the street and at the buildings nearby. "This city is cursed."

"This city intrigues me," said Clement, "and I'd like to learn more about its ... unusual nature." He nodded toward the street where the four knights went down to arrive at the center of town. "Go ahead, brother. I will join you shortly. Tell Captain Steele I am investigating an oddity."

"Yes, sir—I mean—sorry, brother. I will inform the captain. May the gods guide you."

"And you."

Brynden departed his brother's sight. He turned the corner the other knights set down and headed for the meeting with Captain Steele. Clement knelt back to the ground. He scooped up another fistful of gravel from the cobblestone path.

Gabriel stepped out from his hidden position. "You'll not join with the others," he said.

Clement quickly stood, a swift pull freed the longsword from his waist. His eyes darted to the street his fellow knights went down.

"Not yet at least," Gabriel added. "I seek answers, nothing more, but I won't hesitate to kill you if I must."

"Pah," Clement scoffed. "I'm a highly-trained knight. A cult disciple such as you cannot defeat me."

"I am no cult follower."

"Then who are you?" Clement demanded, his eyes scanning Gabriel's clothing and weapons. "Why are you here in the flying city?"

Gabriel ignored the questions. "Why did the Knight's Order march against Duke Lombard's estate? Did the Church sanction the attack?"

Clement snorted and spat. Grey fluid splattered across the cobbles. Gabriel gripped the hilt at his waist and unsheathed his sword.

"Why is the Knight's Order after Vincent Black? Is he to be brought in for an inquisition?"

"Are you ready to burn in the Four Hells?" Clement gripped his longsword in both hands.

The windstriker pulled the round-shield from his shoulder and locked it into his left hand. The bandage made his grip awkward.

This was a mistake.

"I'm through with you," Clement said through clenched teeth. "Prepare yourself!" He thrust an overhand cut at Gabriel's head …

… but the windstriker deflected the knight's sword with his shield and pushed it out to the side. The strike vibrated down his arm. Gabriel felt a sharp pain in his chest. He grimaced.

Damn dragon.

He swung his own blade in an arcing sweep. The knight brought his sword up just in time to parry the blow.

"Twould you like to die a slow or quick death?" Clement drove the point of his steel at Gabriel's chest.

The windstriker shoved his shield over in a left-hook and blocked the sword out to the right. The momentum of the blow left the knight exposed.

Gabriel thumbed the gemstone in his sword's hilt. He swept his blade overhead, and brought it down into Clement's shoulder. The sword's razor-sharp edge, combined with the windstriker's strength, effortlessly cut through the knight's armor. As the blade tore into Clement's flesh, venom released into his body.

Poison, the enchanted sword's killing attribute, coursed through the knight's veins.

He had only moments to live.

Clement grunted in pain and fell to the ground. His breathing grew shallow, a heaving guttural sound. White foam formed at the corners of his mouth. "What vile magick is this?"

"Tell me, Sir," Gabriel was determined to show respect to his dying opponent. *He is a knight. He deserves that much.* "Why is the Knight's Order here in the sky city?"

Clement looked up into Gabriel's eyes. He seemed like he might cooperate before he exhaled his last breath.

"You can burn, sinner!" His head hit the cobbles, dead.

Gabriel breathed out a frustrated sigh. He didn't want to clash steel with the knight. He just needed some answers. The relationship he observed between Clement and his twin made him think the knight might be civil.

Suddenly, a tremor shook the sky city, more violent than the quake experienced in the lair.

Gabriel braced himself in the middle of the street. The buildings around him began to chip and crumble, while flakes of plaster fell to the ground. Cobbles cracked under his feet. Small cracks, at first, but the shaking became more intense and a severe fracture split the ground. It ripped through the street and continued to tear into the side of a building. No longer able to support the roof, the building caved in and collapsed. A huge dust cloud choked the air. When the dust cleared, Gabriel saw that the path to the center of town was cut off—the building in ruins and the street blockaded.

The quaking lessened, the vibrations weakened.

A voice cried out: "Clement!"

Gabriel turned toward the grief-stricken shout.

It was Brynden.

He stared back through the impassable rubble of the collapsed building.

"I shall kill you!" Brynden shouted, tears streaming down his cheeks. "I shall hunt 'n kill you!"

Gabriel said nothing, but he felt remorse. The Knight's Order were supposed to be the good guys, soldiers of the Church. Though their recent actions did contradict their creed.

I only wanted answers, he thought as he looked at the dead knight. *I gave him a choice.* He glanced back toward Brynden, but the knight was gone. *Great, he went to find a way around.*

After he secured the round-shield onto his left shoulder, Gabriel wiped the knight's blood from his sword with a black cloth. He sheathed the blade. Then he knelt beside Clement's body.

"Why couldn't you cooperate?" he asked the knight.

No answer, of course.

He reached up and shut his eyes. Then he stood and hurried back the way he came, to the left of the catacomb's exit this time. No reason to stick around and kill the other brother.

No, he said to himself, *those knights were searching for someone.*

A cult disciple and a girl, he heard them say. Perhaps they were close

48

by. Or perhaps he could find a clue in one of these ancient buildings.

9

THE KNIGHT'S ORDER

Lady Victoria relaxed her right hand on the curve of her hip while her left swayed at her side. "How long must we wait, Lukas?" she asked with a tired sigh.

Lukas Steele, her commander and her lover, knelt to inspect the wide hole they had just stumbled upon in the center of town. "My men should join us shortly," he said. "Look at this."

He motioned toward the deep pit. Its depths descended hundreds of paces into the heart of the sky city, only to vanish into darkness. Its width across must have been fifty paces, if not more. It looked like an enormous well for drawing water.

"This pit is enormous. What think you?" He motioned for her to take a look.

She took a nervous step forward, not wanting to get close to the hole's edge. She leaned over and peered down. The pit was man-made, she saw, with huge slabs of mortared stone. The shadows made the pit seem like a never-ending vertical tunnel. She couldn't see the bottom. Victoria couldn't explain it, but she felt the sudden urge to jump. She took a quick step back, afraid she might give in to the temptation. "'Tis unusual and I do not like it."

Lukas smirked. "It's not like I'm going to throw you in. Come closer."

Victoria shook her head.

"Fine. Stay. I care not." He picked up a small pebble and tossed it into the hole.

Victoria listened for it to strike bottom. Seconds passed, and it did not hit. And did not hit. And did not hit. The strained silence went on, defying understanding. *Gods, surely it would've struck bottom by now.*

"Miraculous," she heard Lukas say.

She glanced up. The pebble floated before them, rising up and down over the center of the hole in a gentle rhythm.

"It defies gravity," Lukas said. "In the name of Lucidus how does this city fly?" He stood. "I wonder what purpose this hole served."

"Honestly, Lukas, I care not." She took another step away from the pit and glanced around the square for signs of his men.

The town center acted as a hub with four intersecting streets. Countless, crumbling buildings flanked each side. And it all, she noticed, encircled this terrifying hole.

"Open your eyes, Victoria." Lukas came closer. He took her hands into his own. "If we are to unlock the mysteries of this city and obtain its ancient power—" he brushed a strand of golden hair from her brow, "—then we must be observant, love."

His touch made her shudder with excitement, made her forget the looming hole. She was spellbound by Lukas. His words, his attention, his love … were her breath of life. And Lukas, well, he was enthralled by her beauty.

And Victoria possessed an overwhelming beauty, Lukas had said as much. He told her she was graced by the gods at birth, given the gifts of lovemaking and affection. The men even called her the *Captain's Affection*, and it was true. He embraced hers, while she reveled in his. But what Lukas called gifts were actually … skills.

Skills she learned working in a grungy, worn-out brothel in the town of Derbent. She had been a creature of the night then; poor, starving, and desperate. It was all she could do to survive. But one wondrous evening Lukas came—her prince—and rescued her. He took her away from the harshness and shame … and the revolting men.

Then, she wore only her midnight gown, grimy and soiled as it was. But now she wore the slender steel armor that Lukas had given her. It was form-fit to her skin, and accentuated her curves well. The men desired her, she knew, but none dared cross their assertive captain.

"I'll be more attentive, my prince," Victoria said as she admired those deep blue orbs piercing into her soul.

He embraced her lips with his, their moist tenderness weakening her senses and her knees.

A deep, muffled voice called out from one of the side streets: "Captain Steele, sir!"

Lukas released his sweet embrace. "See, I told you it would be shortly." He let go of Victoria and motioned toward the approaching knight, who was followed by over a dozen men-at-arms bearing longswords at their waists. "Sir Ellard," he greeted.

The aged knight came near. He removed a heavy helm from his head. His cropped, grey hair reflected the sun's rays in a silver shine. Sir Ellard, according to gossip Victoria overheard among the men, was past his prime, over fifty. Lukas said he once served King Rikard IV personally in his royal army, as Captain of the Kingsguard. After turning fifty the noble knight was forced into retirement, the King citing him to be 'as ripe as a month-old quince'.

"It would take a fool to underestimate the Old Knight," Lukas had once told her. "His prowess with the blade is better than ten good knights combined."

And Lukas was right. The Old Knight, as the men now called him, was unrivaled amongst the men.

Save her prince, of course.

"How fares the hunt?" Lukas asked.

"We've slain a few heretics," the Old Knight replied, "but the hunting is sparse. We managed to pick up a few of Sir Clement's men."

"Oh," Lukas said, no longer smiling. "What's become of Clement's unit?"

Sir Ellard shrugged. "I know not, sir."

"And the twins?"

"They were not among them, sir."

Lukas's right eye twitched. "Do we presume them dead?" He rested a hand on a dagger looped through his belt.

Victoria noticed, fighting back a twinge of fear. Something about that knife never seemed right, with its hilt carved into a four-headed beast and its blade so sinfully black.

"Clement's men say they stayed behind, sir."

"Foolish." Lukas spat. "All right, take his men under your authority until Clement's return."

"Aye, sir."

The sound of clinking metal rang in unison as more knights marched into the square. They arrived from the opposite street the Old Knight and his men had entered from. They were not led by a knight in shining armor, however, but instead by a six foot, brown skin, barbarian woman. She wore bizarre tribal cloth, rattling with multi-colored beads, which barely covered her most feminine of areas. A wooden spear with a metal leaf-shaped tip was strapped to her back. It rose three feet above her head, bound by the same multi-colored beads worn all over her body.

Victoria scowled. *What is she doing here?*

Once among the company of Captain Steele, the barbarian woman greeted him with a strange gesture: two fists curled over her chest, followed by a bow.

"Commander Adanna," Lukas nodded, welcoming her salute. "I pray your report fares better than Sir Ellard's."

Adanna looked from Lukas to the Old Knight, a puzzled squint across her brow, then back to the captain. "I afraid report hunting small and we lose men in battle," she said, still struggling with her limited knowledge of the language. Commander Adanna was not of the kingdom. Her unusual accent, along with her brown skin, was without equal in all the Four Winds.

Lukas said she had traveled overseas from Goa Jaffa, after her warrior tribe was brutally massacred. She came to the Kingdom of the Four Winds seeking death, but instead found the Cardinal. He quickly recognized her skill in combat and placed her in the authority of Lukas Steele. Under his leadership, she became a commander, though she held no knightly title.

At first the men resented her. But their attitudes changed dramatically after witnessing her prowess on the battlefield. Now the men fondly called her Lady Luck, though Victoria could not guess why.

Yet, despite the men's change in attitudes for Commander Adanna, Victoria still held resentment. The barbarian woman possessed an exotic beauty, and from time to time Victoria thought she saw the brown woman staring at her prince. And worse, she caught Lukas eyeing her in return.

Victoria butted in: "Sir Ellard lost no men. Why have you?"

"*Lady* Victoria," Adanna said, emphasizing *Lady*. Victoria knew she had learned enough of the language and Four Wind's culture to understand it meant she and the captain were unwed, a sin in the eyes of the Church. "You no warrior, no understand. You not belong."

"Pah," Victoria scoffed. "Do you hear how she speaks to me, Lukas?" She unsheathed her own slender blade. "She should be punished."

"Enough," Lukas barked. "Losses are inevitable." He looked to both Sir Ellard and Commander Adanna. "Our upmost priority is to determine where the Dräkenkamp rats hide."

"I agree, sir," said the Old Knight, and Lady Luck, "I too," as she peeled her eyes away from Victoria.

"We must conduct a full sweep of the city," Lukas went on.

"All is lost!" a voice cried out, interrupting the captain's orders. "All is lost!" the voice cried again. The disruption came from the street Sir Ellard and his men arrived from. It was Brynden, Victoria saw, panting as he ran toward the company. Sweat dripped from his brow down to his chin. He stopped short of Lukas, hands on his knees. "All is lost, Captain," he said, out of breath.

"Catch your breath, knight," Lukas commanded. "Then tell me, what has become of you?"

Brynden took a moment to compose himself; inhaled several gulps of air, wiped sweat and tears from his eyes, and then fully stood. "It's my brother Clement, sir," he tried to fight back tears. "He's dead." A sob escaped him.

"How?" Lukas demanded.

"A man-in-black," Brynden described, "wielding sword, shield, 'n crossbow murdered Clement in the streets! I tried to get at him, but I was blocked. The quake hindered me, see. I found a way around … but he was gone."

"'Tis unusual weaponry for a cult disciple," Sir Ellard observed.

Lukas answered the puzzled question they all must have been thinking. "Not a cult disciple, this man-in-black. Rather, I believe he may be a dog of parliament … a windstriker."

Victoria sheathed her sword. "Why would a windstriker be here in the Fortress of the Moon?"

"Perhaps he followed," Lukas said. "He may have even caused the disturbance at Castle Lombard last night, just before we saw Vincent and the dragon take flight."

"We did hold the Duke's family captive," Victoria pointed out. "I suppose that in itself affects kingdom security. 'Twould make sense for a windstriker to now be involved."

The Old Knight said, "He's good."

"Yes," Lukas agreed. "To have infiltrated our ranks without my knowing … he most certainly is."

"I like meet windstriker," said Commander Adanna. "Might be man I look for."

"What think you, Captain?" Sir Ellard asked.

Lukas tightened the straps across his chest that kept the greatsword secured to his back. "We marched against Castle Lombard and then on to the Fortress of the Moon without king or parliament's authority," he said. "Our man-in-black may be here to learn why. This windstriker is another obstacle to be dealt with, no more. He must be eliminated."

"What are your orders then, sir?"

"Brynden." Lukas looked to the distraught knight.

"I swore an oath to avenge my brother," Brynden said. He unsheathed his longsword, baring steel. "Give me the command, sir, and our man-in-black is as good as dead."

Lukas squinted at Brynden. "Very well. Take the men from Clement's unit with you. Do not return until you have slain the man-in-black."

"Aye, sir." Brynden sheathed the blade.

"And do not take him lightly," Lukas warned. "He may be only one man, but a windstriker's strength is that of a brigade. This one mayhaps more so."

Brynden nodded. Then he shouted toward his brother's old unit to follow, promising vengeance. He marched away, his newly acquired unit on his heels. They exited the square and disappeared down a side street.

"Sir Ellard, Commander Adanna," Lukas glanced at them both. "I want the two of you to sweep the city streets clean. Determine where the cultist rats hide."

"By your command," Sir Ellard said.

Commander Adanna spoke to the Old Knight, "I sweep left."

"Then I right," he said in return. "Good hunting, Lady Luck."

She curled her fists over her chest and bowed, as before, then headed down the street she had entered from. Her men trailed close behind, armor clinking.

"Captain," Sir Ellard inclined his head. "May the gods guide you."

Lukas nodded.

The Old Knight departed the square with his men-at-arms.

Victoria sighed. "So what are *our* orders?"

Lukas grasped her hands. "Why, my love, we will search for clues."

Victoria didn't understand. "Clues?"

"Clues that will help us unlock the Fortress of the Moon's ancient power."

She arched an eyebrow. "What is this ancient power you speak of?"

"A power," Lukas said with a glint of lust in his eyes, "that can sway men's hearts and minds. A power that can bend souls to a new way of thinking."

"How is such a thing possible?"

"Oh, it's possible." He was enraptured in his own thoughts and words, blankly staring into Victoria's eyes, seeing but not seeing. "But first, we must discover the key to this flying city."

Lukas had never been so intense before. "W-where will we find such a key?" her voice quivered.

"I know not." His focus returned. "But I believe the cult leader, Vincent, knows something of a key."

"Do you believe he has it?" She touched his cheek. She loved being close to her prince.

"Nay, I think he searches for it still." Lukas pulled Victoria closer. He enveloped her in his strong embrace. "That is why we must outwit him, my love. For if we find Vincent, we find the key."

He kissed her then, settling her nerves and resolving her fears.

"Yes," she said, captivated. "Let us search for this key. Let us find this … Vincent."

10

THE MERCENARY

Nothing out of the ordinary made the windstriker choose to enter this particular building, but the clanking armor of approaching knights most certainly did.

Gabriel heard voices outside: "Where we head'n, Bryn?"

There was a desk to his right. Gabriel crept toward it and hid behind, away from the great floor-to-ceiling windows with a view of the street.

"We make for Clement's corpse." The clanking armor and voices grew louder. "I hope to track the man-in-black's steps. I want to see where ..." the voice trailed off as their marching continued down the street.

Gabriel grinned. *Lackwits.*

He stood and circled around from behind the desk. Then he removed a bright golden-yellow quince from his calfskin bag and took a bite. The juice was sour, but Gabriel didn't mind. While most commoners preferred to roast or bake the fruit before eating, Gabriel was used to eating them raw. Living at the Orphanage, you didn't have a choice. Now there was something comforting about the sour fruit.

He glanced around and studied his surroundings.

Shelves upon shelves—twice Gabriel's height—lined the immense room from wall to wall. Hundreds—no, thousands!—of old, dusty books filled the shelves. A second floor walkway circled the room, with even more shelves and books. Gabriel saw a spiraling staircase in the far left corner, books stacked on each step. At his left a long table extended the length of the wall; yellowing scrolls, scripts, maps, and feathered quills scattered atop its dark, ashen wood. Cobwebs hung everywhere.

As long as there are no scorpions, I don't give a—

He scrunched his nose. "What is that smell?"

The old library smelled of mildew and wood rot, mingled with damp books, ink, and leather. Golden light poured in from those tall windows behind him, and from several holes in the rotting rafters above.

Gabriel took another bite of the quince. He walked amongst the rows and rows of books. Sour juice gushed with each bite, fulfilling his hunger. He touched a book on one of the shelves as he passed. Part of the spine crumbled to pieces.

Gabriel stopped his stroll in what he thought to be the center of the library—a circular area with a chipped, fading compass painted on the floor. N pointed toward the rear of the library. A wooden table sat over the middle of the compass, a forest-green book rested on top with golden letters across its cover.

A dome glass ceiling loomed overhead, with several panes broken or missing completely. Dim light streamed in through the broken glass. Specks of dust glittered and sparkled as they drifted through the rays of sunlight.

He finished the quince and tossed its core aside. Then he strode over to the oddly placed book, picked it up, and tried to read its golden script:

LUNAGAESIA
ANZIENCE HYSTEROS

He couldn't make it out. He opened the book and thumbed through its pages, the illegible script throughout.

"That's a good choice," a deep voice said from behind.

Gabriel turned to see a man with black, cropped hair and goatee leaning against a bookshelf, arms folded across his chest. His attire was equally black and close-fitting to his towering build. Fastened all over his body were dozens of belt straps with silver buckles. Strapped to each belt was a decorated, silver dagger. Deadly blades exposed; no scabbards.

The man took out a gold coin from his pocket and began flipping it in the air, catching it, flipping it in the air. And he smirked at Gabriel, almost as though he had been expecting his arrival.

Gabriel dropped the book and drew his sword. The book hit the compass with a resounding bang. Its echo chimed into the extending halls.

"Lunagaesia," the dark man said. He snatched the coin out of air and tucked it away. "The moon city." He walked to the table, ignored Gabriel's threatening behavior and kept talking. "Ancient histories of the Kingdom of Vehayne's capital city."

Gabriel took a step backward from the approaching figure. "You're no knight. One of Dräkenkamp's, then?"

The dark man picked up the fallen book. He blew dust from its cover. Little grey clouds rose, then drifted downward like heavy snow. "No," he scoffed, still staring at the book. "I'm no knight, and certainly no follower of any religious sect."

"Then who are you?" Gabriel demanded, but then he had a realization. "You were at Castle Lombard last night. You took out the guards."

The man smirked, revealing confirmation. He set the book back down where it rested before, and sat himself against the table with both hands gripping its ledge. "Let's just say I'm a friend. Quite possibly your only friend within this dangerous city. Please, put away your sword."

Gabriel hesitated. He did not trust the dark stranger. But he relented and sheathed the sword.

"My name is Slade," the dark man went on. "Jon Slade. And I'm a windstriker, like yourself."

Gabriel moved to grab his sword. The man was proving himself untrustworthy. "Speak fast or draw your blade. Windstrikers work alone."

Slade put his hands up. He quickly added, "Well, I'm a former windstriker. I'm retired."

Gabriel rolled his fingers around the hilt of his sword. "Go on."

"Now I'm a mercenary," Slade said.

"A mercenary?"

"Aye, and the pay's better," Slade joked. "Unlike you, I'm not bound by oath to pay a percentage of my earnings to the Militia. You should consider it. Anyhow, I work for the Lombard family. Last night,

I was trying to secure the perimeter so the family could escape. But now that the Duke's son has been kidnapped, I've been sent to rescue him."

"And you could use my help, is that it?"

"That's right, and I'm willing to help you out in turn. I must admit, I'm no slouch with a blade." He fingered one of the silver daggers strapped across his body. "And you should find me of more use than your captured partner."

"Alivia?" Gabriel said, confused. "How do you know of her?"

"Oh, I know many things." Slade grinned. "But you, on the other hand, know nothing. Especially concerning the Fortress of the Moon."

Gabriel narrowed his gaze. "What do you mean?"

Slade picked up the forest-green book. "*Lunagaesia: Ancient Histories*," he deciphered. "This book chronicles Lunagaesia's founding all the way up to the last few years before its destruction."

"Lunagaesia?"

"See," Slade ridiculed, "you know nothing! Lunagaesia was the capital city for the Kingdom of Vehayne. It stood for nearly three thousand years as the prominent place for commerce, trade, and political power before the Dragon Wars."

"But how does it relate to the Fortress of the Moon?"

Slade sighed. "*This* is Lunagaesia." He made a sweeping gesture. "This city ... the Fortress of the Moon."

Gabriel didn't understand. In all his studies of the Dragon Wars, the Fortress of the Moon was only mentioned toward the end of the war, and always in conjunction with the Great Catastrophe. The name of the city, oddly enough, was omitted in all the writings. The scholars, the history books, all referred to the sky city as the Fortress of the Moon. Even when mentioning the city *before* the Great Catastrophe.

"Continue," he said.

"Over two hundred years ago," Slade began, "before our kingdom became the Four Winds, they were the Four Islands—four weak, desperate countries whose noble aim was to become stronger, more self-efficient. Thus uplifting their citizens from poverty and a barren land.

"The Kingdom of Vehayne reigned north of the Islands, a healthy and prosperous kingdom, with rich resources, flowing rivers, and fertile soil. Vehayne offered to help the Islands, several times over, but their stubborn rulers refused."

Gabriel asked, "Why?"

"I know not. But, they refused all the same. Mayhaps their gods whispered in their ears," Slade said sarcastically. "Alas, an idea formed between the Island countries. A diabolic idea. They would *unite* and *invade* the Kingdom of Vehayne, and take its riches for themselves.

"Individually, the Islands could not hope for victory. United, however, they became a force mightier still. They planned, trained, and prepared ... until they were ready. And the time came. No doubt you've heard this tale?"

"Yes," Gabriel said. "The Dragon Wars."

"Aye. The Islands invaded, catching the peaceful kingdom off guard, and swept through the land like *wind*."

"Thus becoming the Four Winds," Gabriel finished. "After their victory the Islands divided the land into four regions, so naming each region after their invading armies: Highwinds, Whitewinds, Graywinds, and Isle of the Winds. Why the bedtime story? Children know this tale."

"What was the name of the Kingdom of Vehayne's capital city?" Slade asked.

"Lunagaesia, you said?"

"Aye, and though the land was conquered, a mighty force defended the Kingdom of Vehayne's capital city. True victory could not be attained unless the city was taken. Do you remember what force defended Lunagaesia?"

"Dragons," Gabriel said.

"Dragons," Slade repeated. "And one dragon in particular was bigger than all the rest, its scales the color of blood, its wings carrying a dark rider. They called the rider ... the Prophet of the Dragon."

"The Prophet of the Dragon," Gabriel said.

"He wore black, dragonglass armor. Sound familiar?"

"Vincent." Gabriel was mystified. *Who is this cult leader?* "Are you telling me Vincent is a two hundred year old prophet?!"

"Mayhaps." Slade shrugged. "I know not for sure. Anyhow, think you on this ... with a force as powerful as dragons, led by a prophet who could foretell the future, how be it the Islands were able to sweep the land so easily?"

Gabriel thought on this a moment. "Good question. I know not."

61

"The Kingdom of Vehayne let them."

"What? Why?"

"That's the question that needs answering," Slade said. "Mayhaps, there was something hidden beneath the city, something precious, something powerful. Something that needed protecting. Something the Kingdom of Vehayne would go to great lengths to guard, even moving all its force to Lunagaesia."

"What are you saying?"

"The Islands mounted a campaign against Lunagaesia," Slade continued. "A secret campaign to infiltrate the city, to steal an ... artifact ... and to use it against the kingdom to achieve victory. Do you know who led this campaign?"

Gabriel shook his head. "Nay."

"Duke Lombard." He waited for a response from the windstriker, but Gabriel only shifted uncomfortably. "Though he was not yet a duke," Slade said. "He was Knight-General Lombard then, of the Highwinds' army."

Gabriel's head was spinning. "Your story is madness. How can Duke Lombard, and Vincent, have lived through the Dragon Wars over two hundred years ago? You realize how imposs—"

"Impossible, I know," Slade broke in. "Yet true. And what Lombard discovered within the city, and the unnatural events that followed—Lunagaesia torn from the earth as though the hand of a god plucked it from the ground like a flower from soil—led to the creation of this flying stronghold. The Fortress of the Moon."

As if the city itself were listening, the library trembled. Panes from the domed ceiling came crashing down around the two. Gabriel lifted an arm overhead to shield himself, but Slade remained unfazed. He continued to sit atop the table with his hands resting on its ledge.

"This city is starved," the mercenary raised his voice to be heard over the ruckus. "Do you feel her hunger?!"

The quaking subsided, only a brief tremor.

"What did he find?" Gabriel asked. "The artifact, that is. What was it?" He still didn't believe any of it.

Slade shrugged. "I know not. Mayhaps the gods know."

Gabriel scoffed. "Gods, save them."

"Ah," Slade smirked. "I take it you are not a believer."

He shook his head.

"Me neither." Slade stood. "No, I do not believe in the gods of the Four Winds, nor the God Vincent and his lot worship. I believe only in what I see, and I've never seen a god. Yet, magicks are about. If that's not power of the gods, or God, as in Vincent's case, then where does it come from?"

Gabriel shrugged.

"Let me pose one last riddle, Windstriker. Why is the Knight's Order here in the Fortress of the Moon?"

"I'm still investigating that matter."

"Let me help you along," Slade said. "The Cardinal seeks power, and not just any power, an *ancient* power. He has sent Captain Steele to acquire this power for the Church of Lucidus."

Gabriel narrowed his eyes. "What kind of power?"

"Legend foretells that an ancient power exists somewhere within Lunagaesia. A power that can change men's minds and souls."

Gabriel still didn't understand. "What, with magick stones or devices?"

"I know not." Slade shrugged. "But I can tell you, the Knight's Order believes this flying city to be a weapon."

"A weapon?" Gabriel was incredulous.

"Aye, and the Cardinal hopes to use it to control the masses … to convert non-believers and eradicate all who oppose."

"Your words bear much meaning," Gabriel said. "Though, I cannot say I am yet to trust in them. For all I know you are leading me astray."

"Please," Slade put his hands up, showing palms. "I'm a friend. My knowledge is sound and my words ring true."

"Words are wind. Without proof, you're naught but a common sellsword."

"Sometimes, my friend," Slade walked past Gabriel toward the library's front entrance to leave. "You must have faith and ride the winds."

"You said your name is Slade, right?" Gabriel asked.

The mercenary stopped, turned around. A flash of silver gleamed off his daggers like light off a mirror. He nodded.

"You a betting man?"

Slade laughed; a deep rolling rumble. "Of course, mercenaries are. I'm driven by greed."

"I shall rescue the Duke's son before you."

"You're on," Slade grinned wide. "A bit of advice, though, if you'll hear it."

Gabriel nodded.

"Head west for the abandoned mines and through the Forest of Despair." Slade turned and started for the exit.

Suddenly, the rays of golden sunlight between Gabriel and Slade refracted and blurred blue. The windstriker's eyesight distorted, making the departing mercenary look like a shimmering mirage above hot desert sands. The blue light pulsated and formed into the slain boy holding the broken wooden sword.

The ghost spoke: "He plans to hurt me, brother." The image rippled, vanished. The library's front door closed shut, and Slade ran off to the right, out of sight from the window's view.

11
THE HUNT BEGINS

Brynden knelt beside the slab of meat that was once his brother. He fought back the tears, pushed down a lump in his throat. He couldn't show those weak emotions in front of the men, not now, not ever. Clement taught him that. What it means to lead, to demand loyalty, to take the blame and beating for your twin stealing a silver coin from father's money bag.

No, don't go there.

It would only open a sluice of memories, and then the sobs would come.

"What happened to you here, Clement," he said to his brother's lifeless body. "You were a swordsman, a great fighter."

Something strange caught his eye.

Why did the windstriker do that? Why would he even care?

Clement's eyes were shut.

Brynden had seen enough battle to know that when a man died, he did so staring death tirelessly in the face. He brushed the thoughts aside. No compassion for a murderer.

He reached down and removed his brother's gold and silver necklace. It had a locket. Brynden opened it. A portrait of a young girl, freckles on her nose and cheeks, flowing red hair and a heart-shaped face.

Lilyanna.

Clement's fiancé.

Brynden snapped it shut. "I'll get this back to her, I promise."

He stood and faced his men. They hung back, forced conversations and halfway eavesdropped on their new commander.

Only four left, Brynden thought: Aryn, Trevor, Wils, and Pipes.

This morning, Clement's unit was two dozen strong. *Now look at us. So many dead.* Half died attempting to climb those damnable roots; the others, fighting sinners. "We'll make the windstriker pay for our losses," he told them.

Trevor brushed back what few hairs he had on his balding scalp. "Where to now ... Commander?"

Brynden walked toward the building that had collapsed into the street during the quake. He knelt, glanced around at the hill of rubble. He gazed at the cobbles and then down the street, to his right. "He headed west after the quake," he said. "Back the way he came."

Wils grunted and scratched himself. "How do ya know?"

Brynden pocketed the locket and stood. "Back home, I was a tracker. We hunted game—deer and boar mostly—but it taught me something invaluable."

"Yah, and what's that?" Wils asked.

Brynden smirked at the memories, of his brother and their hunts with father. "How to kill a prey," he said. Then he marched down the street, and in the direction he thought the windstriker went. "Let's move, boys. We've a scent to track."

The men fell in line with his step.

Moments they marched, turning corners and into alleyways. Every once in a while Brynden halted their advance to kneel and touch the cobbles, smell the dirt between his fingers. He never once peered into any of the deserted buildings, until they came upon one with soaring rectangular windows. It was the largest building they had seen thus far, with a dome glass ceiling atop a roof two stories up. Brynden vaguely remembered passing it on their journey to pay last respects to his brother.

He wasted no time. He strode inside.

Countless books sat on countless shelves. Dust and cobwebs covered everything, including the floor. The stench was rank, but he pushed it aside.

Brynden scanned the footprints in the dust. "Strange," he said.

"What," Trevor asked.

"There are two sets of tracks. The windstriker wasn't alone."

Aryn spat. "His partner?"

"No," Brynden said. "Windstrikers have no partners." He saw the smaller set of prints leading down an aisle of books. "Spread out, look

66

around," he commanded.

His men went in four different directions to search the library.

Brynden followed those tracks. Halfway down the aisle, he stopped to check out a book. It had been disturbed. The spine had crumbled apart.

Pipes call out: "Hey, Trevor, come have a look at this."

"What?" Trevor shouted back.

"Come tell me if I can smoke this?"

"Is it paper?"

"It's a map," Pipes said.

"You're a damned addict."

Damned men lack discipline. Brynden sighed. He couldn't fault them for it. They'd seen enough of their brothers' deaths for one day. A little humor to sidetrack their thoughts wasn't all bad. Brynden was just surprised they had any at all. He felt nothing but rage, a burning desire to seek vengeance for his brother.

He came across the center of the library, a faded compass painted on the floor. A table sat over the heart of the compass. Both sets of footprints went no farther than this point, he noticed. Dust was kicked up in a light, grey haze.

The two men met here, but they didn't come to swords.

The dust haze made Brynden realize their meeting must have ended mere moments ago. The windstriker couldn't be far.

The core of some kind of fruit—is that a quince?—lay two paces away toward Brynden's right. He moved closer to it and stared at the remains. A surge of anger clenched his gut.

How can he eat after committing murder? Is his stomach not turning over with guilt?!

He stomped on the core, squashing it. "You're dead, Windstriker," he said aloud. Then louder, he shouted, "Boys, to the streets! Our prey's not far."

The knights hooted. Their footsteps pounded as they moved toward the exit.

Brynden dashed for the doors. A satisfying sense of hope kindled his emotions at the prospect of revenge. "The hunt begins," he said to himself, grinning. "The hunt begins."

12

RENDEZVOUS

W hat took you?" Gavin Stone demanded as he scratched at his dark beard streaked with grey. "I'd begun to think you captured by the Knight's Order."

Griff closed the door behind him. "We had a run-in with a few choirboys." He went to the window and peaked outside. "Twas nothing I couldn't handle." He motioned to a small wooden bench shoved up against the wall to the right. "Have a seat."

Alivia did as commanded. Not yet time to form a resistance, she knew. Her wrists burned from the rope binding them. She tried to work them, to make them more comfortable, but that only made it worse. Grimacing, she glanced around the old, apartment loft.

Unlike the stone interior of the ancient medicine shop, this small two-story apartment was wooden, rotting in dampness. Alivia drew in a deep breath, but she only smelled mildew and wet wood. To her left was a kitchen, she saw, with an open wood-burning oven made of brick. Black ash and soot caked the oven's interior and the floor beneath it. To her right, the common area seated two more wooden benches, identical to the one she currently sat on. In front of her, a questionable ladder rose to a second-floor loft.

Must be the sleeping quarters, she presumed. *Wonder where—*

"Where's the boy?" Griff asked.

Stone pointed to the upstairs loft. "Resting. The boy's been through quite the ordeal. I figured he could use it."

Griff glanced out the hazy window pane again. *He searches for knights*, Alivia knew. His nervous tapping went on throughout their journey to join Stone. "Where is Vincent?" he asked.

"He said he would join us shortly." Stone nodded toward Alivia.

"Why did you untie her legs?"

"I didn't have a choice." Griff brought his focus back inside. "I might not have made it if I'd carried her the entire way."

Stone came closer to Alivia. "What think you?" he asked her. "Why is a dog on our scent?"

The windstriker? Alivia thought. She was dumbfounded. "You and your cult seized a Duke's castle," she said. "You jeopardized kingdom security. Not to mention kidnapped a ducal heir. How can you expect to not have a windstriker at your heels?"

Stone looked at Griff. "Do you recall Vincent's vision? Did it entail a windstriker?"

"Nay." Griff shrugged. "Come to think on it, his prophecy didn't mention the Knight's Order either."

I told you, Griff, thought Alivia. *How can you know Vincent shares all he foresees?*

Stone rubbed a hand through his beard again. "Aye, I've already thought on that."

"You think Vincent is hiding something from us?" Griff shot a quick glance toward Alivia. "Like … mayhaps he *saw* them but withheld it."

A strange voice spoke from the apartment's front entrance: "Why, you wound me deeply."

Alivia didn't remember hearing the door open. She turned to see who spoke …

… and saw Vincent Black standing at its entry, blond hair falling across his shoulders and onto black, glassy armor.

Griff fell to his knees. "Vincent, forgive me. I never—"

"—don't beseech me. I care not on your musings." Vincent limped into the dwelling. His left foot scraped the floor and scratched the wood. "My prophecies are never wrong, and yes … I withheld my vision."

"Why would you do such a thing?" Stone had an edge to his voice.

"I sense anger, Stone." Vincent pointed a finger at him. "Control it. Control your fears."

Stone took a deep breath, released a heavy sigh. "Well?"

Vincent stayed quiet.

"Your prophecy, Vincent. What did you *see?*"

"It's naught that concerns you … for the moment." The prophet fingered a dark, red stone dangling atop his breastplate. It hung from a silver chain around his neck, Alivia saw.

Stone cursed. "This city swarms with knights. A windstriker as strong as a bloody titan hunts us. And for what? A game of cat and mouse? Please ... tell me ... what shall my concerns be?!"

"The Duke's son," Vincent said. "Just as before, we stay the course. Our plans remain unchanged."

Stone exhaled a frustrated breath and nodded. He began pacing back and forth.

"V-Vincent?" Griff asked nervously. "How are we to reach the throne room? Those choirboys have infested the streets like ants."

"Yes, they have," the prophet said.

"Well? What should we do?"

Vincent tilted his head back. His eyes rolled to the back of his head, and he began muttering strange whispers beneath his breath. "The knights have divided themselves into three groups," he prophesied. "Ah ... but their numbers have dwindled. They've lost many."

"Damn it, Vincent," Stone said. He stopped pacing. "They still outnumber us ten to one."

The prophet ignored him. "I see two groups sweeping the streets. They search for us. They're led by an old knight and—" he chanted more whispers, "—and a barbarian woman."

"And the third," Griff wanted to know. He drummed fingers against his leg, twitching, twitching, twitching.

"The windstriker," Vincent said. "He has made his presence known, the fool. The third group hunts him as we speak."

"Twould do us a favor," said Stone, "if they killed him. Why did you not kill him when you had the chance?"

Vincent opened his eyes and looked at Stone. "Because he is needed."

"For what purpose?"

"All in due time, Stone, all in due time."

Griff shifted his weight from foot to foot, tapping. "The throne room, Vincent. How are we to reach it?"

Vincent tilted his head back again, whispering strangely. A moment later, he said, "Wait here with our captives 'til dusk. I shall enchant the residence with entry barriers. You will be safe so use the time to rest. At sunset, make way for the throne room. The streets should be less dangerous toward twilight." He grinned playfully. "I foresee our holy knights succumbing to the Forest of Despair."

"If only," Stone said hopefully. His voice became a growl, "And if they should not succumb, what then?!"

"Watch your temper, Stone. Breathe and control it." He placed his scarred hand on Stone's shoulder. Alivia saw that the disfigurement formed a fire-breathing dragon in flight. "We have sacrificed and paid dearly," the prophet said. "Men … good men … have died for the Kingdom of Vehayne. But keep to heart for Adon is in control."

Stone looked at Vincent, the first time since the prophet placed a hand on his shoulder.

"Do you trust me, Stone?" Vincent asked. "Are we not friends, you and I?"

Stone nodded.

"Then grant me your trust, friend," Vincent said. "As you did those many years ago, when you walked away from home and duty."

Stone's stern gaze softened. "Yes, Adon is in control." He placed his right hand on Vincent's shoulder, the two locked in a bond of trust. "Friend."

They released one another. Vincent turned toward Alivia. "You intrigue me, spy," he said. "Quietly listening, more interested in our meddling than for your own safety. Do you find us to be … informative?"

"I find you to be unusual," Alivia said. She rolled her wrists to ease the chafing of the tight rope. It didn't help. "What are you scheming?"

Vincent smirked. "Why, I'm preparing the game board for your friend, the windstriker, and our overzealous knights." He started for the front door.

"Are you not staying?" Stone asked.

"No," Vincent answered. "I'm still setting the pieces into place. Besides, I need to greet our guest, the good captain."

Stone looked concerned.

"Fear not, friend," Vincent said. "I'm the master of this fortress. And I've died before, remember?"

Stone took a deep breath, nodded.

Vincent opened the door and stepped outside. He turned back toward the apartment and scrutinized the door frame and windows. He lifted his left hand, exposing the dragon scar, and chanted,

71

"Dorenze lok."

A green energy shot from his palm. It blasted against the door frame and windows. Green fluid coated them and rippled like water on a lake.

Standing in the street on the other side of the green barrier, the prophet said, "This dwelling is barred from entry." His voice muffled as though he spoke underwater. "Rest up, and make way at dusk. The throne room, my friends, 'til next we meet." He headed down the street, slowly limping to an obscure destination.

Alivia glanced to her captors. The two exchanged nervous looks. *They're worried,* she noticed.

"Get some rest," Stone ordered. "We move out at dusk."

13
CLUES

Victoria knelt beside her prince to examine what he found in the cobbles of the street. "What is it, Lukas?"

"'Tis another clue, my love." Lukas held up his palm to show her the discovery: an ancient relic from a forgotten time. It looked to be a necklace of sorts, the once silver chain tarnished green. Dangling from the necklace was a small object. A stone, or perhaps a jewel? It was tied on with a thin, worn leather strap.

Victoria tilted her head, perplexed. "Okay," she said slowly. "How is this old thing a clue?"

Lukas stood. He sighed. "Open your eyes, Victoria."

She grew tired of hearing those words: *Open your eyes*. Sometimes she felt Lukas treated her like a small child, speaking down to her as though unimportant. Unintelligent, even. She exhaled an irritated breath and fought the urge to slap him. "Honestly, Lukas, is this thing useful?"

"I know not." He clasped his fist around the chain. "Yet it seems familiar to me. I cannot place it."

"What are we to do with such a thing?"

Lukas did not answer. He studied the relic, seeming to contemplate why he felt a strange connection to it.

Victoria waited, growing bored, a common activity she was beginning to loathe.

"Ah," Lukas finally said. "It's a religious relic or … a symbol … if you will. I believe it to be from the Old Kingdom. The cult we hunt has taken it as their banner." He held it up for a closer look. "Perhaps it has something to do with the key to the city."

Victoria brought her face closer to the necklace, too. She scrunched her brow and nose, hoping it would help her see what Lukas saw more clearly. It didn't. "I see nothing special about it. It doesn't even look like a key."

"What do we know about the cult of Dräkenkamp thus far?"

Victoria gave a helpless shrug and started biting her nails.

Lukas rolled his eyes. "Recall, my love, that Dräkenkamp desires to restore the shattered Kingdom of Vehayne. Hundreds of years ago, the Vehaynian Dragon Kings ruled over these lands. When a King died, he passed to his successor a birthright—a stone they called the Heart of the Dragon. I believe this small trinket here to represent that stone." He pointed to the jewel tied onto the chain.

"The Heart of the Dragon?" Victoria asked.

"Yes, a stone believed to contain unfathomable power." He clenched his fist around the chain. "And mayhaps it is the key we search for, the key to unlock the Fortress of the Moon."

"The Cardinal," she said, "is this what he quested you with? To retrieve the Heart of the Dragon?"

Lukas did not answer.

"What is it?"

"It's nothing." He cleared his throat. "All you need know is that the Heart of the Dragon is powerful. We shall not yield its powers to a heretic such as Vincent. 'Twould be folly."

"But what if Vincent already has the Heart of the Dragon?"

Lukas shook his head. "I do not think he has it. If he did, he would have already activated—" he spat and shook his head. "Curse my foolishness."

"What?"

"Vincent wears a necklace with a dark red stone." He clenched his fist, knuckles whitening.

"But if he has the Heart of the Dragon why hasn't he used its powers?"

"Because Vincent must be missing something," Lukas said. "Perhaps he searches for it."

Victoria moved closer to her prince and touched his hand. "Searches for what?"

Lukas shrugged her touch away. "He searches for—I don't know—a part of the stone? Mayhaps something is needed to activate its powers." He looked Victoria in the eye, who bit her lip to keep from storming away. His rejection had hurt and irritated her. "When we stormed Castle Lombard, my men claimed the grounds looked ransacked. Vincent and his cult were searching for something!"

Lukas grinned. "We are that much closer, my love." He brought a hand to her check to brush his fingers against her skin, but she shied her face away. "What is wrong with you? You should be thrilled at my discovery."

"I–I am, Lukas." She forced a smile.

"Then kiss me." He hugged her close and came in for a kiss. Victoria decided to embrace his warmth, glad for her affection to be returned. But she pulled away right before their lips could touch. Something caught her eye just over Lukas's left shoulder.

"What is it?" he asked.

"Vinc—" she tried to say the name, but it stuck in her throat.

"Please, do not allow me to intrude," a voice called out from the direction Victoria stared.

Lukas turned, an effortless pull freeing the greatsword from his back. "Vincent," he growled.

"I only came to welcome my guests," said Vincent, "nothing more." He stood on a nearby rooftop thirty paces away, overlooking Victoria and Lukas and the spot where they found the necklace. "I can return at a later time if you find the moment at hand to be inconvenient."

"Why not greet your guests properly?" Lukas held out his right hand. "Come shake my hand if you would be so bold."

Vincent laughed. "I think not, Captain. But you have my gratitude for your chivalry. No, I overheard you talk of a stone. The Heart of the Dragon, was it? Pray tell, what would you do if you found that stone?"

"I'd get rid of you, heretic." Lukas squared his shoulders. "And I would save this sin-filled world."

"Ever the noble knight," Vincent mocked. "Truth be told, you would know not how to handle such power!"

Victoria took a step forward. "Then you pray tell." She felt emboldened beside her prince. "How would you prefer to die? For surely, sinner, that's where you are headed—a godless death."

"Gods?" Vincent scoffed. "Lest you forget there is only one God––Adon. He is eternal and gracious. A savior God. Adon can even save you, young harlot." The prophet held out his left hand, showing the couple a strange scar. He pointed it at Victoria and chanted her name.

She felt dizzy. The street spun quicker and quicker and her vision darkened. She could feel it, an intrusive presence inside her, searching. Almost as soon as the spell began, it subsided. She regained focus, feeling nauseous.

"Adon can even save you," Vincent spoke, his hand no longer aimed at her. "I have seen your sins, harlot, and Adon will redeem you of them. Your *gods* are merciless. They send the weak and maimed to be outcast, bearing titles of disgrace. That is a godless death. But Adon saves. Your gods know naught of redemption."

How dare he?! Victoria's heart hammered in her chest. She shouted, "Be silent you … you—"

"The unwed love you give to your prince can be redeemed. All you need do is ask."

"Silence!" she cried, tears rolling down her cheeks. *How can he know?!*

"Victoria!" Lukas called out, his voice reassuring. He looked into her bleary eyes and whispered, "Bear your wits, my love."

"Ah," Vincent sounded delighted. "The Cardinal's own pet, the hand of deliverance. The c*aptain.*" He twisted the word. "You would deliver the world to salvation by your gods, through your will. And your will is strong indeed, Lukas Steele."

Victoria tried to regain her composure. She wiped tears from her eyes and breathed deeply. In front of her, Lukas held his greatsword in both hands and glared up at the heretic. He rolled his fingers around the sword's leathered hilt, the blackness of the huge blade reflecting no light.

He was too far away for close-quarters combat, Victoria knew. Once before, she had seen a strong-armed archer attain that distance in competition between the men. Only her prince had no bow. But in truth, he did not need one.

For the sword is blessed with fire, she told herself.

"You have erred, Vincent," Lukas growled," to have entered into my presence." He looped his greatsword overhead with one hand and poised it behind his back. "Taste thy blade and feel its Sinfire!"

He swung the greatsword downward—a strange, incandescent red flame now surrounding the blade—and slashed at the air in front of him.

A scorching fireball flung from the blade's tip. It flew toward

Vincent. In that quick moment, all of the oxygen was sucked from the air and out of Victoria's lungs. The stench of sulfur burned her nostrils.

Vincent appeared stunned. He took a quick step back, seemed uncertain of what to do. But then he jumped leftward, off the roof and out over the street.

He didn't make it—the fire struck him square in the face.

Only the fireball passed through him as though he were naught but a ghost. The flame didn't so much as singe the prophet's hair.

Victoria gasped. *By the gods what is he?*

Lukas reverse slashed, and another ball of fire hurtled for a quick death.

But Vincent—still falling toward the street, now a mere ten paces below him—thrust his scarred hand forward. A green rippling energy shot from his palm. The energy surrounded the fire and smothered the blaze. Before he hit the street, a surge of wind propelled upward, from beneath Vincent, slowing his fall. He landed gracefully on the cobbles.

"So you wield the ancient blade, Sinfire. Interesting," he said. Then he chanted, "Avronze Rok."

The cobblestones around Vincent's feet rumbled and shifted. They broke away from the street and formed into a levitating platform. It lifted him into the air, rising, rising, up and over the buildings and away from the couple's presence.

He had escaped, but not before Victoria noticed a now familiar necklace worn about his neck.

Lukas strapped Sinfire to his back, its color returned to black. "Fly, Vincent," he whispered, "whilst you can. Before this day ends you shall be ours." He turned around and embraced Victoria in a sheltering hug. "How fare you, my love?"

"I'm shaken, but okay." She looked up into his soft, blue eyes. "The fire—did you see what it did?"

"Yes."

"How?"

"I know not."

She squeezed Lukas tighter, not wanting to let go. Never. Silence passed between them, until Victoria felt willing enough to break it. "Did you see what Vincent wore?"

"I did."

"Is it the Heart of the Dragon?"

He nodded.

"Are we to give chase?"

Lukas released his protective squeeze. He faced the direction the fleeing heretic had escaped. "Yes, my love."

14

ABANDONED MINES

Gabriel traversed the rocky tunnel of the abandoned mineshaft carefully. The footing was unsound, the jagged overhang of sharp rock dangerous. He needed to be swift in his crossing of the mines. The dozen holes along the path at his feet opened to a two thousand foot drop—maybe more—and into an emerald-blue sea glimmering in the sunlight.

One misplaced step, Gabriel thought as he stepped over a hole, *and I'll plummet to my death.*

Sunlight poured into the mineshaft from the holes, like beams of torchlight illuminating the most dark of dungeons. Considering that he could see the sea through them, Gabriel presumed he neared the sky city's foundation.

One misplaced step, he told himself again. *One misplaced step and I'll never be seen again.*

He shrugged the thought away, decided instead to focus on his footing.

As he progressed, the mines grew darker and more dangerous.

Gabriel stepped near one of the holes, thinking the ground stable. When he shifted his weight, the ground underfoot groaned.

Okay. Easy.

He lifted a foot to advance forward. The ground cracked.

Hold for me. Hold.

He set his right foot down, gently. But the ground crumbled and plummeted toward the sea. Gabriel hurried to dodge the fall ...

... but he didn't move fast enough and he fell inside the hole. He shouted, then hit the ground with an, "Umph."

The hole didn't widen enough for him to fall completely through.

He lay sprawled on his back with only his left leg dangling inside the hole. He groaned and pulled out his leg. When he looked down, he saw a flock of grey gulls scatter from their perches beneath the sky city.

"Damn, I got lucky."

He cursed and stood and brushed sand from his palms. The shade of a grin touched his lips as he glanced down. The hole was bigger than he thought.

Suddenly, he was laughing. If at barely avoiding death, or the lunacy of being inside the sky city to chase after a possible two hundred year old prophet to rescue a Duke's son, he didn't know.

The ground at his feet cracked.

Gabriel stopped laughing. He quickly eased his way toward what he hoped was more stable ground. Then the small cracks splintered into larger ones and began to spread, like cracking ice across a lake.

He glanced back the way he came. The cracks were breaking into wide rifts. The path began to crumble. Parts of it dropped into the ocean.

Oh, by the Four Hells. Each time the path collapsed, the surrounding surface weakened and more of the ground fell away. And it now spread toward him in a chain reaction.

Gabriel swore, turned, and sprinted down the tunnel. He forgot the cautious demeanor from before, and ran as the ground fell away behind him. He stole a glance as he ran, saw the ground crumbling away, and when he brought his focus back, saw a four foot gap.

He cursed and he jumped, landed and kept running.

A larger tunnel appeared ahead. But before he could reach it, the path beneath his feet fell away. He jumped—

—and caught a ledge. He dangled there by one hand, only air between him and a watery death. His fingers slipped. He reached up with his left hand and slowly pulled himself up.

Grunting, Gabriel stood. Then he clutched his side and grimaced. Pulling himself up just now had agitated his wounds. He turned toward the collapsed mineshaft. The path he had been crossing wasn't there anymore. The ocean's waters glowered back an icy taunt.

"Head west for the abandoned mines," he mocked Slade's advice. Gabriel knew better than to trust a betting man.

With a heavy sigh, he unwrapped the bandage covering his hand and clenched his fist. His hand still hurt like hell, the cut he received when he scrambled away from the dragon and slipped on glass now starting to scab. The bandage was useless, so he tossed it over the edge. Swift winds picked it up and carried it off while it danced and twirled down toward the ocean.

The hand hurts, Gabriel thought. *And the broken rib from the dragon's attack is making it hard to breathe. But I must needs fight through the pain.*

He couldn't afford to let such wounds threaten his life nor the captives he hoped to save.

Determined, Gabriel continued his hike through the unstable mines. There were no longer any holes in the surface. The only light now poured in behind him, from the collapsed passageway. The farther he went, the blacker the darkness. He ran a hand along the tunnel's rough wall to guide his steps.

Just a little farther, he told himself, *and I'll be gone from this deathtrap.*

Moments passed without incident.

Until a strange noise wailed in the distance.

Hawooo! The closer Gabriel crept forward, the louder the howl.

Hawoooooo! A cool, constant breeze flowed into the tunnel.

Hawoooooooooo! The wind moaned.

Gabriel stopped his approach. He now stood with the dark tunnel behind him, a vast cave before him. Across the cave was another tunnel leading farther into the mines. Strangely, the area was basked in warmth and daylight.

The entire left wall had fallen away into the ocean, he saw, and the sun's rays filled the cave with their golden light. It created one hell of a window, a boundless expanse of shimmering sea beyond.

An impressive view, Gabriel mused as he scanned the emerald-blue waters. It was all he could see for miles upon miles, endless ocean.

With his hair and cloak snapping vigorously from the wind, Gabriel strode forward. He made for the cave's edge overlooking the vast ocean. He peered over the cliff. The sheer distance of the drop stole his breath away.

A voice called from behind: "Are you tempted to jump?" It came from one of the other tunnels.

Gabriel turned toward the voice, cursing the wind for muffling the approaching figure's steps.

"Tis quite the fall," the figure added. "How fare you, orphan?"

The windstriker unsheathed his shortsword, ready for combat with the prophet. "Vincent," he said. "Where's the Duke's son?"

"All in due time, Windstriker. No, I merely came to check upon your progress. Are you making friends in the city? You stink as though you have."

Gabriel stayed silent, confused by the riddles.

"Jon Slade is bad news," Vincent said. "Twould be wise to heed that warning."

"I trust nothing from you."

Vincent nodded in reply. Then he limped closer, the scrape of his stride muted from the howling wind. His hair blew fierce, blond tips whipping over his left shoulder. The red stone dangled from his necklace and swayed across his breastplate like a swinging pendulum. "I hope you found my rock giant to be pleasant," he said. "Pray tell, was it courteous?"

Gabriel snorted. He took a step forward, away from the edge.

"Do you not want to share the experience?" Vincent smiled. "Very well. I suppose it is now time for another challenge."

Gabriel scowled.

"Come now," Vincent said. "Do not tell me you have forgotten. 'Tis as I said before … I have laid a few traps of my own." The prophet raised both hands above his head, tilted his head back and chanted, "Konfoth skorpon!"

Black smoke formed along the rock ceiling above, swirling in and out in loops and figure eights. The smoke took shape. It slowly solidified into an eight legged mass—with two pinching claws and a narrow, white, sharp-tipped tail curved over its back. It let go of its grip and fell, rolled in mid-air, slammed into the ground. The abandoned mines shook. A small section near the cliff crumbled and broke away and fell into the ocean.

The giant, white-tail scorpion snapped its claws. With green venom oozing from the tip of its tail, it faced Gabriel.

"Good luck, Windstriker," Vincent said.

Gabriel glanced toward the cult leader, visible through the giant scorpion's legs.

Vincent gave a short, mock bow. Then he left through the tunnel he had entered through.

The windstriker refocused on the threat before him. He drew his crossbow into his left hand, knelt and stabbed the shortsword into the ground. After he pulled the crossbow's string back and locked its catch, he grabbed the dark bolt from his bag. Once loaded, he grabbed his blade and stood. Armed with shortsword in right hand and crossbow in left, he looked into the giant beast's eyes.

"Curse the gods," he spat, his confidence quivering. "Why did I vow to kill all of the kingdom's white-tail scorpions?"

Commander Brynden held a hand up to signal his men to halt.

"What is it, Bryn—I mean, Commander?" Trevor asked.

Brynden knelt to feel the rocky surface of the mineshaft. "The ground is cracked. The path is unstable."

Wils grunted. "Do you want to turn 'round? I saw another tunnel a ways back. Might be safer."

Brynden stood and shook his head. "No, we shall move forward. If the windstriker can make it we can, too."

The knights didn't protest. So he took a step forward, but with more caution than before.

Aryn, Trevor, Wils, and Pipes trailed slowly behind.

They hiked several minutes without any changes in the mineshaft; just the jagged overhang of sharp stalactites and the occasional crack in the ground. Light seeped between the cracks and illuminated the dark tunnel in a dim glow. After a while they saw a golden light ahead. Being in relative darkness, the glow was nearly blinding.

The knights came to an end in the path.

The ground had fallen away.

Where the path had been, an immense drop into the ocean now loomed. He edged closer toward the ledge and peered over. Three grey gulls flew thirty paces below.

So strange, he thought, *to look down on a bird in flight.*

Too much of the path had collapsed to go any farther. Brynden figured it was sixty, maybe eighty paces across. He scowled at the gap. It hindered him of vengeance.

"This buys the windstriker some time," he told the other knights. "We need to turn around and use the other tunnel."

"You sure the windstriker went this way," asked Wils.

"Yeah, he went this way." Brynden spat over the edge and watched as the phlegm was swept away in the wind. "I'll wager his weight was too much for the path and it gave way."

"Mayhaps he fell," Trevor said. "Think he's dead?"

"*NO!*" Brynden said it louder than he meant to. "No. He is not dead. And I shall not rest 'til I see his corpse with my own eyes." He turned from the gap and shouldered through his men.

"Hey," Pipes said. "What's ya problem, Bryn?!"

"Call me by my name again and I'll cut you," Brynden snapped. "It is Commander to you. Now let's go!"

He knew Clement would be reeling in his grave if he saw him treating the men this way. But he didn't care anymore. He only cared for vengeance, and he wanted it now.

15
THE ORPHANAGE

As Gabriel stared the giant scorpion in the eyes, all he could think about was the Orphanage. Helpless. Abandoned. Forgotten. And no one was coming. Like when the Headmaster locked him in a box when he was nine years old because he took an extra roll to give to one of the Littles—newcomers abandoned by their parents. He remembered the infuriated glare on the Headmaster's face. How he despised him, despised all of them. He threw a roll at Gabriel's head, slammed the lid down and locked the box.

"Orphans are worthless," he whispered at Gabriel through a crack in the lid.

After a day, he came back to administer the "real" punishment.

He unlocked the box and opened the lid. "I figured you might be gettin' hungry." He held up a grey bag, then dumped its contents onto Gabriel's head.

Dozens of black-white bugs fell into his hair, inside his shirt, across his bare toes. When Gabriel brushed one away, he saw they were white-tail scorpions. He screamed, flailed his arms, thrashed his feet.

The Headmaster slammed the lid down. "Don't worry, maggot," he said. "There's no venom in their stingers, syphoned it all out meself. But they can still sting. And pinch." He lifted the lid enough to spit in Gabriel's face. Then he locked the box and left.

The white-tail scorpions dug claws into Gabriel's chest, his neck, his thighs. Gabriel remembered their weight, the tingle and itch of their eight prickly legs. The scorpions pinched and they stung; the pain sharp and numbing. Gabriel screamed and screamed, and no one came. He thrashed and hit at the scorpions until his hands bled, and still no one came. He screamed until his voice gave out, thrashed until sleep overtook him.

On the third day, at least what Gabriel thought was the third, the Headmaster returned to find him curled in a ball—crying, red welts covering his hands, body, and face. There were squashed scorpions along the floor and sides of the box, and Gabriel's mouth had dried blood smeared across his lips and chin.

In his desperation, he had even eaten a few.

Fear of the Orphanage, of the Headmaster, of the scorpions, froze the windstriker where he stood.

"Well," he said to the goliath, trying to find his courage. "What are you waiting for beas—" his words cut short as the giant, white-tail scorpion stabbed with its tail.

Gabriel sprang leftward. He rolled into a tumble and nearly fell over the cliff. His crossbow slipped from his grasp, bounced, clanged, and then landed on the edge of the cliff as well.

The scorpion's tail stabbed into the ground where Gabriel had stood. When it tried to yank it out, it was stuck. It pushed its legs forward, but they slipped, so it shook its massive body like a wet wolf drying itself.

Fueled by adrenaline, Gabriel bounded to his feet and grabbed the crossbow. The dark bolt was somehow still loaded. He paced away from the cliff while aiming—fired. The invisible bolt hurtled forward and struck the black beast ...

... but it couldn't penetrate the scorpion's thick exoskeleton shell. The bolt caused only a scratch.

Gabriel snorted. *This is nothing like hitting a scorpion with your fist.*

He thumbed the gemstone and the quarrel returned to the crossbow's barrel. *Six more shots for six more hours.* When the sun went down, if the moon was full, the gemstones would recharge. But if it wasn't—

He fired again, aiming for the same mark. No time to think.

Yet still only a scratch.

The scorpion's tail finally loosened. It yanked again, and fell backwards from the unexpected release. A small crater formed in the ground where the tail had struck. The cracks surrounding it spread, widened, and then dropped into the ocean. A broad hole appeared in the center of the cave.

Gabriel fired again. The specter shot actually dented the shell this time, but the goliath turned on him alarmingly fast and charged in.

A black claw swung forward from the right. He narrowly ducked the blow. A claw swung in from the left. He stumbled rearwards and out of its reach. The scorpion kept swinging, pinching its claws with each strike.

And then the windstriker was dashing backwards—ducking, spinning, and occasionally deflecting claw attacks with his sword as he retreated—until he felt his back press up against the cave's wall.

The beast lunged another rightward strike, missed, but smashed into the wall. Its claw smacked into stone and sent great chunks of rock flying. A claw came from the left, hammered the wall as Gabriel ducked.

Another heavy rain of rock and stone sprayed.

Gabriel knew he needed to do something, and quick, or else it might be his blood spraying next time. He looked around for options.

No escape.

The scorpion's thick shell was too hard to penetrate with his crossbow or sword.

Though I did dent its shell with that last attack.

Then he saw it: an exposed soft spot on the goliath's body.

No, he saw eight soft spots. Eight black, beady eyes grouped in three widely spaced clusters—two on top of its head, two groups of three along the head's front corners. They stared out at him like bare skin seen through a knight's armor, weaknesses without protection.

With a knowing smirk, Gabriel aimed his crossbow and fired. Crossbow thrummed, and the bolt hit one of the beady eyes on top. Black pus squirted. The giant scorpion thrashed and shook in pain. He thumbed the gemstone, the bolt returned, and the windstriker fired another specter shot. The remaining eye on top sprayed dark pus.

Then the scorpion stumbled back, snapping those great claws, now realizing its opponent to actually be dangerous.

Its tail shot forward as it retreated.

Gabriel rolled left. The poisonous stinger struck the wall, green venom spewing upon impact.

Six beady eyes shifted with the windstriker's dash, following his escape. The beast turned toward him and swept in with a leftward claw attack.

Gabriel dove, rolled beneath the blow.

The claw drew back for another assault, and it was then he saw an opportunity. He grabbed hold of the claw, avoiding the pincer, and was lifted into the air. Using the momentum of the lift, he swung onto the goliath's back, just above the head.

The windstriker wasted no time. In one swift motion, he swiped his blade in a low-arcing cut at the three eyes grouped to his right. The cut sliced all three at once, spraying black pus.

All but three of the scorpion's eyes were now blind.

The giant's massive body shuddered in agony.

Gabriel was thrown from its back.

He smacked the ground. Disoriented, he stumbled to his feet. Then he glanced behind and cursed himself. The cliff loomed two feet away, the sea glittering below like a million jewels.

The white-tail scorpion quickly moved to pin him between itself and the edge.

As the scorpion crept forward, Gabriel caught a glimpse of his own reflection in those three milky, black eyes still gleaming with sight.

He took a step back.

Half-blind, the scorpion snapped its claws in intimidation as it approached.

He took a step back. His heels kicked pebbles over the cliff; only an inch of rock and gravel now between him and the fall. He aimed his crossbow at the approaching black threat.

What the hell. Gabriel shrugged. *It worked for the first two eyes.*

He pulled the trigger. The invisible bolt raced through the air …

… and tore into beady eyes. The bolt pierced all three, squirting pus, and then returned to the crossbow as Gabriel touched the gemstone.

Only two shots left, he thought, but snickered at his own luck.

Now completely blind, the giant, white-tail scorpion began wildly attacking with its tail. It struck the surface mere paces short of Gabriel. The ground cracked, and as the beast pulled its tail from the crater, a hole split and spread toward Gabriel and the edge.

Remembering the other tunnel across the cave, Gabriel darted for more solid ground just as the ground dropped away. He made it to the tunnel Vincent had escaped through, and turned around to see the scorpion's demise.

The scorpion kept pushing forward, not seeing the windstriker's retreat. It continued its berserk attack. Venom spewed with each strike. The ground kept falling away, dropping thousands of feet to splash into the ocean. Cracks in the ground now surrounded the giant scorpion, and the holes grew bigger as more rock plummeted.

Then the beast lunged a tail strike that struck an already cracked area of rock. The fragile surface collapsed and fell into the sea.

Taking the scorpion with it.

It desperately clawed and raked with its front legs to stay aloft.

Its massive weight pulled it down.

Gabriel moved closer to the edge of the tunnel. There wasn't a floor to the cave anymore; just a huge gap between the two tunnels. As he peered over, he saw the goliath splash into the water. The impact created sizable waves.

With an exhausted sigh, he bent over and put his hands on his knees. His adrenaline was leaving him. A sharp pain stabbed at his chest, making his breaths wheeze. The few scabs that had started to form on his hand were now torn open again. Blood and pus milked from the wound. He stood and clenched his fist. "How many more challenges will you throw my way, Vincent?"

He wasn't sure if he could survive another fight with one of Vincent's goliaths.

Suddenly, the small gemstone attached to the crossbow's tiller throbbed with an intense light. Gabriel shielded his eyes, remembering the similar event that occurred in the lair after the rock giant's defeat. The blinding radiance illuminated the abandoned mines, the side tunnels and beyond.

Moments passed before the light diminished. But the gemstone continued to shine in a peculiar glow—the red light flowed from within like churning water currents in the ocean.

These glowing gems will be the death of me.

He knelt, cut another strip of black cloth from his cloak, and wrapped it around the crossbow's tiller to muffle the glowing stone. He still saw a faint red light shining through the cloth, but it would have to do.

Sword and crossbow pulsed of energy in his hands.

Gabriel glanced down at them, puzzled. He had possessed these gems since boyhood, for as long as he could remember. He always considered them his birthright—his only legacy from the parents who had abandoned him at the Orphanage. He thought about them—his parents—in that moment. He never knew them.

Why did they leave me to be forgotten? Why did they leave me to be tortured in a place like the Orphanage?

He shrugged the thoughts away. He hated them for it, and chose not to think on them. Ever. He had made that pact with himself long ago, before becoming a man.

He secured his weapons—crossbow to his back and sword at the waist—then looked out to the glorious sight of the shimmering sea one last time. The breeze blew hair from his brow, exposing the wicked, white scar across his eye.

Another inheritance from a forgotten time, he snorted.

He turned to leave.

16

HOW FARES THE BATTLE

W ell?" Victoria asked. "Will the door budge or no?"
Of all the buildings she and Lukas had searched, this was the
only one that would not grant access. It had two stories, same as the
rest of the street's buildings, and the wood was rotting.

Lukas wriggled the handle and shoved his shoulder into the heavy
door. "Nay," he shook his head. "The door holds. Entry is barred."

"'Tis peculiar," she said. "All the other doors opened for us. Can
you see anything inside?"

Lukas cupped his hands around the paned glass window and peered
into the building. "Nay. Pane's too dirty." He rubbed a hand over the
glass, trying to clean it. He took another glance. "It's hazy," he said,
lifting his face to look at Victoria. "More like a fog—a mist."

"Strange."

"Yes," he agreed. "Magicks must be about." He scrutinized the
building again, looking it up and down. "Something is in here."

"How do we get inside then?"

"I know not," Lukas snorted. "Mayhaps it's nothing. The window
may just be smeared of dust, and the door's hinges rusted shut. Alas, I
do not believe Vincent and his lot are holed up in a rotting apartment
like this."

"Where do you believe the rats are hiding?"

"Higher ground." He glanced north, to taller buildings strategically
built on a large hill overlooking the city. "We shall continue to climb.
Vincent may be able to fly, but there's nigh many places left to run.
And a bird must perch to rest its wings."

Victoria looked to the cobblestones at her feet. *Vincent,* she thought.
He scared her now. The prophet so easily caught her off guard during

their previous encounter. The thought of charging in and experiencing another intrusive presence inside her made her wary. Vincent had read her sins, and seen things only she knew disturbed her dreams.

Such as not being wed to her prince, while the two lived in sin.

"What ails you, my love?" Lukas asked, noticing her worrisome change in attitude.

"It's nothing, Lukas."

He strode closer and took her hands into his own. She wouldn't look into his eyes. "Victoria," he said, lifting her chin with a finger and forcing her to look at him. He stroked her cheek and then her golden hair. "What is it? It is plain to see, you look troubled."

A sigh escaped her lips. "I'm sorry, Lukas." She bit her lip to keep it from trembling. "It's just … Vincent … and what he spoke. Does it not disturb you?"

"What?" His voice was calm, soothing. "About us being unwed?"

Victoria nodded.

"Nay," he said sternly. "You are my heart's desire, Victoria. And it's as I've said—we shall wed before year's end."

Victoria smiled. "Do you promise, Lukas? Do you mean it this time?"

"Yes, my love." He kissed her, the warm embrace of his lips comforting.

His words alone soothed her worries. *Gone are the days of harlotry. We are finally going to marry!* Victoria felt overcome with jubilation. Since becoming a believer in the faith of Lucidus, she felt tremendous conviction each time she and Lukas were intimate.

The sound of clinking armor graced the couple's presence, mixed with a rattling noise. The sounds came from behind. Victoria turned, still held close in her prince's arms, to see approaching knights rounding a corner and into the street.

It was Commander Adanna's unit.

The exotic, brown skin barbarian led the procession toward her and Lukas; her multi-colored beads rattled with the swing of her curved hips. Adanna stopped before them, glared at Victoria, and then greeted Lukas with a bow, fists curled over her chest.

Lukas released his strong and loving embrace. "Commander Adanna," he inclined his head. "How fares the battle?"

Victoria frowned. The glorious moment had passed, interrupted by the brown woman's *convenient* timing. She resented Commander Adanna even more for it. "What Lukas means is," she moved her right hand to the curve of her hip, near her sword, "how many men have you lost this time?"

Lady Luck looked at Victoria, shot a quick glance at the hand resting near her sword. "City belong to us, Captain," she ignored Victoria. "Some rats still here. Most run."

"So typical of rats," Lukas said, "to seek higher ground to escape a flood."

Victoria butted back in, "But how many of your men are dead?" She was determined to portray Commander Adanna in a negative light. Surely, Lukas saw what she did: a manipulative woman and a thief.

The barbarian wanted to steal her prince. She was sure of it.

Commander Adanna glared at Victoria. "One score, *Lady* Victoria." She said *Lady* with a sneer. "You know one score? It means—"

"I know what it means," Victoria shot back. Then she drew her sword. "You shall not insult me."

Adanna grabbed her spear and quickly stepped forward to meet the challenge.

"Enough!" Lukas's tone brooked no argument. "I'll not have your squabbles." He glanced behind Lady Luck, observing the number of knights still under her authority. The number had lessened since their meeting in the square. "Despite our victories, we're taking heavy losses. The rats know the city better than we, and we hunt in the open whilst they hide in their holes."

Victoria sighed and sheathed her blade. "What would you have us do differently?"

"Nothing," he said. "No, we knew this day would come. The Cardinal has allowed the cult of Dräkenkamp to withstand too long. And this battle has been long overdue. Losing knights was always inevitable, regardless if we struck the cult sooner or later."

"Then what shall *we* do?" Victoria asked.

"As I've said," he nodded toward the buildings built atop the hill. "We continue to climb. The rats make for higher ground, so we'll open the flood gates. The waters will rise, and we'll drown out the rats."

Lady Luck strapped the spear onto her back, and said, "Rats diseased and need be removed."

"Indeed, Commander Adanna." Lukas grinned. "Pray tell, have you heard word from Sir Ellard?"

She shook her head. "No, sir."

"Mayhaps he still sweeps the right flank."

Lady Luck said nothing. Victoria knew she spoke only when necessary, and that was too often for her liking. After a moment, Adanna asked, "Orders?"

Lukas stroked the evil-looking dagger looped through his belt with thumb and forefinger. "I noticed a wood to the west," he said. "From what I've seen of the streets thus far, it may be the only way to go farther into the city."

Victoria had overheard some of the men earlier in the day calling that wood by an unwelcoming name. They said it held a secret, one someone passing through must know before stepping foot inside the forest. She hoped it wouldn't come to this. She didn't want to pass through it.

"The men were calling the wood the Forest of Despair," she informed.

"Sounds inviting," Lukas teased.

Victoria folded her arms across her chest and frowned.

He must have noticed her concern. "Come now, my love, it is only a wood. No more. The men are a superstitious lot, surely you know this." He touched her arm and tried to pull her close.

But Victoria shrugged his hand away. She took a step back. "I'm just telling you what they said." She hated being teased, especially in front of this thieving barbarian.

"And I'm telling you there is nothing to fear." His voice was stern. He looked at Lady Luck. "Pass through the wood. Do you still remember the secret we were informed about?"

Commander Adanna nodded.

"Good. When you reach the higher section of the city, begin your sweep and wash out the rats."

Lady Luck bowed her unusual bow, acknowledging the orders. "Yes, sir." She walked past the couple, and glared at Victoria as she passed.

Her knights followed immediately. Their armor clinked as they marched.

"And Commander," Lukas added.

Lady Luck stopped the procession, turned around.

"If you stumble upon the cult leader, Vincent," Lukas said. "Engage. He wears a necklace which is of upmost importance. Bring it to me."

Adanna curled her fist together over her chest, bowed, and then resumed the march.

Vincent, thought Victoria. A wave of nervousness sent butterflies to her stomach. She looked at Lukas. *Surely he can protect me. After all, Vincent did flee him.*

Though whether he fled from Sinfire's blazing power or something else, she could not say. Just remembering how the fireball went right *through* him was enough to scare her.

The last of the knights faded from view before Victoria voiced her fears. "What if Vincent uses his diabolic powers against me again?" Her hands began to tremble. "How did the fire pass right through him? It is as though he is a ghost."

"Why, you're shaking." Lukas grasped her hands. He rubbed them as though they were cold. "Does he scare you so?"

Victoria nodded.

He hugged her close, protecting her. "Worry not, my love. I'll not let him hurt you."

"But, everything about Vincent defies understanding." She looked into his eyes, which shimmered in the mid-afternoon sun. "He was inside my thoughts, Lukas. He read my sins ... our sins."

"Come now, Victoria," he soothed. "Do not confuse your sins for mine. You are the harlot, not I."

Victoria blinked. "But—"

"But nothing." Lukas kissed her, but his tender lips didn't offer the same reassurance as before. "Now come, let us see this wood the men call the Forest of Despair."

17

THE PROPHECY

Are they gone?" Griff asked as he tapped fingers against his leg. An anxious behavior Alivia was beginning to find irksome.

"I think so." Stone peered out the window, trying to see if the Knight's Order were still in sight.

"How'd they not see us?" Griff asked. "I mean, the captain, he looked right at me. I thought for sure he saw me."

"I told you before you've nothing to fear." Stone pulled his face from the window and looked directly at Griff. "Vincent's magicks are powerful."

Alivia adjusted her wrists while sitting up. They had left her on the bench, and she grew uncomfortable. She couldn't take being bound any longer. She tried to wrench her hands free of the rope, but that only made the chafing worse. The rope was tied too tight, and she saw blood on the hemp. Hissing, she ignored the irritated burns and glanced around.

I need answers, she thought.

"Is Vincent the only one of your lot who possesses unusual powers?" she asked.

The disciples both looked at her with squinted eyes, annoyance clear across their faces. Neither said a word.

Then, Stone finally spoke, "Aye, the only."

"How does he do it?" She sat forward. "Use magicks, that is?"

Stone walked away from the window and sat on the bench opposite Alivia; just next to the ladder leading to the upstairs loft where the Duke's son lay resting. He lifted his right foot and set it on the bench, rested an arm over a bent knee. "Because," he said after a moment, "Vincent is the Prophet of the Dragon."

"The Prophet of the Dragon?"

"He's gifted."

"Gifted?" Alivia tented her eyebrows.

Stone looked at Griff, who sat on a bench to the right of Alivia. He made a gesture for him to answer the question.

Griff's eyes widened. "You want me to explain?"

Stone nodded.

"Okay," Griff said. "Vincent's gifts—the magicks—are made possible with the dragon scar on his left hand." He held up his own left hand and pointed to it. "Years ago, the dragon touched Vincent and blessed him with the scar. The scar grants Vincent some of the dragon's powers—like the gift of prophecy—and they can talk to each other, too. Without speaking that is. Do you get my meaning?"

Alivia thought she understood. "Like through their thoughts?"

"Aye," Griff said. "They are linked in some way. I don't know how it works." He ran fingers through his black, unruly hair. "Anyhow, Vincent's magicks are channeled through that scar, which the dragon blessed him with. When Vincent desires to use his magicks, he uses the words of power—a prayer, in the Vehaynian tongue—and wind and earth, water and fire bend to his will."

A blessed scar? Words of power? Prayer in an ancient tongue? The words echoed in her head. "I do not see how that's possible."

"Tis possible, woman," Stone cut in, "because the dragon is God——Adon incarnate. Vincent lifts his voice in prayer, and Adon answers his call."

The room filled with an awkward silence. Alivia felt uneasy. Up until a couple of days ago dragons no longer existed, having disappeared over two hundred years at the close of the Dragon Wars. Now, one not only exists, but people are claiming it to be the god, Adon?

The whole entirety of events was lunacy.

Stone interrupted the silence. "Regardless if you understand, or believe, that's how it is."

"Well, I do not believe." She believed in reason, science, the study of chemistry, philosophy, alchemy, psychology, not in a faith she couldn't see.

"And that's fine," Stone said. "But one day, you'll find your beliefs put to the question." He pointed a finger at her. "You've seen oddities

97

this day you cannot explain. Can you?"

Alivia didn't answer.

Her silence was all Stone needed to hear. "I thought so."

Another awkward silence followed, this time interrupted by Griff. "But Vincent's powers," he said, resuming the discussion about the prophet and his magicks, "they are strong, but they can be stronger."

"How so?" Alivia asked.

"His necklace," Griff said. "The Heart of the—"

Stone cleared his throat, a grunt clearly indicating Griff to stop speaking.

Alivia wanted to know more. "What?" she asked, looking from one to the other. "The Heart of the what?"

"It's naught that concerns you," Stone said harshly.

The discussion was over.

Both disciples stared off, perhaps thinking on answers she wished she knew. But Alivia lifted her chin, straightened her posture. She wasn't through questioning her captors.

"What about the Duke?" She changed subjects. "Why did Dräkenkamp seize Castle Lombard?"

The disciples met eyes, exchanged words without speaking.

"Why?" Alivia demanded.

"She is unrelenting." Stone chuckled.

Griff agreed, "Aye, that she is." He got up and walked over to the ladder. "I'll leave you two to your words. I need to get some rest whilst I can."

Stone nodded, and Griff climbed. Once he was out of sight, Stone focused back on Alivia. He looked serious. "So you want to know of the Duke?"

Alivia nodded.

"I fear we've said too much as it is." He leaned back against the wall, observing how she sat with hands bound behind her back. He gestured toward her ropes. "But seeing how you're not going anywhere." He released a heavy sigh and scratched at his beard. "And mayhaps, if you survive this mess, you can tell the world ... how it is and how it was. Of what really happened here in the Fortress of the Moon."

Alivia nodded again. She was determined to survive this ordeal, or better still, steal a dagger and kill her captors so she might save the child. But she also needed to learn as much about Dräkenkamp as she could and report back to parliament. Though she would never be a voice of reason for the cult, despite what Stone may believe her to do once free.

"The Duke," he began, "turned against us."

Alivia leaned forward. "So you *were* in dark league with him after all."

"Aye."

"Then why the falling out?"

Stone lowered his foot from the bench. He leaned forward, put his elbows on his knees, and whispered, "The Duke stole something from us. Something of great importance."

"What?"

"Something needed to aid our cause."

"So you seized the Duke's castle to find what he stole," Alivia said. "And when you couldn't find it, you kidnapped his son so you would have a hostage to barter with."

"That's right," he said. "In order for us to inherit the Fortress of the Moon—to access its powers—we must have the *key.*"

Alivia arched an eyebrow.

"A stone," he said. "The Heart of the Dragon. What Griff started to say before. It's the key to the city."

Alivia couldn't believe how his tongue had loosened. "And the Duke, he has this stone?"

"Nay." Stone shook his head. "Vincent, he has it. But the stone is … incomplete."

"Incomplete?" She paused. "What is missing?"

He didn't answer, so Alivia repeated the question.

"I know not." He exhaled a frustrated breath. "All I know is that we searched Castle Lombard for artifacts. Enchanted artifacts, according to Vincent. Which the Duke stole."

"Did you find them?"

He shook his head.

"What are they, these artifacts?" she asked.

Stone's eyes narrowed. He was hesitant to answer.

"What are they?" she asked again.

He turned his gaze from her and stayed quiet.

"You do not know," she realized. "Vincent won't tell you, will he?"

Seconds ticked by and Stone still muttered no words, his silence betraying him.

"He hasn't," Alivia confirmed. She shifted her weight and rolled her wrists to ease her discomfort. "If Vincent had these artifacts, then the Heart of the Dragon would be complete? Is that right? The *key* would be complete?"

Stone snorted. "Aye."

"Then what?" she asked. "When you have the key to the city … what happens?"

"What happens?" He smiled. "Vincent's greatest prophecy will be nigh close to fulfillment."

Prophecy? Stone speaks in riddles similar to Vincent.

Alivia shrugged. "I always wondered if our morrows could be foretold," the cynicism barely hidden in her voice.

"Vincent's prophecy," Stone ignored her doubt, "heralds the coming of the shattered Kingdom of Vehayne." He closed his eyes and recited a verse: "He will die to save what is broken."

Alivia felt a chill come across her, the hairs on the back of her neck standing on end. *Prophecy and death.* She didn't believe, so why the sudden feelings of dread? "W-who will die?"

Stone shrugged. He unsheathed a dagger. "Mayhaps it's your windstriker friend."

Alivia gulped. "What is broken? Is it the incomplete Heart of the Dragon?"

Stone shook his head.

"Do you think Vincent knows the answers to his own vision?"

He didn't answer; just tossed the blade from hand to hand.

"Do you think Vincent knows?"

Stone stabbed the dagger into the wooden bench. "This discussion is over."

His harshness startled her. Their conversation had seemed friendly enough. She lowered her head, and looked at the floor. She could see where Vincent's sharp-tipped boots had scratched the wood earlier.

Vincent. Heart of the Dragon. Key to the city. Her mind whirled like an unsolved puzzle, and she couldn't put the pieces together. *I must know more,* she thought. *I'll not survive otherwise.*

Perhaps she could change the subject to something less … provocative. "Earlier," she said. "Before the Knight's Order walked past our door, you slept."

"Yah, so." Stone rested his head against the wall. He glanced to the upstairs loft where the other two lay resting.

"You spoke in your sleep," Alivia went on. "Mentioned a name: Logan."

Stone's gaze shot forward, a stare so hateful Alivia's stomach churned in fear that he would dash across the room and strike her. "Speak not on him! You hear me?!"

A rustling stirred from the upstairs loft.

Alivia glanced toward the disturbance, and then back to the infuriated Stone. To her surprise, his eyes were closed and he inhaled deep breaths of air. She remembered Vincent's words: *Watch your temper, Stone. Breathe and control it.*

Temper indeed.

"M-my apologies," she said. "I did not intend—"

"Never you mind," Stone said, his calm demeanor returned. He looked away, seeming distant. A moment passed before he deeply sighed, "Logan, my little boy."

"Oh," Alivia remarked. "I did not realize you had a son."

"How could you." His eyes glossed over with a look of remembrance. "Alas, I do no longer."

"I am sorry to hear it. To lose a child must be unbearable." Although the conversation had become delicate, Alivia felt if she could learn something of Stone's past, she might be able to learn of his—and quite possibly Dräkenkamp's—motives. "What happened?" she asked in a tender, soft-spoken voice.

"You ask too many damned questions!" Stone ran strong hands through his beard. "But now that I think on it, it might be best if you knew."

Alivia nodded.

"He was taken from me, 'bout five years ago," he began. "Murdered by the kingdom with which you so serve."

Alivia kept quiet.

Stone snorted. "Curse the Four Winds, they murdered my boy!" He was fighting back tears, Alivia saw.

"How?" she asked.

"My home is Shade Town of the Graywinds," he continued. "The region's ruler, Duke Garasoan, raised our taxes knowing our poor town could not afford to pay them. When the collectors came for the money, we didn't have it. At least, not all of it.

"They said they'd be back. To collect the rest, that is." He balled his hands into fists. "And return they did, with a raiding party led by Duke Garasoan himself. He demanded the payment, and when the townspeople could not pay, he ordered his men to enter our homes and take what was 'rightfully his'."

Stone punched his legs, tears beginning to trail down his cheeks. "They raped and pillaged us! Burned our homes," he cried. "Amidst the chaos, I lost my boy. He got away from me. I don't know how. Everything happened so fast."

A sob escaped him. "Then I heard Logan's voice. Yelling for me, calling 'Papa'. I ran toward his terrified shout and found him in front of our home. It burned, oh how it burned. And the heat, I can still feel the heat."

Alivia gasped.

"He thought I was trapped inside. He yelled for me, and I yelled for him. When he heard me he turned, and seeing that I was safe, brightened his crying face in a joyful smile." Stone smiled himself and wiped away a tear. "Oh, what a smile. I can still see it."

After a moment, Stone continued, "Logan ran toward me, smiling and yelling 'Papa'. He never reached my arms." He brought his clenched fists up in front of his face, seething in anger. "An arrow struck him in the back," he wailed.

The horrendousness of his story and the howl of his anguish were unbearable. Alivia blinked, and tears fell from the corner of her eyes.

Stone resumed his sad tale. "My boy fell to the ground. He didn't move and I knew … he was dead." He exhaled a long and slow breath. "Behind him, his murderer sat mounted upon his robust steed, bow in hand, laughing with his men. It was Duke Garasoan," he said through clenched teeth. "He killed my boy as though he were hunted game!"

Alivia's mouth fell agape.

"I charged at him," Stone continued, "intent on killing him. I cared not if I died then. How could I live without my boy? When the Duke saw me running toward him, he nocked another arrow and fired. It struck me, giving me this scar." Stone pulled his jerkin down off his neck, revealing a scar on the right side of his chest, just under the shoulder.

Alivia gasped, "My word."

The wound was reddish, in the shape of an X. The arrowhead must have been crossed to cause more damage to its victim.

Stone let go of the jerkin and it settled back into place over his chest. "I blacked out, and the Duke didn't even bother to come finish his work. He left me to die from my wound, or to live. He cared not."

After a pause, he went on. "I awoke to the sound of screams. Mothers held their dead sons. Husbands held their dead wives. We were left to the ruins of our misery. Garasoan's raiding party was gone, and the town was no more—just smoldering ash and a choking smoke.

"I lay there, in the street where I was wounded," he continued. "Wishing I were dead. It was then that I saw him, walking amongst the rubble—a man in dark armor with long, blond hair. He was so out of place."

Alivia whispered, "Vincent?"

Stone nodded, and said, "Aye. He came over, knelt beside me, and offered his hand. And he said, I'll never forget what he said: *Keep to heart for Adon is in control.*"

Alivia asked, "The Hero-King deity?"

Stone nodded. "I took Vincent's hand. He looked over my wound, withdrew the arrow, and miraculously healed me. He told me he was in need of good men—men desiring to overthrow the Kingdom of the Four Winds. It was all I needed to hear. I wanted revenge for my boy's murder. I followed."

"So revenge is your game?" Alivia asked. "That's what you and Vincent are scheming?"

"The Kingdom of the Four Winds is filled with sin," Stone said. "And the masses worship undeserving gods. Revenge may be my aim, but not Vincent's."

"Then what is his aim?"

"Cleansing," he answered. "To wash clean the sins of the misguided, and to bring them to Adon—the one, true God."

"The prophecy," Alivia said.

"Is the answer," Stone finished.

Moments ticked away, neither speaking. Alivia contemplated the meaning of the disciple's words. She understood Stone's plight, and felt sorry for the loss of his son. But scheming to overthrow the Four Winds was treason.

Dräkenkamp is clearly a threat to kingdom security, she thought. *I must try to stop them, by any means.*

A commotion stirred from the upstairs loft.

Alivia looked up and saw Griff standing at the top of the ladder.

"Stone," Griff called. He motioned toward the front window of the apartment. "It nears dusk."

Stone glanced toward the window, as did Alivia. The sun was low in the sky and the colors of sunset were close at hand. Only an hour, two at most, until the Fortress of the Moon would be thrust into darkness.

"So it is," Stone sighed. "All right, bring the boy."

"Aye," Griff said. He disappeared from view.

Stone stood and focused on Alivia. "Stand up," he demanded.

She scooted off the bench to her feet.

The disciple pried free his dagger from the bench and came closer. The dwindling sun reflected off the blade's metallic shine.

Alivia's eyes widened.

"Turn 'round," he ordered.

Alivia did as commanded, and Stone cut the ropes free from her wrists. Immediately, she felt relieved to not be harmed; but, moreover, to be rid of those burning restraints.

"We've quite the trek ahead of us," Stone said. "Do us no good to have you slowing us down."

Alivia turned around, nodded. *And now that my hands are free I'm more likely to kill you.*

"But mind you," he resumed, sounding serious. "If you attempt to flee, you'll find this dagger in your back." He held up the blade to make certain she knew he meant it. Then he sheathed it at his waist.

She nodded again, unimpressed.

From behind Stone, a stomp thumped against the floor as Griff dropped the last few steps of the ladder. He gently lowered the boy to the ground, who blinked tiredly and rubbed his eyes.

"The Duke's son," Stone introduced. "Our ... honored guest." He focused on the boy, and asked, "Did you sleep well, Patrick?"

Patrick nodded. Then, upon seeing Alivia, walked closer to Stone and hid behind him.

"He seems quite taken with you," she said, noting the strange behavior.

"Aye, he is," Stone said. "Though he is timid and does not speak." He placed a hand on Patrick's blond head, the size of his hand nearly consuming it, and ruffled his hair. "He reminds me of my own boy ... Logan."

Alivia now understood Stone's attachment to the young heir. "Does he know why you have taken him? Why you have brought him here?"

Stone shook his head.

Griff grunted to interrupt. "We should get going. We need to reach the throne room by nightfall."

"Aye," Stone agreed. "Let's get moving."

The four walked toward the front door of the apartment, led by Stone. He opened it, and Alivia saw that the green, rippling energy still pulsated around the door's frame. Stone walked through and into the street. He held up a hand for the other three to remain inside while he inspected for safe passage. Once satisfied, he waved his hand for them to follow.

"Safe," called Stone from outside, his voice muffled like he spoke underwater.

Alivia stepped through, followed by Griff. She glanced over her shoulder and looked back inside the door, astonished. The green energy could not be seen. Instead, a foggy mist loomed inside the apartment's interior and hazed the onlooker's view.

Vincent's magicks are impressive.

"Let's go," Griff said. He ran past to catch up with Stone and Patrick.

She started to sprint after, but her foot caught on a cobble in the street and she fell to the ground and scraped her hands. She put her hands under her chest to push up and spring back to her feet, but halted. Right in front of her face, to her utter disbelief, was a flower boasting a bright, red bulb centered amongst green pedals.

The poisonous Redoulz.

Knowing how to handle such a deadly plant, she hurriedly, yet delicately, broke its stem and pocketed the flower.

Griff turned around to see her lying face-down. He rushed over and helped her to her feet. "You all right?" he asked.

"Y-yeah," Alivia said. She brushed her hands together to remove the small rocks embedded into her skin. "I think so."

"Come on," he said, unaware of her discovery. "We need to catch up."

18

FOREST OF DESPAIR

The windstriker climbed the stairs exiting from the abandoned mines two at a time. Unlike the entrance to the mines, the exit boasted square-cut stones seamlessly blended into the cave's floor and walls. As Gabriel reached the top step, he saw that the stones spread out into a small courtyard just on the edge of a lush, green wood.

From here, he couldn't see any of the buildings, nor the ocean below and beyond the Fortress of the Moon. But he could see how the courtyard looked like the rest of the sky city, ancient and forgotten. Weeds rose up between cracks of stones, their once clean cut edges weathered rough and uneven. A stagnant fountain—green sludge floating atop the water's surface, a trio of stone dragons frolicking in its filth—was the focal point of the yard.

The forest is consuming this place, he thought. The forest had overgrown into the courtyard; grass and weeds stretched across the stones to strangle the life from something that was once, perhaps, beautiful.

At least the air smelled fresh and clean, accentuated by all the grass.

He passed the fountain, and kept heading toward the edge where the courtyard and wood met. Here, the stones ended, marking the outer border of the yard. Wind stirred leaves in the distance, dancing toward him until his tousled hair joined their rhythm. Then the wind ceased to dance, and silence followed.

Gabriel narrowed his eyes and tried to peer deeper into the deserted forest. He saw nothing unusual.

"This way," a frightful voice whispered amongst the trees.

Gabriel took a step back, away from the forest's edge.

"Come, Gabriel Lost" the voice beckoned. *"This way."*

Gabriel felt a chill, and he tightly pulled his cloak about him. But he noticed the air felt warm and no breeze stirred.

Then he saw her—a slender figure walking between a pair of oak trees covered in moss. She wandered aimlessly, skipping at times and running at others, but all the while she looked directly at him. Her hair was long and white, though she was not old. She was very fair, and very beautiful. And Gabriel could see she wore no clothes, though she was not naked. Her flowing white hair covered her most womanly features.

She beckoned him, holding her hand out and curling her finger. And her voice was the chill in the wind. *"Come to me, Gabriel Lost,"* she whispered. *"This way."*

Then she skipped behind a tree and vanished.

Gabriel took a step forward, compelled to follow. "Who goes there?" he shouted.

"Don't let the wood spook you," a deep voice said from behind.

Gabriel turned around, and saw the dark mercenary, Slade, leaning against a stone wall next to the abandoned mine's exit. His arms were folded across his chest, and he looked as though he might have been waiting a while.

"It's the Witch of the Wood," Slade said. "She's the wind that speaks." He pushed off the wall and made his way toward the center of the courtyard, near the fountain. "Took you long enough."

Gabriel squared his shoulders to the mercenary.

"At the rate you're going," Slade smirked, "I'll win our bet."

Gabriel grabbed the hilt at his waist and drew his sword. He didn't trust the man, not after the ghostly vision in the library.

Slade put his hands up. "Please, I thought I told you I'm a friend."

"I've been told otherwise," Gabriel said.

"Well, I'm sorry to hear it." He paced toward the forest's edge, staying clear of the windstriker. "I've been waiting for you," he said, peering into the forest. "So I could advise you how to pass through this wood." He looked at Gabriel. "There's a secret it holds. Most men don't know it, and they pay dearly for their ignorance."

"Like your advice to pass through the mines?" Gabriel sneered. "The mines were unstable. The falls alone nearly killed me."

"Then you are not as skilled as I'd first believed," Slade ridiculed. "The mines are the quickest and surest way to reach the wood. And this wood is the *only* way to reach the higher portion of the city."

Gabriel stayed silent. If Slade's words were true, then he may need to hear what *secrets* the wood held.

Slade motioned toward Gabriel's weapon. "Your sword?"

Gabriel sheathed it, then got to the point. "What secret does the wood hold?"

"The Witch of the Wood," Slade informed, "entices men. She's beautiful and alluring, sure, but she's deadly. The wind stirs and she speaks, beckoning you to follow her. Most men pursue in their lust, the fools, hoping for her warm embrace. But to follow her is to follow death."

Gabriel asked, "Then what is the secret?"

"Don't follow," Slade said simply.

"What mean you?"

"What I mean," he said with a grin, "is to travel the opposite direction. The Witch beckons you one way, and you walk the other."

Gabriel didn't see how anyone could reach the other end of the wood in this manner. "How does it work?" he asked. "How does one reach the other side?"

"This wood is enchanted," Slade said. "The Witch leads you farther and farther into the forest, until you reach her dwelling. Then you're hers. No escape. But to not follow keeps you on the *true* path toward the exit."

Gabriel said, "I see."

Slade nodded.

The windstriker headed into the forest to join the trees.

"Going so soon, my friend?" Slade called after.

Gabriel stopped, turned to face the mercenary.

Slade looked serious. "Don't take the Forest of Despair lightly. The Witch is cunning. She'll play tricks on you."

Gabriel nodded. He moved to leave again, but halted. "Why's the wood called the Forest of Despair?" he asked over his shoulder.

"Because the men who follow the Witch are lost to despair."

"Ah," Gabriel mused. Then he said, "I've some advice for you, if you'll hear it."

Slade nodded.

"I'll not sheathe my blade, next we meet. Prepare yourself to face me. If you want to live, though, you'll leave the sky city before nightfall."

Slade grinned.

Gabriel resumed his hike amongst the trees, to try his luck with the so-called Witch of the Wood.

Victoria squeezed Lukas's right hand tightly as the two climbed the stone stairs. After meeting up and ordering the rest of the men to head through the Forest of Despair and to higher ground, she and Lukas made their way for the abandoned mines. Lukas had been told by an informant that the mines were the "quickest and surest way." And the couple needed to make up precious ground to catch back up with the men. Rounding up Sir Ellard and his men-at-arms had taken time.

They reached the top of the steps. A weed-infested and stone-surfaced courtyard spread out before them. In the center of the yard, a disgusting fountain with vile byrds sat in a pool of green muck. Across the yard, leaning against a tree on the edge of the wood, was a dark figure with arms folded across his chest.

Why is he *here?* Victoria squeezed her prince's hand tighter.

As the couple drew closer, Jon Slade grinned deceitfully. "Took you long enough, Steele."

"And greetings to you, mercenary," Lukas said with no trace of a smile. "We had to make certain my men knew to head for higher ground."

Slade unfolded his arms and pushed off the tree. "Did you tell your men the secret of the wood?"

"Of course," Lukas said impatiently. "I'm the last of my men to pass through."

Slade nodded. He gazed toward the forest. "Five of your knights went in, no more than ten minutes ago. I hid, not wanting to draw their attention. They are quick on the heels of your man-in-black."

Lukas snorted. "Good, Brynden and his men will see to the windstriker's demise soon enough."

Slade faced the couple. "No, I fear the Witch will mark all their graves. She's too cunning a foe."

At the mention of the wood's Witch, Victoria shivered. She didn't want to go in there.

Lukas asked, "What can you tell me about this windstriker?"

"He's bloody strong," Slade answered. "But he's been ill-informed."

"That's not surprising. Parliament likes to keep their attack dogs in the dark."

Slade nodded.

Victoria wanted to know she and Lukas could make it through the Forest of Despair. "Are you sure the Witch will not harm us?" she asked for reassurance.

Slade said, "As long as you stay clear of her, she's no threat. But she'll play her tricks all the same. Keep your wits and you can survive the wood. Fall to her deceits, though, and you're dead."

Victoria tore her gaze from the mercenary and stared into the wood. She rubbed her arms as though she were cold.

Slade returned his focus to Lukas. "Are you to follow the windstriker?"

"Nay," Lukas shook his head. "I've a unit hunting him. I trust my men will perform their duty." He released a contemplative sigh. "No, my business lies with Vincent."

"Ah," Slade mused. "And what business would that be?"

Lukas narrowed his eyes, hesitant to answer. "What's it to you?" He spat. "Didn't we have a deal? You've been paid, have you not?"

Slade motioned with his hands. "More or less."

"Then join with Vincent," Lukas demanded, "and find the key."

Slade grinned knowingly. "The Heart of the Dragon, you mean?"

Lukas's gaze turned to anger. "How do you know of the stone?"

"I know many things."

"So it would seem."

"But I must inform you," Slade said, looking serious. "There is something odd about Vincent and that windstriker."

"What mean you?"

"Vincent," Slade began, "seems to have a strange attachment to the man-in-black. For what purpose, I cannot guess." He paused as though he were finished speaking.

Lukas said, "Go on."

Slade smirked. "I knew you'd find me to be useful." Then he continued, "Vincent is challenging him—calling forth the fabled Goliaths of Old."

Victoria scoffed. "Surely he lies, Lukas. No such beasts exist."

"No?" Slade shrugged. "As you say. But, I must tell you it's true.

For I have seen it."

Lukas snorted. "Explain yourself!"

Slade nodded. "As I was saying, Vincent's powers are beyond what we first believed. He has somehow discovered how to summon the mythical Goliaths, and he's pitting them against the windstriker."

"And you say you saw it?"

"Aye," Slade said. "In the mines."

"Describe what you saw."

"You may recall I'm a former windstriker," Slade said. He hooked his thumbs underneath two belt straps at his waist. The exposed, silver daggers gleamed in a clean shine. "Keeping to the shadows was once a specialty of mine."

"Get to the point."

"Anyhow," Slade went on, keeping his calm demeanor despite Lukas's impatient one, "I'd hidden myself, knowing the windstriker would pass near. I wanted to observe him. See how my skill might measure up to his. He's too strong a foe to take lightly."

"So I have heard," Lukas said.

"I didn't expect him to encounter Vincent. He approached the windstriker. The two exchanged words I could not hear. The wind blew too fierce. After their exchange, Vincent lifted his arms and chanted something. Then the Goliath materialized before him—a Scorpion."

Victoria gasped.

"And you say the windstriker fought the beast?" Lukas asked.

"Aye," Slade said, "and won."

"Impressive."

"Indeed."

Victoria didn't understand how anyone could possess such powers. She feared the pagan prophet enough; now, though, her fear intensified. "But how?" her voice quivered. "And ... and why is he doing it?"

Slade said, "I know not why, or even how, Vincent summoned the Goliath. But he did it all the same. Alas, there's more to these strange tidings ..."

Lukas sighed with impatience. "What is it, then? I need to catch up with my men."

"After the Scorpion's defeat," Slade continued, "the windstriker's weapon illuminated itself in a most bizarre glow. Its intensity was blinding. If it had not been, my cover would have been exposed."

"What did you make of it?" Lukas asked.

Slade shrugged. "That's the question, is it not? Seems significant, though."

"Mayhaps."

A moment passed before Slade spoke again, "Anyhow, you've got your update." He turned away from the wood, and started back toward the mines.

Lukas called after him, "You're not going through the wood?"

Slade stopped and shook his head. "Nay, I've some business of my own to attend to on this end of the city. I'll catch up, soon enough." He continued his exit from the couple's presence.

Victoria looked at her prince. He didn't meet her eyes. Instead, his face was worked up in a sneer as he glared hatefully at the mercenary's back.

Why is Slade so needed? she wanted to ask.

The mercenary stopped as though he had overheard her thoughts. He glanced at Victoria, grinned. Then he focused on Lukas. "Stay clear of the Witch," he advised, reminding Victoria why he was needed. "She'll entice even you, my good captain." He descended the steps leading back into the unstable mines.

Once the mercenary was out of sight, Victoria asked, "Can he be trusted, truly?"

Lukas shook his head, and said, "Nay. But alas, we've no choice. His knowledge of the sky city is too great to ignore." He turned away from the mines, and focused on the ominous wood.

Wind stirred behind the couple and wafted into the forest. Victoria felt as though the wind were pushing her, urging her forward.

The Witch is expecting us. She was certain of it.

"Is—is there no other way?" she asked. She *really* did not want to go in there.

"No other," Lukas answered.

Victoria sighed.

He grabbed her hand, a strong touch of protection. "Tis time to go, my love," he said. "Stay close."

19

WITCH OF THE WOOD

This wood," Griff said as he pushed away a branch sticking out over the path. It swung back into place as he let go. "There is so much fog."

"It's the Witch," Stone said. "She's playing her tricks. Mayhaps she aims to disorient us."

"Well, it's working," Griff said. "I can no longer tell which direction we came from."

"Just keep your wits and follow my lead. Now be silent."

Alivia ducked beneath a low-hanging limb. The wet air felt cool pressed against her skin and the dampness clung to her hair. The musty smell of wet leaves filled her nostrils. They seemed to be walking endlessly, keeping to narrow paths with Stone leading them onward.

The boy, Patrick, kept pace close behind the disciple. He never strayed far from arm's reach, and had still not spoken a word. But every once in a while, he would turn and look at Alivia, the extent of their interactions. If the boy was nervous, he didn't show it.

Griff, on the other hand, was far from quiet. He trailed behind Alivia to make sure she did not escape. All the while he rambled on about the wood and the mist and asked absurd questions about this yet-to-be-seen witch.

"Wonder what happens if you follow her. Do you think she's really a demon in disguise?"

A branch snapped underfoot as he finished that last question.

"Enough with the questions," Stone growled. "Silence."

"Come on, Gavin, I'm just curious is all."

Stone said nothing. Sighing, Griff finally gave it up.

Alivia still couldn't believe what she had witnessed these past few days: a dragon, men wielding magicks, the wonders of the flying sky city—the Fortress of the Moon. And now loomed the threat of a Witch, a so-called predator of this ancient forest.

I feel like I'm walking through a fairy tale.

They continued to hike through the wood in silence, with only the occasional snapping stick to cause any disturbance.

Then, from the right, Alivia heard wind sigh through the trees. The leaves rustled, and it reminded her of the wooden wind chimes on her parents' front porch back home in Voss. She glanced toward the commotion, but could see no farther than a few feet past the fog.

How can Stone possibly know where he is going? This mist is too thick.

Stone stopped abruptly, causing the other three to halt just as quick. He held up a hand, motioned for them to stay quiet.

No one moved.

Alivia lowered her head and listened. She couldn't hear anything, save the rhythmic breathing of her company. Without thinking, she lightly pat her coat pocket to make sure the Redoulz lay undisturbed. She thought about taking the flower out now, poisoning Stone, and grabbing the boy to make a run for it. But she knew she couldn't outrun Griff, especially blind from the mist, not knowing where she was going.

Stone took a sudden step forward. He gasped with what sounded like excitement.

Alivia lifted her head.

Stone took another step forward, arms held out to his sides.

"Gavin?" Griff asked nervously. "Is–is everything all right?"

He didn't answer.

Alivia tilted her head to the side to see what Stone was staring at. She could make out nothing, only fog.

But then she saw something—a slender shape—skip through the mist. The shape pranced from behind a tree, and Alivia saw a woman: ankle length, white hair covered her neck, shoulders, and chest; her pale skin glistened from the wet touch of moist air; while her eyes shone silver like the haunting gleam of moonlight.

The woman raised her hand and curled her finger, beckoning Stone. She whispered to him, but Alivia couldn't hear what was said. Then the woman skipped away and disappeared into the mist.

Stone took another step forward.

"What is it you see?" Griff called out. He moved up to stand near Alivia, to get a better view.

Alivia grabbed his arm. Griff looked at her with alarm. "It's the Witch," she whispered.

Griff's gaze shot forward, mouth agape.

Stone shouted, "Can you believe it? It's my boy ... Logan!" He turned and looked at them, face beaming with excitement.

Right before he ran off into the fog.

"No, no, Gavin!"

"Come back, Stone," Alivia yelled. "It's not your boy!"

Only Patrick remained still.

"I can see him," he yelled back. "He calls for me!"

Griff looked at Alivia expectantly.

"Do something!" she urged.

He hesitated for a brief moment, uncertain of what to do, but then he bolted for Stone. Alivia saw him close the gap between them and dive. He tackled Stone around the waist and brought him to the ground.

Stone stood, wrath in his voice. "You'll not keep me from my boy!"

Griff pleaded, "It's not your boy, Gavin!"

Laughter filled the air, a sound of bells and wind.

Stone looked back to where he saw the false vision—the direction of the Witch. "See," he said. "Can you not hear his sweet voice?"

"No," Griff argued. "It's not your boy. It's the Witch!"

Stone charged at Griff like an enraged bull. He screamed his fury, and Griff took a startled step back. But then Griff charged at him in return, desperate to save his friend.

The two clashed as rams and tumbled to the ground. They scuffled around, rolled in the leaves, wrestled for control.

Until Stone finally broke free and started back for the Witch.

Griff stumbled back to his feet. He lunged after Stone and grabbed him around the shoulders, trying to keep him back. But Stone was stronger. He grabbed Griff's wrist, then flung him over his back and to the ground. Griff quickly tried to get back on his feet, but Stone swung a strong, right hook into his jaw and dropped him to the dirt.

He stepped over Griff's motionless body and continued his determined pursuit.

It was then that Alivia noticed she was alone. In the chaos of the commotion, she never saw Patrick leave her side. She looked around, frantic, calling his name. She hoped to grab the boy and make an escape. A rustling stirred from ahead, toward Stone, and she saw the disciple halt his advance.

Stone just stood there, staring down at something in front of him.

Alivia took a few hesitant steps forward so she might catch a glimpse of what he was seeing. And then she saw *him*.

Patrick.

The boy stood in front of Stone and prohibited him from moving. His tiny arms were held out to his sides, and he looked up at Stone as though he were expecting a father's hug.

Stone snorted. He moved to go around the boy, determined to pursue the Witch.

Patrick said nothing in response. He held his arms out farther, stepped closer to Stone and stopped him once more.

The sound of bells and wind filled the air again.

Stone looked out to the beckoning Witch, then back down to Patrick. Seconds passed away to uncertainty.

Finally, Stone shook his head to come out of the trance. He sighed, "No, it's not my boy." His voice was choked with sadness. "It can't be … he's been dead for some time."

He knelt and looked Patrick in the eye. Alivia heard his faintest whisper of: *Thank you.*

She breathed a sigh of relief as Stone hoisted the boy into his arms, and carried him like a father holding his son.

He walked over to Griff, who was rocking back to his knees and spitting blood. Stone offered his free hand, and asked, "You gonna live?"

Griff nodded, a shade of anger still in his eyes. But he said, "Aye," and took Stone's hand.

The three approached Alivia.

Stone arched an eyebrow at her. "I'm surprised you didn't run."

If I'd been in a right mind, I would have. "I gave you my word," she said.

Stone nodded. "That you did, and kept it." He glanced over his shoulder, back to where the Witch had beckoned him.

Griff and Alivia exchanged nervous glances.

After a second, he turned away, and started walking in the opposite direction. "Let's be off," Stone said. "The sooner we leave this accursed wood, the better."

"Lukas!" Victoria shouted into the fog. "Please, if you truly love me, answer me!" She let go a quivering sigh, fighting back the fear. "Where did you go?"

Victoria had stayed close to Lukas, as he advised. But somewhere along the way he disappeared, no longer embracing her in his firm grasp of protection. Now she was alone, frantic, and trembling. And the Witch loomed near, she was certain of it.

She called his name again, and again. He didn't answer.

She tried to return the way they came, but wondered if she walked in circles.

She stopped to listen for his footfalls, but heard nothing save wind rustle the leaves.

And now, she put her head in her hands and despaired. "Why won't you answer me, Lukas?"

"What ails you so?" a voice called from the mist.

Victoria looked up to see her prince standing in the distance. Fog rolled in. It made him appear ghostly. "L-Lukas," she said. "Is that really you?"

"Of course," he replied. *"Come to me, my love."*

She started to move closer, slowly. "Oh, Lukas," she felt relieved. "I thought I lost you!"

He turned from her and ran between the trees, vanishing into the fog.

"No, Lukas," she shouted. "Wait! Where are you going?"

"This way, my love," his voice beckoned.

She ran after and tried to catch up. "Have you found the wood's exit?"

"I have," he said. *"And it is glorious. You should see it."*

Victoria rounded a tree and found herself staring at Lukas in the distance, still unattainable. He held out an arm, and opened his hand. He wanted to take hers, she realized. To make sure she wouldn't lose him again. As she got closer, he ran back into the fog.

"Stay close."

"No, Lukas. Why won't you wait?!"

"You are almost there."

She continued her pursuit, panting and shouting. Moments passed as she ran and yelled his name. But he wouldn't answer. She slowed to a walk.

Then she saw a strange shape weave in and out of the mist.

It was a home, she realized as she got closer, planked with oaken slats painted yellow and white. It boasted a wrap-around porch and a swing out front. Two children ran across a green lawn, and Lukas scooped a little girl into his arms and twirled her around in the air. After the girl giggled with delight, he set her down.

Victoria took a step closer, smiling. "Lukas?" she said.

He glanced up.

He looked at her.

He smiled back.

Then a torrent of fog gusted across the beautiful home and lawn, covering it in mist. When it cleared, the home, the lawn, the children, even Lukas … were gone. In its place loomed a wooden shack splattered in dry blood and decorated with bones. The smell of the air shifted from the green of leaves to the rot of death.

Victoria gasped, realizing her folly.

She had followed the Witch.

Laughter filled the air; it came from all directions.

Gooseprickles shivered down her neck and spine. She backed away from the shack, shook her head, and said, "No. This can't be. I must be—"

She backed into a tree and it grabbed her wrist.

Victoria turned, startled, and saw that Lukas clutched her, not a tree. She pushed against him, fighting and screaming, as she tried to break free from his strong embrace.

"Victoria," he shouted, his grip tightening. "It's me!"

She kneed him in the groin and raked his face with her free hand. A grunt escaped him and he doubled over. Victoria broke free and drew her slender sword. "Take another step and I'll shorten your member!"

"Vict—" he gasped in pain and clutched his groin. "Victoria, it's me."

"How do I know?" She squeezed her grip tight around the sword.

"Victoria." Lukas swore beneath his breath. "Do you remember what you were doing when first we met?"

119

She didn't answer. Instead, she gripped her sword into both hands.

"You had your knee on Simon Temple's throat," he went on. "Oh, I liked your bold demeanor. He had grabbed your rear and demanded a dance free of charge, do you remember?"

Victoria blinked.

"You made him promise to lick the dirt off your boot before you let him go. And he did." Lukas laughed. "The town of Derbent must have jested of it for days."

Victoria lowered her sword.

Lukas started to walk closer. He kept talking.

"Do you remember our conversation that evening?"

Victoria nodded. Tears started to form at the corners of her eyes.

"Do you remember how we talked of Lucidus and the Faith?" He gently nudged the sword aside, stepped closer and looked her in the eye. "Do you remember the first time we kissed?"

Victoria looked into his soft, blue eyes.

"It's me," he whispered.

She inhaled a deep breath, her nerves relaxing on the exhale. Only Lukas could know those things. "Oh, Lukas—" she sheathed her sword and then threw herself into his arms.

He hugged her back. But then he grasped her by the shoulders and forced her to look at him. "Why did you run from me?"

Victoria shook her head, not understanding.

"You wrenched yourself free of my hand, and ran off into the fog."

"I ... I ..." she began. All she remembered was one moment she held her prince's hand, and the next, she was alone.

"Never you mind." Lukas looked away from her and toward the shack. He shook his head. "You have erred, Victoria."

Laughter filled the air again, a screech of despair.

"This is wonderful," the Witch spoke, and it was the wind. *"Two love birds I've ensnared."*

The door to the shack creaked open, and Victoria saw a bare foot step through.

The Witch exited, and she was not the trim, curvaceous beauty the men had described, but instead an old and withering hag. She was sickly thin, nearly down to the bone. Her back was stooped, and her skin rotting. And her thin, white hair hung limp from her balding head.

The Witch lifted her hand and curled her finger, calling the couple over. *"Come to me,"* she whispered, a raspy voice of death.

Lukas drew his greatsword into both hands. "Run, Victoria."

Victoria glanced from Lukas to the Witch, and then back again.

"Run!" The huge, black sword began to glow red.

She did. And as she ran, she stumbled and tripped, feeling as though a monster breathed at her neck.

From behind, Victoria heard Lukas shout, "Die, repulsive hag!" Then the fog radiated a brilliant red, and she felt an intense heat on her back.

The Witch screamed, a shriek of horror.

The wind howled ferociously and forced Victoria's hair to snap into her eyes.

Then she heard the Witch shriek again. *"No, you shall not escape me!"*

Victoria ran onward, not looking back.

Lukas is alive, Lukas is alive, Lukas is alive, she told herself again and again. *He can't die here, not here.*

The fog slowly lifted. It thinned enough to see twenty paces in front of her. And then, finally, a clearing beyond the wood. The exit!

Victoria stumbled from the forest and fell onto her hands and knees. After she caught her breath, she glanced up.

Before her loomed the higher portion of the sky city. Ancient buildings, greater in size and grandeur here than the shops and apartments from the business district they had searched throughout the day, rose and grew taller upon a gentle, sloping hill. The houses were dark, with red tile roofs, stacked stone walls, and painted wooden flower boxes adorning most windows. Though the flower boxes were barren and their paint faded.

Atop the hill, and overlooking this district, sat a building larger than the rest, with four, soaring spires at each corner, and a round stained glass mosaic that glimmered from a low, afternoon sun.

The throne room.

Victoria stood and brushed dirt from her hands. She turned to stare into the forest, hoping to see Lukas approach.

But moments passed, and nothing stirred.

Despite her efforts to remain calm, she found herself pacing the wood's edge. "Come to me, Lukas," she repeated again and again. "Come to me."

Still no movement.

She unsheathed her sword, continued to pace. Though it panged her to do so, she readied herself mentally to go back in. "Okay," she sighed. "It looks like I must save my prince." She stepped over a tree's exposed roots and started to reenter the forest.

A movement stirred in the distance and stopped Victoria in her tracks. The shape walked amongst the trees. Lukas! He had his greatsword strapped to his back, and he seemed to favor his right leg as he walked. He reached Victoria in the clearing, and she embraced him, kissing him over and over.

"Oh, Lukas," she cried between kisses. "I thought you done for."

"I am fine," he said. "Please, let me breathe."

She let go of him, and took a step back. "What happened in there?"

"The Witch became a wraith," he answered. "A diabolical spirit. Greater than any foe I have ever encountered."

"Did you kill her?"

"Nay."

"How did you escape her, then?"

Lukas looked back into the Forest of Despair. "I think I surprised her with my enchanted sword. I attacked and the wraith's form split. She turned back into the hag and cowered into her shack." He glanced at his leg. "I am thankful to have only sprung a foot."

Victoria moved closer to soothe him.

"Pah, it's nothing," he waved her away. "I shall heal soon enough. Anyway, I did not stay to finish the battle. I hurried here to ascertain your safety."

Victoria smiled.

"I could feel her presence as I ran, though," Lukas said, "as the wind at my back. I think she was hesitant to follow, after witnessing Sinfire's strength." He shrugged. "I know not."

Victoria felt ashamed that her foolishness put them in harms way. She apologized, "I am sorry, Lukas. I do not know what came over me. This wood confuses the senses."

Lukas turned away from the forest and glanced up at the city. "It matters not now," he said. He took Victoria's hand and pulled her forward. "Come, let us explore the city."

"The hunt is in my blood," Brynden told his men. "And the

windstriker is close, I can smell it in the air."

The five knights trudged through the wood, following Brynden along a narrow and overgrown trail. The fog pressed against them, promising to rust their heavy plate and mail.

"First the sand in the mines, and now this damned mist," Wils said. "My armor cannot get a rest from the elements."

"Stop ya whining," Pipes said. He took up the rear. "Hey, Bryn, whatcha see up there?"

Brynden snorted. He could choose to deal with Pipes not calling him commander now, or he could keep to the hunt. *If I continue to let this go, the men won't respect me.* He stopped and started to turn around. But then he remembered that Pipes had always called him Bryn. He couldn't fault him now that he had been promoted to commander. With a shrug, he picked up the trail again.

But before he could take three steps, a dark figure moved fifteen paces ahead.

It was a man, Brynden saw, about six feet tall. He plowed through the underbrush and disappeared into the fog. Brynden dashed closer for a better glimpse.

It was the windstriker.

He wore a black cloak, with a crossbow and round-shield strapped to his back. He cut his way through the forest with his shortsword, swiping it this way and that to clear a path.

Brynden grinned. He slowly, quietly, unsheathed his sword.

"Commander," Aryn said. He was first to catch up. "What do you see?"

"It's him," Brynden whispered. He stalked into the brush.

"What, the windstriker?" Aryn called after. "How can you be sure? Remember, there's a Witch in these woods. The captain told us."

"Quiet."

Aryn sighed, but he made to follow.

Wils shouted, "What are you two doing?"

"The Commander says he saw the windstriker," Aryn said. "We're sneaking up on him. So stop loafing and spread out."

Pipes said, "I ain't going in there. I'd say Bryn saw the Witch and she's playing her tricks. How we know for sure ..."

Their voices drifted away as Brynden went deeper into the wood. He wasn't going to wait around for them. No. Not with vengeance so close at hand.

He crept through the thicket, making sure to watch his footing so he wouldn't snap any twigs. As he took his next step, he peered ahead into the fog.

Nothing.

But then a torrent of wet air gusted past a group of pines in the distance and he saw the windstriker again. He grinned, and took another step. Fog rolled in and cloaked the windstriker in mist.

Brynden swore beneath his breath. He stopped and looked over his shoulder for his men.

"Aryn. Wils. Trevor." He called their names in a hushed tone.

No response.

"Pipes."

No answer.

He squinted to see clearer: only the thick underbrush, group of pines, and a murky fog.

Suddenly, Brynden felt alone. He swallowed.

Clement. Lilyanna, he reminded himself. *I must catch the windstriker and avenge them.*

He turned around, and came face to face with a stunning white-haired beauty. He stumbled back and fell, startled.

The woman laughed, and the wind sighed high in the trees overhead. *"Why, you frighten so easily ..."* her face grew stern. *"Brynden Lifebringer of House Gossimer."*

Brynden cursed and climbed to his feet. "Who—who are you? And how do you know that name?"

"I, too, seek vengeance. And I, too, have lost loved ones. Will you help me? Will you be my judge and justice, my sword and shield?"

"You haven't answered my question," Brynden said. Despite his commanding tone, his grip on the longsword went slack. And he couldn't steal his eyes away from the woman.

She smiled, and something warm passed through Brynden's body, like the sun breaking free from the cover of clouds on a cold day. *"All know of Brynden Lifebringer, savior of the weak. Why, your deeds are renown throughout the kingdom. When others feared to burn, you passed through fire."*

Brynden's eyes widened in remembrance:

The barn ablaze, animals squealing, people shouting. And coming from inside, a desperate scream for help.

Lilyanna's voice.

Without a second of hesitation, Brynden soaked a blanket and wrapped it around himself, charged into the burning building to find her. He managed to pull her from the fire, barely, while the barn collapsed and burned into the long hours of the night. Once safe and illuminated by the shifting dance of flames, he saw to her wounds. She kept calling him Lifebringer, saying he had given her another chance at life.

She kissed him.

And in that moment, he loved her.

But the next day, Clement announced his betrothal to Lilyanna. A part of him hated his brother for it, a part of him was thrilled. The mixed emotions churned in his gut, threatening to tear him apart. How could two brothers love the same woman, and preserve a relationship stronger than friendship, stronger than marriage?

Yet this event happened ages ago, and no one knew of his deeds— save Lilyanna, of course, and the two families. How could this woman know?

He glanced into the white-haired woman's eyes, and it was like looking into two orbs of pale moonlight. And then, strangely, they started to look more like Lilyanna's: brown, gold around the edges, and pretty. A smile curled up at the corner of her mouth, and her hair became as red as fire. Then freckles appeared along her cheeks and nose, and her face rounded like a heart.

"Will you serve me, Lifebringer? Will you be my knight, and I your queen?"

Brynden smiled. "I will serve, Lilyanna."

She kissed him.

And in that moment, he was hers.

* * * * *

"Blasts this fog. It's maddening."

The windstriker walked moments on end, and still saw no sign of any Witch of the Wood. He hoped to see her, and soon. If the forest was truly enchanted, and the only way to reach its exit was to *not* follow the Witch, then he needed to find her quick. Time ran short, and the sun would set in less than two hours.

After thirty more steps, he stopped and peered into the mist. Nothing except a heavy fog, trees with wet bark, and a thick overgrowth covering the ground.

125

He sighed. *Where are you, woman?*

Gabriel shook his head and continued his discouraging search. Finally, after another thirty or fifty paces, he grew impatient enough, and yelled, "Damn it, woman, show yourself!"

"I am here," a voice breathed on his neck.

The hairs on Gabriel's neck bristled.

"Will you join me?"

The wind picked up, and Gabriel felt its chill. When he turned around he saw the fair beauty standing five steps away. Her long, white hair flowed in wisps of entrancement, and the wind twirled around her like she was the eye of a storm. Her locks squalled across her flesh, giving Gabriel brief glimpses of her thighs, her hips, her … he tore his gaze away. Mystified, he felt an urge to follow the woman to all four corners of the kingdom if she wished it.

An urge to do more than just follow.

She curled her finger, beckoning him. *"Come to me, Gabriel Lost. This way."* Her voice angelic, filled with longing.

Gabriel grinned. He took a step forward, and then another.

She skipped away into the mist.

"No, stay here!" He held a hand out toward her, and dashed to where she had stood.

But then he stopped and shook his head. "What am I doing?" he said aloud.

The Witch's captivating powers were stronger than he had anticipated.

I need to be more cautious. Now realizing this, he walked the other way.

A long time passed as he hiked, and only the wind stirred. High above, leaves rustled in the trees. Gabriel looked up to them and remembered Slade's words: *She's the wind that speaks.*

As if she overheard his thoughts, the Witch skipped before him. *"You did not follow,"* she pouted, appearing shy, an innocent girl who could cause no harm. *"You have saddened me."*

Gabriel moved to exit her presence.

"Don't go," she pleaded. *"I can show you things. Things of your past. Answers you yourself have forgotten."*

Gabriel stopped. He faced the beautiful creature. "What things?"

The Witch smiled, her beauty beyond most women. *"I know of your life, how your parents abandoned you. I can show you who your parents are … and*

126

were." She paused. *"If you will follow me."*

She flicked her wrist out to her right. The mist swirled and formed into an image of a crying boy. He was about seven or eight years old, Gabriel saw, with a scar across his brow. Rain droplets took shape within the fog, pouring down on the boy.

It was an image from the past.

The boy looked out to something, or someone. He reached with his hands, and cried, "Why, father? Don't leave me here. Please!" He fell to his knees, now soaked and dripping. "Father," he begged. "Don't go …"

The image vanished, leaving only mist.

"I can show you your past," the Witch spoke.

Gabriel felt compelled to go. He didn't remember the boy, but he wanted to. He wanted to know of the boy's past—his past. For strange reasons, Gabriel couldn't remember a time before the Orphanage.

He took a step closer toward the Witch.

But then he stopped and narrowed his eyes as another boy entered his thoughts.

The Duke's son, Patrick Lombard.

He shook his head to shake the Witch's charm from his conciousness.

She waited expectantly, a ghostly woman with fog thickening around her.

"Not a chance," Gabriel finally said. "I'll not believe your false visions." He continued his pursuit for the wood's exit.

"So be it," the Witch spoke, and she was no longer welcoming. Her voice grew louder the farther Gabriel walked. Not a whisper, nor a woman's voice, but that of a demon. *"You shall have me loose my knight upon you, Gabriel Lost. A knight wrought for vengeance. A knight who is mine and does my bidding."*

The wind howled violently, making trees, branches, and leaves sway as though a storm brewed. Gabriel's hair and cloak snapped and fluttered like flags weathering a squall.

"Men named him Brynden Lifebringer of House Gossimer, but I name him Knight of the Witch, bringer of death. With dark powers granted upon him, he is able to leave this cursed wood, which I cannot. He will come for you. He will hunt you. And he will kill you!"

Gabriel snorted. "Let him come." He kept walking onward.

The wind died, the Witch's presence gone.

Gabriel *tsk*ed. "Seems everyone in this damned city hunts me."

After what seemed like an eternity, the windstriker finally saw light and a fading fog—the wood's exit. Gabriel approached hesitantly. He heard harsh voices in the clearing past the trees. It sounded like two men arguing. He made his way over to get a better view, and hid behind a tree on the edge of the wood. He knelt and listened.

"It's hopeless," one of the voices shouted. "You cannot defeat me!"

"You are a fool," another voice replied. "If you followed the Witch and lived, you are doomed. None pass her grasp without falling to despair." The voice paused, Gabriel sensing a familiarity to it. "You may already be dead!"

"Nay, you are wrong," the first voice shouted again. "I am her knight! Lilyanna has given me powers. Powers you cannot hope to fathom. I can feel her strength, and it surges through me." Gabriel heard steel ring as the man unsheathed his sword. "You are dead!"

Gabriel dared not step out to interfere. Let enemy fight enemy and save him the work. But he was curious to know who quarreled. He stole a glance, and then hid back behind the tree with a furrowed brow. He didn't believe what he saw.

It was the Prophet of the Dragon and the Knight of the Witch— Vincent and Brynden.

They prepared for battle.

20
KNIGHT OF THE WITCH

Vincent and Brynden met sword to sword. The first stroke from Vincent split the air in a green, rippling energy upon blade's impact. The next strike came from Brynden, and the air was wrought in a black blast of surging power. At the third, both struck together, and the clearing illuminated in an explosion of green and black. And then at the fourth, Brynden fell.

"Tis as I told you," Vincent said. "You are a fool. There are limits you cannot attain, and my magicks are beyond yours."

Brynden stood to his feet, and reset his stance. "We shall see," he scoffed. "Mayhaps you've reached the limit of your magicks, but mine are just beginning!"

He held up his sword, pointing it to the heavens. It swirled in a smoky, black power that spiraled from the tip of his blade down the length of his arm. "Once I'm finished with you," he poised the sword overhead and locked eyes with Vincent, "I shall hunt and kill the windstriker!"

He dashed forward and attacked.

Vincent darted rearwards as the knight swung in, parrying blows left and right. Green and black energy sparked each time their swords clashed.

"Why. Won't. You. Stand still?!" Brynden yelled with each strike. He swung his blade downward with his right hand.

Vincent dodged the attack.

The knight's sword went to the hilt into the dirt. A black energy flared upon impact, and the lush green grass of the clearing withered and died to brown and grey. Brynden yanked his blade from the ground. He pulled with it soil that was no longer rich, but instead a powdery dust.

Gabriel, who watched the battle from his hidden position, gasped astonishment. It would seem the Witch of the Wood granted her knight with a touch of death.

Dark powers indeed.

"Do you see," Brynden said. "One touch from my magicks, and you will age to your death in seconds."

"And what do you think will become of you," Vincent ignored his taunt. "When you have accomplished the Witch's tasks?"

"If these powers allow me to kill my brother's murderer, then it matters not!"

"Well, you won't get that chance." Vincent pointed his slim rapier at Brynden. Then set his fencer stance, right hand resting behind his back. "For you have yet to defeat me."

Brynden scoffed, "Only a matter of time. My strike will come!"

"Alas it will not. You are too slow." Vincent gestured toward his leg and disability. "Even with my hindrance I am quicker."

"You ridicule me?" Brynden said through clenched teeth. "You're dead!"

He charged.

A wind surged beneath Vincent, and he jumped, a leap no mortal could make. Brynden's gaze followed the prophet up, and he leaped to follow. An unusual wind also gusted beneath him, and it propelled him up to meet Vincent.

The two soared fifty feet off the ground, heights only birds dare reach.

They clashed in mid-air, hacking and slashing, and green and black energy danced about them. In one swift motion Brynden swung his blade out to the right and reversed it to the left ...

... only to find Vincent's rapier stabbed through his heart.

Brynden dropped his sword and it fell back to the clearing. He put a hand to his chest and felt the blade, looked down at it, unbelieving. Coughing blood, he glanced at Vincent with shock. A gasp escaped him, though it turned to a gurgle. And then he fell back to earth like his sword and thumped against the dirt.

Vincent landed lightly on his feet. He limped over to the fallen Knight of the Witch. After inspecting his body, he placed a foot on his stomach and ripped the rapier out of his chest. He swiped a low-arcing cut toward the ground. Blood flung from his sword and sprayed the grey grass red. He sheathed the blade.

"I hate that I had to kill you," Vincent spoke to the dead knight. "But you would have wrought a multitude of death in your vengeance against the windstriker." He peered into the Forest of Despair, scanning the wood's horizon from left to right.

Gabriel ducked low behind the tree, hoping the prophet didn't see him.

After a moment, Vincent turned from the wood and headed toward the city beyond the clearing.

Gabriel knelt and checked the Knight of the Witch's pulse. Nothing. He was most certainly dead.

"I thought I smelled your presence," a voice called out.

Gabriel looked up, and found himself staring at Vincent ten paces away.

"You reek of Slade's stench," Vincent said. "I could smell you beyond the trees."

Gabriel said nothing. He stood and unsheathed his sword, ready for combat.

Vincent glanced at the dead knight. "Did our match entertain you?"

Gabriel shook his head.

Vincent smirked.

"Slade told me of the Dragon Wars," Gabriel said, "and of you being a two-century old prophet." He paused. "Are you?"

Vincent shrugged. "Who's to say?"

Slade's words rang in Gabriel's ears: *One dragon in particular was bigger than all the rest, its scales the color of blood, its wings carrying a dark rider.* He scanned the sky for the red dragon, then focused back on Vincent. "Where is your byrd?"

"Des'tok?" Vincent said. "Oh, resting. Mayhaps in his lair." His face turned grim. "You recall our meeting in the lair, do you not?"

Gabriel hesitated, but nodded.

"Pray tell, orphan, when you killed the boy, did you enjoy it?"

"You speak nonsense," Gabriel growled.

"Do I?"

Silence.

"Secrets, Windstriker," Vincent went on. "Deep secrets. Dark secrets." He paused briefly, and his eyes narrowed. "And your secrets are dark, indeed."

Who does he think he is to speak of my *past?* "What are you getting at?"

"Memories. For that is what you saw in the lair. A memory. Your own."

"That was no memory of mine."

"No?" Vincent raised his left hand, palm open, and showed Gabriel his scar in the shape of a dragon. He aimed it at the windstriker. "Then let us have another look."

Gabriel's vision blurred—darkness weaving in and out—and he fell to his knees too heavy to hold up his own weight. When he looked up he saw that Vincent now stood over him. And standing beside Vincent, which the prophet did not seem to see, was a boy. It was the boy from the dream in the lair—the ghost. He held two halves of a broken wooden sword, and he watched Gabriel with interest.

"Look with your eyes," the slain boy spoke, "and see with your heart."

Then Gabriel's head hit the dirt, and he heard no noise and saw no light.

Only darkness.

Whack! *The clack of wooden swords shot through the silence like thunder.*

Whack! Whack! *The noise awoke Gabriel. He opened his eyes, and found himself lying on stone. A stone surface to a stone courtyard.*

Whack! *The scene of boys playing knights took place before him again. He stood to his feet and brushed gravel from his hands. Then he walked slowly toward the boys. Two boys sparred while the third—the one who would be slain—watched from the side.*

Whack! *The symphony of their swords clacked in concert, the only notes Gabriel could hear.*

The boy watching began to speak, but no words came out, same as before. Gabriel tried to recollect the event taking place before him, but he couldn't recall it. Vincent had said it was a memory, his memory.

He doubted it.

One of the boys—the eventual killer—relinquished his turn and left the scene, kicking a rack of wooden swords over in his temper.

A voice called from behind, "What think you, Windstriker?"

Gabriel turned to see Vincent limping closer.

He smirked as he approached, then turned his gaze toward the angry boy marching away. "Is that you there?" Vincent asked, pointing. "The unhappy child?"

Whack! *The newcomer's mock battle began.*

Gabriel snorted. "I'm not that boy. This vision of yours is false, a foul deception aimed to trick me!"

"Oh, is it now?" Vincent now stood beside him. "I assure you, this is real. Or at least it used to be. This is a memory. One from your past."

"I don't believe you."

Vincent clicked his tongue. "Well, whether you believe or not is of no importance ... for the moment. In time, you will believe."

Gabriel wasn't convinced. He shook his head.

"As I said," Vincent continued, "this is your memory. Which means one of these boys is you." He focused on where the angry boy exited, and to the stone, arched entry he went through. "Pray tell, orphan. If you're not that boy, which boy are you?"

Gabriel's eyes narrowed as he watched the two boys sparring. Could he truly be one of them? That is, if this vision was a thing from the past, as Vincnet continued to assert. He watched them for a moment, studying their faces and movements. Both showed promise with the blade, yet both of their techniques were different. Which was he more like?

The killer returned, hiding the real sword behind his back. Though Gabriel knew what was about to befall the two unsuspecting boys, he felt fear well up inside him. A fear he'd felt before, but had forgotten.

Vincent said, "See with your eyes."

Gabriel glanced at the prophet with a raised brow, then brought his attention back to the impending massacre.

The killer attacked.

The boy to be slain fell to the stones as his wooden sword was split in two. Gabriel looked into his eyes as he lay there, and saw terror.

Then the killer turned on the other boy. He slashed a flurry of relentless attacks, but the boy dodged and ducked, refusing to use his wooden sword as he waited for an opportune moment to strike back. His efforts were useless. A cutting strike came to close, and the boy had to lift his wooden sword to defend.

Steel struck against wood. Splinters went flying into the air. The toy blade was cleaved in two, and the steel bit into the boy's face and blood sprayed across the stones.

Without realizing it, Gabriel was touching the scar across his brow. He had the scar for as long as he could remember. He never knew how he got it.

Until now.

"Aghhh," the boy wailed in pain as blood gushed from his face and through his fingers. Gabriel could hear him! And it was his cry—his pain—from so long ago.

"That's it, Windstriker," Vincent whispered. "Remember."

The first boy lay there, trembling, as the killer headed back for him.

"Stop this," Gabriel said through clenched teeth. "Stop this now!"

"No," Vincent said. "I want you to watch. I want you to remember."

"No," the windstriker growled. "End this madness or I'll end you!"

Vincent laughed.

Gabriel turned around—the soldiers now tackling the killer—and swung a punch at Vincent's jaw. The prophet did not attempt to dodge. He held his ground and watched as the punch closed in. But Gabriel's clenched fist did not hit Vincent's jaw, it didn't hit anything. Instead, it passed right through *him. The image of Vincent rippled as though he were only an illusion, and the momentum of Gabriel's swing and the weight of his muscular build sent him hurtling forward and to the ground.*

Vincent laughed again. "You still don't get it, do you?"

Gabriel stood to his feet, faced the cult leader. He'd busted his lip on the stone. He spit blood and wiped his mouth with the back of his hand. "What are you? A ghost?"

"Me?" Vincent gestured toward himself. "Mayhaps, but who really knows. You cannot hurt me, Windstriker, not here." He looked all around, observing the castle and courtyard. "I exist in this place no more than you do."

Gabriel pulled a black cloth from his calfskin bag and dabbed it against his lip.

"This is all in your head," Vincent went on. "A memory. As I've told you."

Gabriel still didn't believe him.

Vincent sighed. "This is only a vision. One from the past. You and I are only observers here, no more. It's like a dream, really. But sometimes," he motioned toward Gabriel's bleeding lip. "You make it more real than it is."

The windstriker spit blood again to the stones. "I see."

"Do you, truly?" Vincent asked. "Your memory is broken. Unclear. You do not remember it all, so you do not see it all. Nor do you hear *it all."*

"Ah," Gabriel mused. Strange as this was, the prophet's words were beginning to make a bit of sense. "If this is a memory from my past," he said, "then why have

I forgotten it?"

Vincent smirked. "Easy enough. Men tend to forget that which pains them. You have suppressed the tragedy from your mind. Or perhaps someone else suppressed it for you. Regardless, this memory was buried deep inside you."

Gabriel looked at the stones, and to the blotches of blood he had spat. He stared at them for a moment, pondering the prophet's words.

In the background, he heard a boy sobbing profusely, the only sound he could hear. He took one last glimpse at him—the young him—holding his face as blood and tears streamed through his fingers. Beyond, the slain boy lay motionless in a pool of his own blood. While the killer struggled to free himself from the firm grasps of three soldiers.

"Come," Vincent said. "There is no more to see here."

Gabriel's vision blurred, and he was blanketed in darkness. A strong gust lifted, and he was thrown into a swift upward flight. The wind subsided. He opened his eyes. And saw the dead grass of the clearing pressed against his cheek.

With Vincent standing over him.

"Did you sleep well?" Vincent asked. He no longer held his dragon-scarred hand out toward Gabriel.

Gabriel grunted and stood to his feet. He brushed off dead grass and dry soil as he did. Then he grabbed the hilt of his shortsword and set his stance for close-quarters combat.

Vincent showed no reaction to the windstriker's threatening behavior. "You would attack me now? After all I have shown you?"

"You have shown me nothing."

Vincent *tsk*ed. "But I have. You just refuse to believe."

"Nay, you are deceiving me. With foul deceptions."

"You deceive yourself, orphan. It is your memory that misguides you, not I."

Gabriel wasn't convinced. "What's your game, Vincent?" He pointed his sword at the prophet. "You pit giants against me, show me foul dreams, and try to spook me with ghostly images of that slain boy."

Vincent squinted. "A ghost boy? I know naught of that."

Gabriel was surprised. He thought for sure the ghost was one of Vincent's schemes. He lowered his sword, but pressed on. "Why are you pitting giants against me?"

"To challenge you, Windstriker."

"For what purpose?"

"So you will learn," the prophet smirked, "and as a horse of war you and your gemstones need strengthening."

Always the riddles. "You speak nonsense," Gabriel snorted.

"You need to learn the truth, orphan."

"And what truth would that be?"

"The truth," Vincent said, "as to why your parents abandoned you. Where your true destiny lies." He paused. "The truth to what really happened on that fateful day."

"I spit on your truth."

"So it would seem," Vincent said. "In time, though, you will come to believe. Alas I think you have already begun. Am I mistaken?"

Gabriel didn't answer.

Vincent smirked again. "I am a prophet, orphan. My visions are never wrong."

"You think you can see my past?"

"Nay, I see it not. Though most of my visions are *seen,* yours I know."

Gabriel's eyes widened. "Know? What mean you? Wait!"

Vincent had started for the city. But he halted, and faced back toward the windstriker. "Let me pose one last riddle for you to ponder. If you didn't murder the boy, then who did?"

Gabriel shook his head.

"I shall leave you with that." He raised his hands overhead, looked to the sky, then chanted, "Avronze rok!" The dead grass and soil beneath Vincent broke away from the ground, elevated him into the air. "If you seek answers to these questions," he said as he floated around the clearing on his levitating platform. "Then continue your chase. I await your capture."

The platform rose. It carried the prophet away from the clearing and toward the city.

Gabriel sighed and sheathed his blade. "Curse you, Vincent."

He knelt beside the dead knight. He felt sorry for him. The twin brothers shared doomed fates, and it was unfortunate. Gabriel remembered overhearing their conversation about their hometown, Lorenta, and how they hoped to return after leaving the sky city. But it was to be their last conversation together, and neither of them would

THE PROPHET OF THE DRAGON

ever see Lorenta again.

I killed one brother, he thought solemnly, *and Vincent the other.*

Gabriel lowered his head, swallowed the lump in his throat, then stood to leave.

He had a mission to complete, and captives to save.

A slight breeze whispered through the trees. *"Arise, my knight."*

The dead knight opened its eyes, and they were blackness, wrought of death and despair. The once motionless body stirred, and the Knight of the Witch stood to its feet. It didn't stand upright like a mortal man, but with a hunch as though it were a puppet attached to strings.

It groaned; a guttural noise, a cold noise.

It walked over to its fallen sword, picked it up, and sheathed it at the waist.

"Go, my knight," the wind spoke through the trees. *"Hunt the windstriker. Kill the windstriker. For your brother. And for your Queen."*

The Knight of the Witch staggered its pursuit toward the city. It stepped from the dead grass of the clearing onto a patch that was lush and green. When its foot lifted, the green had turned to brown, dying upon the dead knight's touch.

Dark crimson ran down its chest, onto its arm, and through its fingers. Dangling from those fingers was a gold and silver necklace, its locket—a portrait of a red haired, freckled face girl with the smallest hint of a dimple—dripped of blood.

Wherever the windstriker went, the Knight of the Witch would follow. And it would stalk him always, from this day forward to the next. To avenge his brother, and to obey the Witch.

21

THE THRONE ROOM

Alivia, Patrick, and her captors panted as they ran from the Forest of Despair. Knight's Order patrols paraded the streets, breaking windows and searching buildings, as they looked for the disciples of Dräkenkamp. But the disciples and Alivia had darted in and out of alleyways. They eluded the knights and rushed for the throne room, to the safe haven of its walls.

Stone carried the Duke's son, to keep a steady pace and not tire the boy. He managed to free a hand and point. "There it is."

Alivia glanced up, over the houses flanking the alley and beyond their red tile rooftops. She saw a building with four, heavenly spires and a circular stained glass window. The last rays of daylight made the aging throne room look holy, somewhat divine. Its architecture—gothic, with pointed arches, ribbed vaults, and flying buttresses—loomed over the Fortress of the Moon like a menacing demon with teeth. As the central hub of the city, it was a structure hard not to notice.

"Bout bloody time," Griff said, out of breath.

The group halted at the end of the alleyway. A wide intersection loomed before them. Before treading out into open space, they pressed their backs up against a building's wall and edged closer to its corner. They made sure to stay inside of the building's great shadow. Stone poked his head out and peered around the corner, toward the direction of the throne room. After a moment he motioned with his hand, signaling all clear. Then he darted into the open. Patrick bounced in his arms with each stride. Griff and Alivia stepped out to follow.

When Alivia rounded the corner, she saw that the magnificent throne room loomed before them. It soared seven stories tall, and the great, oaken double-doors leading into the building were banded with gold. They climbed the steps and reached the doors, which were three times Stone's height. He set Patrick down, grabbed one of the door's handles—ornately carved into the likeness of a dragon—and heaved it open. The door groaned in protest, its rusted iron hinges screaming.

Mayhaps they have not been opened since the Great Catastrophe, Alivia thought.

"Let's go, Gavin." Griff fidgeted with nervousness. He scanned the streets to make certain the noise was not overheard by any knights of the Order. "Those choirboys might come running."

Stone grunted. "Stop your whimpering." Then he opened the door a little further and slipped inside.

Patrick, Griff, and Alivia followed him in.

Once inside, Stone shut the door. It closed with a solid bang, its echo resounding throughout the great hall.

Alivia turned from the door, and toward the room. Her mouth fell open in astonishment.

Large dust-covered tapestries hung along the walls, each depicting a different battle. A few tapestries had knights on horseback fighting alongside soldiers on foot. Some men were shown slain, while others gained victory. But the central feature of each was a dragon. In each tapestry a different colored dragon slew an enemy, while a rider in dark armor straddled its back. And in each, the rider wore a silver necklace tied to a bright, red stone which glowed about his chest.

The Heart of the Dragon, Alivia remembered Stone's words about the sky city's key.

Beneath the tapestries, and flanking a fading, red carpet the length of the hall, stood empty suits of armor; dark and dusty. The hollow knights stood guard, but seemed as though they could step off their platforms any minute and seize them. The armor reminded Alivia of Vincent's, and the slim blades strapped to each knight's waist made her think of him as well.

But neither the room's armor, nor tapestries, stole her attention nearly so much as the throne itself. It was polished onyx, glimmering, and centered against the back wall on a raised dais. Alivia counted thirteen steps, which climbed to meet the great seat.

Centered above the throne was a round, stained glass window. The mosaic portrayed a colossal bloodred dragon, which carried a dark rider who wore a golden crown. The Heart of the Dragon hung from a necklace around the king's neck, and blazed a blinding radiance. Through the round mosaic the setting sun illuminated the throne beneath it. It cast a wonderment of colors across the kingly chair.

A Divine Right of Kings, Alivia thought. She imagined the king's subjects seeking his audience during this hour each day. Kneeling before him, awed as their king sat haloed from this vivid, multi-colored spectacle. *They must have thought he was a god, or that he held a god's favor.*

Stone interrupted Alivia's admiration of the throne room. "Damn, where is Vincent? He should be here!"

"Do you think he was delayed?" Griff asked.

"Mayhaps." Stone inhaled a deep breath.

Alivia glanced at Patrick. He was admiring a suit of armor. *What is it with boys and knights?* She walked closer and knelt beside him. "Do you want to be a knight when you grow up?" she asked him.

He didn't answer, but he looked at her.

Alivia squeezed his arm. "Look at you, and already so strong. You'll make a great knight someday. You sure are brave, Patrick."

Still no response.

Maybe he doesn't trust me. "Tell me," Alivia pressed on, "what is the first thing—"

He backed away and hid behind Stone.

Alivia stood. "You treat your prisoners well."

Stone looked down at Patrick, then up at Alivia. "Yeah, well, I could never harm a child ... no more than a woman."

Alivia narrowed her eyes. "What about thrusting your dagger in my back if I ran?"

Stone grinned knowingly. Then he glanced back to Patrick. "Are you hungry?"

The boy shook his head.

Griff asked, "What's the plan?"

Stone scanned the throne room. He sighed. "I guess we'll rest up while we wait for Vincent. We can catch our breath and—"

The great double-doors burst open. The sound of heavy wood scraped against stone and complained throughout the room.

"Halt in the name of the Cardinal!" a voice boomed.

Alivia and the others turned toward the entry.

A score of knights hurried into the throne room, like rushing water after opening a flood gate. The knights quickly surrounded the group, the sharp points of their longswords aimed at their chests threateningly.

Stone went for his sword, and found the tip of a knight's blade pressed under his chin. Alivia saw Stone grip his weapon tighter, so the knight poked his sword harder into his neck.

Blood began to trickle.

"Easy … friend," Stone struggled to say. He let go of the hilt. Then he put his hands up to show he wouldn't try anything.

The knight backed away, lowered his sword. "You disgust me, sinner!" He spat in Stone's face.

Griff grabbed one of the blades strapped across his chest, and quickly stepped forward to challenge the knight.

But Stone put a hand on his arm and pulled him back. "Don't. He is not worth it."

"Are we done?" the knight whose voice boomed asked. He still stood near the great, oaken doors. "You rats are tough to find." He marched over to the circle of knights now surrounding their captives.

As he got closer, Alivia saw that his attire differed from the other knights. While the rest donned the traditional crimson on white and grey, along with their silver chainmail, their leader had his crimson trimmed with gold and his chainmail interlaced in golden ringlets.

The circle of knights made room for their leader to join their ranks. He joined them shoulder to shoulder. "Who leads this motley group?" he asked, resting a hand on his sheathed sword.

"I do," Stone said.

Alivia put a hand in her pocket and felt the Redoulz.

No. Not yet time.

The leader focused on Stone. "Tell us, rat," he said with disgust. "Where is the key to the Fortress of the Moon?"

Stone scoffed. "Why don't you go and—"

One of the knights threw a punch into Stone's jaw.

His head whipped back and he tumbled to his knees. He spit blood and stood, working his jaw back and forth.

"Once more I will ask," the leader said. "Where is the key?"

Stone cocked his head to the side and spat more blood, which landed on the knight's boot who had prodded his neck a moment ago.

"So that's how this is gonna go?"

141

"Yah," Stone said. "That's how this is gonna go."

"Hmph," the leader said. "Well, the captain will join us shortly." An evil smirk twitched across his face. "Then, you shall talk."

22

TRAINING GROUNDS

Lady Victoria pulled strands of moss and vines away from the wall. "Tis as you say," she said with a touch of excitement. "There is something here."

Lukas came closer, walking past racks of rusty swords, spears, and axes. Upon entering the area, he had told Victoria it must have once been the city's training grounds. Weapons were strewn about everywhere. He reached the wall and brushed back a lock of vines with the back of his hand. "So there is."

"Is it another clue?"

"Mayhaps." He grabbed the vines touching the back of his hand, pulled them down and dropped them to the cobblestones at his feet.

Victoria saw what he meant to do. So she ripped and pulled the vines down as quickly as she could. Little by little more of the clue became visible. At last all of the vines were removed.

The couple stepped away from the wall to see what they had uncovered.

A wall painting.

The mural depicted the Fortress of the Moon, a floating island with a city on top. Its paint was flaking and cracking, with some areas no longer visible—colors faded or worn away completely. But there was something strange about the depiction.

A cylindrical, metal mass protruded from beneath the sky city.

The tangle of blackened roots was warped around it.

Victoria pointed. "What is that?"

Lukas didn't answer. He stroked his chin with finger and thumb, studying the wall. "The citizens," he said after a moment. "They must have known all along."

"What?"

Lukas stepped closer to the mural. He touched the area depicting rock and dirt and tangle of blackened roots, and ran a finger across the unusual metal cylinder. "This painting," Lukas said. "How old do you think it is?"

Victoria shrugged. "Mayhaps, a few hundred years."

"Precisely. That means this mural is older than the Great Catastrophe."

She arched an eyebrow.

"My love," he said, and pulled her closer and drew her attention back to the mural. "Before this flying city became the Fortress of the Moon, it was the capital city Lunagaesia. A city on land, near the sea. The fact that this mural is here, painted before the city was torn from the earth and raised up into the heavens," he paused and looked at her. "Means that the citizens must have known. They must have known that this city could fly."

"Ah," she mused.

"Yet, there is more. Look here." He touched the bottom part of the mural again, the tangle of blackened roots. "Is this what you are referring to?" He pointed to the metal mass protruding from underneath the sky city.

Victoria nodded. "Yes, what is it?"

"It appears man-made," he said. "Like steel or some other metal. Look at how it juts out from beneath the Fortress of the Moon. It reminds me of what King Rikard had on display several fortnights ago when last we were in Wyndsor."

"Oh, yes, I see the resemblance," Victoria said. The king's display had involved strange black sand; powder, that when ignited, caught fire rather quickly. Lukas had said the black sand would change how wars were fought. "What did the king call his? A cannon?"

"Aye," Lukas confirmed.

"But this sky city has no cannon. I did not see one when we climbed those great roots."

Lukas shook his head. "No, and you wouldn't have. Not until we have the key to the city—the Heart of the Dragon."

"Oh."

Lukas knelt and examined the huge cannon depicted beneath the flying city. "There is something I must tell you, Victoria. Before the

Cardinal sent me on this quest, he called me to his quarters."

Victoria narrowed her eyes. She stayed quiet. It was rare for the Cardinal to have private meetings, in his quarters no less.

"He told me," Lukas went on, "it was now or never. Follow Vincent and the cult of Dräkenkamp, he said, nigh wherever they may go. Capture the Fortress of the Moon, 'tis the only way. I urged him, years ago, to take this floating island from the grasp of Dräkenkamp. But he said it wasn't yet time."

Lukas stood and came closer to Victoria. He held her hands. "The Cardinal is dying."

She gasped. "Oh, Lukas, I am sorry."

The Cardinal had always been like a father to him.

"That's why it is now or never," he said again. "The Cardinal wants to save the kingdom before he passes. It is filled with sin. He hopes to convert the non-believers to the gods of the Four Winds."

"And we are," Victoria said. "It's what we have been doing all these years."

"I know," Lukas said, but he shook his head. "It hasn't been enough. The people haven't truly changed. They continue their sinful ways. They are heathens."

Victoria squeezed his hands to reassure him she was here to help.

"So we shall make them change," he growled. "Through force."

Victoria dropped his hands and stepped away, taken aback by his sudden fierceness.

"You see, my love," he said with a slight fury still to his voice. She'd rarely seen this side of him. It alarmed her. "This city has power, ancient power. And it is power we can use to *change* men's minds. That's why we hunt Vincent. He has the key to the city. And that key will unlock the power hidden inside the Fortress of the Moon. For this glorious sky city—" he pointed at the mural and to the cannon, "—is a weapon."

Clink. Clink. Clink. Clink. The noise rang out behind the couple.

They turned toward the sound, and Victoria saw the dark mercenary, Slade, clapping his hands together. His bare daggers clinked against the many belt buckles latched across his body.

"Impressive." The mercenary grinned, a smirk exuding arrogance. Victoria loathed that grin. "Truly quite impressive, Captain. Your reasoning is stupendous. 'Tis no wonder the Cardinal hand-picked you

145

to lead his holy knights."

Lukas squared his shoulders to the mercenary. "What, you knew?"

"Of course." Slade strode closer to the couple. "The Fortress of the Moon is a weapon, just as you surmised. One containing a destructive power the likes no one has ever seen. 'Twould make the king's black sand look like a mere magick act." He gestured toward the mural. "Its name is Ragnarok."

Ragnarok, thought Victoria. *Doom of the gods?* Fear caught in her throat. Her mother told her bedtime stories of a monster named Ragnarok, so vicious and mean it killed the gods and devoured the world.

Lukas glanced at the wall painting, then focused back on Slade. "Why have you withheld this?" He spat. "Has your purse been lined by another?!"

Slade put his hands up, seeming truly hurt. "Please, you wound me. Your coin is still the greater … for the moment."

"Where is your honor?"

"I stopped fighting for honor long ago," Slade said. "Now, I fight for gold. It is what rules the world, after all."

Lukas's lip curled up in a sneer. "You are naught but a common soldier. Your presence sickens me."

Slade bowed, and said, "My thanks for your kind words." Then he stood straight. "You may think me a common soldier, but I am much more. For I am skilled with the blade and with the mind. You need information, and I am at your service."

"Then tell me," Lukas demanded, "everything you know about the Fortress of the Moon being a weapon."

Slade pointed at the weapon in the painting. "You say this is a cannon, and in a way that is true. It is somewhat similar. But it is more than that."

"Then what is it? What does it do?"

"It is Ragnarok, the doom of the gods." The mercenary smirked. "And it can rain destruction from on high. You position the Fortress of the Moon over any city, with that weapon exposed, and you can so *change* men's minds. Men would beg to worship your gods. For Ragnarok is a ray of death. A city can be annihilated from the map of the Four Winds in only seconds."

"You mean to tell me this sky city can fly? I mean, actually fly?"

146

"Aye, I do."

Lukas grinned.

"But, of course, you need the key."

"The Heart of the Dragon."

"That's the one." Slade latched thumbs behind two belt straps at his waist. "Without it, this city is nothing more than a mound of floating rock."

Lukas began pacing, lost in thought.

Victoria's mind whirled as well. *The Fortress of the Moon can fly? Can destroy cities?* With that kind of power one could easily rule all of the Four Winds from their perch high in the heavens.

"Now I understand what the Cardinal meant," Lukas spoke, more to himself than to Slade or Victoria. "But why has he waited so long to take this city?" He stopped pacing, and looked at Slade with a grim glare. "What's the catch? Why has Vincent not used Ragnarok against the Four Winds?"

Slade shrugged.

"He has the Heart of the Dragon. I have seen it."

"I know not, why," the mercenary said. "Mayhaps something is wrong with the stone. Mayhaps something is missing."

"Yes, yes," Lukas said. "But what could it be?"

Slade shrugged again. "I know not. But I do know something else you may find to be of importance. It involves the windstriker."

"What is it?" Lukas asked.

"Ah," Slade said, rubbing his thumb and forefinger together.

Lukas snorted. "You disgust me." He reached into his pouch and pulled out a round, gold coin. Then he flipped it in the air toward the mercenary.

Slade caught it, bit it, then tucked it away. "Now, where was I? Oh yes, the windstriker." He smirked. "After you entered the Forest of Despair, I made my way for the library. To conduct some ... research."

"For what?"

"The incident I encountered in the mines puzzled me," the mercenary said. "Why did the gem on the windstriker's weapon glow as it did? Does it involve the Goliath in some way? Then, I remembered—"

"Get on with it," Lukas interrupted.

"I remembered," Slade continued, unfazed by the captain's short-temper toward him. "The story of the Onion Knight."

Lukas arched an eyebrow. "I've heard the tale. Goliaths swarmed the land and terrorized its citizens. They kidnapped their children in the dark of night. No one could defeat the beasts. Knights of both valor and honor stepped up to challenge the Goliaths. All died in defeat."

Victoria butted in, remembering the tale, "But a boy of low birth, a boy who was no knight, who was both courageous of heart and clever of mind succeeded where all others failed." Her mother told her this story each night at her bedside, before she died. "He challenged the Goliaths."

"That's right," Slade said, "and won. Thus he freed the land of tyranny. The people made him a knight, and called him the Onion Knight for he had come from such squalor. Onions were the only food his family could afford to buy."

"Yet, he rose to power," Lukas added. "He became a king."

Slade nodded.

"'Tis quite the child's tale," Lukas said. "How does it relate to the windstriker?"

"How did the boy defeat the Goliaths?"

"A stone, was it?"

Slade nodded again. "And after each Goliath was slain, the stone used to kill the beast glowed red—red with giant's blood." He paused. "That's why I headed for the library, to seek answers to this riddle."

"Did you discover anything?" Lukas asked, sounding genuinely interested.

"I did," Slade answered. "The legend foretells that when each Goliath was slain, its blood seeped into the stone and made it stronger. And the stone ..." he paused, smirking.

Victoria knew he must be savoring the moment, of having the upper-hand over her prince. She hated the mercenary for it.

"Go on," Lukas demanded.

"The stone was lost."

Lukas narrowed his eyes. "What do you make of it?"

"Is it not plain?" Slade asked. "What stone do you know of that possesses a strange power?"

"The Heart of the Dragon." Lukas shook his head. "How have I not seen this before? But, the windstriker?"

"The windstriker's weapons hold gems. Those gems give his weapons power. They are not normal stones."

"Do you think they are the something missing?" Lukas asked. "Do you think that's what Vincent searches for?"

Slade shrugged. "Mayhaps."

"But what is Vincent's purpose for the windstriker? Why does he not just kill him and take the stones?"

Slade shrugged again. "I know not. But I think Vincent is recreating something here in the Fortress of the Moon, by challenging the windstriker against the Goliaths. For what purpose, I cannot guess." He strode away from the mural and past the couple. "Mayhaps, the windstriker represents the Onion Knight."

Lukas nodded. "He may be of low birth, possibly an orphan even. One cannot succumb lower than an orphan in all the Four Winds."

The mercenary stopped and faced the couple. "Too true." He folded his arms across his chest. "So, what do we know?"

"That the windstriker may have the missing pieces to the Heart of the Dragon," Victoria answered.

Slade nodded.

"That Vincent is challenging the windstriker," Lukas added, "against Goliaths."

Slade nodded again, and then said, "And with each Goliath slain, the stones shine red—from giant's blood—giving them strength."

"So," Lukas said, "Vincent is making the windstriker stronger."

"In a way, yes," Slade said. "Though it may be the stones he is truly strengthening."

Bang! Something shattered a short distance away from their group. Each of them turned toward the clamor, and then looked at one another with tented brows. Lukas and Slade exchanged knowing glances. Then Lukas made a nod with his head, motioning them all to leave.

"Let us quit this place," he said a little louder than needed. "I believe the throne room is near."

23
WINDSTRIKERS

Gabriel entered the now deserted training grounds. He nudged a rusty sword with the toe of his boot as he went to examine the mural.

I cannot believe what I overheard.

After sneaking up on the captain, his lady-knight, and the mercenary he swiftly took cover behind an overturned wagon. He was just close enough to overhear their exchange of words, and was taken aback: the Fortress of the Moon could rain destruction from on high and annihilate cities? The gems attached to his weapons, stones he'd had for as long as he could remember, belonged to the Heart of the Dragon?

Truly absurd.

But his luck of overhearing their conversation had diminished. A *bang* had crashed against the cobblestones at his feet, and something shattered. Startled, he looked up to see where the object came from, and saw a grey gull taking flight. It had perched on a red tile roof above, just long enough to dislodge a tile out of place. The bird took to the air, so sending the tile falling to the ground. It broke at Gabriel's feet and created the noise. When he returned his focus to the party at hand, they were exiting the area.

He had hoped to overhear more of the stones.

And of Vincent.

Gabriel reached the mural, a pile of dead vines and moss heaped in front of it, and stopped short to examine the painting.

The Fortress of the Moon, he thought. *Look at the size of that weapon.*

Ragnarok, Slade had called it.

If a lunatic wanted to, he could easily destroy all of the Four Winds. And who would stop him? Who could *stop him?*

He took a deep breath, squared his shoulders. "It will have to be me," he spoke to himself. "I am the only one who can stop this city from being made into a weapon."

"Why, that's not entirely true," a deep voice said to Gabriel's left.

The windstriker turned toward the voice, instinctively curling his fingers around the hilt of his sword. His gaze caught sight of Jon Slade, who stood next to the captain with his huge black sword strapped to his back. The blond and steel clad lady-knight rested a hand on the curve of her hip, near her own slender blade.

"For you see," Slade said, smirking, "there will be others. When word of your death reaches parliament, they will most surely send another windstriker." The mercenary's grin widened. "And we shall kill him as well."

Gabriel unsheathed his shortsword. The blade's steel rang a sharp song in preparation of battle. "I warned you to leave before nightfall," he said. "When you beg for your life, remember that."

Captain Steele laughed. "A song shall be sung of this battle— windstriker against windstriker." He scanned the old training grounds, and glanced at the multitude of weapons strewn about. "And such an appropriate setting."

Slade popped his neck left and right.

Just then, a lone knight of the Order came running up from behind the couple and mercenary, his armor clinking. He halted, caught sight of the windstriker. Gabriel saw he was dripping of sweat. The knight took a few slow steps toward the captain, but his eyes never left Gabriel. Then he leaned in and whispered something to Steele.

Captain Steele grinned. "Well, it seems I must make haste. My men have captured some rats in the throne room, and it is far past time I discovered where Vincent is hiding." He nodded toward the knight, and the knight departed the way he came. "'Tis a shame I won't get to see the battle."

Gabriel saw the captain's gaze shoot toward his shortsword, and to the faint red glow illuminating through the cloth wrapped around its gem.

"Bring me his gemstones," Steele told Slade. "And you will be handsomely rewarded."

Slade grinned. "Aye, I can manage that." He unsheathed two silver daggers from belts across his chest. "What of the Heart of the Dragon?"

"Leave it to me," the captain answered. "Vincent is mine. I have hunted him too long."

The mercenary nodded.

Captain Steele took the lady-knight's hand. "Show this man-in-black what it truly means to be a windstriker. Make him kneel. Make him beg." He exited the training grounds, leading the blond woman away from the impending battle.

"With pleasure," Slade spoke, and it broke Gabriel's focus from the retreating couple. The mercenary rolled his shoulders and bounced a few times, loosening up. "This will be fun."

Gabriel pulled the round-shield from his shoulder, grimaced from the movement, and readied it in his left hand. Squeezing the shield made his sliced-open palm sting. Not wanting to show weakness, he banged the flat edge of his blade against the shield. Then he set his stance—left foot forward and shield out front.

Slade started pacing to the left while he twirled the daggers in his hands. To Gabriel, they looked like sharp mirrors.

"I hoped it'd come to this," Slade said. "It has been a long time since I last fought an opponent as strong as you."

Gabriel ignored the taunt. He circled the mercenary, keeping an even pace and distance.

Slade grinned. "You know," he said, "tis a shame our fates brought us to this. Imagine what we could accomplish—the two of us—together. We could make one hell of a partnership."

Gabriel scoffed. "Are you asking me to join you?"

"Why not?" Slade asked. "Think of the profits we'd make. Two windstrikers turned mercenaries. Nobles and lords would throw money at us for our skills. We could make a killing."

"No," Gabriel said. He tightened his grip around the leathered hilt of his sword, felt the surging power of the gemstone flow into his hand, tiny vibrations of strength.

"Come on, think about it."

Gabriel dashed forward in response.

"Tis a shame," Slade managed to say before the windstriker closed in. He threw the dagger in his right hand, and then the one in his left. They flew through the air, two razor-sharp blades of silver, and struck

Gabriel's shield with a *clank, clunk*. They stabbed into the wood and stuck.

Did he aim for my shield? There was no time to contemplate it further. He was on him.

He swiped the shortsword in a high-arcing cut; the poisonous blade reeled in for its killing bite.

But the mercenary removed two more daggers from the many belts latched across his body, and lifted them to defend. Steel rang against steel, and windstriker contended with ex-windstriker for the glory of victory, and the honor of living.

Gabriel charged forward, falling into a smooth rhythm. Swing sword from right, shield-punch from left. *Sword, shield, sword, shield,* the words sang in his thoughts with each strike.

But Slade was fast, blazing fast, as quick as any man Gabriel had ever fought. He deflected each attack with those slim daggers. And if Gabriel disarmed one away from the mercenary's grip, he pulled another blade from a belt latched across his body.

Now it was the mercenary attacking, driving Gabriel back on his heels. Gabriel darted rearwards and parried the sharp, silver blades with his sword and shield—occasionally dodging and ducking or rolling to the side. Slade stayed with him, though, like a quick, black cat with razor-sharp claws.

A dagger was thrown and Gabriel swiped it out of the air with his sword. When he refocused on Slade, he saw the mercenary smirking. Always smirking—a sly and overconfident grin. He studied it for a moment, lifting his shield up in time to stop another dagger with a *clunk*. The mercenary had a way of looking as though he held some secret, and Gabriel didn't like it.

"Why are you smiling?" he asked, stabbing a low thrust aimed at Slade's knees. "You are always—" he ducked a high slash aimed at his head, "—smiling."

Slade stopped his swift offensive attack and leaped rearward, putting some distance between them. "Because," Slade said, with a wide grin, "I know something you don't."

"What?"

"That you are not the only one here with unique weapons."

Gabriel squinted. "What in the Four Hells are you—" he started to say, but then he saw it.

In the space between him and the mercenary a thin, white line glimmered, then disappeared. Then another white streak flashed, vanished.

Are those wires? Attached to my shield?

No. Not his shield.

Gabriel's gaze followed the wires with a focused eye, and saw Slade wrapping them around his right arm like a determined sailor coiling rope. And then the mercenary jerked his hand back, and the wires went taut. They flashed white.

Gabriel felt the round-shield tug away from his hand, and then the tug slacked off.

The wires are attached to Slade's daggers, he realized.

But before he could reach around and slash them away...

... Slade yanked his arm back.

The shield tore from Gabriel's grasp, bounced and clanged against the cobblestones. Then it lunged into the air, and revolved around the mercenary as he twirled his arm like he twirled a lasso.

Gabriel's cut hand suddenly felt like it was on fire. When the shield had jerked out of his grasp it split his wound into a wider rift across his palm. He grabbed his hand and gritted his teeth.

Slade looped his left hand around more thin wires, and began twirling his left hand as he did his right. And all the daggers Gabriel disarmed from Slade's grasp took to the air—becoming revolving knives along with his shield.

The air filled with the sound of humming and whistling. The blades and round-shield zipped through the air; the daggers looked like flying pieces of a broken mirror. Wires danced in flashes of white about the mercenary, and Gabriel saw they were not only attached to Slade's daggers, but to his belts.

Slade took a step forward, grinning. Then he took another step. "Here I come, Windstriker."

The mercenary was an approaching tornado, a storm of sharp death.

Gabriel took a step back, rethinking his strategy.

Crossbow, he thought, and he pulled the weapon from his back. With his cut and bleeding hand, he clumsily locked the dark bolt into the catch and took aim. Fired. The invisible bolt thrummed forward...

... and was deflected out of the air by a twirling dagger. He thumbed the gemstone and the bolt returned.

Only one more shot and then I'll have to retrieve the bolt each time I fire.

He reloaded the crossbow and fired again …

… but it was blocked by his own shield and deflected away. The bolt landed next to the overturned wagon.

Slade laughed. "It is useless." He kept pressing forward.

Gabriel strapped the crossbow to his back, and glanced behind. *Damn, nowhere to go.* Only three feet between him and the mural. He glanced back at the mercenary, only to have his round-shield slam into his face and knock him to the ground. He got to a knee, but before he could stand a sharp blade sliced his cheek, drawing blood.

Slade laughed again. "You should have considered my offer."

The tiled rooftop, Gabriel remembered. He grabbed the hook and rope from his calfskin bag, but a dagger clipped the rope and flung it from his grasp. Desperate, his hand brushed something at his side. Gabriel glanced down to see what it was: the pile of dead vines.

Useless. I need something I can use. He looked up at Slade. *Only a matter of seconds before this walking dagger-storm rips me apart.*

But then he had an idea, and knew what he had to do.

He grabbed a lock of the dead vines, and began wrapping them around the hilt of his shortsword. The knot was secure. He stood. Then he spun the vine round and round, and hurtled the tied sword into the air. It caught on a tiled shingle, the sword acting as a grappling hook.

Gabriel glanced one last time at Slade, then jumped into the air—and scaled the wall and hoisted himself onto the roof.

Below, the mural was slashed and cut. Slade's daggers ripped deep scars into the wall.

Gabriel grabbed his sword, untied the vines, and darted from rooftop to rooftop while keeping to shadows. He ignored the pain in his hand and the ache in his side. Survival depended on pushing out the hurt and focusing on the threat at hand.

"Where did you go?" Slade yelled, still twirling and spinning the wires and blades around him.

Gabriel stayed silent. He now crouched in a dark spot overlooking the mercenary.

Slade's temper flared. "Damn you, Windstriker. Show yourself!" He turned away from the mural and moved toward the center of the training grounds, still twirling the daggers. "Are you a coward?!"

Gabriel studied his movements. *He has set into a rhythm.* He tightened his grip on his sword, and counted. *One. Two. One. Two.* When the shield spun round each second time, there was a gap between the wires and blades—an opening, a weakness. He felt the tinge of vibrating power surge into his arm from the sword's gemstone.

One. Two ... he leaped out over the training grounds, and down onto the mercenary.

Slade must have heard him, because he looked up just in time for Gabriel to slam the pommel of his sword into his nose. Gabriel landed into a roll. Then he scrambled to his feet and turned around.

Slade was knocked out and on his back, nose busted and bleeding.

Gabriel scanned the area. He slowly moved toward to his shield, hugging his side with his wounded hand. After removing the daggers from the shield he strapped it onto his shoulder. Then he retrieved the crossbow bolt from the cobblestones near the overturned wagon— just as Slade was regaining consciousness.

He took a few steps toward the mercenary and pressed the tip of his blade underneath his chin.

Slade moaned and opened his eyes. "Agh-agh ... please, I yield."

Gabriel dug the sword in deeper. But then he thought: *There may be more I can learn from him.* So he took a step back and sheathed his sword. He swallowed and kept his breathing shallow so Slade wouldn't realize he was hurt.

"Thank ... you," Slade struggled to say. "Damn ... you broke my nose." He clutched it between his thumb and forefinger, and snapped it back into place. "Aghh!"

"Consider yourself fortunate," Gabriel said. "I could have done worse."

Slade nodded. "I believe you. You are a bloody titan!"

Gabriel walked to the nearest wall and leaned against it. He folded his arms across his chest. It seemed to help the pain. "I will let you live," he said, "on one condition."

"Yah, and what would that be?" Slade got to a knee.

"You are going to tell me all you know about the Fortress of the Moon ... and how it's a weapon."

Slade asked, "Does this include the Heart of the Dragon?"

"Aye, it does."

"All right, "the mercenary wiped blood from his face with the back of his hand, "that's fair enough." He stood to his feet. "I'll tell you what I know."

24
THE LUNAGAESIA CAMPAIGN

Nigh two hundred years ago," Slade began, "during the Dragon Wars. Duke Lombard embarked on a secret campaign to capture the city of Lunagaesia."

Gabriel started to say something about it being impossible for a man to have lived for centuries, but Slade put a hand up.

"You thought it impossible when I mentioned it in the library," the mercenary said. "But I assure you it is true. Duke Lombard is hundreds of years old."

Gabriel sighed, unbelieving. He gave a slight nod for Slade to continue anyway.

Slade drew in a deep breath. "Anyhow, like I told you, Duke Lombard embarked on a secret campaign. The Kingdom of Vehayne had moved their mighty dragons to defend the capital city. And the Island countries, so calling themselves the Four Winds, could not attain victory unless the city was taken."

Gabriel nodded, remembering the mercenary's history lesson. "You said Duke Lombard discovered something," he said. "An ancient power hidden inside the city. And that discovery led to the creation of—"

"—the Fortress of the Moon," Slade finished. "Though Lombard was no duke at the time. He was Knight-General Lombard, then. Commander of the Four Winds knights and sworn swords."

While the mercenary's words rolled from his tongue in a low bass, Gabriel rested his head against the wall and listened to his story ...

"By the gods," Dondro exclaimed as the city of Lunagaesia came into view. "Tis

no way! We must turn back, sir, or die by the fangs of those vile beasts."

"What? Are you afraid of dragons, boy?" Knight-General Lombard asked with just the dawn of a smile.

Dondro did not recognize the jest. He was young, only twenty, and awed in the presence of knights. But he hoped to join their ranks some day, and being squire to the Knight-General was too great an honor to act cowardly now. "Dragons are dragons, sir," he said. "And they'll die by the sword just the same."

Despite his courageous banter, he couldn't peel his eyes away from the city. While the moon hung high, dancing in and out behind clouds to create an aura of tranquility, the city lay low, massive and stark against the ocean beyond its walls.

Must be warriors by the thousands in there, *he thought.*

Yet that was the least of his concerns. For circling the city, flying low at times and high at others ... were dragons. Hundreds of them—greens, blues, golds, whites, and blacks—defended the stronghold, defended its people, and defended ... something.

But what?

"Ah," Lombard said, grinning. "For a moment there I thought I'd chosen the wrong squire. Now come on. The sewer's entrance lies west."

Dondro swallowed the bile curdling in his throat, and nodded. Then he fell in line behind the Knight-General as they marched through the wood. They kept to the edge of the forest, the city an ominous sight across the plain. He tried not to focus on it ... but the dragons. They were not easy to ignore.

Gods, this mission is madness!

He ducked beneath a low-hanging limb, trying to muster the courage needed for the battle ahead. From time to time, his eyes darted back to the city, despite his best efforts to keep his sights on the path before him.

A massive red byrd launched into the air from the center of the city. It brought Dondro out of his thoughts and made his stomach lurch. The dragons scattered, frantic, darting this way and that like a swarm of bees after having their hive disturbed.

Dondro gasped.

"Worry not," Lombard said. "She'll die, same as the rest."

Dondro nodded, though unconvinced. He watched her—the bloodred dragon that had joined the swarm—mouth agape. "She must be three times the size of the other byrds."

"Aye, reckon so." Commander Lombard pointed toward the red dragon's back. "She's got her a rider. There."

Clouds rushed by to uncover the moon, illuminating the red dragon and its dark armored knight, before it disappeared behind the clouds once more.

"Do you think that's the king?" Dondro asked, twigs snapping underfoot.

"Mayhaps." Lombard stopped. "We are here."

A thicket of brush had overgrown into the side of a hill. Lombard stepped closer, pulled away limbs and leaves and moss, until a rusty round grate appeared. A fat iron padlock secured the sewer's entrance.

Just great. Guess we can turn around now and head back to camp? *Dondro didn't dare ask.*

A rustling stirred from behind. Dondro turned to see two knights approaching— —Rikard and Grenn—the remainder of their small party.

"The others are in position, sir," Rikard informed the Commander. He was clad in the colors of his house, red on gold, his coat of arms depicting a red lion on hind legs pawing. He scratched at his beard, glanced out to the city, and then hooked a thumb toward the swarm of dragons. "You sure this plan of yours will work, Lombard?"

"Aye, it will work," the Knight-General said.

Grenn grunted. "Those byrds are nothing to fear," his voice thick and gruff. The immense knight had a reputation for being a giant among men, with a giant's temper to boot. Once, it was said, he killed a man with those bear-sized hands of his, and all for the pleasure of hearing the man's neck snap. "I wager I'll kill more o' them byrds than you," he said, speaking to Rikard.

Rikard grinned. "I'll take that bet."

Dondro sighed. How can I be expected to kill a dragon? They may be knights, but me?

"Hey look," Grenn said. "It's Lombard's pet, Dondro."

"Leave him be," said Rikard, as he handed the Commander an unlit torch. "It's his first mission, you know that."

"Enough," Lombard commanded. He looked at Dondro. "Boy, you got the key?"

What?

How could he have forgotten? The key was his charge, one granted to show his readiness to take responsibility. In his haste, and his nerves, he left it back at camp, next to his journal, next to his bed. He was lucky to have remembered his sword. Even seeing the padlock didn't trigger the memory He was just that damned nervous.

Gods, people died to get that key.

He opened his mouth to speak, then looked to the ground and shook his head.

"Boy, I thought you were ready to be a knight." Lombard's words cut deep.

Rikard glanced up at the moon high above the trees. "The might of our Four Wind's army will be upon Lunagaesia's front gate soon. If the diversion's going to work, we've gotta get inside the sewers."

"Rikard's right," Lombard said. He looked at Grenn. "I didn't want to make noise, but do you think you can manage?"

The big knight stepped forward, unstrapping a battle axe from his back. "Aye, I can manage." He struck the padlock with his axe; once, twice, and on the third, it sliced in two and fell to the dirt.

Rikard opened the rusty grate, its iron hinges screaming protest. He stepped inside.

Grenn followed.

But Knight-General Lombard stayed behind. After glancing around the forest for signs of movement, he faced Dondro. "Boy, you get your act together, and you do it now. You say you want to be a knight, so prove it."

"Y-yes, sir." Damn it, Dondro, how could you forget the key?! He followed the Commander inside.

Rikard and Grenn had already lit their torches.

Shadows stirred and moved, lurking like black-faced demons ready to devour a prey. Flickering lights graced the round pipe at Dondro's feet and swept against a brown watery muck ankle deep. It reeked of human waste. Dondro fought against gagging. The stench filled his mouth and crawled down his throat.

Rikard sloshed closer, crouching, and handed Dondro one of his lit torches. "Hey," he said, "don't worry about it. You let one mishap dictate your actions from here on out, and you're dead. Focus on the mission. You'll have a chance to prove your worth."

"Right," Dondro sighed.

"Let's get on with this." Grenn kicked sewage from his boots. "This mission just got rank." He laughed, his deep cackle booming throughout the sewer pipe.

"Quiet," Commander Lombard ordered. He ignited his torch with flint and stone. "No more noise. Now let's move." He took the lead, Grenn and Rikard followed, with Dondro at the rear.

Moments passed in silence, save the splashing of sludge underfoot and the clinking of their heavy plate and chainmail. Every once in a while, two glowing red orbs could be seen in the shadows. Until they got closer and the rats scurried back into their dens. Some had even chewed holes into the very pipe itself, burrowing tunnels deep into mud and earth.

Any longer of this stench and I am going to vomit. Dondro was glad he took up the rear so the others couldn't see the trembling torch in his hand.

161

"So, this artifact we are looking for," Rikard broke the silence. "You say it's a stone?"

"Aye, a stone," Lombard answered.

"And you think it'll be hidden in the throne room?"

"Yep."

Grenn grunted. "What's it do?"

"We'll know naught until we get our hands on it," Lombard said. "But legend foretells that the possessor of the stone, possesses power. A power that can change men's minds and souls."

This is suicide, thought Dondro. We're risking all for a stone? He didn't see how a stone could be the answer the Four Winds sought. They needed victories, not miracles. "But how ..." he hesitated, unsure of himself. "How will a stone give us victory?"

"Dondro," Rikard said. "When knights go looking for stones, it's not to make necklaces."

"Oh."

"You ever hear the story of the Onion Knight?" Rikard asked.

Of course he had. What child hadn't heard the tale? Four Hells, the Onion Knight was the reason why Dondro wanted to become a knight in the first place. A tale of knights and goliaths, of valor and honor, of blood and redemption. And the Onion Knight—gods, did he defeat all with a stone?—freed the land of tyranny, rose to power, and became a king.

"You telling me the stone we're looking for is from the Onion Knight?" Dondro asked. "That the fairy tale is real?"

"That's right, boy" Lombard said. "And that stone has become our only hope for winning the war."

"Who gives a damn," said Grenn. "Let's just get to the surface so I can kill me some dragons."

"We're almost there," the Knight-General assured. "I see light."

Dondro squinted past the three knights and saw a hazy orange-red glow, maybe fifty paces ahead. It flickered off the walls of the tunnel. And the tunnel opened up, he saw, into a chamber of some kind. But the chamber wasn't round and mortared like the arched brick of the sewer pipe. It was more rocky and rough, like a cave, rather than a structure man-made.

"Extinquish the torches," Lombard commanded.

The squire and knights stuck the flaming torches into the sewage at their feets. Putrid smoke rose into their nostrils, blackness enveloped them. Then they crept toward the light of the chamber.

Oh gods, oh gods, oh gods! This is it, this is it, this is it!

The sewer pipe opened up into a cavernous cave—no, not a cave!—a lair. One small fire was lit, twinkling a hundred paces in the distance. Its smoke rose into a massive hole in the ceiling. And it was empty, except for thousands of glimmering jewels scattered across rock and stone.

No, not jewels, *Dondro realized, seeing the various colors: greens, blues, golds, whites, blacks, even reds.* "They are scales," *he said.*

"It's a lair," Rikard said, and he unstrapped a spear from his back.

Grenn grunted. "Damn right. Now where be the dragons?"

"They fly above," Lombard said, "while we sneak below." He pointed. "I see a wooden door, no, two doors. On both ends of the lair. We'll take the left." He strode out from the sewer pipe, and into the expanse.

The knights and squire moved to follow.

They were halfway there when a low snarl pierced the air.

The four halted, Dondro's stomach tinged with fear. The knights turned, quick pulls freeing weapons from their sheaths—Lombard his longsword, Grenn his axe. Dondro drew his own sword, and his eyes darted left and right for the source of the noise. But there was nothing there. Only the small fire and surrounding darkness.

The low snarl reverberated again, growing louder and louder until it became an angry growl. Something shifted in the shadows past the fire, and the ground trembled as it moved forward into the firelight.

Another shift of shadows, another tremble of stone.

Then two green, cat-like eyes appeared out of blackness. They studied the knights, shifted to the squire.

"Yah, boys," Grenn hooted. "We got us a dragon!"

The great byrd crept closer, prowling like a tiger amongst the brush. As it stalked nearer, its green scales became clear, its golden spikes, its pink, forked tongue, its ivory teeth the size of longswords.

Gods, its thrice as big as a mammoth!

Dondro took a step back.

The knights took steps forward.

"Remember," said Lombard, pacing to the right to meet the dragon head-on. "It's a Green—claws, tail, teeth—all poisonous."

Rikard and Grenn spread out and tried to surround the beast.

Only Dondro remained behind.

Then the dragon hissed and flicked its pink, forked tongue. Green phlegm came spitting forth from the back of its throat, toward the Knight-General. He dove, and the acidic mucus splattered against the stone, smoldering green smoke as it ate through rock. The place filled with the sharp smell of rotten eggs.

Grenn attacked first. He charged the dragon's right-side, and swung his battle axe down with all his strength behind the blow.

But the byrd swatted him away with the back of its talons.

The big knight flew into a wall of rock and smacked the floor. Then he stumbled to his feet as he shook the daze from his head.

Rikard moved next. He flanked the left, his halfhelm now on his head. The dragon's focus was on Grenn, Dondro saw, and Rikard saw it, too. The knight stepped closer, spear poised, then dashed for the beast's ribcage.

At that moment, Lombard charged the dragon's head. The beast turned its green gaze on the Commander, not seeing Rikard's attack. It spit more acidic phlegm—which Lombard sidestepped, dove, and rolled away from as he ran—then chomped those massive jaws down for a killer bite. But before the bite could sink teeth into Lombard, Rikard stabbed the tip of his spear between its ribs and twisted the blade.

The dragon reared up with a roar of pain. Then it turned on Rikard with an angry glare. It whipped its tail around to pummel the knight, but he ducked the blow.

Then Grenn was staggering back—he shook his head, still dazed—but he had enough composure to keep his battle axe gripped tight. "Damn byrd, you'll pay for that." He ran back for more.

Dragon clawed and slashed, bit and spit, but still the knights fought on—narrowly avoiding poisonous strikes with each encounter. And watching it all, a mix of dread and awe entwined across his face, was Dondro. His mouth was drooped open, his sword gripped weakly in his hands.

He mustered enough courage to take three steps forward.

The byrd let out another roar as Lombard slashed the beast across the underside of its neck. It flailed its body in rage, flicked its tail and thrashed its head. Rikard and Grenn were hit. They went hurtling across the lair and tumbled into rolls. They dropped their weapons.

Knight-General Lombard was alone to fight the beast.

Dondro took another step forward.

The dragon faced the Commander, snarling, and crouched low to pounce. And behind its back—which Lombard could not see—was poised its sharp-edged tail.

Watch the distraction, Dondro tried to yell, but no words came out.

He took another step, and another. His legs were moving, and he didn't know how.

Rikard and Grenn were back on their feet. They both recovered their weapons, *and ran forward to aid their Commander.*

The dragon lunged. Jaws snapped shut as the Knight-General leaped rearward and away from the crunch. But the poisonous tail was whipping down at the same time, Lombard's sights still set on the dragon's eyes.

At the last second Dondro shoved his commander aside, sending him tumbling to the floor.

Something hot lanced through his arm. He turned to see what, and saw his arm bleeding from an open cut. Green venom oozed from the wound. The byrd wrenched its tail back, and Dondro faced the beast. He raised his sword in defiance with his good arm, hand trembling.

The dragon hissed at the squire, and opened its jaws to spit acidic phlegm ...

... then Rikard stabbed his spear into the beast's jaw. It pierced into its mouth and impaled its forked tongue.

Grenn struck next, and in three great swings, he severed the byrd's head from its neck.

A hush fell over the knights and squire, save their heavy, labored breaths.

Dondro slowly lowered his sword. He inspected the deep cut in his arm, and felt a sudden queasiness. I'm to die a slow death, aren't I? *He looked at the Commander.*

"One kill for me," Grenn boasted, as he strapped his bloodied battle axe across his back.

"You got lucky," said Rikard, who wiped blood and saliva from his spear with a dark cloth. "And you wouldn't have gotten the kill without me. Thank gods it was a small."

A small, *thought Dondro.* That was a small? *He couldn't imagine going against anything more massive.* And there are a hundred more dragons flying above?

"Let's move." Lombard was back on his feet. He met eyes with Dondro. His expression said: Thanks, boy. *"Our army will be at Lunagaesia's front gate any minute. Let's get to the surface." He strode toward the wooden door they had been marching for before the attack.*

Grenn turned to follow, but Rikard stayed behind. "What a save, Dondro, I'm impressed. How is your arm?"

"The cut's not too deep, but I feel ... different."

Rikard took the rag he wiped blood and saliva on, and handed it to Dondro. "Wrap that around the wound. It's not an antidote, but the dragon's blood will slow the effects of the poison. Hopefully it'll be enough to get you through 'til we get back to camp."

"Right," Dondro *took a deep breath. He wrapped the cloth around the cut, giving the knot an extra tug to tighten it. Then he followed Rikard to the open wooden door, and stepped into darkness …*

"I don't understand," Gabriel said.

"What's not to understand?" The mercenary motioned with his hands. "You asked for me to tell you all I know, and so I am."

"How do you know these things?"

Slade grinned. "I know many things. Have you not learned this by now?"

Gabriel narrowed his eyes. "Tell me," he demanded. "Or you'll *know* my steel."

Slade put his hands up. "Easy, friend." He chuckled. "You aren't one for jests, are you?"

Gabriel rested his palm on the hilt of his shortsword, and gave it a little pat to make certain the mercenary knew he meant it.

"All right," Slade sighed. "I have seen Duke Lombard's journals and documents. Secrets spanning back hundreds of years."

"How?"

"I have my ways."

A former windstriker. A mercenary. A thief is more like it. "Go on."

"Most of the documents detailed useless information, but some," he paused, studying the windstriker's face, "chronicled the Dragon Wars. One journal in particular was that of his squire."

"Dondro," Gabriel said.

Slade nodded. "Dondro was dear to Knight-General Lombard. The squire kept a journal, detailing his service to the Commander and his deeds in the war. Most notable among his entries was that of the Lunagaesia Campaign."

"I see. So it describes how this city became the Fortress of the Moon."

"Aye, it does" Slade said. "As well as how the Heart of the Dragon was discovered within the city. But his entries end shortly thereafter."

"Why?" Gabriel asked. "Did something happen to the would-be-knight?"

"Ah," Slade smirked. "The tale is just beginning …"

25

HEART OF THE DRAGON

The cries of battle rang louder as the party reached the door leading to the surface streets. Dondro's stomach was twisted in a knot, and only grew tighter as he heard the great war drums of the Four Winds boom outside the city gates. A Lunagaesia warhorn bellowed, its deep moan signaling catapults to creak and thud and fling heavy stones. Yet beneath the drums, and beneath the horns, were the cries of dying men.

I may join them shortly, *Dondro dreaded.* If not from an enemy sword, from that dragon's poison.

The torch in his hand flickered—they were fortunate to have found more after entering the door, inside an iron container and ready for use—and shadows swayed and shifted. The smoke burned his eyes, and he rubbed at them with the palm of his hand.

"To the gates!" a soldier shouted on the far side of the door.

Knight-General Lombard turned around. "Throw your torches down the hall," he whispered.

The squire and knights did as told and tossed them behind into the gloom. They bounced down the steps, landed thirty paces away, and washed the nearest tombs in a glimmer of red and orange.

Dondro heard footsteps pound on the pavement outside as a rush of soldiers ran off to the right. The footfalls faded. Knight-General Lombard eased open the door. Moonlight seeped in through the cracked opening as he peered out onto the street. After a moment he closed the door, leaving a small gap for a trickle of white light to illuminate the hall's foyer. He faced his company.

"The diversion is working," he told them, his silhouette all Dondro could see. "But we must make haste. Our armies won't be able to hold off those dragons for long." He looked to both Rikard and Grenn. "The two of you head east, Dondro and I will head west."

"Aye, sir," Rikard said, and Grenn responded with a hoot.

"Find the stone," Commander Lombard continued, "and we'll find a way to victory. I assure you."

Dondro wasn't so sure. The Onion Knight is a child's tale, *he wanted to tell the Commander.* This plan of yours will not work.

"At the ready," the Commander said, and the four of them unsheathed their weapons. Steel ground against steel, and Dondro felt the leathered grip and weight of the sword in his hand. My palms are sweating, *he noticed.* He didn't know *if it was from his nerves, or from the slow effects of the poison.* Gods, he hoped it was his nerves.

"Let's go!" Lombard flung the door open. They rushed out and onto the street. Immediately, Rikard and Grenn bolted right, the Commander left.

Dondro stumbled out just a shadow darted across the street, almost like a cloud had passed in front of the moon at a high rate of speed. He glanced up to see a black dragon soaring low over the rooftops. It flew toward the front gates of the city. My gods, *he swallowed to keep from vomiting.* The beast is massive. *He quickly ran after the Commander.*

The two journeyed through the streets, heading toward the center of the city on their way to the throne room. To Dondro's surprise, fewer sentries guarded the streets. And those that did were felled by a swift strike of the Knight-General's sword. Dondro had yet to lift his blade against a foe.

Only a matter of time.

"There it is," Lombard said, pointing to something over the rooftops as he ran.

Dondro glanced up, and saw the tall, pointed spires of the throne room he'd seen from his position along the edge of the wood. Behind it, dragons swooped and dove and roared while joined in battle.

I wonder how our blades are faring against them ... .

They turned a corner and came into view of the ominous throne room.

No guards, *Dondro saw.* Mayhaps the Commander is wrong ... and the stone lies elsewhere. Or it doesn't exist.

After reaching the top of the steps, Lombard grabbed a dragon-carved handle to open one of the great, oaken doors. Dondro glanced behind. In the distance, he could see a hundred dragons fighting tooth, claw, and tail at the front gates.

They look like crows swarming a carcass. We must be losing down there. *He scanned the byrds, looking for the giant red dragon.* Where is the king?

Lombard pulled the handle and the door creaked open. "All clear. Let's move," he said.

Dondro returned his focus to the throne room. He entered behind the Knight-General. The door groaned once more as Commander Lombard closed it shut. Torches lined the walls on both sides of the long hall, making shadows dance. And it was as Dondro feared—dark knights stood guard and flanked a deep red carpet toward a raised black throne. Panic caught in his throat and he froze. He tightened his grip around the hilt of his sword.

But then he felt a wash of relief.

The knights were just statues, hollow suits of armor.

Damn it, Dondro, get hold of your nerves!

They looked so real.

A round, stained glass window loomed above the throne. It depicted a ruby dragon carrying a dark rider, who wore a crown and necklace. Dangling from the necklace was a bright, red jewel. 'Tis the king who rides the red dragon, Dondro realized upon seeing the colorful mosaic.

Lombard started walking down the length of the hall, toward the throne. "Look around," he commanded. "Find the stone."

"Aye, sir," Dondro said. He slowly walked behind the Knight-General. He kept ten paces between them and glanced left and right. There is nothing here, he thought, save these hollow knights. "Commander," he said, looking up to see where Lombard stood, "are you sure this stone truly exists—" he stopped himself; a jolt of fear shuddered the length of him as he saw movement to the right.

Three statues marched off their platforms in front of the Commander, swords at the ready.

Lombard took a quick step back, away from them. "It appears some of these statues are not statues at all."

The dark knights charged, and without hesitation, the commander charged to meet them with his sword poised, perilous. There was a blur of fast movement. Grunts and clangs of steel. Then with three swift strikes, three men lay dead at the Commander's feet.

Dondro heard a shout from behind. He turned around just in time to parry a blow from a fourth dark knight. The knight launched a series of attacks, aiming for a quick kill, but Dondro managed to block each strike.

"Keep him busy," Lombard shouted. "Whilst I search!"

The knight was tireless, his speed unrelenting, and the weight behind his strikes profound.

Oh gods, thought Dondro, he is stronger than me.

He rolled to the side in time to dodge an overhead strike. When he came back to his feet, his own sword seemed heavier and he felt dizzy. The dark knight

169

redirected his stance, but now Dondro was seeing two of him, doubles, through his bleary vision.

The dragon's poison was taking hold.

Dondro struck an attack of his own, but the dark knight blocked it out to the side with ease. Then he ducked a blow, returned one of his own.

Sweat began to drip from his brow and touch his lips. Dondro thought he tasted something metallic in the back of his throat. He ignored the taste, and launched a series of attacks at the dark knight. Each was blocked, but the squire noticed the knight had lost some speed.

Then the dark knight attacked. Steel clashed against steel as Dondro defended. An even weaker strike, he noticed. Another strike came near, but Dondro parried the blow and flicked his wrist. The move sent the dark knight's sword flying from his hands. Full of adrenaline and fear, Dondro dashed forward…

… and thrust the point of his blade up and under the knight's helm, into his neck. The knight spluttered and choked, eyes wide. Dondro withdrew the sword, shaking.

The knight stumbled back. He clutched at his wound and fell to the floor. He removed his helm and gasped for air, but choked as blood gushed from his throat. Dondro felt like he was going to be sick. He is so young. Mayhaps my age or younger. The knight's hands fell to his side and thumped against the throne room's floor with a sickening slap.

Dondro couldn't take his eyes off of him. He felt the need to puke. That metallic taste wouldn't go away. He touched fingers to his lips, felt something wet. When he pulled them away, green mucus coated the tips of his fingers.

Gods, save me!

"You did well, boy," Lombard said. Dondro didn't even hear him approach. "I had to let you face him on your own. You know that, right? A squire must prove his worth." The commander paused. "Was he your first kill?"

Dondro nodded, eyes still locked on the dead man.

Lombard nodded as well. "Battle is never an easy thing." He sighed. "But war is war, and you'll get used to it. Now, help me find the stone."

"The stone," the squire said, making it a question.

"We still have a mission to complete, boy."

"Right." Dondro spit the venom from his mouth and wiped green mucus from his lips with the back of his hand.

Lombard climbed the steps to the throne. "There must be a clue about somewhere, perhaps a lever or a switch." He knelt beside the dragonglass chair to inspect it.

170

Dondro began to walk toward the commander with quivering legs. He eyed the stained glass window as he did. Its dragon was fearful, menacing, as it ripped apart a foe. While the king boasted confidence upon his monstrous steed. The red stone dangling from his necklace was—

"Uh, sir," Dondro said. *If the stone existed, that's where it would be.* "What if the stone isn't hidden?"

"What do you mean?"

"What if the stone is out in the open, for all to see?" *He nodded toward the mosaic.*

Commander Lombard followed his gaze. "Ah, yes," *he shook his head, disappointed.* "So we won't find the stone here. Of course it is with the king. There is no safer place. His Majesty is protected by his kingsguard ... and by a dragon!" *He descended the steps of the dias and started down the carpet for the exit.* "Come, boy, we need to get that necklace."

"But how?" *Dondro asked as he fell in step beside him.* "The king rides a red dragon—the largest of all the byrds."

Lombard grinned. "We shall find a way." *He pushed on one of the great, oaken doors, and it groaned open.* "For now, let's head for the city gates and see the battle. If the Dragon King directs his soldiers, he'll be out in the open."

"Ah." *Dondro understood now.* "Find the king and we find the stone."

"Precisely."

They reached the street. Dondro scanned the sky and searched for the red dragon. "I don't see the king," *he told Lombard.* "What if we can't find him?"

The Knight-General picked up his pace. "Then all may be lost. That stone is our only hope of winning the war. Without it, the Four Winds will be annihilated. Lunagaesia is too powerful. So I say we push onward until we can no longer."

You mean until we die, *Dondro thought.*

"Let's see the gates," *Lombard continued.* "Let's see the battle. Then, if we still cannot find the Dragon King, we will rendezvous with Rikard and Grenn. Mayhaps they have seen the king and his dragon—"

An explosion of cobblestones flew as a giant, red mass slammed into the street before them. It happened so fast, Dondro didn't have time to shield himself. A sharp piece of stone stabbed into his left eye—cutting deep and so blinding it. The squire fell, reeled in pain, and clutched his face.

My gods, *he screamed, though no words came out.* What was that?!

"You stray far from the battle, knight," *a deep, loud voice bellowed in an accent Dondro knew at once to be Vehaynian.*

"Aye," *Knight-General Lombard shouted.* "To retrieve that jewel you fancy *about your neck!"*

Dondro tried to glimpse whom the Commander spoke to, but he struggled to see through only one eye. Blood streaked the left side of his face and down his neck. Then his focus came, albeit distorted.

Knight-General Lombard stood poised for combat before the Dragon King himself. The king straddled his fearsome red dragon, a hand brushing against its bare scales, and another hand gripped around a wide broadsword. The byrd was massive, its great size three times the size of the green dragon fought in the lair.

The Dragon King laughed; a laugh so boisterous one could have thought Lombard told some jest. "A knight of valor! I like that. I like that very much. Mayhaps you are a worthy opponent for me and my byrd. So few are …" He ran a hand down the dragon's neck and along its red scales.

The beast craned its neck upward, toward the grey-black sky. Then it unfurled leathery, crimson wings out to the sides, and lunged its triangular maw toward the Knight-General as though to eat him. But it did not charge, and instead opened its jaws to release an ear-piercing roar.

Dondro quickly staggered to his feet. He fumbled to keep his sword in hand as the dragon's shout blew the wind fierce.

But Knight-General Lombard stood his ground. He stared into a mouth filled with teeth like blades of ivory, unfazed—his cloak fluttering and snapping wildly behind him.

The beast yielded the taunt. It flicked its tail like a cat readying to pounce on a defenseless mouse.

The Dragon King laughed again. "Good. Good. You will do." His boisterous smile faded to a grim scowl. "Now, to battle!"

The dragon's maw lunged forward, its jaw poised for a killing bite.

They snapped shut, but Lombard managed to leap rearward in time to avoid the crunch. He swiped his blade down from the right and slashed the byrd's snout. Its scales were like hardened armor, though, and the strike caused no damage.

Dondro teetered between joining the battle or running for safety. The dragon is too powerful, *he told himself.* But Lombard needs me. *He ran forward, his legs weak, his body trembling. Then he ran back as the dragon's tail whipped round toward the Knight-General.*

Commander Lombard dove out of the way, and the tail slammed into the street. Great chunks of cobblestone smashed to pieces. They hurtled into the air like a blast of cannon fire.

"Oh, you are fast," the Dragon King laughed. "But are you fast enough?"

The byrd flapped its wings, lifted itself and the king into the air. The two hovered over the street, rose and fell in a smooth cadence like a ship swaying up and down over rolling waves.

Smoke began to billow from the dragon's nostrils, and Dondro knew it could mean only one thing—fire. He ran back toward the throne room, stumbling and tripping, as he sought cover. A popping sound erupted from behind.

I won't make it!

He jumped to the left, and slammed into an adjacent building's wooden door. It wouldn't budge, though, locked from the inside. He glanced back toward the battle, just as the dragon breathed fire into the street—bright and hot.

"Please," he cried, shoving his weight and shoulder into the door again and again. "Open!"

Fire raced for him. It filled the area from wall to wall.

He shoved again, and the door gave. He tumbled inside, just as flames licked the air outside.

The heat's intensity blazed in a deafening roar, until the inferno finally died.

Dondro stood to his feet. He picked up his dropped sword and staggered toward the door. He peered out hesitantly, scared the dragon would breathe fire again. Small fires were ablaze throughout the street, remnants from the fiery blast. The smell of charred wood and smoke filled Dondro's nose. And to his utter surprise, the Commander lived.

"He ran beneath the byrd," he said aloud, amazed at Lombard's wit.

"Fast and sharp," the Dragon King bellowed. The red byrd propelled itself upward, then flipped around toward the Knight-General. It landed back to the street. "Truly, a worthy foe!"

Dondro stumbled out from his protected shelter. He moved down the street, the pain in his left eye excruciating, the poison curdling his stomach. His skin felt agonizingly hot. He tried to focus on the Dragon King, but the smoke irritated his good eye.

I must do something, he told himself. I cannot stand aside whilst Lombard fights for his life. But, what can I do?

Then he remembered the purpose of their plan: diversion. The might of the Four Wind's army caused a distraction at the gates, took the focus off the real threat of those that would steal the stone.

That's it, he realized. I can be the distraction. He looked around for something to use.

Three crates were stacked within a dark alleyway to his left, smashed cobblestones scattered all across the ground.

He glanced at the rooftops.

Then at the crates.

Then at the dragon.

In minutes, the squire was climbing the crates and rolling onto the rooftops. He made his way toward the building's edge, overlooking the street. Below, he saw Lombard spin and dive, his sword slash and stab, but still he couldn't get inside the dragon's tremendous reach.

A rock hit the Dragon King in the back of the head.

"Hey, Byrd Queen," Dondro shouted. He picked up another shattered piece of cobblestone and threw it. This time he hit the dragon's hind side. "Over here, ya crow!"

"What is this?" The Dragon King looked up, and then laughed. "A boy? Move along. Before my byrd crushes you." He turned his focus back to the Knight-General, who seemed to be contemplating where best to attack.

Dondro clenched his fists. I'm tired of being called a boy. *He felt a surge of courage come upon him, from some deep depth, a berserk bravery fueled by a desire to help his comrade. He took ten steps back, then ran toward the edge and leaped out from the rooftop, toward the dragon's back.*

"Die!" he shouted.

At that moment, Lombard made his move. He darted left, feigned an attack, and dove right as the dragon snapped another killing bite. But Lombard stumbled, lost speed, those ferocious teeth closing in.

The squire tackled the Dragon King and unsaddled him from the byrd. The impact flung them both into the street. The sudden shift of weight sent the dragon off balance, and its jaws snapped shut mere inches from Lombard's face.

The Dragon King hit the ground first. The stone around his neck smacked the street and chipped upon impact.

Then Dondro hit the cobbles. He thumped his head against a wall. Blacked out.

When he came to, his head felt like a horse had kicked it. His vision was blurry, and he could feel warmth spreading down the back of his head, down his neck. He reached up and touched the wetness.

Gods, that's a lot of blood.

He rubbed the liquid between his fingers. A mix of red and green coated them.

Is that the dragon's poison? The venom is in my blood?!

If he remembered his dragonlore correctly, it would be only minutes now before the poison traveled to his heart, infected it, and caused it to explode within his chest. He glanced around for the Knight-General.

To his surprise and confusion, the dragon was sitting, no longer aggressive. And

Lombard—gods, he must have moved quick!—stood over the Dragon King with the tip of his blade pressed beneath the king's chin. A large dagger-sized splinter stuck out of the king's chest. Crimson pooled across his stomach and into a puddle beneath him.

He fell on a crate, *Dondro thought,* must have shattered the wood.

"Give me the stone," the Commander demanded.

"N-never." The Dragon King struggled to speak with a sword at his throat and a splinter in his chest. His eyes darted back and forth between the Knight-General and the dragon. "You are not worthy to wield the stone, you repulsive rat of the Four Winds." He coughed blood. "You are not worthy of its power!"

Lombard poked the sword harder into his neck. "Want to say that again?"

The Dragon King swallowed, said nothing. Then he looked up at the red dragon. "What?" he asked. A pause. "No, it is mine and I won't give it to him." Another pause, and the king took a rasping breath. "Blasts, you won't change your mind?"

Can he talk to the dragon, *Dondro wondered.*

"What are you doing?" Lombard asked.

"I see." The Dragon King focused back on the Knight-General. "The byrd tells me ... to give you the stone."

"What are you talking about," Lombard asked. "You can talk to the dragon?"

"Yes," he answered. "The dragon and I are linked."

"Meaning?"

"Meaning we share a bond." He tried to pull his neck away from the sword, but Lombard kept his blade pressed close. "Agh, all right, damn you. We share a blood bond," he went on. "We can hear each other's thoughts. We are linked."

"And the dragon told you to give me the stone?" Lombard asked.

"Yes." He looked back at the dragon and asked again, "Are you sure?" After a brief pause, he said, "Okay." He focused back on the Commander. "He tells me ... you are the next successor."

"Successor?"

"Yes, the successor," the king said, "of the stone. The Heart of the Dragon."

Lombard stayed quiet, but slowly lowered his sword.

"It has been passed down throughout the ages," the Dragon King continued. "Wielded by those destined to possess it. I am among that line." He reached up and touched the splinter in his chest, coughing up more blood. "Agh, your squire did me in, I'm afraid."

"Such is the way of war."

The Dragon King nodded. "True." He took a deep, grating breath. "As much as I want to, I cannot deny the dragon's will. So the stone ... is now yours." With shaky hands, he took off the silver necklace. "The possessor of the stone, possesses power. Power with magicks and power with the dragon. Power … over this city."

"I thought the power could change men's minds and souls?"

"Ah, you mean the prophecy. In time … that will come to pass. But not 'til the prophecy has been fulfilled."

Lombard asked, "Then what is the prophecy?"

"You will come to know, in time. For you … are now the Prophet of the Dragon."

"You speak madness," Lombard said. "You are dying. You know not what you say."

"I did not believe when I first became the successor," the Dragon King said. "Nigh one hundred years ago."

Dondro gaped. "One hundred years?"

"But, believe me," the king continued. "I speak true. Hold out your hand."

Lombard hesitated, but after a moment he held out his right hand.

The king took a dagger from his waist, grimacing from the movement. Then he grabbed Lombard's hand and sliced his palm.

Lombard cursed and yanked his hand back.

"A blood bond," the king said, coughing. "'Tis the only way to pass the stone between successors." He sliced his own palm, and blood spilled onto his lap. Then he grasped the Heart of the Dragon in his cut hand.

The stone radiated a dim redness.

Dondro saw a mark, or a scar, of some kind on the back of the Dragon King's hand. What is going on? *he wondered as he wheezed for air.*

"Take the stone into your hand," the king told Lombard. "Grasp it with me."

"What will happen?" Lombard asked.

"Take it, and see."

The Commander reached out to grab the Heart of the Dragon.

"But, I must warn you …"

Lombard pulled his hand back. "Warn me? Warn me of what?"

"People will die," the Dragon King said, his voice grim with importance. "Tonight, and in the coming days of your life. Loved ones you cherish will pass before your eyes. You will live longer than any, for you will be changed." He coughed and gasped, and this time it seemed like it would be his last breath. But then he calmed himself and said in a grating whisper, "You will no longer see the world as you now perceive it. You will see with new eyes, a new mind, and a new heart. You will see … as the dragon sees."

"See as the dragon sees," Dondro repeated. "Aggh." Pain shot through his

chest, his heart pounding as though trying to escape. His breathing quickened, and the vision of his good eye wove in and out in distorted blurs.

"What do you mean?" Lombard asked. "See as the dragon sees? And what of the city? How will I have power over the city?"

"Take the stone," the Dragon King said, "and see for yourself."

Lombard reached for the Heart of the Dragon, slowly, as blood trickled down the underside of his palm.

They grasped it together, linked as one, in a bond of blood.

The dimness of the stone pulsed and intensified, until the light became the brightness of a red sun.

Dondro shielded his eye whilst the stone blazed. After a moment, the red glow faded. When he lowered his hand to look, the Knight-General stood holding the Heart of the Dragon by its silver chain and gazed up at the red dragon. While the king lay motionless, head slumped on his shoulder with eyes set into an eternal stare of death.

The city began to quake.

It shook the streets and buildings.

Windows shattered in the distance, exploding down the street in a chain reaction that made its way toward Dondro. The pane above him smashed. Shards of glass fell on him like a dangerous rain. He shielded himself with his arms.

A tumult of shouts bellowed from the direction of the city gates. Those joined in the battle, from both sides, yelled in alarm.

Something was happening.

Something so big, armies trembled.

"Boy," Lombard shouted. Dondro lowered his arms to see the comander making his way over to him. He now wore the Heart of the Dragon. And a strange scar was on his right hand, which Dondro saw as he helped him to his feet. "We must make haste. The city is waking!"

"Waking? Aghh!" Lombard lifted him onto his shoulder, and not with care. "Des'tok will carry us to safety."

"Des'tok?" Dondro asked as the Knight-General ran back toward the byrd. "Please," he grimaced in pain from the jolting movements, "not the dragon."

"'Tis okay," Lombard assured. "The dragon will not harm you."

The red dragon crouched low, and bent its front legs for Lombard to climb onto a small hollow at the base of its neck.

The Knight-General set Dondro onto the dragon's shoulders. Then he vaulted on himself. "Blasts, the stone fragments!" Lombard jumped off. He scrambled toward the three broken shards that had chipped away from the Heart of the

Dragon when it smacked the street.

The city continued to quake.

Lombard struggled to stay on his feet, but he managed to scoop the shards into his hands. Then he stumbled back toward the dragon as the city's shaking intensified.

Dondro gripped the Commander's waist as he seated himself onto Des'tok once more. His heart still raced, and green sweat poured from his skin in a mixture of poison and water. He feared the massive byrd, but feared what was about to happen inside his chest more.

Commander Lombard ran a hand down the dragon's neck. Dondro could feel the unpleasant, rough scales between his thighs. The byrd lowered its head, and then reared up, flinging itself into the sky. Its crimson wings cracked like thunder, and suddenly the cobblestone streets and buildings were falling away beneath them.

Dizzy, Dondro closed his eyes. Wind rushed past his cheeks. He could hear the whoop-whoosh, whoop-whoosh *of the byrd's wings, and feel warm air grow cold as they rose higher and higher. When he opened them again, he glimpsed Lunagaesia beneath him, now smaller, and he let out a weak yell. He swallowed and tried not to vomit. The dragon leveled off, so Dondro mustered up enough courage to glance around.*

Underneath, the battle at the city gates had become chaos. A monstrous crack had broken into a wide circle around the city, and troops fell into it by the hundreds. The Four Wind's armies poured out of the city, while the forces of Lunagaesia back into it. And to Dondro's confusion, the dragons that once were joined in battle flew north, like a great migration of birds after winter's end.

"Where are they going?"

"Beyond the kingdom's borders," Lombard said. "Into seclusion. Until a Prophet calls upon them in a time of need."

Dondro scrunched his brow, not understanding what was going on. Then his stomach turned as the dragon descended into a shallow dive. He clutched at the dragon's scales, his fingers scrabbling for purchase. Des'tok's wide crimson wings beat the air. Dondro could feel the heat of the byrd between his legs. His heart felt as if it were about to burst.

He looked ahead and saw they headed for the edge of the wood where their evening began. The byrd landed in a clearing, and allowed the knight and squire to dismount. Lombard set Dondro gently in the grass, and then turned to look at the devastation.

Dondro could hold it back no longer ... he vomited. When finished, he glanced at the Commander. His mouth fell agape.

Beyond the silhouetted Knight-General, who stood poised next to the giant red dragon, loomed what once was the city.

The immense crack now completely surrounded Lunagaesia. And as Dondro watched, the city suddenly tore itself from the earth, uprooted its foundation, and ascended into the sky. As it rose, a loud boom erupted and an uproar of screams sounded. Bodies fell from its edges. Dirt and rock crumbled, trees and roots snapped, buildings and streets burned.

Until all that remained was a floating sky city, a tangle of great blackened roots stretching from beneath its foundation toward the surface hundreds of feet below.

Most of the city remained intact, Dondro saw, and part of the forest that once was on the outskirts of its walls, now joined it in the heavens. Its size reminded Dondro of a small mountain, and it continued to climb in elevation until it floated among thin, grey clouds skirting across a pale, crescent moon.

"The city is now a fortress," Lombard said, "as high as the moon."

"Yes," Dondro agreed, turning his gaze skyward. "A Fortress of the Moon ..." his voice trailed off as he stared at the otherworldly city.

For it now flew above, suspended in air—a floating island.

Beneath the sky city, the sea flooded into the great crevasse left in the destruction's wake.

The sea thirsts, and the city has quenched its parched lips.

Dondro glanced back to Commander Lombard and the dragon. Both of them continued to gaze at the flying stronghold. "The Prophet of the Dragon," he whispered, remembering the Dragon King's words.

What have you become, Lombard? What will become of us all?

"We will win the war now, boy," the Knight-General said with a heavy sigh. "We will win the war." He knelt beside his squire. "Dondro," he said. "You saved my life today, twice no less. You fought valiantly—bravely—and I commend you for it." He took Dondro's hand into his own. "You have earned your knighthood."

Knighthood, *Dondro thought. He coughed, spitting red and green phlegm onto his chin.* But the price. The price is too great!

Then he clutched his chest, grimacing as his heart pounded its last, desperate battle for life. And as he closed his eye, a sharp pain exploded from inside. It gushed a strange euphoric warmth throughout his body.

Everything went white ...

"So, did Dondro die?" Gabriel asked. The mercenary's tale had been quite extraordinary.

"Aye, he did," Slade answered. "But somehow, miraculously, the Knight-General healed his squire and gave him back his life's breath."

"How?"

Slade shrugged. "A priesthood of healers would kill to know that answer. Anyhow, after the incident, the two sought refuge. For Lombard wanted to keep his discovery of the Heart of the Dragon hidden. It was then that Dondro scribed the events of the campaign into his journal."

"Why would Lombard want to hide his discovery?" Gabriel asked. "Seems to me, the Commander of the Four Winds would want to boast of his newfound power."

"Ah, too true," Slade smirked. "But Lombard had been changed. He saw with new eyes, a new mind and heart. He had become the Prophet of the Dragon." The mercenary shrugged again. "I cannot explain it."

"In other words, he turned against the Four Winds."

Slade gestured with his hands. "Seems that way, does it not? A few days after the Lunagaesia incident, Lombard returned to his Four Winds armies. What remained of them, that is. He spun a tale of deceit and battle, and how he'd barely escaped the city's quake."

"So he lied," Gabriel said. "Becoming a traitor, becoming a spy."

Slade nodded.

"But Lombard has been a high-reigning duke over the Highwinds for all these years. Are you telling me his service to the Four Winds has been a ruse?"

"I am," Slade answered. "He has used the Four Winds. Whilst he's plotted and schemed to achieve his true ambitions."

"And what would those ambitions be, exactly?"

"Restoring the Kingdom of Vehayne. Taking this flying city for himself, and out of the firm grasp of those that seek to misuse its power."

"People like you," Gabriel snorted, "and the immoral Knight's Order. You all want the power this city holds."

"Of course," Slade said, grinning. "And Vincent holds the only key. Well, most of it." He motioned toward Gabriel's weapons, and to the three gemstones attached to them. "You have the missing pieces. The three shards that broke away from the stone the night of the Lunagaesia Campaign. Without those, the Fortress of the Moon won't—" he raised an eyebrow, searching for a word, "—operate."

Gabriel looked down at his sheathed sword. Beneath the cloth wrapping, the gem swirled in a dim, red glow.

I've had these stones since I was a boy. For as long as I can remember. How is my childhood inheritance a part of the Heart of the Dragon?

He glanced at Slade. "What do you mean, operate? Are you referring to the city being a weapon?"

"Precisely," Slade said. "For this city is a weapon. One with more destructive power than anything the world has ever seen." He paused. "But the stone is incomplete, making it faulty."

"Faulty?"

"Aye. Imagine trying to shoot an arrow with a cracked bow. How might the arrow fly?"

"It would be inaccurate," Gabriel said.

"Correct." The mercenary crossed his arms. "And seeing as how the Heart of the Dragon is broken, the city is not responding as it should."

"But you said the city did activate, when Lombard and the Dragon King made the blood bond."

"Ah," Slade smirked knowingly. "That wasn't supposed to happen. But since the stone chipped, it did happen, and the city activated without the *Prophet's Command.*"

As if the sky city had overheard, the ground began to shake. A rack of rusty swords along the outer edge of the training grounds fell over and spilled onto the cobblestones. Gabriel took a step away from the wall he had been leaning against, sand and pebbles dusting his hair.

"This city hungers," Slade shouted over the ruckus of the quake. "She's made for flying—for destruction!"

The tremor settled to a low vibration, and then stopped altogether.

"What do you mean?" Gabriel shook flakes of rock and dust from his hair. "What is the Prophet's Command?"

"The Fortress of the Moon will not bend to just anyone," the mercenary said. "Only to the Prophets—those chosen by the god, Adon." He laughed. "If you believe such things."

"Adon and the gods of the Four Winds," Gabriel scoffed. "I care for none of them."

Slade nodded, agreeing with the windstriker. "It is said a prophet can *feel* the city, know the movements of all who walk within it,

181

manipulate the very ground, even direct its course through simple thoughts."

"Ah," Gabriel mused. *Explains how Vincent knew I was in the lair this morning, and how he flies on that levitating platform.* He glanced in the direction the captain had fled. *Time is running short,* he reminded himself. *Just a few more questions.*

"Why, if Duke Lombard was a prophet all those years, did he not just take the city? Seems the best way to keep it from falling into the wrong hands is to control it yourself."

"Tis like I told you," Slade sighed. "The stone is broken. The city is too unpredictable. If he'd tried, there's no telling what destruction might be wrought. And besides—" he began pulling on those thin wires, dragging the silver daggers strewn about the ground toward him, "—Lombard has not been a prophet for some time."

That's right, Gabriel realized. "How long has Vincent been a prophet?"

Slade shrugged. "I know not. But he is now the successor—the Prophet of the Dragon—while Duke Lombard lies rottting in his bed, dying." He sheathed a dagger into a belt loop across his chest. "No longer possessing the stone, he no longer possesses the vitality of a long life."

"How has he kept his age secret?" Gabriel asked. "Seems like someone would have noticed that the Duke would not die."

"One of the many mysteries surrounding the man," Slade said. "Mayhaps, he used magicks to keep it hidden all these years. I truly know not, though."

"I see."

Slade nodded. "Ah, that reminds me of another who sits awaiting to die: the Cardinal." Gabriel's face must have shown his confusion because the mercenary said, "What, you did not know?"

Gabriel shook his head.

"Tis another reason why Captain Steele seeks the stone, to save the Cardinal. I am not the only one who knows of Dondro's miracle of resurrection." He sheathed the last of his daggers. "Tis common knowledge the Cardinal has been like a father to Steele."

"Yes, the captain," Gabriel said, more to himself than to Slade. He glanced the way the captain went again. "Tis time I take my leave." He turned to make his charge for the throne room.

Slade called after him: "You really going to let me live?"

Gabriel stopped, faced the mercenary. "I gave you my word."

Slade grinned. "I will not yield so easily next time, my friend."

Gabriel nodded. He glanced at the daggers strapped across the mercenary's body. "Then you'd better sharpen your blades." He smirked, and then continued to pursue the captain's trail.

The windstriker was gone. The mercenary grinned.

"'Tis not the throne room you should be heading for, my friend. But the temple ..." Jon Slade began his own pursuit, and not for the throne room.

26

PORT COALCLIFF

How much farther, Lukas?" Victoria grew tired of their journey to the throne room. The distance seemed too great.

"It is just ahead, my love. Look." He pointed her attention to the red tile rooftops and beyond.

She glanced up, and saw the immense building she had seen throughout the day. The throne room. Its four spires loomed over the manses along the street, like dragon's teeth jutting from the heart of the city. She shivered. "Thank the gods. This day is never-ending and I've grown weary."

"We shall rest soon," he assured her, armor clinking with each stride. "The city will soon be ours. Vincent's doom is nigh, I can feel it."

I pray it to be true this time. "Do you think the rats your men captured have Vincent among them?"

"One can hope." His jaw clenched.

She knew the cult leader angered Lukas like no other. "And if he is not?"

"Then I will make those there tell me where he hides."

"What if they won't talk?"

"Oh, they shall talk," he said. "And if they won't, well, I shall loosen their tongues for them."

Victoria knew he meant it, too. She hated to admit that Lukas could be so cruel, but she remembered what happened to a couple of sinners off the coastal town of Port Coalcliff a few months ago.

Cardinal Rominas had sent her prince there to enlist coal miners and fishermen for the Knight's Order. Lukas had said the Cardinal was planning something big, but he wouldn't tell her what. Though now she realized this was it—capturing Vincent and the Fortress of the Moon.

On that day, two sinners were brought before Lukas, shoved roughly to their knees by Sir Stevron and his knights.

"These men refuse to enlist, sir," Stevron told Lukas.

"Is that right?" her prince replied.

Victoria remembered looking from Lukas to the sinners, and noticing how one had the appearance of hardness and the toils of labor, while the other looked like a young replica of the older, but with a softness about him.

A father and son, she realized.

"Tell me," Lukas demanded, "is our Knight's Order not good enough for you?"

"'Tis not that, sir," the hardened father replied, looking at the ground. When he opened his mouth, Victoria caught a strong whiff of fish. The sinners reeked of it. "We be but poor fisher folks, sir. We's not made for war'n."

"Uh-huh." Lukas smirked at Sir Stevron. Then he scowled at the father. "Show me your hands."

The old, fisherman glanced up for the first time. He looked at Lukas with confusion across his face. His eyes darted to Victoria, but she couldn't stare the man in the eye so she looked away. "Me hands, sir?"

"You heard me."

He held out his trembling hands, showing callused palms and fingers.

"Stevron, tell me what you see," Lukas said.

"I see sword-bear'n hands, sir. *War'n* hands, sir."

"Well now," Lukas said, "my knight tells me you are the war'n type. You calling my knight a liar?"

"No sir, no sir," the fisherman pleaded. "'Tis just ..." He glanced to the boy at his right. "My family needs me, sir. I work the sea and—"

"—my Knight's Order needs you."

There was a brief silence, broken by the father, his face distraught with worry. "I sorry, sir." He shook his head. "I just can't do it. My family would starve."

Lukas *ts*ked. He looked at Sir Stevron, gave a slight nod.

"Hold out his hands," Stevron demanded, drawing his sword.

Two knights stepped forward. They grappled with the old man to hold out his hands. The fisherman was strong, though, so a third knight came up from behind and pummeled him with his sword. The father went limp, and the knights forced his hands out and exposed his wrists.

"Father! No!" the boy cried, and he rushed forward to help. But another knight kicked his legs out from beneath him, and he went sprawling in the dirt.

Sir Stevron raised his sword overhead, grinning, and brought it down just as fast.

Victoria turned away, thinking: *Why, Lukas?!*

The father screamed an agonizing, stomach-wrenching scream. As his scream turned to sobs, Victoria brought her focus back thinking the deed was done.

But the hands didn't sever completely, and the knights played tug-o-war with the man until the skin holding them together ripped apart. They fell from the release of tension and stumbled to the ground. Then, of all things, they threw the hands at one another, laughing as though it were all fun and games.

The sickening smell of blood wafted under Victoria's nose.

The memory still burned vividly in her mind.

"Let us see how you provide for your family now," Lukas said to the wailing fisherman. "It will be difficult to work your nets and rigs without hands. You should have joined the Order." He turned his attention to the boy. "What say you? Are you the war'n type?"

Please, Lukas, leave him be.

The boy looked at Lukas, and then at his father who shook his head. Victoria saw it in the old man's eyes—a plea for his son not to go, but clearly torn for the boy's safety. The boy wiped his wet and dirtied cheeks, and brought his attention back to Lukas. "Y-yes, sir. I ... I's the war'n type."

The father's howl of anguish swelled, and Victoria knew he cried more for his boy, than for his hands.

The throne room came into view as she and Lukas turned a corner.

"There it is," Lukas said.

Victoria brought her attention away from the passing cobbles beneath her feet. Tears blurred her vision as she remembered the boy. *Gods, he died in the Castle Lombard skirmish with the cult of Drächenkamp. He was so young.*

"I hope Vincent is inside." She didn't want another Port Coalcliff incident to occur. She didn't want more harm brought upon others. Not for the sake of Lukas's ambitions.

They climbed the steps to the great entrance of the throne room. Lukas pulled on a dragon-carved handle, and the large, oaken door groaned open.

Please, let it be Vincent they have captured.

Torches sputtered along the walls leading the long walk down the hall toward the throne. Shadows danced off the many dark knight statues; which made them seem half-alive, marching in place. At the base of the raised black seat knelt four figures—two men, a woman and child—bound by rope and flanked on both sides by knights with swords drawn down upon them.

And none, she saw, were Vincent.

Oh, by the gods, Victoria despaired. She released a long, quivering sigh. *This will not turn out well. 'Tis going to be Port Coalcliff all over again ...*

27

GHOSTS & DRAGONS

The sound was the faintest whisper in the air, a sighing breeze from the coast. Gabriel peered across the grassy path beneath his feet, and gazed out over the ocean. Moonlight rolled across the waves in a silvery, white gleam thousands of feet below, just beyond the steep cliff along the winding trail he had found.

So peaceful, he thought, though he knew the sky city was anything but.

The path climbed steadily, narrow at times and wide at others. He was fortunate to have found it. Quakes had caused buildings to crumble and block the streets leading to the throne room, so this path was the only chance he had to get there.

But will I make it in time to rescue the Duke's son, he wondered. And he couldn't forget about Alivia. *She might have been captured by the Knight's Order, too.*

Grass swayed in the wind. His cloak began to flutter. The breeze died, and the blades of grass bent back tall. Then it happened again—grass swayed and cloak snapped—but this time fiercer.

Unusual weather, Gabriel observed. He glanced to the sky, surveying the clouds. *No storm brews.*

He heard a sound: faint, like a distant crack of thunder, followed by the wind, crack of thunder, wind. It repeated itself again and again. Gabriel stopped and listened. As the sound of thunder claps grew louder the wind blew stronger.

Then there was silence. No wind.

Whoop-whoosh! The wind suddenly howled as though a tornado approached. Gabriel's eyes widened as he saw the source of the storm.

The red dragon flew up and over the ridge of the cliff. It landed before him.

Gabriel stumbled back and fell. Frantic, he stood, drew his sword and shield, and readied his battle-stance to face the massive beast. No pain entered his thoughts—there was only his foe.

The byrd roared, and spread out its wings to give the appearance of enormity, to intimidate.

Gabriel swallowed down his fear, mustered courage. "Yeah, yeah," he taunted back. "We know you're a goliath."

And then it struck him for the first time—in the child's tale, the Onion Knight, the boy had to slay one last goliath to save the kingdom.

A dragon.

A popping sound erupted and Gabriel saw smoke billow from the dragon's snout. The beast lunged its triangular maw forward, opening its jaws. A red, fiery glow ignited from the back of its throat and flared up to the ribbed topside of its mouth. The dragon flicked its pink, forked tongue, and fire spewed forth, bright and hot. Red and yellow flames licked the path, scorching the grass and charring the cliff.

Gabriel had a decision to make: jump from the cliff and plummet to his death, or embrace the inferno and burn.

"I choose neither," he yelled defiantly, and he slumped to his knees and took cover behind his round-shield.

Fire surrounded him on all sides, sparking past in a sweltering blaze. But his shield absorbed the fire and heat, broke the dragon's fire-breath like it broke most magicks—blocking spells as shields block swords.

The inferno burned out, though sparks still flickered off his round-shield. Gabriel looked down and saw that the grass beneath his feet—which swayed in the wind a moment ago—was now a scorched wasteland.

Whoop-whoosh!

Gabriel stood to face the dragon ... but it was gone.

He strode toward the cliff, the rocks aglow in an orange glimmer, and glanced over the edge. "Hmph." He didn't see the byrd. He whirled back toward the path, squeezed the shield in his left hand and twirled the sword in his right. "'Tis not good to lose your opponent," he scolded himself.

Whoop-whoosh! He heard it from above.

The windstriker looked up, and saw the dragon in a steep dive swooping down toward him.

189

"Oh, damn you, byrd." Gabriel ran, and then leaped, as the dragon slammed into the path. Chunks of rock and dirt exploded upon impact. Gabriel was thrown into the air. He landed on his back, the wind knocked out of him.

He didn't have time to recover. The dragon spun round and whipped its tail downward for a crushing blow. But Gabriel rolled aside and got to his feet. Quick as a cat, the byrd thrust its head forward and snapped its jaws shut, snarling.

As they snapped closed, the windstriker leaped rearward.

There we go, he saw a chance to strike. He shield-punched the byrd's snout.

The dragon craned its neck away and shook its head from the blow.

The dragon didn't hesitate, though, and kept pushing the offensive. Black, razor-sharp talons slashed at the windstriker, and he blocked with his shield.

Blinding pain lashed through his hand and into his arm from the impact of defending the blow. When last he fought the dragon, Gabriel remembered that the byrd feigned an attack—slashed at him with its talons but hit him with its tail. The dragon must have thought to do the same, because Gabriel saw the tail swooping around. He blocked another talon slash with his shield, and timed his jump with precision.

The tail whirled beneath his feet.

Gabriel felt a surge of power course through his arm from the sword. He sensed the gemstone's radiating glow, and felt its tiny vibrations swell into his fingers.

His arm acted as if on its own, and his blade arced in and split the dragon's hardened scales like a knife cutting through cheese. He landed to his feet as the byrd retreated from his attack range; jade, cat-like eyes wide in alarm.

The dragon crouched low, snarling, and Gabriel locked eyes with the fearsome beast. In the smoldering green pits of Des'tok's eyes, Gabriel saw his own reflection. How small he looked, how weak and frail.

I must not show fear.

The dragon blinked. It peered back in a haunting gleam.

A chill shuddered down Gabriel's neck and spine. He sensed something strange deep inside those otherworldly eyes. Like an emotion, though one he had rarely felt.

The byrd roared, the sound so loud that Gabriel almost dropped his sword. Its teeth snapped at him.

Whoop-whoosh! Then its wings cracked like thunder and the dragon took flight. Rising, rising, rising … it was gone.

Gabriel watched the dragon until he saw it no more. "Did you send your byrd to challenge me, Vincent?" He glanced down at the gem attached to his round-shield.

It didn't glow. Still looked like a common rock.

The last Goliath, Gabriel thought. *To activate the stone, the dragon will have to die. That's what Slade said, at least: The stones are strengthened with giant's blood.*

"Do you know this, Vincent?" he said aloud. "Do you know this city won't fly 'til your dragon's blood has been shed?"

Suddenly, a ripple of blue light pulsed in front of Gabriel. It formed into the ghostly apparition of the slain boy.

"He knows," the boy spoke.

Then the ghost vanished.

Gabriel sheathed his sword, and strapped the shield onto his shoulder. "Ghosts and dragons," he scoffed. "I must be mad." He shook the thought away, and resumed his hike up the path.

The throne room, he reminded himself. *I must make it in time.*

28

HOSTAGE CRISIS IN THE THRONE ROOM

Tell me," the Captain of the Knight's Order demanded. He sat brooding on the black throne—a leg draped over an arm, his greatsword propped against the high-backing of the grand chair. "Where is Vincent?"

"I know not," Stone said, hands bound behind his back with rope. He sat slumped on his knees, occasionally rocking his weight to get comfortable. To his left knelt Alivia, Griff, and Patrick.

All cuffed with rope.

Alivia thought binding the Duke's son was unnecessary. She had said as much, but the captain ignored her remark. It seemed the Knight's Order were here in the Fortress of the Moon for something else entirely. Saving the boy was not part of their plans.

Captain Steele leaned forward and pointed at Stone. "Do you take me for a fool? You are Vincent's right hand—his confidant. You know where he hides!"

Stone shrugged.

"I can be merciful, but only if you tell me." The captain grasped the blond woman's hand standing to his right. "Am I not just, my love?"

"Yes, my prince, you are just."

He clapped the shoulder of a knight standing to the left of the throne—the leader of the knights who had captured them. His interlaced gold and silver chainmail glittered from torchlight. "Am I not merciful, Sir Stevron?"

"Aye, sir, you are merciful."

"You see," the captain said, and he looked at Stone. "Now speak.

Where is Vincent?"

Stone snorted. He spat.

The captain *tsk*ed. He raised a hand.

Two knights stepped forward. One circled around behind Stone, the other stopped in front of him. Both placed the tips of their blades inches from his head.

Please, Stone, Alivia wanted to say. *Tell them. Before this gets bloody.*

"Last chance before I loose my dogs. Where is Vincent?"

Stone cleared his throat. He opened his mouth to speak, then snapped it shut.

Captain Steele sneered. He nodded to Sir Stevron, who stepped forward and descended the steps of the dias.

"All right, men," Stevron said. "'Tis time to *make* him talk."

Stone grunted, and Alivia saw the knight behind him grab a handful of his hair. He forced Stone to look at the knight who stood before him.

"Do it," Stevron ordered.

The knight in front pummeled his sword into Stone's nose. Blood squirted. Alivia heard the crack of cartilage. Stone moaned, spit blood, and tried to free his head from the knight who held it. But the knight gripped his hair tighter, brought the edge of his sword underneath Stone's throat.

"Again," Sir Stevron commanded.

The knight hit his nose in the same spot with the end of his sword. Stone cried out in pain.

Oh gods, Alivia prayed. *Let this end. Save us all.*

She turned away from the beating, and looked at the round, stained glass mosaic above the throne; its king and dragon dancing in a rainbow of colors as the torches flickered throughout the hall.

"Again."

The knight hit Stone again, and his moan became a whimper.

Alivia tried to ignore the sounds of torture. She wanted to focus on the mosaic, to bring her attention away from the beating and the man who ordered it. A shadow moved behind the glass, and Alivia squinted.

"Again."

Hilt of sword smashed Stone's nose, but the knight's aim was poor. His mouth took the blunt of the blow.

"Enough," Captain Steele ordered.

The knight let go of Stone's hair. Stone slumped to the floor and spat out a tooth.

The captain shifted his weight in the chair. "Get him back on his knees."

The two knights who beat him grabbed Stone under the arms and lifted him up. Hunched and broken, blood dripped from his nose and mouth to the floor.

"Now, cultist rat, are you like to talk?"

Stone glanced up and looked at Steele, eyes already swelling and bruised purple from a broken nose. "He … He is," Stone started.

"Yes?" Captain Steele leaned forward.

"Adon is in control." Stone spat more blood. "You can burn for all I care, Steele."

The captain leaned back in the chair. "No, you can burn sinner." He waved a hand at the other three captives. "Make them talk."

Six more knights stepped forward, toward Alivia, Griff, and Patrick Lombard—three in front and three behind—same as they did to Stone.

"Start with him." He pointed at Griff.

The knight behind Griff grabbed for his hair, but Griff threw his head back and into the knight's fingers. Alivia heard bones snap.

"Aghh!" The knight jerked his hand back. Griff tried to stagger to his feet, but the knight in front of him punched him in the jaw. He went sprawling onto the floor. Then both knights began to beat him, while Griff tried to protect himself with his hands.

"Men can be stubborn," Captain Steele said to the blond woman.

Alivia saw she had turned away and wasn't watching. *She wants no part of this,* Alivia realized.

"Boys are another matter. Sir Stevron."

"Aye, sir." Stevron gestured toward the two knights nearest Patrick, and the one behind grabbed the boy's hair. Patrick let out a weak cry.

Alivia could stay quiet no more. "He is Duke Lombard's son," she told Captain Steele. "As a knight of the kingdom you are charged with protecting the weak, not threatening them."

The captain waved the comment away. "I serve the gods, woman, not the realm of men."

"Regardless, if you harm him you commit treason against the Kingdom of the Four Winds. Your gods cannot protect you then!"

Captain Steele stood, and shouted, "Who is to say the boy didn't die by the hands of this one!" He pointed at Stone. His voice echoed off the walls of the long hall. He sat back down onto the throne, and nodded toward the knights and boy.

The knight in front of Patrick reared back to punch him with the pommel of his sword.

"Wait!" shouted Stone. "I ... I will talk."

The knight hesitated, waiting for his captain's command.

Captain Steele smiled. "I knew you'd come around. Now, where is Vincent?"

"The Temple of Adon ... he is there."

"The Temple of Adon? Then why are you here in the throne room?"

"We were s'posed to meet up here, before heading to the temple. However," Stone motioned with his head toward the surrounding knights. "Plans changed."

"The temple," Steele said. "And if I take my men to the temple, what awaits us?

"Your demise, that's what."

Captain Steele snapped his fingers. Patrick cried out in pain as his hair was pulled back roughly.

"All right, all right," Stone pleaded. "Vincent and his byrd await you. And he ... he awaits the windstriker."

Alivia turned her gaze toward Stone. *Gabriel?*

"Why does Vincent await the windstriker," Captain Steele asked. "What is his interest in the man-in-black?"

Stone spit blood. "He has the missing pieces to the Heart of the Dragon. I don't know how, though."

"Vincent won't tell you?"

Stone shook his head.

"What will happen when Vincent has the windstriker's stones?"

"The city will fly," Stone said, "and the *successor* will have the power of the Fortress of the Moon once more."

A malicious grin swept across Steele's lips. "And *only* the successor?" he asked.

"Aye, only the successor. The Fortress of the Moon responds only to the chosen—those destined to wield the Heart of the Dragon—the Prophets."

Captain Steele leaned forward in his chair, fidgeting with anticipation. "How does one become successor?"

Stone hesitated.

"Sir Stevron." Captain Steele snapped his fingers again.

Stevron strode toward the boy, sword drawn, and placed its tip at the hollow of Patrick's throat. Blood trickled down his neck. Patrick began to sob.

Stone watched this all, fear clear across his face. Alivia knew it was not the Duke's son being threatened in Stone's eyes, but his own.

She knew he'd talk.

"A blood bond," he said desperately. "The blood of both men— prophet and successor—must seep into the Heart of the Dragon at the same time. Only then can you claim the Fortress of the Moon."

"Is that all?" Captain Steele asked.

"N-no." Stone's voice quivered. "Before the blood bond can be made, all the Goliaths must be slain. The windstriker has killed two. There is one left."

The captain's voice was sharp as steel. "What is the third Goliath? In the child's tale it was a dragon." He paused. "A dragon," he said, realizing.

Stone swallowed. "Aye, it's the dragon. Des'tok is the last Goliath."

Captain Steele slumped back into the throne, released a contemplative sigh. "And Vincent knows this? He knows that his byrd must be slain?"

"Aye, he does. He says that the dragon needs to die for the prophecy to be fulfilled."

Steele waved a hand in the air. "I care not for your cult's prophecies." He looked at the blond woman. "What say you, my love? Would you like to see this temple?"

She placed her right hand on the curve of her hip, and smiled. "I would. Mayhaps we can finally capture Vincent once and for all."

"'Tis settled, then." The captain addressed his knights: "My boys, it's time to go. We march for the city's temple!" He nodded to Sir Stevron.

"Slit their throats," Sir Stevron ordered.

The knight behind Alivia grabbed her hair and pulled back hard, exposing her neck.

She heard Griff yell and curse.

Patrick began to sob.

Stone shouted and got to his feet. He shouldered into the knight behind him and knocked him to the floor. But the knight in front drove the pommel of his sword into Stone's gut. He doubled over. Then the knight stabbed him in the back; its tip impaled out of his chest.

And then the stained-glass mosaic shattered.

A dark figure came launching through.

Alivia felt the knight gripping her hair loosen his grip. He almost sounded like he was choking—his breaths became gurgles. She yanked her hair free and turned around. The knight was falling back, dead, before he even hit the ground. A crossbow bolt was pierced into his throat.

When she brought her gaze back toward the throne, she saw the windstriker tumble into a roll. He slashed a knight across the chest with his sword. The knight wheeled around, face contorting in pain, and Alivia saw white foam splutter from his mouth.

And then all the knights were on him, hacking and slashing, as they tried to kill him. But Gabriel was too skilled. He blocked with his shield and parried with his sword, slashed with its edge and stabbed with its tip—slicing knight's armor and cutting deep—so injecting the blade's poison. Knights fell and died, and more knights rushed into the throne room through the great, oaken doors. They ran to aid their brothers against such a foe—a titan!

And watching it all, sitting the throne with an amused grin across his face, was Captain Steele.

Oh gods, Patrick, Alivia remembered.

She got to her feet and moved to help him. But Griff was already cutting the boy's ropes with a knight's fallen sword. It must have landed next to him. The ropes cut free from Patrick's hands, and Griff darted closer to do the same for her. Her ropes came loose and fell to the floor.

"We have to get out of here," she told him, rubbing her wrists.

He nodded, and ran over to Stone who lay motionless. "Aye," Griff said. "Get the boy!"

She moved toward Patrick and grabbed his hand. When she whirled back around to make for Griff and Stone, she ran into a heavy, gap-toothed knight.

"Ye not goin' anywhere, missy," the knight said. He grabbed her by the shoulders, licking his lips.

The redoulz, she remembered. She told Patrick to hold his breath, reached into her pocket and pulled out the deadly flower. Then she shoved it into the knight's face.

Red pollen dusted his eyes and mouth.

The toxic smell of redoulz spores filled the air.

The knight gagged and fell to his knees. The pollen burned his flesh, and as he took a rasping breath, the plant's toxins seeped into his lungs. He screamed.

Alivia ran past him with Patrick in tow. Her fingers started to tingle, felt a little raw. There would be scarring. But she ignored the sensation since she hadn't breathed in the fiery poison.

She reached Griff as he was standing. He half-carried Stone, who had an arm draped over Griff's shoulder to help carry his weight.

"Where to?" she asked, glancing back at Gabriel. The knights were circling the windstriker, more and more hesitant to attack. They looked like a group of boys playing with a viper, afraid of its poisonous bite.

Griff paid the battle no mind. He made for the great, oaken doors. "Let's head for the streets," he said. He moved slow carrying Stone's mostly dead weight. "Your boy is distracting the knights. Now's our chance!"

He is right, she realized. The Knight's Order had assembled here in the heart of the city—the throne room—and Gabriel's riot sent them into the hall in droves. It seemed their focus was on killing the windstriker ... and surviving.

She tugged at Patrick's hand, and kept pace with Griff.

They reached the open doors. Alivia stopped to take one last look at Gabriel, while Griff and Stone descended the steps to the street. Two knights rushed in on the windstriker, and in two quick cuts they each tasted death. Another came from behind, and the windstriker turned to defend with his shield.

Alivia saw movement from the throne. Captain Steele stood to his feet. He grabbed his greatsword—its black blade turning red.

Gabriel stabbed a knight through his mail, and cut off another's hand.

And then she saw what Gabriel could not, his back facing the throne, locked in combat with a score of knights. Captain Steele slashed his greatsword at nothing but air, and a fiery blast flung from its tip.

"Behind you!" she shouted, but it mattered naught.

The fireball exploded into Gabriel and surrounding knights. A scorching blaze tore through them all. Men screamed and flailed and burned and died. Captain Steele seemed to care little if he killed friend or foe.

My gods, she thought, as billowy black smoke rose from the ashes. *This can't be.*

Gabriel lay motionless, face down in the midst of blackness.

He was dead.

Griff shouted from behind, "Let's go! Before those choirboys find us missing!"

"Gabriel," her voice caught in her throat.

"Come on, or we are dead!"

Reluctant, she descended the steps with Patrick in hand.

Griff led them as quick as he could manage. They staggered down the street and to one of the larger buildings Alivia had seen on their journey to the throne room. He came to a rotting wooden door and shoved it open.

"An old manse," he said. "Once a house to a noble or lord." He hauled himself and Stone over to a door in the back, near a cobweb infested kitchen. "If the city were ever sacked—" he kicked open the door, and they began to descend a set of steps confined within a narrow stairwell, "—they could escape underground."

Stone groaned. "V-Vincent."

"I know, Gavin." Griff shifted his weight, hoisting Stone's arm over his shoulder for a better grip. "But there's naught we can do. He is on his own now."

Stone groaned again, seemed to weep.

"He still has Des'tok," Griff reassured, "and that windstriker just killed a good many of those choirboys. Vincent will survive."

The stairwell grew darker. Alivia felt along the rough bricks to guide her steps. Ever lower they descended, into the deep depths of the Fortress of the Moon.

Alivia couldn't steal her thoughts away from Gabriel. *I thought for sure he'd save us.* She felt the boy's small hand, and the wiggle of his delicate fingers. *Patrick is my charge now, and only mine,* she told herself. *I have to get him to safety …*

29

WARRIOR'S DEATH

Victoria fought back the vile taste of vomit in the back of her mouth. *So many knights,* she thought, scanning the bodies strewn before the throne. The stench of blood made her stomach churn. *So many dead.*

"Can we leave here?" she asked Lukas. "Please."

"Shortly." He knelt beside the face-down windstriker. After rolling him over and onto his back, he leaned down and placed an ear to his mouth. "He breathes." Lukas brought his attention to the windstriker's hand. He unclenched the shortsword from his grasp.

"Then kill him and let us begone."

Any longer and she was going to lose it. Among the faces of the dead, she recognized several. Waymen and Vylar had eyed her often, desiring more than looks. Now they both lay still, their once gawking eyes now stared up at her unblinking. Bryce had supped on roast venison and drank of Lorenta's finest red wines with her and Lukas, after winning a tourney in honor of King Rikard IV last year in Wyndsor. His mouth now hung open, and he supped on white foam drooling from his bottom lip.

Anders, Trents, Hackett, and Ethon. *So many dead.* Travis, Ed, Qynn, and even Sir Stevron—he'd lost his sword-bearing hand, Victoria saw.

Justice for the fisherboy's father, she thought bitterly, as she brought her gaze back to Lukas.

Lukas unwrapped a black cloth from the windstriker's sword. There was a red gemstone attached to its hilt beneath the cloth. He touched the gemstone, and then with a strong twist, it came loose. He examined the stone.

It radiated in a dim, red glow, drinking the torchlight throughout the hall; and it was far from symmetrical, more like a broken shard than a piece of jewelry.

"Remarkable," he said, turning the stone over to see the other side.

"What about that one?" Victoria pointed to the windstriker's round-shield. Anything to take her mind off the dead. "It does not glow."

Lukas picked up the round-shield, and removed the stone. "Yes, the stone is dull. It looks more like a rock." He found the windstriker's crossbow and took its stone as well. "Two are ablaze, and one is not." He dropped the crossbow and stood. The gun thumped against the windstriker's side and clanged onto the floor.

Victoria placed her right hand on the curve of her hip, swaying her left. "What do you make of it?"

Lukas shrugged. "I suppose we'll have to ask Vincent, won't we?" He smirked. "Andison," he called for the Weapons Master.

The stout, balding man came scampering at once, short brawny arms swinging quickly.

"These stones—" he handed them to Andison, and then drew the greatsword from his back, "—can you attach them?"

Andison mulled over the stones, squinting at them and at Lukas's sword. "Yes, sir. I think so."

"See to it."

The Weapons Master took the stones, and Sinfire, and scampered out of the throne room.

Victoria was puzzled. "Why did you do that?"

"Do you not remember what Slade said about the Onion Knight?"

How could she not remember? Among her favorite childhood memories, her mother reciting the tale before bedtime had been the best. She liked that the boy hero became king in the end, after he defeated the Goliaths. Defeated them with the most simplest of weapons, too, a stone.

"Yes," she said slowly.

Lukas inhaled a heavy breath. "Giant's blood strengthens the stones," he reminded, "and there is one Goliath left to defeat. With the gemstones attached to Sinfire, I shall have enough power to slay a giant and activate the Fortress of the Moon."

I wish you lusted for me as you lust for power, she wanted to say, but bit her lip instead.

"Captain Steele, sir." The Old Knight approached, and to Victoria's utter resentment, Lady Luck followed. The knight and commander stopped and saluted—Ellard with a slight nod, Adanna with a bow and fists across her chest. "We gave chase as you ordered, sir," the Old Knight said. "A unit pursues the cultist curs now."

"Where did they get off to?"

"An old manse, sir. We found a secret passage leading underground."

Lukas snorted. "So the rats have scurried off to another hole."

"No worry," Commander Adanna said. "Our men will find them." She gave Victoria a quick, distasteful glance, then looked down at the windstriker. "Ah, man I look for."

Lukas drew the menacing, black dagger from his waist; the one with its hilt formed into a four-headed beast. "His days are numbered. You need not look for him any longer."

"*NO!*" Lady Luck drew the spear from her back. "Bad omen to kill foe while sleeping. I take care of him." She motioned toward the windstriker with the leaf-shaped spearhead. "He warrior. I give him warrior's death."

Lukas sighed. "Not bloody likely. He's a warrior, all right." He knelt beside the windstriker, the dagger's sharp edge gleaming in his hand. "One I'd sooner see dead than given a fighting chance."

Sir Ellard cleared his throat. "Adanna has the right of it, sir. 'Tis dishonorable to slay a knight while unconscious. He should be given a chance to defend himself."

Lukas shook his head and spat. "Damn the two of you and your omens and honors." He stood, gave both the Old Knight and Lady Luck a stern gaze. But he sheathed his blade.

Victoria knew her prince had to relent. The barbarian woman held her superstitions too closely, and as the men's luck charm, they would sooner see to it that no ill-will befell her. Sir Ellard was another matter altogether. It was well-known throughout the kingdom that he held his honors high. He had served as Captain of the Kingsguard, after all—a most honorable title for any knight. And what was there in life for the Old Knight, if not but honor on the battlefield?

"You can take the head from a snake," Lukas said, "and its venom can still kill." He glanced to the unconscious windstriker. "Remember that. When he wakes, see to his death."

"By your command," Sir Ellard said with a nod.

Commander Adanna twirled the spear in her hands. "It will be so."

"When it is done, bring your men to the temple," Lukas ordered.

"Aye, sir," said the Old Knight. "But, what would you have us do with Brynden's men?"

Lukas furrowed his brow. "Brynden's men? What has become of *his* unit?"

"The men say he was lost passing through the Forest of Despair."

Lukas snorted. "He must have followed the Witch, the fool. All right, his men will come with me."

Lady Luck shifted nervously. "Bad omen. Men cursed."

"Then it's good I am not a superstitious fool." Lukas marched to exit the throne room. "Let us begone, Victoria." His tone was short.

She hurried after. They descended the steps to the cobblestone street. Knights were everywhere—sharpening blades, eating what rations they had left, or resting their eyes before heading out.

The Weapons Master scampered forward, Lukas's greatsword in hand.

"I have done it, sir," Andison said. "I attached the stones." He handed Sinfire to Lukas.

Lukas embraced the heavy, black sword. Victoria saw the gems were now attached in a neat row along the flat of the blade. It was by no means castle-forged work, for the stones were tied to the blade with leather straps. The two glowing stones were closer to the hilt, while the dull one was just above them, nearest the point of the sword.

"Are you certain the stones will stay attached to the blade?" Lukas asked.

"Ah," Andison fidgeted with his hands. "Under the circumstances, and with our limited resources, this was the best that I could do. But they should hold."

"Should?" Lukas arched an eyebrow.

"Will," Andison corrected in a hurry. "The stones will hold."

Lukas grunted. "I suppose this will suffice, for now." He looked out to the many knights spread throughout the street. "Brynden's unit, with me," he shouted.

Knights darted into motion—sheathing blades, finishing meals, waking their eyes and getting to their feet. All quickened their stride to stand before their captain.

But when Lukas saluted his men, he frowned. "There are only four of you. Where is the rest of your unit?"

"They died, sir," a thickset knight with sand coating his armor said.

"Hmph," Lukas said. "What became of Brynden?"

A scrawny man chewing on a pipe spoke up. "He ran off into the woods. Disappeared."

Lukas cocked his head and spat. "Only the weak of mind fall to the Witch's deceits. No matter. Gather six more men and come with me."

"Yes, sir," they said in unison, and then hurried off.

Lukas didn't wait. He turned from the hustle of men, and began heading down a street with a slight upward rise. Victoria followed beside him. She noticed that the street led toward a building sitting higher than the throne room; its silhouette all she could see a hundred paces ahead.

Is that the temple? She felt Lukas take her hand.

"Are you ready to slay a dragon?" he asked with a grin.

30

FOR HONOR, FOR DEATH

*A*re you lost?" *a woman asked Gabriel, brushing a strand of flowing yellow hair from her eyes. "Why look at you, you are trembling." She reached out and took his hand, and Gabriel saw that hers was bigger than his.*

I am a boy, *he realized,* no more than six or seven.

"Hey, I recognize you," the woman said. "You are the boy from down the road. Your father is ... and your mother is ..." she spoke their names, but Gabriel could not hear them.

Everything shook so violently when she said them.

What's that? What are my parents' names?

"They must have people out looking for you, surely." The woman knelt and scooped little Gabriel into her arms. "I shall take you to them."

Yes, *he thought,* I would like that very much.

She trudged along the dirt road. A green grassy plain stretched for miles on end to either side of its winding path. Hours they walked, neither talking. Gabriel felt the gentle bounce of each step as she carried him. Felt the tender touch of her warm and soft embrace.

Comfort, *he thought.* Safe.

He felt the cool breeze of the day's sunny springtime air, which drifted the woman's scent underneath his small, boyish nose.

She smelled of jasmines and lilies, *he remembered.*

In the distance, over the next bend, Gabriel saw the fist-like towers of a castle come into view. Is that my home, *he wondered.*

A boy ran down the road toward them.

The woman set little Gabriel down, and greeted the approaching boy with a curtsy. "My Prince."

"You found him," the boy said, gasping for breath. "We thought we'd lost you, brother." Gabriel recognized the boy from Vincent's dream—the boy who sparred

with wooden swords, and was slain with steel. "Come on. Mother and father will be happy to see you." *He grabbed Gabriel's hand and pulled him along.*

They will be happy to see me? *he thought.* My parents *want* to see me?

The castle gates grew larger and larger, and two figures stood beneath its raised portcullis—a man and woman. My parents, *he hoped.*

Everything shook violently, and Gabriel's vision blurred until darkness took him. "No, come back," *he shouted.* "Don't leave me!"

But he knew they had left him long ago, before he became a man ...

"Are you lost?"

Gabriel opened his eyes.

The woman brushed a strand of flowing yellow hair from her eyes. "Why look at you, you are trembling." *She reached out and took his hand, and Gabriel saw that hers was bigger than his.*

Is this déjà vu?

The image of the pretty woman shook, and darkness took him ...

"Are you lost?" the woman's tender voice asked again. Gabriel opened his eyes, and saw her brush flowing yellow hair aside.

The image shook, blurred, and then darkened ...

"Are you lost?" the woman's tender voice deepened. It was more masculine this time. "Are you Lost? Agent Gabriel Lost, the windstriker?"

What? Gabriel opened his eyes. Two figures stood over him—an old knight and a brown-skinned woman.

"It is him," the brown woman said.

"I wanted to make sure," the knight said. "Twould be dishonorable to fight the wrong man."

A spearhead was thrust into Gabriel's face. "He wakes."

Gabriel tried to blink the bleariness away. *That's right,* he remembered. *There was an explosion.* He swatted the spear aside and scrambled to his feet. "Where is the Duke's son," he croaked. He sounded half-dead.

The old knight ignored him. "You killed our brothers." He drew a longsword from his waist. "The men say you are a titan." He scanned the bodies strewn about the throne room's floor. "It would seem they speak so."

Gabriel swayed from side to side, off-balance. His entire body ached from the explosion, and the inside of his head felt like a tiny blacksmith was striking an anvil with a hammer. What is more, the cut on his hand and his broken rib hurt worse than ever.

I feel horrible, he thought.

"Come, let us see you fight," the brown woman said. "See if you man I look for." She started for the great, oaken doors to make for the city streets.

The knight followed, rolling his neck and shoulders.

So they want a fight, huh?

Gabriel looked around for his weapons. He found each in turn— the sword he sheathed at his waist, the crossbow and shield he strapped to his back. The dark bolt he had fired at the knight threatening Alivia was still pierced into his throat. So he walked over to the corpse and knelt beside it. After yanking the bloody bolt from its flesh, he wiped away the gore with a black cloth and tucked the bolt inside his calfskin bag.

My stones are missing, he noticed. Where the gemstones had been, hollow depressions now resided. *The weapons' enchantments are gone.*

"You coming, Windstriker?" the old knight called.

Gabriel looked up and saw he now stood next to the barbarian woman beneath the open foyer.

"He come," the brown woman said.

They turned and descended the stairs to the street.

"Twould seem I have no choice in the matter." Gabriel started after them; a slight limp in his gait, a sharp pain in his side. He descended the steps and staggered onto the cobblestone street.

A score of knights had circled around, eager to watch the fight. Some chanted, "*Old Knight*," while others, "*Lady Luck*." Some spat at his feet, cursing him for killing their brothers, while more cast lots, taking bets and exchanging copper pieces.

"No one interferes," shouted the Old Knight, as he paced to flank Gabriel on the left. "This is a battle for honor!"

"And for death," Lady Luck bellowed, moving to flank Gabriel's right.

Gabriel studied his foes. He glanced at the knight. *They called him Old Knight.* "I know you." He remembered the man once served as Captain of the Kingsguard, before being forced into retirement. It was said he was "past his prime," though Gabriel figured otherwise. "You are Sir Ellard." Gabriel drew his sword. Its weight felt shaky in his hand. "Hate that I have to face you. You are a noble knight."

The Old Knight nodded, and said, "Thanks."

Gabriel turned his focus to Lady Luck. "You I know not. Why do they call you Lady Luck?"

The barbarian woman twirled the spear in her hands. The beads on her weapon and clothing clattered against one another as she did. "Because I cannot die," she said. Then she held up a leather cord necklace dangling from her neck. Gabriel saw that it was tied to a thick lock of hair bound by red ribbon. "My tribe killed, save me. I take hair from my dead kin and keep it with me always. I want to join them in afterlife so I seek death on battlefield. But it never so. Men call it luck, I call it curse."

A whoop of, "Lady Luck!" hollered from the crowd of knights.

She paid them no mind. "Are you man I look for? The one to give me death?"

Gabriel drew his round-shield into his left hand. It hurt to raise his arm higher than his shoulder now. "Guess that depends on how lucky I feel."

"One can hope," said Lady Luck, though Gabriel sensed doubt in her voice.

He heard a scrape of leather against stone behind him. When Gabriel whirled around, he saw the Old Knight coming down fast with his longsword. He got his shield up, and the blade clanged against it. The impact shot a sharp pain through his arm.

For a knight of honor, he thought, swiping a cut at the Old Knight's open left-side. *He did not hesitate to attack from behind.*

The Old Knight blocked the strike with his sword, and pushed Gabriel's blade out with ease.

I am so weak.

"You—you fight well, Windstriker."

A noise rustled from Gabriel's side: a slap of skin against stone. Lady Luck made her charge, bare feet and all, and jumped. She hurtled down on him with spear thrust forward—its reach near twice his size.

Gabriel swiped the spear's wooden shaft aside with the flat of his sword, just as he raised his shield in time to block another of the Old Knight's sword strikes.

Lady Luck landed behind him, then smashed him across the ear with the spear's shaft.

Gabriel stumbled forward, ear ringing—its sound mixed together with the triumphant shouts of watching knights and men-at-arms.

"Give him no praise," Lady Luck told the Old Knight.

Then the two rushed in on the windstriker together.

Gabriel took a step back, though not too close to the surrounding knights in fear one might stab him with an unseen blade.

Spear jabbed and longsword swung, and Gabriel twirled in a dance of shield and sword, blocking both. The Old Knight and Lady Luck fought as though their thoughts were linked. If Gabriel sliced at the Old Knight, Lady Luck was on him; if the barbarian jabbed her spearhead, Sir Ellard defended her strike.

The three were locked in arms—a waltz of blades and shield and spear—when the city quaked.

The watching knights yelled in alarm. Buildings crumbled into the street. Men ran, frantic.

Sir Ellard leaped rearward and out of the fray. "By the gods," he said. "What abomination is that?!"

Lady Luck stopped her attack, dashed from Gabriel's range, and stared in the same direction as the Old Knight. "This city births bad omens."

Gabriel turned to meet their gaze. Men screamed and scattered, dodging falling debris and breaking stone, but more were desperate to get away from—

"Yeuuu!" shrieked the Knight of the Witch.

The undead knight staggered through the throng of knights and men-at-arms, casting death upon anyone it touched. Gabriel saw a knight charge forward to cut it down, but the Knight of the Witch grabbed his throat. The knight kicked and fought … then aged and died. His skin shriveled like a dried raisin, decayed into rotting flesh. The knight went limp, and the Knight of the Witch thrust the body aside.

It locked eyes with Gabriel. "Yeuuu!" it shouted again, voice hissing and cold. Gabriel saw breath steam from its undead mouth as it spoke.

"Yeuuu killed ... my brother. Kill. Uhoooohhh!"

The Old Knight took a step forward. "Is that walking corpse ... Brynden?"

"It is," Gabriel answered. "He fell prey to the Witch."

"He has joined the cold ones," Lady Luck said.

"Adanna." Sir Ellard said. "You finish off the windstriker. I will end our brother's misery." He charged toward the Knight of the Witch. While all the young knights fell back, and away from the aging touch of the undying corpse, the Old Knight ran forward poised to face death.

Lady Luck tightened her grip around the shaft of her spear. "Come, warrior. Kill me, and end my pain." She rushed in, bare-feet slapping against stone.

This is madness, Gabriel thought, but he ran to meet her halfway. His side ached in sharp stabs with each stride.

Spearhead thrust forward.

Gabriel side-stepped.

She jabbed again.

He blocked with his shield.

I have to get inside, he told himself, darting away. *Her reach is too great.*

Lady Luck closed the gap. She jabbed at Gabriel's head.

He ducked, and a *whoosh* of wind rushed by his ear as the spearhead swiped past. *That's it,* he saw a chance. Gabriel lashed his sword upward, and cut the spear's wooden shaft in half with the blade's sharp edge.

Adanna fell back, holding the spear's two splintered ends. She smiled. "You are man I look for." Then she dashed forward, shaft with spearhead in one hand, stick in the other. "Give me death," she shouted, and she hacked and hit in a fury.

But she no longer had the advantage. Gabriel blocked the overhead strike of the spearhead, trimmed the wooden stick even shorter with his steel, then reeled around and sliced open Lady Luck's leg—which released no poison. Without the gemstone, the sword no longer bit like a vicious snake.

Lady Luck fell to her knees. When she tried to stand, she stumbled. The wound was deep. "Aghh," she groaned. "You *are* warrior I look for. Please, end my luck. Kill me." She reached for the lock of hair about her neck.

Her slain tribesmen, Gabriel recalled. He tightened his grip around the leathered hilt of his sword.

The city stopped trembling. Gabriel heard the cries of dying men——of those pinned beneath heavy rock, of those running in terror of the undead knight's touch. He glanced to see where the Old Knight had gone. Nowhere in sight, nor was the Knight of the Witch. *What became of those two?*

He turned his gaze back to the brown woman. "No."

Lady Luck looked distraught with grief.

"You need to survive," he told her. Then he sheathed his blade and strapped the round-shield onto his shoulder. "Otherwise, the memory of your tribe will be lost forever."

"I ... I ..." she looked to the cobbles, at a loss for words. "Please, grant my wish. Kill me."

"No." Gabriel turned to leave.

"Wait," she called after him.

Gabriel stopped, and faced the brown woman.

"I owe you my life," she said. "Let me help you. It is way of my people."

"You'd slow me down." He motioned toward her cut leg. Blood gushed and glistened dark red on her thigh. "But if you want to help, tell me what has become of the Duke's son."

"He runs. Captives escape us, taking boy. Men hunt them now."

Run Alivia, thought Gabriel, *get him to safety.* There was nothing he could do for them now. Captain Steele had his gemstones. If reunited with the Heart of the Dragon, the city could fly and destruction would reign. *I have to stop the city from falling into the hands of a lunatic.* "What of your captain, where has he run?"

"To temple. He gives chase on Vincent's heels."

"The temple," Gabriel repeated. "Of course, Vincent flees to his God." He locked eyes with the barbarian woman. *Brown, like her skin,* he noticed. "Thank you." He turned to leave, but stopped. "You said you owe me your life ..."

She nodded.

"Then live. Don't let the death of your kin be the death of you."

He spun on his heels, and began his march for the temple. Thus leaving behind the destruction wrought by quake and undead, and leaving Lady Luck with thoughts of life, not death.

211

31

THE TEMPLE OF ADON

Quiet," Lukas ordered his men. "We approach the temple."
Victoria glanced ahead, not wanting to go any farther. She feared what awaited them inside—mostly Vincent and his mind-invading magicks—and she couldn't forget there was still a dragon to contend with. She shivered at the thought.

"Look at it," one of the men said. "'Tis as old as the Never-Never itself."

Lukas gave a stern glare of warning. "Quiet, I said."

The knight who spoke shunned his face toward the ground.

Victoria saw the soldier was right, though. The temple loomed before them, more ancient than the rest of the city. Thick, green moss crawled up its walls and stained glass windows, threatening to strangle the man-made structure. The building rose high and spread outward into two towering flanks. In the center, a domed roof thrust into the sky, supporting a massive golden cross that shone in the moonlight. Countless archways decorated the bone-white façade, sheltering dragon statues or hiding ornate windows.

The summit of the city, Victoria observed. She glanced over her shoulder and at the buildings behind her. The throne room's rooftop was still visible, three hundred paces away. *This temple sits atop the Fortress of the Moon,* she thought, *like Adon sits atop his throne.*

Though, she didn't believe anything so base. The gods of the Four Winds were the true divine, not Dräkenkamp's god. Theirs was false——pagan.

Oh, save us you gods, she prayed, *for we are about to enter the mouth of a dragon.*

Lukas made a gesture with his hand, silently ordering his men to spread out. The knights and men-at-arms did as commanded. They ran to surround the building and block the exits.

"Victoria, with me," he said. Then he took her hand and pulled her along. The two sneaked and crouched their way to the temple's front entrance—two rotting doors adorned in dragon carvings. One was cracked open.

Victoria overheard voices inside.

Voices she recognized:

"What are you planning for the windstriker?" That was Jon Slade's voice, no doubt. He had an arrogant tone Victoria came to loathe over the years of dealing with the mercenary. *But what is he doing here?* She assumed the windstriker had killed Slade, before wreaking havoc in the throne room.

"Ah, I thought I smelled your stench, Slade." Victoria shuddered at the sound of Vincent's voice. She squeezed her prince's hand for reassurance. "Have you come to seek redemption," Vincent said, "before the altar of Adon?"

"I care not for your God, Vincent." Victoria heard shuffling footsteps. "No, I'm here for *that*."

"The Heart of the Dragon? 'Tis just a rock, I am afraid. 'Twill do you no good."

"Mayhaps not in its current state. But when I have the windstriker's gemstones, this city will be mine." Slade paused. "Oh, you didn't think I knew? I *know* about the Heart of the Dragon—of the broken shards and the Goliaths. The blood bond. Everything."

The blood bond, thought Victoria. She didn't like it when the sinner in the throne room spoke of it. She liked it even less coming from Slade's own mouth. "Are we going to take them?" she whispered to Lukas.

He shook his head. "Let the rabble take care of themselves."

"Tell me," Slade demanded. "How are you summoning them, the Goliaths?"

"Those giants?" Vincent *ts*ked. "Why don't you pray and ask Adon. They are his creations, after all."

Victoria heard a scrape of metal against leather. *Slade's daggers,* she recalled. "Why is the windstriker so important to you?"

Another thin rasp of metal rang. Vincent must have drawn his own blade. "Not yet figured it out, have we? Your arrogance blinds you,

Slade."

"Has it?" The scrape of another dagger being drawn sounded. "He is to succeed you, isn't he?" Slade snickered. "I thought so, it's plain across your face. He is the next Successor."

Victoria felt her prince's hand clench. *Lukas wants that power*, she knew. *He won't hesitate to kill them all, if he must.*

"He is," Vincent said. "He shows all the signs of a *true* prophet. The Fortress of the Moon's ancient powers will be his. The windstriker will rule this city, and herald the coming Kingdom of Vehayne."

"That unknowing fool?! He is like a child. He knows naught of this city, and less of his own past!"

"Children have the unquestioning faith of saints. Better a child than the lusting greed of a mercenary."

Slade laughed. "That windstriker you speak so highly of cares less for your God than I do. He has told me as much."

"He shall believe. He is almost ready. And unlike you, he will not misuse the city's powers."

"Is that so?" Slade sighed. "Well, Vincent, I'm afraid your plans will not come to be. For I will have that stone from you. Whether you hand it over, or I pry it from your dead corpse. Prepare yourself!"

A *clink, clank* sounded, followed by pounding footsteps. Steel clanged against steel, and Victoria heard the puffs and grunts of struggle. Then a crash clamored. Something hit the ground with a *thump*.

Silence.

Did they kill each other? she hoped.

Lukas drew his greatsword into both hands.

A *clink* and scrape disturbed the quiet within. *Clink* and scrape.

Lukas raised a closed fist into the air. Then he opened it and motioned for his men to infiltrate. They moved forward and rushed inside the temple. "Let's go," he told Victoria, and he kicked open the rotting doors.

She followed him inside ...

... and saw Jon Slade pinned beneath a great dragon statue of obsidian and gold, face down in a pool of his own blood. Vincent's back was to them as he knelt at the temple's altar, praying.

Pray, Vincent, she thought, *your end is now at hand.*

Vincent stood, and turned to face them. "Why, if it isn't my good friend, the captain." He met eyes with Victoria. She cowered at his glare. "And his most loyal companion, the young harlot."

I won't show him fear, she decided. She unsheathed her slender blade. "You have nowhere left to run, Vincent."

Lukas stepped forward. "I have waited too long for this moment. All these years I have hunted you, and each time you have eluded me." His voice became a growl. "No more."

Vincent spread out his arms. "Well, here I am. What would you have of me now ... since you've 'caught' me?"

"I shall have that stone." Lukas nodded to the surrounding men who came in from the side and rear entrances to the temple. Their longswords were drawn, poised to strike at Lukas's command. "And you will name *me* successor to the city."

Vincent scoffed. "How 'bout I name you maggot, successor to eat the dead."

"You would like that, wouldn't you?" Lukas snorted. "Then how 'bout I start with *your* corpse, thus making you a martyr for your false religion."

"Oh, it is not false, Captain. I assure you." Vincent pointed a finger at Lukas. "Pray tell, with Heart of Dragon in hand, what would you do? How would you rule this city? I am curious to know."

"I'd rule with fear," Lukas growled. "The Kingdom of the Four Winds suffers from sickness. King Rikard abuses his power, whilst nobles and lords profit from the poor. Merchants are thieves, and thieves are rewarded. And lest us not forget—" he gestured toward Vincent, "—pagan religions have spread, corrupting the masses. I will cleanse them all of their sins and bring them to the true gods of the Four Winds." He rolled his fingers around the hilt of Sinfire. "Starting with you."

Vincent smirked. "Ah, so you'd become a tyrant—a ruler with no value for human life. But I feel I must warn you ... tyrants die alone. In the end the kingdom will burn, and you will be the only one left standing in its ashes. Not what I'd call ... *cleansing.*"

"Enough," Lukas barked. "This squabble is needless. 'Tis time you name me successor. Perform the rites."

"If the soul is not pure of heart and mind, the rites are meaningless."

Lukas raised his greatsword overhead, and the blade ignited in incandescent red fire. "As you can see, my own gods have blessed me with magicks. Now, the rites."

"You are a fool," Vincent said.

Lukas squeezed Sinfire's hilt, knuckles whitening. "Name. Me. *SUCCESSOR!*"

Victoria's heart raced. "You are a fool, Vincent. Name him!" She worried what Lukas might do if he got any angrier ... or who he might harm.

Vincent inhaled a deep, calming breath. "I shall never consent to the blood bond with the likes of you."

"No?" Lukas said. "I'll beg to differ—" he poised Sinfire behind his back with one hand, and its fire burned brighter, hotter, "—for I shall have your blood, and you *will* name me successor ..."

32
THE DOOR OF DELIVERANCE

Faster men! They are close at hand, I hear them." The voices of pursuing knights grew louder, Alivia noticed. Clanking armor echoed off the walls of the underground tunnel. Footsteps pounded against the stone beneath the knights' feet like the hammering of a blacksmith.

We are too slow, she thought. *Patrick's legs are too short, and Stone's wound too grievous.*

Griff hoisted Stone's weight up for a better grip. "They are gaining on us," he told Alivia.

She nodded, and gave Patrick's hand a tug to speed him along.

Over the last half-hour they had picked up their pace, at least as much as they could manage. But their efforts seemed futile. They were four—wounded and with a child—whilst the knights were seasoned soldiers accustomed to the hunt.

"How much farther to this door you spoke of?" Alivia asked.

"Not much." Griff led the party down a left-turning corridor, narrower than the first, with darkness just as black. "It should be ahead."

If only we had torches, thought Alivia. Her fingers felt raw from the constant scrape of rough brick as she felt along the tunnel's walls to guide her steps. She glanced behind, expecting to see more darkness, but instead saw a faint orange glow flicker off the walls in the distance. *The knights have light.* "Let us hope you speak true. The knights can see whilst we cannot." They turned right this time. "Are you sure this door can lead us to safety?"

Griff panted. "Aye, it will lead us to safety."

"But how? This city floats thousands of feet above the ocean.

Where does it lead?"

"The Door of Deliverance is an enchanted gate, ancient magick. It has delivered people into and out of this city for centuries. It will deliver us to freedom."

Stone groaned, reminding Alivia he was still there. "F-freedom."

"That's right, Gavin." Griff stumbled and nearly dropped Stone. He recovered. "We are on our way."

If we can use the gate, surely the knights can, too. Alivia needed reassurance. "How can we be certain the knights will not follow?"

"Unless they can read the ancient script of Vehayne, they'll be hard pressed to enter the door. There is a puzzle that needs be solved, one written by the citizens of the Old Kingdom."

"I've heard tales about the Old Citizens having a fondness for riddles," Alivia said. "'Twas said they could make keys out of sounds, words that when spoken unlock doors. I'd always thought it was a fairy tale, though."

"'Tis no fairy tale," Griff said. "The Old Citizens could craft locks and keys with precision. Many believe they used magicks to do so. But worry not, the knights will need to know how to read Vehaynian in order to solve the puzzle."

"Well then," Alivia said, "let us hope they are illiterate."

The knight whose voice boomed before echoed off the walls again. "Damn, a split in the path." *They reached the fork we just passed,* Alivia realized. "All right," he bellowed. "You three take the left tunnel, me and Wylomar will take the right."

Now only two follow, she thought upon hearing the orders. *Better two knights than five.*

Griff led them right and then right again. It was with that last turn Alivia noticed a faint, bluish glow emanating ahead.

The Door of Deliverance, she hoped.

"We are almost there," Griff said.

Oh, thank the gods. Alivia squinted the closer they got to the blue light, trying to adjust her eyes to something more than just black shapes in the darkness.

They reached a small, round chamber. Its brick walls stretched overhead and formed a low-hanging vaulted ceiling. Opposite from where they stood, Alivia saw the source of the blue radiance—a door——arched, with curving vine-like scrollwork. It was embedded amongst

218

the brick and rock of the fortress. A thin script, written in glowing blue ink, was carved into the door's frame—the long-forgotten language of the Old Kingdom.

Alivia could not read it. "What does it say?"

"'Tis the door's riddle," Griff said. "To open the door, we must solve the puzzle. It reads:

> *What is born to die, arises and flies;*
> *sleeps in death, but awakes for breath?*
> *What lays in wait, to alls debate;*
> *will conquer the knife, for eternal life?"*

A ghost, she thought. *No, that can't be right.* "What is the answer?" Patrick's hand fidgeted in hers. "You okay?" she asked him.

Patrick nodded. The boy looked exhausted.

Alivia glanced back at Griff. He was setting Stone down nearest the door, leaning him against a wall. He stood and focused on the ancient script. It illuminated him and the small chamber in hues of blue. "Open in the name of Adon," he suddenly shouted in a commanding tone, his voice echoing between the bricks of the vaulted ceiling.

Nothing happened.

"Open in the name of Adon," he shouted again.

Alivia glanced behind nervously, expecting the two knights to be upon them any moment. "I thought you knew the answer to the riddle?"

Griff spun around and fixed Alivia with a withering stare. "I do."

"Then why is the door not opening?"

A shout echoed off the walls from the tunnel. "A light, sir! Ye see it?"

"That's right," Griff thumped his forehead with a knuckle, "it's what the Vehaynians called Adon." He faced the door again and shouted, "Adonaiz!" Still the door remained closed. "No, that's not it. Odonaiz!"

Nothing.

Alivia heard the knight's armor clinking louder now. "Better remember quick, they are almost upon us!"

"Adonsyn! No—"

The rasp of steel being drawn sounded. "Ye rats are ours!"

Alivia moved her and Patrick closer to the door, ready to make haste when Griff recalled the right word.

"Adon'ton." Still nothing.

"Well, what do we have here?" a gruff voice called from behind.

Dread filled Alivia. The knights were upon them, slowly approaching with swords drawn.

One knight closed in on her left with a chuckle. "Looks to me we caught us a few rats."

"Hiding in their hole, no less," the knight with the gruff voice said.

Not here, she despaired, *we can't die here. I have to get Patrick to safety.* "What is the answer?!"

"Adon'tok," Griff yelled.

The chamber shook. Sand and dust fell from the mortar between the bricks. The glowing, blue script brightened, and the door began to rumble open—thus filling the area in a blinding white light.

The knights cried out.

But Alivia lifted Patrick into her arms and ran toward the intense glare. She heard Griff yell, "Go on ahead, we'll be right behind—" but his words cut off as she stepped through the door.

Everything went dark.

She hurtled forward, desperately trying to keep Patrick within her grasp as hot winds whipped around her. Her stomach tingled with weightlessness, and her skin burned. The sharp scent of ozone stung her nostrils. Patrick slipped, and she tightened her hug to keep him close. A dot of light gleamed ahead, growing. Patrick let out a timid squeal ...

... then they tumbled onto hands and knees in cold sand.

Alivia grabbed Patrick's hand and glanced behind toward the door, just as Griff came tumbling through. He fell to the ground, and after a second passed, Stone crashed down on top of him.

The two moaned. Griff got to his feet. He shook sand from his pants and hair.

Alivia saw that the Door of Deliverance looked the same on this side as it had on the other. It was embedded into a mountain—Mt. Shade, she presumed. The glowing, blue letters brightened and then dimmed. The open doors began to slowly close. They started to meld into the mountain and look more like rock and stone as they did.

No wonder the door has stayed hidden, she thought.

She helped Patrick get to his feet, and then got to hers. She surveyed her surroundings. All around were dunes of sand, beach grass dotted the landscape, and ocean waters lapped against a shoreline twenty paces away. Behind her loomed the mountain, but before her, just off the coast, loomed the Fortress of the Moon as it floated high above the ocean's black waters.

Thump. "Oof."

Thump. "Umph."

Alivia turned toward the clamor. The two knights were standing to their feet. They had followed them through! One of them went for Griff before he could draw the daggers strapped across his chest, while the other went for a longsword that had fallen from his grasp. Griff began to fight the one who charged him, fist to fist. The other knight picked up his fallen blade from the sand. He turned around to stab Griff in the back.

Alivia shouted and tried to warn him before it was too late.

33

VINCENT BLACK

A few torches had been lit, but most of the temple's sanctuary remained in darkness. Gabriel Lost entered and stepped over the remnants of a busted door lying on the floor. The room was empty; save two rows of pews covered in dust, unlit candles lining the walls, and a raised altar with two goblets and a plate blanketed in cobwebs.

He took another step toward the altar.

An obsidian dragon statue lay crumbled on the floor—its teeth, spikes, and eyes gilded in gold. Beneath it was a pool of blood and—

Jon Slade, Gabriel saw. The mercenary's body was pinned beneath the heavy weight of the statue. His cheeks were smeared in blood and his eyes stared tirelessly forward. "You should have left the sky city at nightfall," Gabriel told the dead mercenary.

A meager groan sounded from behind the altar.

Gabriel drew his blade. "Who goes there?"

"H-help ... me."

He stepped over Slade's feet and crept around behind the altar. "What's this?"

A pale, white hand reached up. "What took you ... Windstriker?"

Gabriel knelt and helped him to sit up.

Vincent leaned against his arms and chest, ragged and bloodied. His blond hair looked thin, and he wheezed between breaths. Deep gashes were cut into his breastplate, showing open wounds across his chest and belly, and both hands were slashed deep to the bone. Blood pumped out and ran across the floor. His skin was ghostly white from all the blood that had seeped from his body. He looked almost transparent—ethereal—and his face was lined with pain.

"Twould seem you finally managed—" Vincent coughed blood, "–

—to capture me."

Gabriel scoffed, then glanced up and scanned the temple to make certain they were its only occupants.

"This city is yours, Windstriker. Its powers ... *nggh* ... are yours."

"I want nothing to do with this accursed city. Where is Captain Steele? Where is—" Gabriel glanced at Vincent's neck. "Where is the Heart of the Dragon?"

"I am afraid ... the captain has acquired it." He coughed again.

Gabriel heard a gurgle in the cough. *The blood is in his lungs.* "Tell me," he said. "Where is he? I must stop him. I think he plans to misuse the city's powers. The kingdom may be in danger!"

"Worry not, Windstriker. For you are a horse of war, as I prophesied."

"You said that to me before." Gabriel remembered Vincent saying something about war horses when he dangled from Duke Lombard's cathedral tower. "What do you mean?"

Vincent raised his left hand—no longer disfigured with a scar of a dragon. "The captain," he said, "has taken my powers. He forced me to make the blood bond." He wheezed, coughing blood onto his chin. "And since he has taken the stone, I am beginning to fade. Yet ... I still have some of the gift within me. Take my hand."

Reluctant, Gabriel grasped Vincent's hand.

"I have shown you your past, and you have learned some truth." He squeezed Gabriel's hand with what strength he had left. "Now see ... and know all."

Gabriel's vision turned double. He saw Vincent bloodied in his arms, but another vision swirled before him: a stone courtyard. The flickering torches of the temple popped and crackled, but they grew fainter. Then another sound filled his ears.

Whack! The sounds of swordplay.

Gabriel's eyesight adjusted to the image. He saw two boys' wooden swords clack together.

"Hear, as well as see," he heard Vincent's voice inside his head.

Whack! Whack! "Come on, Gabriel," the eventual killer called, bringing his sword overhead to strike. "You can do better than that!"

Whack! Whack! Whack! "Be silent, you!" cried little Gabriel, returning the assault.

The boy watching the mock battle began to speak. "'Tis my turn," he said. "I'd like to spar with Gabriel."

The two stopped their skirmish and turned to the watching boy. "We just began," the soon-to-be killer said. "How 'bout you sit down and watch a while longer."

"It has been longer than you think. 'Tis my turn."

The boy was reluctant. He twisted the hilt of the wooden sword in his hands. "Fine!" He shoved the toy blade into the newcomer's palm, walked to a rack of sparring swords and kicked them over. "All you highborn are alike," he shouted. "You all think you're better than the rest of us. I am no peasant, mind you. I shall return!"

"Ignore him," little Gabriel said.

The newcomer nodded and readied his stance.

Where did he go? Gabriel wondered as he watched the angry boy depart.

"I will show you," Vincent's voice said.

For a split second, Gabriel thought he saw the cult leader in his arms. But the image vanished, replaced by two boys standing before him with wooden swords ready.

Whack! The new mock battle began, but Gabriel's vision swirled and the scene dissolved.

He felt like he flew as a bird-of-prey, chasing after the departing boy. His eyesight was as such, too. He looked down over the boy's shoulder and wind rushed past his cheeks. His eyes began to water.

The boy exited beneath a stone, arched walkway—a gate leading into and out of the castle's courtyard. He crossed a dirt road and moved under the shade of a tall oak tree.

Beneath its limbs, a shady figure leaned against its thick gnarled trunk. He wore all black—black boots, black pants, black cloak—with the hood of the cloak pulled up over his head. The face underneath was masked in shadows.

"Are they distracted?" the dark figure asked, voice deep and gruff.

The boy nodded. "Yes, sir. The soldiers are too engrossed in their training to notice us boys playing Knights. I do not think they have looked our way once."

"You do not think? If you are to be my apprentice, you know. Uncertainty is unacceptable. Uncertainty is death."

"I–I know," the boy's voice quivered. "They are distracted."

"Good." The man pulled back his cloak, and unsheathed his sword.

He handed it to the boy. Gabriel saw that the boy's hands trembled as he took it. "Calm your nerves. Assassins act swiftly, calmly. What is the Blind Brotherhood's motto?"

"Ours is the way of shadows, ours is the way of death."

"Good, remember it." The man glanced left and right nervously, then to the castle. "Do not fail me, you hear? Kill them both. Do this, and I shall accept you as my apprentice into the Blind Brotherhood."

The boy smiled, but the man grabbed him by the throat. His joyous face turned to fear as he clawed at the man's hands.

"Do not smile at me, boy." The boy gasped for air. He gave his head a strong shake to show he wouldn't smile again. The man let go. "Now begone, before someone notices you missing."

The boy nodded and turned to depart.

"And remember," the dark figure called after. The boy stopped. "Do honor to the Brotherhood, Jon Slade, and you shall be rewarded. We brothers look out for our own."

The image swirled and vanished, leaving Gabriel with the sight of Vincent cradled in his arms.

"I told you," said Vincent, "Slade is bad news."

Gabriel looked up to the crumbled dragon statue, and to Slade's motionless body pinned beneath it. "He is the killer? I do not understand ..." he focused back on Vincent. But when he opened his mouth to speak again, Vincent squeezed his hand and everything went dark.

Whack! Whack! His vision returned. He saw the newcomer lunge sidelong at little Gabriel with each strike.

The boyish Jon Slade came back to the bout, hiding something behind his back. "'Tis my turn," he told them.

The boys stopped their match and looked at him. "Go home, Jon," the newcomer said. "Me and Gabe have to pick up all those swords you kicked over."

"Just come back tomorrow," little Gabriel said. "We can play Knights again then."

Jon Slade gave a knowing smirk. "No, I think not. I'd like to take you both on. You two want to play Knights against me?"

The newcomer pointed his wooden sword at Slade. "You can't be serious. We'd kill you."

"Oh, I think not." Slade revealed what he was hiding—the sword–

—its edges honed sharp and its tip like the spike of a thorn. "I think it is I who will kill you." He attacked.

The newcomer yelled in alarm and tried to parry, but his wooden sword was cut in two and he fell to the ground screaming.

Slade turned to deal with his other armed opponent. Little Gabriel ducked and dodged the sword strikes, refused to parry with his toy blade. Until it was too late, and the steel cut into his face sending a spray of blood across the stones. Little Gabriel reeled to the ground and clutched his wounded face, howling in agony.

Slade went back for the newcomer, grinning wickedly. He stopped before him. Blood dripped from the tip of his sword. He lifted it overhead in both hands. "You highborn disgust me." He rolled his fingers around the sword's leathered hilt. "This'll teach you to think less of me."

"Please," the newcomer pleaded. "We never thought less of you, Jon!"

"Yah, right—" Slade swung the cruel steel down, and it tore into the boy's flesh producing a gut-wrenching scream. The newcomer lifted his hands to defend, but the sword sliced into them and his body until he lay motionless in a pool of blood.

The training soldiers were finally upon them. They tackled Slade and disarmed him. He screamed and kicked, punched and cursed. But they were stronger and they had him in custody.

Gabriel heard his old self—his boyhood self—sobbing while he held a face covered in blood. Then he heard one of the guards speak: "By the gods, the madness." Gabriel glanced at the soldiers. Three had Slade in their arms, while a fourth stood between them and the boy's unmoving body.

Slade gave up the fight. He began to cry.

"Why'd you do this?" the fourth guard demanded. "Do not start crying. You are a killer now and will be treated as such." He slapped Slade across the face. "Why'd you do this, boy?"

"Because," Slade shouted in the guard's face, tears streaking his cheeks. "He deserved it, that's why!"

The guard ignored the outburst. He knelt beside the dead boy. "By the gods." He released a heavy sigh.

Gabriel sensed the severity of the moment had finally sunken in. People throughout the castle were now gathering around—squires, men-at-arms, cooks, serving girls, stable boys, stewards. All, it seemed, but the lord of the castle.

The guard looked up, and spoke to anyone and everyone. "Inform the master," he said. Nobody moved. He stood to his feet and pointed at the slain boy's body. "By the gods, go tell the master. His son, Vincent, has been murdered!"

The scene whirled and dissolved into blackness.

Gabriel's focus returned, and he saw he was back in the dimly lit temple. He looked down at Vincent, who lay in his arms on the brink of death. "I ... don't understand. How could you—"

"Have died those many years ago?"

Gabriel hesitated. "Yes."

"Slade's sword did me in, I am afraid." Vincent gave a weak smirk. "But it was the dragon who gave me life once more."

"The dragon? But ..." Gabriel narrowed his eyes. "How?"

Vincent took a rasping breath. "When my father learned of my death, he brought me before his God—the dragon named Des'tok, who is Adon made flesh. The dragon became my savior. He blessed me with my life-spirit, but only for a time. It could not be permanent. Death is unavoidable. So it was made that I would live only while wearing the stone—the Heart of the Dragon. There were other benefits, too. As long as I wore the necklace, I could not be harmed. But now Steele has stolen it from me and wounded me grievously. 'Tis only a matter of time before my body fades away completely."

Gabriel opened his mouth to say something, but Vincent interrupted him.

"Gabriel. When the dragon touched me and brought me back from death, I saw a vision—the horses of war."

"What?"

"Last night when you dangled from Duke Lombard's tower, I saw the vision again ... one I had not seen since. It can only mean one of two things—that you are destined to save the Old Kingdom of Vehayne. Or to destroy it. Since Captain Steele has Sinfire, a prophetic blade wrought for destruction, I believe you are the one foretold to save the kingdom from the demonic gods of the Four Winds—the white horse. And there is something else. Since you are the white horse, that means," Vincent met Gabriel's eyes and reached up and clasped his hand. "I am your brother."

227

Gabriel's head swam. "Brother?"

"Yes, Gabriel. Brother. Another revelation revealed in the dragon's vision."

For the first time in a long time, Gabriel's memory started to resurface from the dark depths of confinement. "I remember," he said. "On that day ... we were playing Knights as we always did when the soldiers trained." Gabriel glanced at the motionless body of the mercenary. "Jon Slade. He was a friend we would play with. He had a temper, but he was skilled, so we allowed it so we could have another knight to spar with. Only ... something happened. He killed you and hurt me." Gabriel touched the scar across his brow. "And ... and ..."

He felt a warm tear streak down his cheek. He was remembering! All his life he had tried to remember a time before the Orphanage, but could not. And now the memory was fading. "For the life of me I can remember no more. I want to, but ... I cannot. It is so dark."

Vincent nodded. "Give it time. You shall remember all, eventually."

Gabriel shifted Vincent in his arms. *My brother.* He felt exultant and sorrow, hope and fear. *And now I must watch him die once more.* And there was another void that needed fulfillment. "I must ask ..."

"You want to know of our father?"

Gabriel looked to the ground for a long moment before answering, "Yes."

"Have you not pieced it together?"

Gabriel shook his head.

"Think of the castle from your memory. Think of the courtyard from your past—the stones, the oak, the towers."

"Castle Lombard," he said, realizing. "Duke Lombard. He is my father?"

Vincent nodded. "He is. And it is for him, our father, that I am here in this city."

"What?"

"Father has kept the Fortress of the Moon within his grasp for many years. But now, the corruption of the Four Winds has taken charge, and the city will likely fall into the wrong hands. It cannot be so." Vincent squeezed Gabriel's hand. "He implored me—do not let them use it—the power. If the city fell into the hands of one who would misuse the power, people will die." Blood came coughing up onto Vincent's lip. "You must ... stop him. Stop Captain Steele. Those who lust for power cannot control the power."

"Steele," Gabriel said. "Where is he?"

Vincent pointed toward the rear of the temple. "Out there."

"What—what's out there?"

"The city's *true* throne of power," Vincent answered. "From there, he can see all of the sky city, and control its course once activated." He coughed. "You must stop him, before his gods suck his living soul dry. They are an evil thing—his gods—demonic. The people have been led astray into darkness. You *must* become their light. You *must* bring them to the one, true God. Be their messenger. Become their prophet."

"Their prophet," Gabriel repeated.

"To defeat Steele," Vincent said, "you must know what has happened here ... to me. I must show you."

Gabriel nodded.

"But I must warn you: to do so, you will feel what I felt, see as I saw, think as I thought. You will become me in that moment, and it will not be an easy thing."

I must keep the city from falling into the hands of lunatics, thought Gabriel. *I must keep the kingdom safe.* "I understand."

"Good." Vincent lifted a hand to Gabriel's forehead, who felt his body stiffen as a vision began to overwhelm him. "See, brother, what has transpired here. See ... the price of freedom."

34

THE PRICE OF FREEDOM

Name. Me. SUCCESSOR!" shouted the Captain of the Knight's Order.
Vincent took a long, slow breath. "I shall never consent to the blood bond with the likes of you."

"No? I'll beg to differ— " he poised Sinfire behind his back with one hand, and its fire burned brighter, hotter, "—for I shall have your blood, and you will name me successor." Steele swiped the sword down, and a blazing, red flame spewed from its tip.

But Vincent held his ground, unconcerned. The flame licked at his skin and roared near his face, yet he felt no pain. For I have died once before and the stone protects me, he thought.

The fire extinguished.

Captain Steele sneered in disgust. "The diablerie," he said.

"Not diablerie, good captain— " Vincent raised his left hand, showing the couple his palm and dragon scar, "—a gift."

He flicked his wrist, mumbled a prayer beneath his breath. Green energy rippled from his palm and blasted toward Captain Steele. It hit him square in the chest and he went flying onto his back.

The surrounding knights rushed in on Vincent.

"Ah, I'd almost forgotten the loyal dogs." He spun on his heels, and hit them each with a surge of power from his palm, encasing the knights in a green, webbing cocoon.

They froze in place, stuck in their last movements with eyes blinking stupidly.

He turned back to face the captain ...

... and had the necklace ripped from his neck.

Captain Steele took a step back, the Heart of the Dragon clasped in one hand, his greatsword gripped in the other. "I know not why my sword failed," he said while staring at the necklace. "But I bet it has something to do with this stone."

Vincent fell back against the altar. His hands seared in pain. His chest began to re-open from old wounds. Smoke rose from his opening abrasions as if his body were filled with fire. The stench of burnt flesh drifted up.

The stone kept them at bay, kept the old wounds healed, but with it removed, the damage Slade had caused when he was a boy could not be restrained.

The pain, *he gasped, trying to scramble to his feet, disoriented.*

"Sit back down." Steele strode forward and kicked Vincent in the jaw.

Blind agony shot across his face. He slammed into the altar and then tumbled down its steps.

"What is happening to you?" Steele must have noticed all the blood, and the opening abrasions. "Get up."

Vincent tried to stand, his arms shaky beneath his weight.

Steele kicked him in the ribs.

The cuts across his chest opened wider, skin tore, and he gasped in agony.

The spell cocooning the knights released. They began to recompose themselves; readied their swords and circled around the altar.

Captain Steele strapped the greatsword to his back. He knelt beside Vincent and grabbed a handful of his hair.

This is it, *he thought.* The moment I have seen in my dreams.

Steele pulled back hard and leaned in close to his ear. "You disgust me, sinner," he whispered. "You and the rest of your lot. But mostly you." He flung Vincent's head down and stood. He paced back and forth. "Call your byrd," he demanded.

Vincent looked up.

"You heard me true," said the captain. "I know the dragon is the last Goliath. I know it must be slain to restore the windstriker's gemstone." A smile brushed his lips. "As a matter of fact, your good friend told me before one of my knights impaled him on a sword." His face grew dark. "Now, call your byrd."

Never, *thought Vincent. He shook his head, coughed up blood.*

Steele snorted. "I thought so." He reached down and grabbed a handful of Vincent's blond locks. Then he dragged him by the hair toward the rear of the temple. "Come, Victoria," he said. "'Tis time we summon a dragon."

She rushed to follow, as did the knights and men-at-arms.

Too weak to resist, Vincent let himself be dragged from the temple's sanctuary, through a hall leading to a set of arched double doors, and outside to where a cool breeze stirred and moon and stars filled the sky like a million witnesses.

Before moon and stars, Adon, *Vincent prayed,* it happens here. Give me strength.

Steele shoved Vincent bodily into grass and dirt. "I shall ask again, call your byrd."

Vincent glanced up. He looked past the captain and to the clearing behind the temple. There was a pond, behind Steele, and its still surface cast a perfect reflection of the starlit skies above. An arched bridge spanned across those waters with thirteen guardian statues placed between its rails. Each statue faced toward a great, stone throne thirty paces away.

The Seat of Power, *Vincent thought. It sat near the edge of a cliff and overlooked the Fortress of the Moon.*

A smirk touched his lips. It will be done out of free will. *He met eyes with Steele.* "Never."

The captain drew a dagger from his waist. "How about this, I open a few more wounds—" *he rolled the black blade over, letting the moon's white gleam flash from its steel.* "Now that your stone has been removed, I bet this knife will hurt you." *He stepped forward and nodded to his knights.* "Seize him."

Two knights grabbed Vincent by the arms and hoisted him to his feet.

Captain Steele put the blade beneath Vincent's chin. He prodded. Warm blood began to trickle down his neck. "Here is your choice, sinner: you can die, or you can call your byrd and it can die. Which will it be?" *He turned away, still holding the blade threateningly into Vincent's neck, and shouted,* "DO YOU HEAR ME, DRAGON?! IT WILL BE YOU, BEAST, OR HIM! WHICH DO YOU CHOOSE?!" *Steele looked back at Vincent with an expectant glare.*

Vincent hesitated. He opened his mouth to speak, but closed it.

Steele tsked. "So be it." *He jabbed the dagger in deeper. And deeper.*

The sharp pain stabbed at Vincent's neck, slow and stinging. He shut his eyes and suppressed a cry from escaping by biting his lip. He let the darkness take him, allowing the sounds around him to enter his thoughts: Steele's provoked breathing, knight's laughing and jeering, the young harlot's gasps of disgusts, the distant claps of thunder from over the ridge …

… and the sudden roar *of a dragon.*

Vincent opened his eyes, and saw Des'tok swoop down and land next to the Seat of Power in the distance.

A thin smile stretched across Captain Steele's lips. "So it will be him." *He loosed the dagger from Vincent's neck and sheathed the blade. Then he drew the greatsword from his back, and turned to face the dragon.*

He will die, *thought Vincent,* to save what is broken.

He glanced at his body, bleeding and lacerated, and then back at Des'tok. "The prophecy."

"Come to save your rider," *Steele shouted, pacing toward the byrd. His greatsword's black blade ignited in a red, fiery glow.*

Des'tok came forward to meet the captain. The dragon's scales drank in the pale moonlight in a captivating aura, its tail flicked wildly from left to right, and its triangular maw was clenched and full of strength.

"You attempt harm," Steele told the dragon, "and my men will kill Vincent." The captain moved closer, yet it seemed to Vincent he was staying back, mayhaps afraid of what he planned to do. When Steele saw he was met with no resistance, a triumphant grin stretched across his face. "Men," he said, "come roll this beast on its back."

Reluctant, the knights and men-at-arms—save the captain's blond harlot and the two knights holding Vincent—approached as commanded. Then, working together, they rolled the huge dragon over on his back. Des'tok made no sound, no noise of protest. He landed on his back with a loud thump, *and the men scampered away cheering and hooting. Several, feeling emboldened by their "brave" victory, taunted and spit on the dragon upon retreat. Though Vincent knew, had Des'tok desired it, each knight and man-at-arms could have tasted death in a flash.*

Steele drew near and stood by Des'tok's head. His knuckles were tight and clenched around Sinfire's hilt, while his chest heaved up and down in deep, heavy gasps. But the dragon's rose in a smooth, calm rhythm, eyes looking up toward the heavens in a still and quiet gaze. The goliath byrd seemed neither frightened nor angry, almost peaceful, almost sad.

The captain raised his greatsword overhead, its blade afire in a sweltering blaze. Then, before he swung the killing blow, he spoke, "You lay your life down, beast, for a crippled sinner. Fool byrd. Alas, your death is needed to restore strength to the stone. Strength that will now be mine! I will rule this kingdom, forever, from this seat of power—the Fortress of the Moon." His voice became a whisper. "Yet know this before you die: you have lost your life, and when the deed is done, I shall kill him as well."

Steele's Sinfire struck, and Des'tok's massive body shuddered as the flaming blade speared into the underside of his maw.

Vincent closed his eyes during the actual moment of the murderous deed. He couldn't stand to watch. Though, he'd seen the moment a thousand times before, in his dreams.

A blinding red light stung through Vincent's closed eyelids. The strength of the stone has been restored with the blood of a giant. *The intense glow throbbed and, after a moment, died away.*

Mean laughter filled the air. Knights and men-at-arms rushed forward to join their captain, swords drawn. They stabbed, spit, and kicked Des'tok's body, mutilating it.

Salt in the wound, *Vincent thought as he saw Captain Steele meet his eyes.*

The captain strode closer. Dark crimson dripped from his now black blade. "Tis time we perform the rites." He looked to the knights holding Vincent. "Release him."

They did as commanded. Vincent slumped to the ground too weak to stand.

The captain held the Heart of the Dragon up to his face. As he scrutinized the dark red stone dangling from its chain, an eager smile swept across his lips. "I can see where the shards fragmented." He stabbed the tip of his greatsword into the dirt before Vincent.

Vincent glanced up at the sword, seeing Des'tok's blood wash down its side. The price of freedom, *he reassured himself.* The price of freedom. The price of freedom.

"Here, my love," Steele said to his young harlot. "Hold this." He handed her the Heart of the Dragon. Then he knelt and untied the leather straps holding the three glowing gemstones to his greatsword.

With the windstriker's gemstones in hand, he stood and took back the necklace from his lady-knight. Then he toyed with them a moment—the three broken shards and the Heart of the Dragon—twisting and placing the small fragments into the larger piece like one would fit a puzzle. Before long, the fit was made, and a thin outline from where the break had occurred gleamed bright red. The glimmer faded, leaving the stone with no sign of having ever shattered.

Thus, after nigh two hundred years, the Heart of the Dragon was whole once again.

Captain Steele wasted no time. He unsheathed his dagger and slashed Vincent across the chest. Its demonic edge seared into his breastplate and opened a wider cut from shoulder to belly.

Vincent clutched his chest and doubled over. He cursed and screamed and blood spilled from the deep wound. The pain was excruciating.

Steele sneered. "Now, the blood bond." He knelt, necklace in hand, and wet the Heart of the Dragon with Vincent's blood. Then he sliced open his own palm by running it along the sharp edge of his greatsword, and grasped the stone.

It gave off a faint red glow, pulsated, then blast its radiance into the night sky.

The city quaked and basked in momentary daylight, then faded away to stillness and darkness.

Steele grinned, a wicked lust in his eyes. "My love," he said, "we have the key to the city."

The blood bond had been made.

Gabriel Lost touched his chest and hands to make certain he was still whole. The vision felt so real he thought *he'd* been the one cut open. He glanced to Vincent—his brother—bloodied and dying. "I ... there are still things I do not understand."

Vincent took a gurgling breath. "Go on, then. Ask."

"How did you make it back here to the temple? How did you escape Steele and his knights?"

"I crawled," said Vincent. "After the blood bond, Steele and his men succumbed to power lust. In his fervor the captain forgot of me." Vincent gasped for a moment. "Steele sits his new throne now, out there, mayhaps still trying to figure out how to activate the city."

"Activate the city," Gabriel repeated. He recalled the mural in the training grounds, and how it depicted a cannon beneath the sky city—Ragnarok. "So the Fortress of the Moon is a weapon, then?"

"Yes. But—" He grimaced, and blood gushed from the open wounds.

Gabriel put a hand over the cuts to try and stop the bleeding.

Vincent bit his lip, then continued. "They all think the Fortress of the Moon can change men's minds and souls. With—damn it—with the city's weapon. Ragnarok. They all think they can rule through fear." He wheezed. "But it isn't so. That weapon is not the ancient power, and tyranny is not the answer."

Gabriel scrunched his brow. "Then, what is?"

"The dragon," Vincent said.

"But Steele killed your dragon."

Vincent nodded. "I know." He grinned, red smeared across his teeth. "The prophecy has been fulfilled, Gabriel. He has died to save what is broken. Me. Though, truly, Adon has saved us all. We are all broken, in one form or another." He grasped Gabriel's hand, weakly. "Des'tok's sacrifice was the price of freedom."

Gabriel didn't understand, but he remembered the mercenary's words about the stones being strengthened with giants blood. "The Goliaths," he said, "each was slain to restore the stones. My gemstones."

Vincent nodded.

"In that way, the broken shards could be reunited with the Heart

235

of the Dragon. Right? Thus making it whole and allowing the Fortress of the Moon to fly.

"Yes, Gabriel."

"Why did you pit them against *me*?" he asked. "I thought you were trying to kill me, now I learn we are brothers."

"Ah, 'tis understandable you'd think as such. But the vision I had, of the two war horses, showed them warring for power with mankind as the prize:

They will ascend on the fortress in triumph and sorrow.
Slay the giants and send them to barrow.
One rides the black, and one rides the white.
For the horses of war will clash and they'll fight.

"You are the white horse, Gabriel. You bring triumph and nobility to the Fortress of the Moon. Steele, he brings nothing but calamity and sorrow. He is the black horse."

"But what does it mean?"

"It means that you are the only one who can defeat him. Steele is strong, and his gods have given him demonic gifts. Such as the greatsword he carries. If he has learned any words of power—Vehaynian words of prayer—then he'll be able to cast magicks as a prophet." Vincent let that sink in. "So I have been challenging you against the Goliaths. To make you stronger, and to restore the shards for the Heart of the Dragon." He squeezed Gabriel's hand. "In other words, I have been preparing you, brother."

"Preparing me? Preparing me for what?"

"For succession," Vincent answered. "The dragon has shown me that you are the next prophet."

"But Steele now has the Heart of the Dragon. It has been made whole. The city will fly straight and true." Gabriel let go of Vincent's hand. "*Steele* is the prophet now, and *he* has the key to the city."

That lunatic has the power to destroy the kingdom, he thought, *and your dragon allowed it.*

"Worry not, Gabriel. I have lured the Knight's Order here as well. Lukas Steele was destined to kill Des'tok, and you are destined to stop him. And you *can* stop him. Believe, and defeat the Dragonslayer."

The Dragonslayer, thought Gabriel. "He's still out there?"

Vincent nodded. "He is."

Gabriel peered down the hall leading out of the Temple of Adon, and to where Captain Steele awaited. He focused back on Vincent. "I am going to leave you here, for now." He propped his brother against the altar in a sitting position. Gabriel stood and unsheathed his shortsword. "Will you make it by yourself until I return?"

"Yes, I think so." Vincent clutched his blood-soaked chest. "Gabriel, I am d—"

"—I know."

A low rumble shook the temple—another of the city's tremors. Unlit candles lining the walls spilled over and onto the floor.

"It is happening," said Vincent. "Steele is activating the city."

Gabriel unstrapped his round-shield into his left hand. "Then it's time I take my leave and stop him."

Vincent looked up at Gabriel; a blue-grey gaze, sad yet hopeful. "May Adon guide you, brother."

Hesitant, Gabriel thought about that a moment: Adon. He never believed before. Ever. Not when he was abandoned to the world of men at such a young age. Not when he was deserted by his parents and left to an orphanage. Adon. He cursed them all, his parents, Adon, and the gods of the Four Winds.

Why did they all abandon me? He looked down at his brother, elated, yet uncertain. *But I'm not lost anymore. I have a brother now.*

He swallowed his pride and steeled his resolve. "Adon shall guide my blade," he said, "and be my shield."

Vincent smiled.

And Gabriel prepared to face Captain Steele.

35

DEPARTURES

Alivia Corwyn was desperate. She didn't have a weapon and the knights had followed them through the Door of Deliverance. One now fought with Griff, fist to fist, while the other had picked up his fallen blade from the sand. He was turning around to stab Griff in the back when Alivia suddenly had an idea.

She grabbed a handful of sand and threw it in the knight's eyes.

The knight staggered back, blinded, and rubbed at his eyes to see.

Alivia charged him and tackled him around the waist. In any other place, she wouldn't have had enough weight to bring the big knight down. But his heavy plate and mail made him clumsy in the sand. He toppled over with her right on top of him. She tried to pry the longsword from his grasp. They wrestled in the sand and fought for the blade.

Then the knight punched her with a gauntleted fist. The side of Alivia's face screamed in pain and the momentum of the blow sent her sprawling to the ground.

The knight scrambled to his feet, still gripping the longsword.

"Alivia!" shouted Griff. He broke free from his struggle long enough to toss her a slender blade. It landed in the sand three feet away.

Alivia rolled toward the blade—just as the knight's sword struck the sand where she had been a split second before. She picked up the weapon, realized it was the same blade Gabriel had given her, and got to her feet.

The spy crouched into a knife fighting stance.

"Watch it, woman," the knight said with a thick, gruff voice. "Ye might get hurt carrying that toy."

Alivia ignored him. Instead, she paced to her left and scanned for weaknesses. The knight had the advantage. The longsword gave him a greater reach, not to mention his steel plate and mail. The only places she could strike were the soft areas of flesh around his neck and face. Perhaps if she stabbed him under his arm where the armor left him exposed ...

"Defend this, woman!" The knight swung his sword down with all his strength behind the blow.

Alivia dove aside. She couldn't deflect a sword with a knife. As she got back to her feet, the knight turned and attacked again. Alivia jumped rearward and avoided the strike.

"Ah, come now, don't ye play coy with me." He staggered forward. The sand made him slow.

I must attack. 'Tis my only chance. She lowered her own blade, inhaled a deep breath. *Let him come.*

"Decided to play nice, did we?" The knight raised his sword overhead.

Alivia lunged forward. She stabbed the knight beneath the arm, in the ribs, repeatedly. First, shock registered across the knight's face. Then he fell to his knees and onto his cheek. Strangled gasps escaped his lips. Blood soaked into the sand.

Alivia took a step back from the dying knight, trembling. As a spy of parliament she had killed before, but it still never came easy. She wanted to curl up into a ball and disappear. But then she heard grunts and groans and remembered Griff. She turned toward the sounds of struggle.

Griff lay on his back, both of his large daggers strewn across the sand and out of his reach. The knight was on top of him with a slim knife in his hands. He was trying to force the point of the knife into Griff's face. Griff had his hands locked around the knight's, and through brute strength, kept the point of the knife an inch away.

But his strength was failing, Alivia could see.

So with quiet footfalls, she sneaked up behind the knight. With cautious movements, she brought her dagger around to bare on the knight's neck. And with fluid motion, she slit his throat.

Dark crimson spilled out and across the knight's chest. His body twitched and weak breaths sputtered from his mouth. Then he tumbled over and onto the sand as Griff pushed the body off of him.

Griff climbed to his feet. "Thanks," he told Alivia.

She nodded in reply.

Griff picked up his fallen daggers, slid them into the sheaths strapped crossways on his chest, and then went over to Stone. Stone was propped up against the dunes. Patrick sat beside him. Throughout the struggle, the boy hadn't once left his side. Griff reached them and knelt to inspect Stone's wound.

Alivia inhaled a large gulp of salt air. She looked up at the sky and to a full moon above, trying to calm her nerves. She had just killed two knights of the Church of Lucidus. A faith she did not necessarily believe in, but one she considered holy all the same.

What have I done? she thought. *I am a spy of parliament. Now what am I? A turncloak?*

Kingdom and Church often worked together—a government linked through faith in the gods.

Contemplating the ramifications of her "crimes," Alivia moved closer to the shore. Cold sand crunched beneath her boots as she walked. She stopped short of the lapping water and stared at the Fortress of the Moon as it gloomed over the ocean. It looked otherworldly. The tangle of blackened roots twisting beneath its foundation were warped and knotted. The city was darkened in shadows, with buildings and alleys illuminated here and there from pale moonlight. She recalled seeing the sky city this morning from atop Mt. Shade with Gabriel. It was just as ominous then, but now she had walked its streets and rested inside its buildings. She had much to report about when she returned to inform parliament.

A sudden red flash shone from the highest point of the sky city. It flickered and then disappeared.

Alivia stepped away from the shore. "Something is happening," she called over her shoulder to the others. Dread filled her voice.

"What is it?" Griff yelled back. He was cleaning Stone's wound, while Patrick held his hand trying to add comfort. Stone slipped in and out of consciousness.

She faced them. "You may want to have a look."

Griff recovered Stone's chest with his jerkin. He stood and came closer toward Alivia, stepping past the two dead knights on his way.

Alivia quickly wiped blood from the slim dagger against her pant leg. She tucked the blade away so Griff wouldn't be reminded of it.

When Griff stepped up beside her, she pointed toward the Fortress of the Moon. "There was a flash of light, a glowing red blaze near its peak."

Griff narrowed his gaze and stared at the sky city. "A red flash of light?"

She nodded.

He sighed and ran fingers through his unkempt hair. "Mayhaps the city is activating. But if that's the case, the question is," Griff faced her, "who is activating it?"

Who is activating it? thought Alivia. If it were Vincent, what intentions did he plan for the sky city? He was the enemy, or so she thought all this time. But Griff, Stone, and Dräkenkamp seemed different somehow. Then and there, Alivia decided not to return to parliament until she knew more about the cult and its purposes. Despite her efforts to see them as enemies of the kingdom, their actions spoke differently.

The Knight's Order, on the other hand, are fearful. They were supposed to be holy knights—the Church's knights—charged with protecting the Cardinal and the divine right of the gods. But instead they had hunted the disciples of Dräkenkamp, from Castle Lombard to here in the sky city. *The Church should not be involved,* Alivia thought. Castle Lombard's takeover was a security issue, a kingdom issue. Hence the windstriker's involvement.

But Gabriel is dead now, she despaired.

"Do you think it is Vincent?" she asked.

Griff shrugged. "We'll have to wait and see."

Alivia raised an eyebrow. "Wait and see? For what?"

"If it is Vincent," Griff said, still staring off toward the Fortress of the Moon, "the city will fly out to sea." He glanced over his shoulder to Stone and Patrick, then focused back on Alivia. "It was our intention all along to activate the city and remove it from those that vie to misuse its power. We want to save the kingdom, not destroy it. Though Stone still wants revenge for his boy, Logan." He sighed. "Vincent was confident he'd get Stone to see that revenge is never the answer." He glanced at Stone.

Alivia did the same. Patrick was holding his hand and staring at the sand with a sullen look.

The boy has grown attached to him, Alivia realized. *Could be that he loves him.*

"He won't get that chance now," Griff said in a choked voice. "His wound has festered. It is only a matter of time."

Alivia took a deep breath and turned back toward the sea. "And if it is not Vincent, how will we know?"

"Ragnarok will be uncovered from its earthy tomb. And then," Griff faced her again, but this time with a grim look. "All may be lost."

All may be lost. The words lingered in the air amongst them, echoing, though in truth the only sound to fill her ears was the sighing coastal breeze.

Alivia felt helpless. *I can only watch and wait now,* she thought as she gazed at the sky city.

Suddenly, a huge chunk of rock and roots crumbled from beneath the flying fortress and splashed into the ocean. Then a group of trees on the edge of the city broke away and plummeted. They took with them another tangle of huge black roots. A large area of rock calved off, revealing a gleam of metallic steel.

"What is that?" she asked.

Griff took a step forward. "No, this can't be." More rock gave way and splashed to deep depths below. Then, beneath the sky city, a huge cylindrical metal mass appeared. "Oh, Adon," he prayed, "save us all."

Alivia gasped. "Ragnarok."

A bright red ball of light ignited from the cannon's tip, growing ... and growing. It grew in size—nearly as big as the floating island—until it lit up the evening sky. But as Alivia and Griff watched, a fierce wind squalled off the coast, kicking up a sand storm. They covered their eyes, and Patrick leaned over Stone's face to protect them both. A shout filled the air, like a wolf's howl, only louder ... much louder. Then the flare of energy spawning from the cannon shot into the ocean.

A giant cloud of fire and smoke filled the sky.

All of the oxygen was sucked from the air.

The ocean's waters imploded on themselves.

And the next thing they knew, a shock wave was speeding toward them across a boiling sea.

"Run, Alivia! Run!" cried Griff.

They did. And as they ran at full speed away from the terrifying wave, fire seemed to rain down around them.

She reached Patrick and Stone, grabbed the boy, and darted for higher ground.

Griff stopped long enough to hoist Stone up, and together they scrambled for the small hill she and Patrick now rested on.

Boooom! An explosion knocked them all on their backs.

When Alivia came to, she heard the others moaning. She climbed to her feet, ears ringing, head spinning. Then she brushed sand from her hands and glanced around. It seemed like every bush and tree along the coast was on fire. Patrick let out a weak cry. "You okay?" she asked, helping him to his feet.

Patrick looked to her, startled. But he nodded and dashed over to Stone—who was groaning and grimacing from the blast. Crystals of sand had entered his wound.

"It's moving," Griff called. He'd gotten to his feet and was heading back toward the shore.

Alivia made to join him. "What was *that*?!" she yelled as she neared. To her disgust and astonishment, dead fish, dolphins, even a whale were washing ashore.

"A test blast," Griff answered. He pointed. *"Here it comes!"*

The sky city approached, flying closer and growing larger. Loose dirt and rock continued to fall as it flew. The unworldly shriek Ragnarok had made before was now a droning hum.

"Where is it going?" Alivia asked.

Griff shrugged. "I know not. But wherever it's going there is nothing good that will come of it."

In only a matter of minutes, the Fortress of the Moon soared overhead. Alivia watched it as it flew above. She could see a red fiery glow inside the cannon, Ragnarok, and feel a hot sulfurous wind surge against her face from its thrust.

The flying island ascended over and beyond the mountains, and into the heart of the Kingdom of the Four Winds.

"It flies southeast," she shouted.

"Southeast," Griff echoed. He rubbed his face and chin, distraught. "It–it's heading for Wyndsor!"

Alivia's eyes widened. "The kingdom's capital?" She couldn't believe this was happening. "If they destroy Wyndsor—"

"Then King Rikard, members of parliament, and the city's subjects are like to fall."

"They must be warned!"

"Warned? Warned how?" Griff started back for Stone. "And if they *are* told, how can they stop it?"

Alivia fell in beside him. "I do not know. We must do something!"

"What are *we* going to do? The Fortress of the Moon is a flying fortress. Even if we had an army, we'd never defeat the thing." They reached Stone and Patrick. Griff knelt to inspect Stone's wound again. "The sky city is too powerful," he continued, "and nigh unreachable!"

Alivia glanced at the mountain, and to where she thought the Door of Deliverance loomed. "That's not entirely true."

Griff followed her gaze. "Madness! What are you suggesting?"

"We still have access to infiltrate the sky city," she said, trying to reason. "Mayhaps we can use the door to get back inside and stop Lukas Steele from destroying the kingdom."

Griff stood and motioned toward Patrick and Stone. "There are only four of us. One's a child and you can see *he's* no good for battle. So that leaves just you and me ... against a score or more of knights and men-at-arms. 'Tis not possible!"

Alivia took a heavy breath, determined not to give up. "Where are your followers?" she demanded. "Dräkenkamp is more than you, Stone, and Vincent. I know. I have investigated your group for years."

Griff's face turned to anger. "Most of us died in the Fortress of the Moon," he growled, "at the hands of those choirboys."

Alivia looked at the sand. She should have realized that. "I'm sorry, I did not mean to insult. I just ..." tears began to streak her cheeks. "People are going to die. Innocent people." She sobbed. *I am so weak*, she thought. She had been strong for so long, a spy of parliament no less, and now she was breaking.

A touch embraced her, strong, warm.

"It will be okay," Griff comforted. "Sometimes, there's naught we can do. "He nodded toward the Door of Deliverance. "To go back through that door will mean our deaths. And we would gain nothing."

"But ..." another sob escaped her.

He embraced Alivia in a consuming hug. "I'm not letting you go back through. I'm not." Griff let go and drew her attention to Patrick Lombard. "The boy needs you. You must be the one to get him safely back to his father, the Duke."

Alivia turned her gaze to the boy, and let it linger.

Patrick met her eyes, full of innocence.

He is right, she realized. *I must see him safely to his father. He is my charge now, not Wyndsor.*

To her utter despair, the capital would be on its own.

Stone raised a hand and groaned.

Griff knelt beside him. "G-Gavin ... save your strength."

"The ... city flies," Stone's thick voice croaked. "The ... p-prophecy has been fulfilled."

"What are you saying, Gavin?" Griff clasped Stone's hand. "The city *does* fly. It flew past nigh a moment ago. What do you mean, the prophecy has been fulfilled?"

"Des'tok ... has sacrificed self and saved us all. The," Stone grimaced in agony. "The chosen warrior ... will rise from the ashes." His voice grew faint and his eyes drooped.

"Stay with us, Gavin," pleaded Griff. He rubbed Stone's brow and gently lifted his head into his hands. "The warrior will rise from the ashes. What do you mean?"

Stone opened his eyes. "The warrior ... the windstriker ... will rise and conquer false gods. He will reclaim the sky city."

The windstriker? Could Alivia dare to hope? "But I saw him die," she told them. "Lukas Steele killed Gabriel in the throne room."

"He will rise from the ashes," Stone said again.

Alivia recalled the manner of Gabriel's death, and how he was blasted in a fiery blaze. Last she saw of him, he was face down in blackness—ash—she realized now.

"Boy," Stone spoke, interrupting her thoughts. He raised a shaky hand and ran fingers through Patrick's hair. "I am sorry ... for putting you through all of this. You are a brave one ... truly." A tear fell across Stone's cheek. "You remind me of my own son. I will miss you, Patrick."

"Nooo!" Patrick cried. "Don't leave, Stone. Stay with me!"

"You speak at last." Stone smiled and wiped away the boy's tears. "I am sorry." The last breath sighed from his lips, and his hand fell from Patrick's head and thumped against the sand.

Patrick wept. His tears splashed into Stone's open palm.

Griff reached up and closed his eyes.

Now he sleeps, thought Alivia. She wiped away her own tears. Patrick stood and rushed to her. He threw himself against Alivia's legs, and buried his face into her, sobbing. She hugged him, comforting him.

Griff stood. "'Tis up to your boy now."

"Gabriel," she said, gazing toward the mountains and to where the sky city soared moments before.

Stone departs for the life beyond this one, she thought, *while the Fortress of the Moon departs for Wyndsor to destroy the kingdom.*

"Save us all, Windstriker." She looked down to Patrick embraced in her arms. "And I shall look after him."

36

BEAUTY & THE BEAST

His moist lips tasted of sweat and, oh, how she loved that taste on Lukas. He removed his lips from hers and gently released his strong embrace. *Too short,* thought Victoria, wishing she could stay in his arms forever.

Lukas sat down on the great, stone throne overlooking the flying city. She moved to stand beside it and rested her left palm on its rough backing. Opposite her, leaning against the throne as well, was the greatsword, Sinfire.

My prince's most prized trophies, she thought with a smile. *His sword and his bride.*

Though Lukas paid neither of them any mind at the moment. He was leaning forward in his seat, gazing out into passing darkness.

"She flies swift," he said.

Victoria glanced ahead. Wind brushed against her cheeks and fluttered through her hair like fingers. The moon's shining, white light illuminated enough land to see rivers and trees, hilltops and villages pass beneath as the sky city soared into the night. "Aye, she does," Victoria agreed. "Does that please you, my prince?"

Lukas grunted.

"Where is it we fly?"

"To Wyndsor," he answered. "That is, if the Fortress of the Moon is responding to my command as it should be." Lukas brought a hand to his bare chest and groped for the Heart of the Dragon.

He makes certain it is still there, Victoria noticed.

Lukas had taken off his plate and mail so he could feel the necklace against his skin. The men advised against such doings, but he told them all he felt the surging power of the stone better that way.

Oh, how he lust for power. And, oh, how he has attained it.

Though the sky city's powers did not bend so easily at first.

After the blood bond was made, it took Lukas several attempts to activate the sky city. There were no orders to follow, no listed commands. The Fortress of the Moon had not been activated in hundreds of years. So no one knew what directives to take, exactly. Lukas seemed to think the city would respond to his touch. He sat the throne behind the temple, yet nothing happened. After a while, his own men started shouting suggestions, which only angered him.

But finally, when all hopes seemed dashed, the city responded and Lukas claimed he could *feel* its presence; like he knew all of the city's inner workings and operations. "Not my touch," he had said, "my thoughts. Let us see what she can do."

The men all shouted their agreements, and he focused on firing Ragnarok. When it was done, they were in awe of the sky city's destructive force … Lukas especially.

The memory made Victoria wonder why her prince aimed to fly for Wyndsor, the kingdom's capital city. "What awaits us at Wyndsor?" she asked.

"The King." Lukas leaned back in his seat. "And parliament, all those subjects—sinners, the lot of them. We shall start our cleansing there. And what better place? Wyndsor leads this kingdom, and this kingdom is led into darkness." He looked up into Victoria's eyes. "Sin is a plague, my love. We shall cut away the bad growth from the Four Winds and *force* sinners into salvation."

Victoria swallowed, uneasy. "What if they won't convert?"

A smile swept across his lips. "Why, death of course."

Madness, tyranny, she thought, but she dare not say those words.

Lukas stood to his feet. "My quest is nigh at an end." He pointed. "We have arrived."

Victoria glanced beyond and saw that Lukas spoke true. The large capital city of Wyndsor loomed a thousand feet below; sleeping, mostly, though some fires were lit. Distant lights glimmered red and yellow through windows of buildings, mayhaps pubs and inns, and nightwalkers strolled along the streets. Guards patrolled their ramparts, of those surrounding the city and the castle on its high hill.

They look out over land for signs of trouble, she thought, *not to the sky. Though no doubt the Night's Watch is ought to have noticed us by now.*

"We shall make the Kingdom of the Four Winds bend to the gods it has so strayed from," Lukas said as he strapped Sinfire across his bare back. "And this flying city is the key." He pulled the sword belt tight across his chest, then touched the Heart of the Dragon. "I will put fear in their hearts, Victoria, starting with Wyndsor."

He moved closer to her and grasped her hands. "What say you, my love? Is it cleansing *you* want? Do *you* want to free this world of sin?"

His touch was warm and soothing, caring and affectionate. *Yet strong,* thought Victoria. *He protects me ... loves me ... provides for me.* "You are my prince, Lukas." She smiled. "I want what you want."

Lukas grinned. He moved in and kissed her again, passionate and with vigor as though it were their first kiss. Victoria embraced his lips eagerly, losing herself. *No other love in all the world—*

A sharp pain pierced her gut and a trickle ran hot down her thighs. Lukas let go, and Victoria found herself clutching a dagger—his dagger—protruding from her belly beneath the slender, plate armor.

"M-my prince," she gasped, falling to her knees. "Why?"

"Cleansing, Victoria." She made to grab for him, but Lukas took a step back, disgusted. "You have sinned against your gods."

"W-why?" It was all she could say. Tears fell unbidden, turning to sobs. Her heart was breaking, and it hurt worse than the steel in her stomach. "Why ... L-Lukas?"

"Why?" Lukas snorted. "You have given me your unwed love. A sin before the eyes of gods and men. Are you so blind?"

"But ... but ... you—"

"—me? I am the Bringer of Salvation. You should feel honored, you are thy first to be saved." Lukas knelt beside her. He moved in for a kiss, but instead touched his cheek to hers. "Rejoice, my love," he whispered, "for you are now forgiven."

Then he ripped the dagger out of her and wiped clean its blood-soaked blade upon her golden hair.

No, she thought, *you love my hair.*

He stood. "You truly are a beauty, Victoria."

And you are a beast, she realized as she took her last breath. A beast with a bite as sharp as steel, and as cold as a devil.

37

LUKAS STEELE

The once beautiful lady-knight lay unceremoniously at the captain's feet.

Only a demon would kill his own, thought Gabriel as he moved closer toward the city's Seat of Power. Lukas Steele's bare back faced him as he brooded over a sleeping city far below the Fortress of the Moon. Gabriel recognized the castle on its high hill, the city's twisting alleys and cobblestone streets, the manses and lesser-homes.

Wyndsor. He is going to destroy the capital.

He tightened his grip around his shortsword and readied his round-shield.

"Hey, who's this?" someone shouted to his left.

Gabriel turned to see a group of knights and men-at-arms looking directly at him. With longswords drawn, they stood next to the slaughtered dragon, Des'tok. The byrd was an unmoving mass of scales and teeth. Its leathery wings were torn and slashed, and dark crimson pooled beneath its head and neck.

"Tis that windstriker," one of the knights said, approaching.

"Hey, Captain," a voice like thunder boomed from Gabriel's right. When he glanced that way, he saw a towering, thick-set knight—standing head and shoulders above the men-at-arms—moving closer. "We got us a guest!"

Captain Steele turned around and locked eyes with Gabriel. His bronze breastplate had been removed and the huge greatsword was strapped across his back. The Heart of the Dragon hung limp from its silver chain. It dangled against the center of his robust chest.

"Ah, our man-in-black," he said with an amused grin. "I see that Lady Luck and the Old Knight could not finish the job. I should never have listened to those two. Omens and honors. Pah!" He spit, then stepped over the dead woman and slowly walked closer. He nodded to his men as he walked.

The knights and men-at-arms quickly formed a circle around Gabriel and their captain.

Gabriel knew he was outmatched in every sense. He had always survived on his wits as a trained windstriker, but mostly on the reliability of his enchanted weapons. They were his steadfast companions, getting him into and out of the most dangerous situations. But now, those companions were no more. That left him with nothing but a sword and a shield, and a crossbow with one bolt. What is more, he was hurt and tired with scarcely any strength remaining him.

He crouched and studied his opponent.

Lukas Steele stood opposite him, surrounded by soldiers ready to act upon his command. *And he is gifted,* Gabriel reminded himself. *He may wield magicks, since he has the Heart of the Dragon and might know some words of power. The captain is a prophet now.*

The thought was not encouraging.

He sheathed his sword. Then he grabbed the crossbow from his back and loaded the dark bolt.

"I'm so glad you could join us." Steele motioned to his men. "We can use a little entertainment before destroying Wyndsor. My men have grown restless, and they enjoy witnessing my newfound powers."

The knights and men-at-arms hollered their agreements.

Gabriel stood. He aimed the crossbow at Steele. "Why destroy the city?" he demanded. "I thought you were a sworn knight of the Four Winds?"

"A sworn knight?" Steele laughed. "I serve the gods, Windstriker, not this sin-filled kingdom. This city is corrupt. Its king undeserving. And let us not forget parliament … those greed-lusting harlots care not in their faith." He touched the Heart of the Dragon hanging from his neck. "Alas, I am merely honoring the Cardinal's dying wish: to cleanse the Four Winds of sin and bring its people back to the gods they have so strayed from."

"You will achieve naught through force, Steele."

"No?" The captain sneered. "But I think I will. For I am the Sword of the Gods! People are more like to bend their knees in fear than they will to kindness." He laughed, and his men along with him.

Gabriel tightened the pressure on the crossbow's trigger. "I have heard enough."

Steele stopped laughing. He clenched his jaw in disapproval. "You have heard enough?" He scoffed, then began pacing to Gabriel's right. "The windstriker has heard enough," he shouted to his men.

Laughter rolled throughout them.

He stopped and glared at Gabriel. "Hear this, *Knight Killer,* you want to save the city of Wyndsor, whilst I want to destroy it. I have the means, and you have naught but a toy sword and a bee's sting. So do not tell me when you've 'heard enough'."

Gabriel narrowed his eyes, focusing, aiming. "I'm tired of your clichéd speech, Captain." He fired the crossbow. The bowstring gave a dry twang and the bolt raced for Steele's neck.

The knights and men-at-arms shouted their warnings.

But Captain Steele only grinned. He waved a hand in the air, mumbled something beneath his breath. A shielding red energy shot from his palm and formed into a fiery wall. The bolt struck the barrier and burst into flames, disintegrating.

The magick wall dissolved. Steele laughed. "The viper is an eager one, isn't he?" He glanced at Gabriel's un-enchanted weapons. "But his venomous fangs have been removed. Good, I liked them not. You killed too many of my men with them." He touched the Heart of the Dragon. "Tis time we make this … complicated." Steele looked to his soldiers. "Stand aside," he commanded them. "I want him to watch as I destroy Wyndsor."

He raised his hands overhead and closed his eyes. The Fortress of the Moon began to rumble. A screeching howl pierced the air. And coming from beneath the sky city, a reddish glow was emanating— growing brighter and brighter.

Gabriel strapped the crossbow to his back. He readied his shield and sword. *I have to stop him. I am the only one who can!* He charged forward.

Loyal to a fault, the knights and men-at-arms stood aside and did nothing.

Gabriel reached Lukas Steele. He swung the shortsword down with all his weight and strength behind the blow …

… but Steele opened his eyes and sidestepped the strike.

252

He lost his concentration on firing Ragnarok, though, so Gabriel pressed the attack. The windstriker shield-punched and slashed, then found himself lying on his back from a searing blast to the chest. He rolled onto his side, breathless, and saw Steele walking closer. Red flames sparked and disappeared from his hand as he lowered it.

Behind the captain, along the sky city's edge, Gabriel glimpsed the reddish glow still growing brighter.

Damn, he cursed his luck. *Ragnarok is still charging!*

"I will make you bleed for your impudence," said Steele, now towering over Gabriel. "You should have felt honored to witness my power."

"Power?" Gabriel laughed, remembering Vincent's words, trusting in them. "You are naught but a pawn, Steele. You were destined to slay that dragon, and I am destined to stop you. For it is all how my brother has foreseen."

Steele scrunched his brow, puzzled. "Who are you, Windstriker?"

"Naught but a lowly orphan. *Captain.*"

The wind howled, growing louder and louder as though a pack of wolves had joined the cannon's shrieking song. Gabriel looked up at Steele, as *he* looked down on him. His chest throbbed from the blast and he felt too weak to stand.

I have failed, he thought. *Ragnarok is going to fire and destroy the city. I may speak bold, but I am too late. All those people will die.*

Lukas Steele raised a hand, while the other grasped the Heart of the Dragon. "I shall know who you are before I destroy you." He snapped his fingers and chanted Gabriel's name.

A sea of images suddenly engulfed Gabriel, surfacing from the deep depths of his consciousness—

Gabriel as a boy of seven, playing Knights with his brother, Vincent, in the stone courtyard of a castle. Their wooden blades clacked *together, and they laughed at their jests and taunts toward one another. Warriors and heroes, they pretended to be.*

"Gabriel, Vincent," a man called from an open window. It was their father, and the soldiers and servants called him m'lord and master. "Come inside," he said, "I have something I must show you."

Lukas Steele reached up and grabbed the hilt of his greatsword. As he took the blade into both hands, Gabriel tried to stand, but the flood of memories was too great, and they rushed his thoughts.

Standing before an altar in a hidden room in an abandoned tower. "No one knows of this place," their father told them. He set a box atop the altar and opened it. It was lined in black velvet, with a bloodred rock attached to a silver chain resting safely inside. Three broken shards lay next to it. "This, my sons ..." He held the rock up by its chain for Gabriel and Vincent to see. "Is the Heart of the Dragon."

The greatsword's black blade ignited in an incandescent red fire as the captain brought it overhead. With hatred in his eyes, he mumbled a silent prayer to his gods.

How father looked when he first saw Vincent lying dead in a pool of his own blood. He wailed in agony, before sending his son's killer to the dungeons below Castle Lombard. He went missing with Vincent's body, days on end, and servants and soldiers searched for their master to no avail.

How the killer, Jon Slade, escaped the dungeons and mysteriously vanished.

How Gabriel awoke to the sound of his father's voice. "Quiet," he whispered, "I must get you someplace safe."

Gabriel was kneeling now. He dropped his shield to grasp the shortsword with both hands. He heard the shouts of knights and men-at-arms, and the constant howling of the charging cannon. Too late. Not enough time.

It was raining on that day. Gabriel stood before the Orphanage and its headmaster, crying. "Don't make me stay here," he pleaded with his father.

"I am sorry, son," he said, "but this is for the best. You must be kept safe."

"Why, father? Don't leave me here. Please!" He fell to his knees, soaked, with water dripping from his clothes and hair. "Father, don't go!"

"I am sorry, son." He knelt before Gabriel and touched his brow. Darkness shrouded his thoughts and he lost consciousness. When he came to, a strange man

stood a few feet away. Gabriel sensed that he knew the man, but he couldn't place him in his thoughts. "I have wiped away your memory," the man told Gabriel. "You knew too much and I want you safe." He turned to leave, but stopped. "There will be a day when a man with one eye comes for you. On that day, give him those gemstones you have there in your pocket. He will want you to join the Windstriker Militia."

The captain was swinging the burning greatsword down, red and orange flames trailing like ribbons behind it.

The countless days spent training, learning to use the new weapons Owyn attached the three gemstones to. "They will give you power," he said, tapping his eye-patch. "Give you the advantage. Learn to use them."

"I will," Gabriel promised. He grew stronger and more confident every day. It gave him pride. He learned to fight, to sneak, to kill, how to be a windstriker. Then one day …

The greatsword neared … not enough time … he would die, and the city of Wyndsor along with him.

"Your father loved you," Owyn told him.

"My father? You knew him?"

"Yes, I did long ago." Owyn placed a strong hand on Gabriel's shoulder. "He told me, to tell you, that when the time came you should learn of your inheritance. That time is now."

"My inheritance?"

"Those gems," he said, "are gifts from your father. They belong to something greater than you can imagine. And one day, you will have to make a choice between preserving the power of those stones, or saving all of mankind. The choice, your father said, will be yours."

With what strength Gabriel held inside, he curled his fingers around the hilt of the shortsword. *To preserve the stones,* he thought, *or to save mankind.* He lunged forward …

… and stabbed the Heart of the Dragon. It shattered to pieces, just as the tip of Gabriel's blade pushed into Lukas Steele's chest.

The greatsword's flame snuffed out. The black blade fell from Steele's grasp and to the dirt. He looked down, stunned, at the sword protruding out of his chest. He opened his mouth to speak, but only blood gurgled out. Then he fell backwards and hit the ground with a *thump.*

The captain was no more.

The next few moments were chaos.

Knights and men-at-arms sent up a tumult of shouts and cries. Gabriel readied to face them all, readied to die. But they ran away, instead, losing sight of vengeance in order to save their own skins.

Confused, Gabriel whirled to see what they ran from. But there was nothing to be found. He saw, to his relief, that Ragnarok ceased to fire, had stopped charging altogether. The night shone pale from moon and stars and from the dim, glimmering lights of the city below.

Then he felt it, and knew why the soldiers ran.

The sky city was falling.

A tremor shook, more violent than any before. Gabriel scrambled to Steele's body and recovered his sword. He turned to make for the temple and his brother, but stopped as a sudden thought came to mind. He glanced back toward the captain's body, and to the shattered pieces of the Heart of the Dragon.

Afterwards, as Gabriel Lost stumbled and ran for the temple to save his brother, the Fortress of the Moon was crumbling back to earth. Returning to the land from whence it came, after nigh two hundred years of floating in the heavens.

38

HONOR & TORMENT

I shall dance with you 'til the end of days," the Old Knight shouted to the walking undead one. "And this flying city will mark our graves well."

His sword danced, and steel rang against steel as the Knight of the Witch defended. A swirling, black power encircled the combatants when their swords kissed.

The Knight of the Witch grunted, cold breath misting from its undead mouth. "Kill. Vengeance. Uhoooohhh!" It hacked and slashed, but the Old Knight parried and thrust. His sword went to the hilt in Brynden's gut, but the corpse felt no pain, felt no fear.

Sir Ellard unsheathed his sword from the cold one's stomach. "Abomination!" He staggered back a step.

"End this now," Lilyanna's voice whispered inside Brynden's thoughts. *"The sky city falls. Find the windstriker. Kill."*

"Kill," the undead knight groaned. It lunged forward to grab the Old Knight by the throat.

But Sir Ellard leaped rearward and slashed. The edge of his blade clanged against Brynden's gauntlet.

Locked in eternal combat the two fought on, one for life, one for death.

Then, through a thicket of pines behind Sir Ellard, the Knight of the Witch saw something move: the windstriker, running, into a temple. "Yeuuu!" it shouted, and it staggered past the Old Knight to pursue.

"Where do you think you are going?!" Sir Ellard swiped a cut at Brynden's neck to behead.

But the Knight of the Witch parried.

"He keeps you from vengeance," Lilyanna whispered. *"He keeps you from me."*

With that, Brynden felt rage. The corpse brought its attention back on the Old Knight in a fury and shrieked an inhuman scream. Then it hacked and slashed and stabbed and charged.

Sir Ellard evaded the blows, riposte and thrust.

But in that same moment, the constant quake of the falling city intensified. The ground beneath the Old Knight's feet cracked and the earth fell away beneath him. He fell with it. He shouted and grasped for something to stop his fall. Dirt slipped through his fingers. Then he managed to get hold of a root. The sudden halt in momentum jarred him. A pop erupted from his shoulder. Groaning, Sir Ellard tried to hoist himself up.

The root would hold. He might yet live.

It snapped and he fell over the edge.

Brynden lurched toward the edge and peered over.

Twenty paces below, hanging from a tangle of roots, was Sir Ellard. The Old Knight had caught another handhold! But he was struggling. His heavy plate and mail made it difficult to pull his weight up. The fall beneath him was a thousand feet, but lessening quickly as the sky city descended. After a third attempt to pull himself up, Ellard let go of his sword and took the roots into both hands.

The Knight of the Witch watched with curiosity, craning its neck to the side as it looked on.

"Lifebringer," Lilyanna said. *"Kill the windstriker. Avenge your brother and obey your queen."*

"Obey," the Knight of the Witch echoed. Then it reeled away from the edge and the fallen knight, and staggered toward the temple. With each step, grass wilted and death followed. As it stalked, rage consumed what once was human. It thought only of vengeance, and Lilyanna. Death. And Lilyanna. Brynden was no longer himself, wasn't aware of a self.

There were only his queen, hate, and the windstriker, who must be struck down.

39

RIDE THE WINDS

Vincent was unconscious when Gabriel shook him awake. "Quick," he told him, "the temple is collapsing."

"W-what?" Vincent grimaced in pain as Gabriel helped him stand. "What about Steele? What happened to Steele?"

Gabriel placed Vincent's right arm around his neck to help carry his weight. "Dead."

A loud *crack* sounded overhead and a support beam in the domed ceiling collapsed. It fell upon the altar the two brothers stood next to. Splinters the size of daggers sprayed into the air. Gabriel twisted and placed himself as a shield between the onslaught of shattered wood and his brother. The splinters assaulted his back, like arrows and knives from a score of foes. The debris bounced harmlessly off his thick, leather cloak—

"Aghh!" One stabbed Gabriel in the lower, left half of his back.

He reached around and clutched the large splinter, grinding his teeth. The wood went deep. With short, labored breaths, he yanked it from his flesh. Hot blood poured out and ran down his back. The stench of blood drifted up.

When he looked at the splinter, he saw that it was the size of his shortsword. Dark, red blood covered halfway up its shaft and dripped to Gabriel's feet.

"We have to get out of here," he said through gritted teeth, "before the ceiling comes down on us." He hoisted Vincent's weight onto his shoulder, started to move, but stopped.

"What?" asked Vincent, coughing. "What is it?"

"He is gone."

The obsidian dragon statue—with teeth, spikes, and eyes gilded in gold—lay crumbled atop a pool of wet crimson. But Jon Slade was missing. Splotches of blood trailed out the front entrance of the temple.

"There is no time," Vincent said, bringing Gabriel back to the dire situation at hand. "We must go. Now!"

Gabriel nodded. Then he half-carried, half-dragged Vincent toward the rear exit of the temple. Each jolt of movement was agony in his side.

They made it to the clearing overlooking the sky city, with its arched bridge and reflection pool, guardian statues and stone throne, yet barely. As soon as they exited the temple the ceiling broke and plummeted. The building collapsed with a thunderous crack.

"Where to?" he asked Vincent, as a huge dust cloud enveloped them from the destruction.

Vincent coughed and pointed. "The Seat of Power."

They started for it, breaking free of the choking dust.

Halfway across the arched bridge, a shrill scream pierced the air. "Yeuuu!"

Gabriel stopped and turned toward the noise. A dark figure emerged from the trees along the clearing's edge. Pale moonlight revealed its metallic garb—silver armor, dented and covered in dark spots, presumably blood, with a longsword held loosely in one hand. It staggered closer, dragging a foot and twitching wildly, and Gabriel noticed that the grass beneath its feet shriveled to grey.

Death.

The Knight of the Witch.

If that corpse touches us, we're dead.

The smell reached him first, thrust forward by the strange winds of the falling sky city. The stench threatened to knock Gabriel to his knees—a foul combination of the fetid bite of urine and the bloated ripeness of a corpse left in the sun. He fought his heaving stomach, wondering if this reek was as much a weapon of the undead creature as its sword and touch, meant to incapacitate its prey.

"Yeuu killed … my brother. Uhoooohhh!"

Gabriel would not succumb.

It was more than his life in danger.

With a shaky hand, Gabriel shifted Vincent's weight onto his shoulder and scrambled for the throne. The quicker movements shot a rush of pain to his back. He felt the open wound gush warm blood down his side. "Keep moving," he told himself.

They reached the throne. Gabriel sat Vincent into its deep seat. He glanced toward the undead knight and drew his sword. It was now only thirty paces away. He scanned for any options to escape.

Wyndsor loomed nearer, he saw, now big enough it seemed he could reach down and touch its rooftops. And its citizens were now awake. People cluttered the streets and roofs. Some ran for safety, while others pointed toward the flying city, astonished. The ground was coming up fast, and it would be only moments before the Fortress of the Moon crashed back to earth.

"Mayhaps we'll overshoot Wyndsor!" he yelled to Vincent. "But we might hit the castle on its high hill!"

Its lofty towers were approaching fast.

He whirled around. The Knight of the Witch now loomed twenty paces away.

"What do we do?" Gabriel asked, desperate. He didn't know how to kill something already dead. He didn't know how they could get off this falling island without doing the unthinkable.

"Do you believe, Gabriel?"

Gabriel looked to Vincent, confused. "What?!" He glanced up. Ten paces. Cursing, he drew his round-shield.

"Do you believe in Adon—"

The words cut short as the Knight of the Witch shrieked a guttural scream. Gabriel charged to meet the undead knight head-on...

... but a blur of flesh streaked across Gabriel's vision and tackled the Knight of the Witch around the waist.

"Our dance has not yet ended!" Sir Ellard shouted as they went sprawling to the ground.

Gabriel gasped and jumped out of the fray.

Ellard stood—defenseless without his sword, plate and mail—and grabbed the undead knight's wrist. Then, grunting and shouting, aging and dying, the Old Knight dragged the undead one closer to the edge.

The Knight of the Witch shrieked, groaned, and thrashed. Then it reached a hand toward Gabriel. "Noooo! Kill ... my brother. *LILYANNA!*"

As the name sounded from its pale, cracked lips, the two knights went over the edge and plummeted to their deaths.

Honor and torment, thought Gabriel.

"Brother," Vincent's voice sounded faint. "Do you believe … that Des'tok … is Adon incarnate?"

He is still going on about this?

Gabriel glanced toward the slain byrd. "Your dragon is dead," he heard himself say.

A fierce tremor suddenly shook the sky city. The Fortress of the Moon dropped twenty feet in the air from the turbulent quake. Gabriel felt his stomach lurch and turn over. He looked to see where Castle Wyndsor loomed.

"Damn," he cursed. "We are definitely going to crash into the castle!"

"Do you believe, Gabriel?" Vincent's voice was so calm, compared to Gabriel's frantic one.

Gabriel furrowed his brow, uncertain what to make of his brother's cryptic banter. "Your dragon is dead," he said again.

"Ah, but Adon can save us." Vincent smirked, blood still glistening on his teeth.

"No god has ever saved me."

"All you have to do is believe," Vincent went on. "Ride the winds."

Gabriel whirled around to see the sky city's edge. He couldn't believe what he was hearing. "Ride the winds? You mean jump! Are you mad?!"

The tallest tower of Castle Wyndsor came into view.

"Ah, hells. Brace yourself!" He threw himself atop Vincent.

The bottom half of the Fortress of the Moon slammed into the castle's tower, sending great chunks of stone raining down. The sky city jerked violently, but kept soaring past. Shouts and cries sounded from the castle below.

Gabriel stood. *We only hit the top of the castle,* he realized. *Wyndsor will survive.* He glanced ahead, and to the flat clearing of land behind Wyndsor. *But we won't. Once we crash down, we're dead.*

"Help me to my feet, Gabriel." Vincent held out an arm. Gabriel put it around his neck and together they stood. "What would *you* have us do, brother?" He coughed up blood. "Believe, I say, and ride the winds."

Gabriel took a deep breath. "Ride the winds, you say?" He walked closer to the edge, half-carrying Vincent to help him along. Once he was next to it, he peered over. A twinge of fear clenched his stomach. Land soared past three hundred feet below, coming closer by the second.

I have survived worse than this, he told himself. *Haven't I?*

He took another deep breath.

"Gabriel," said Vincent.

Gabriel looked to his brother, but didn't answer.

"Adon will save us."

Do I believe? Gabriel asked himself.

He thought of the Orphanage, his father, of the abuse and abandonment. All those times left forgotten, all those times filled with longing.

He glanced into Vincent's eyes, and the emotion he saw inside them reminded him of another's—the dragon's, Des'tok. Those jade orbs were otherworldly, and they left Gabriel confused; for he had seen an emotion within them, too, an emotion he had rarely felt, not even as a boy. It wasn't until he witnessed Des'tok's sacrifice that he understood what that emotion was, what it truly meant. He was seeing that same emotion now, in Vincent's eyes.

It was love.

With a deep breath, Gabriel answered, "I believe."

And the brothers leaped from the Fortress of the Moon.

Their feet weren't touching the flying city anymore. They were plummeting back to earth at breakneck speed. The wind whistled in Gabriel's ears as the ground came up fast to meet them.

"If Adon is going to save us," Gabriel yelled, "then now might be a good time!" Tears began to form at the corners of his eyes. He blinked them away, just as he heard the unimaginable.

The deafening blare of trumpets.

"I told you Adon would come!" he heard Vincent shout.

Gabriel looked to the sky. Moon and stars shone dimly, dancing in and out behind dark grey clouds. The Fortress of the Moon flew past to crash into the clearing, and another resounding blare of trumpets sang.

The sky parted.

A stinging, white light illuminated all the land as the heavens opened. Amidst the white—shining brighter than the rest—was a figure crowned in glory. It was a man, Gabriel saw, a man whose shape was morphing as he came closer. Wings sprouted from his back and his neck elongated like a crane. His legs merged into a tail, while his skin hardened into ruby scales. As he changed and grew, Gabriel saw he was no longer a man, but the most magnificent and terrifying image he had ever seen.

A bloodred dragon.

"Des'tok?" Gabriel said, though later he didn't remember saying anything at all.

The byrd went into a free-falling dive and raced toward the falling brothers. Gabriel spun his head to see where the land below him was, and then shut his eyes tight upon realizing the dragon would never make it in time.

But the impact never came.

When Gabriel opened his eyes, he saw he now stood on land. His brother lay withered upon the grass at his side. The dragon loomed protectively over them. Des'tok was a specter of his former self, with a streak of white light illuminating him from the heavens above. Gabriel tried to look at Des'tok, but his glory was too great to behold. Then the great byrd nudged Gabriel with his snout and pushed him toward Vincent. When Gabriel turned to his brother, he saw he was taking his last desperate breaths.

He knelt beside him. "Brother ... I'm here."

"Gabriel." Vincent smiled. "I knew you would jump."

Gabriel laughed, though he felt like crying.

"I knew you would ... believe."

"I do." Gabriel glanced behind at the dragon and then back to Vincent.

Vincent's eyes sparkled full of life, yet his body was failing him. He coughed up blood. "Now," he said with pain, "you must share what you have witnessed with the people of the Four Winds."

"You mean I must become a messenger to the kingdom?"

"Yes," answered Vincent. "Tis time you to take your place as a prophet." He raised a hand and Gabriel clasped it. "You told me before that you saw ghosts—visions of a slain boy?"

Gabriel nodded. "I'd never seen the visions before, or any, 'til my time here in the Fortress of the Moon. Why is that? What did I see?"

"You are a Seer, Gabriel. A *true* Seer. One who can see images of the past, present, and future. The sky city is steeped in mystery and magicks. It may have brought forth the gift within you."

"A Seer?" Gabriel didn't understand. "What do you mean?"

"To see visions as you have—ghosts, as you described them—means you have a touch of prophecy." Gabriel felt Vincent squeeze his hand, tightly, though it felt frail and weak. "A gift passed down from our father. Duke Lombard. When he sired you and I, he was a prophet at the time. He passed down part of the gift. You see?"

Gabriel narrowed his eyes. "I think so."

"Good." Vincent coughed. "Then go to him."

"Go to him? Go to who?"

"To father."

Anger seized Gabriel. "I'll do no such thing." *The man abandoned me at the Orphanage,* he told himself. *He left me in the hands of a cruel headmaster.* "Father dropped me off at the Orphanage and never looked back," he told Vincent. "I was only seven years old, yet he abandoned me to the world of men. When I fought Steele, I remembered. Why should I go to *him?*"

"Because," Vincent replied, "he is expecting you."

Expecting me? Gabriel opened his mouth to speak, but was at a loss for words.

"Go to him," Vincent said again. "Father *wants* to see you. He has words you must hear. Answers."

Gabriel was hesitant, but ... answers. "I will," he said reluctantly.

Vincent smiled. "I am glad." And with that, he sighed—long and slow—taking his last breath. The light left his eyes, and Vincent Black departed to the world beyond.

Warm tears splashed to the dirt beneath Gabriel. *I haven't cried since that day,* he remembered, *when father left me.* He wiped the wetness from his cheek, then reached up and shut Vincent's eyes. "Rest, my brother."

A voice boomed behind him, and only then did Gabriel remember the dragon. "Be at peace, my child. Your brother now rests in my kingdom."

Gabriel stood and turned around to face Des'tok.

"Be not afraid," the dragon said, yet he did not speak. It was in Gabriel's thoughts he heard him. "It is time. You now, are my prophet. Spread word of what you have witnessed here in the Fortress of the Moon."

Gabriel tried to look Des'tok in his eyes, but the light surrounding him was too bright and his image too great. And Gabriel tried to speak, but found only enough courage to nod.

"It is time," the dragon's immense voice boomed. "Time to rally the Army of Believers. Time to call forth the last of the dragons. They have stayed hidden too long. For you, my child, will help me restore the lost Kingdom of Vehayne. Together we shall save this kingdom from the demonic gods of the Four Winds."

Gabriel went to his knees, and still, he could not speak. He nodded.

Des'tok spread out his leathery wings. *Such strength*, Gabriel thought, *such majesty*. "It is for this task," the dragon said, "you have been chosen. Godspeed, my child." He flapped his wings to ascend back to the heavens, and as he flew, a flurry of fiery embers glimmered behind whilst he vanished into the sky.

And then, the dragon was gone.

Gabriel knelt beside his brother. But as he did, Vincent's body disappeared in a swirl of sparkling, red light. The body faded away, and Gabriel was left there alone. His back no longer ached, nor did his hand and broken rib. He reached around to touch the wound the splinter had caused, and felt it healed.

Miraculous, it was all that came to mind.

The Fortress of the Moon lay broken in ruins across the clearing, smoldering. Thick black smoke rose whilst fires raged. Buildings and streets alike were ablaze. And no survivors, Gabriel saw, were crawling away from the wreckage.

Wyndsor is safe, Gabriel thought. *Though the kingdom is far from it.* The Four Winds worship demonic gods and its leaders are corrupt. *I must be a voice for the people. I must restore the lost Kingdom of Vehayne.*

The first rays of dawn broke over the horizon. The moon and stars faded from view; the sky turning purple, then orange and red, then golden blue. Gold rays heated Gabriel's face.

Rally the Army of Believers, he thought, *call the last of the dragons.* He sighed. *There is something I must do first.*

"I must see my father."

EPILOGUE

Before the golden knight entered the Duke's tower, he inhaled deep breaths to calm his nerves. Once he was ready, he opened the door and began to climb a spiraling staircase that wound its way upward to the top floor. With each step, his steel-plate boots echoed off the stone walls, too loudly for his liking.

He reached another closed door. Torchlight filtered through its cracks. When he reached for the iron rung, he saw his hand trembling. He clenched his fist. *No,* he told himself, taking another heavy breath. *It is now or never.*

He had waited all his life for this moment.

Sighing, the golden knight opened the door.

A long hall stretched before him. Torches flickered smokily in their iron sconces. A large painting in an elegant frame held a Kingdom of the Four Winds map, showing all four regions in defining detail.

And a guard, he saw, stood watch before the Duke's bedchamber.

He swallowed the lump in his throat, hoping his voice wouldn't quiver, and entered the hallway. *Mayhaps the guard will let me pass,* he thought, as he gave a stiff nod and reached for the bedchamber door handle ...

... only to be blocked by the lackwit's longspear.

"Sir, no farther." The guard was a broad-shouldered man with streaks of white peppering his temples. "Duke Lombard is resting. He seeks no audience at this hour."

The knight lifted the visor on his helm to show significance. "I'm here on King's business."

"I manage the Duke's affairs. He seeks no audience."

"Is Duke Lombard aware that Wyndsor was attacked?" He couldn't take his eyes off the door. *I have waited all my life for this moment.*

"He is," the guard said. "A messenger bird was sent."

"I must see the Duke," he told the guard, growing impatient with him. "It regards a matter of utmost importance."

"He seeks no audience," the guard said again. "The Duke is not to be disturbed."

"Step aside, *guard*." He gripped the hilt of his shortsword, thumbing the notch where the gemstone used to be. There was no other choice. "Or I shall take that spear and—"

"—Samuel," the frail voice came from inside Duke Lombard's sleeping quarters. "Let the knight pass. I will take his audience."

Fear gripped the knight's stomach.

The guard named Samuel jerked his longspear upright and opened the door. He stepped aside. The knight gave him a smug grin as he stepped past and into the room.

"Samuel," said Duke Lombard. He was abed, the knight saw, sitting up with feather pillows behind his back. "Wait without. If you will."

Samuel was reluctant, but he conceded to his master's orders.

"Shut the door behind you."

"Yes, m'lord." The chamber doors clicked shut.

And before truly realizing it, the golden knight was alone with the Duke.

A dying flame crackled in its large, marble hearth in the corner. The drapes were pulled back from a window leading out to a small balcony. It overlooked the stone courtyard with the dead oak tree, as well as the rest of the castle. The room smelled of sickness and death, an over-sweet odor of sweat and decay.

When the knight brought his focus to the great, four-post bed, he couldn't help but stare at the feeble man lying under sheets of satin and silk. Duke Lombard was nothing he had ever envisioned: a strong man with a strong will, a healthy desire and a fierce ambition. Instead, the Duke was pale and clammy. A sickly man with no apparent life-purpose, who struggled to take weak wheezing breaths.

It was the Duke who spoke first. "Come closer," he croaked. "Knight of the Kingsguard."

The golden knight was hesitant, but he moved to the right side of the bed.

Duke Lombard raised a trembling hand. "Please, knight. Your helm."

The knight nodded. Then he moved his hands to both sides of the golden helm and removed it from his head. Brown hair fell across his brow. He set the heavy helm atop a dark mountain wood table, and turned to face the Duke.

"Come closer," he croaked again.

The knight knelt beside the bed. He met eyes with the man he longed all his life to meet.

"That scar," said Duke Lombard. "It never quite healed, did it?"

The knight shook his head.

"At last." The Duke sighed. "At last, you've come." He touched the knight's brown hair with a thin, pale finger and brushed it aside. "My son ... Gabriel."

Gabriel jerked his head away from the Duke's touch. Yes, he had come. But he wasn't sure if he had come out of anger or curiosity, or even of what he intended to do.

Where shall I start? "Vincent," he began.

"Is dead," finished the Duke. "I know."

"How do you know?"

"Vincent died long ago, I'm afraid, when the two of you were but mere boys." His father's voice trembled. "It is a day I wish I could forget, but a day I shall never forget. No more than I could forget of you, my son."

Don't you say that. He hated his father for abandoning him to the world of men, leaving him behind at the Orphanage. "But you did forget me," he growled.

"No, my son. Gabriel ... that is not the way of it. I merely—"

"—what? Wished me the best? Hoped the headmaster tortured me enough?" Gabriel hadn't waited this long to hear excuses and apologies. "Why did you leave me?"

"On that day. When Vincent was killed ..." Duke Lombard cleared his throat. "It was then I knew someone had learned of my secret, the one I'd harbored for so many years—that I was a Prophet, hiding the Heart of the Dragon."

Gabriel touched his golden breastplate.

"They came after the family," Duke Lombard continued. "By using a child."

"Jon Slade," Gabriel knew that now.

"Aye, Jon Slade. At the time, he was but a mere boy. But even then he was one of the Blind Brotherhood."

269

"The dark brood of assassins." Gabriel knew their lot well. Years past, he foiled an assassination attempt against the King's Hand. Three members of the Brotherhood placed into custody, and none would talk. "*We brothers look out for our own*," was all they'd say.

"He killed Vincent in the courtyard and tried to kill you, too." There was bitterness in his father's voice. "Afterwards, I had Jon Slade locked in the dungeons. I sent you to have your face tended to in the infirmary, and I took Vincent's lifeless body to the dragon."

"Des'tok," said Gabriel, reverently.

"Des'tok," Duke Lombard repeated. "Adon incarnate. The dragon gave him back his life's breath by making him a Prophet, and only by wearing the necklace would Vincent be free from his wounds. But he couldn't live long. The dragon said he'd survive long enough to name the next successor—the one foretold to restore the Kingdom of Vehayne." He gave Gabriel a solemn look. "You, my son."

Gabriel stole his eyes away. "Why did you leave me?" he asked again. "I will know why I was abandoned, old man." It was an easier question than the weight of restoring a shattered kingdom.

"When I returned to the castle," Duke Lombard said, "I discovered that Jon Slade had escaped from the dungeons. The Brotherhood look out for their own," he reminded Gabriel. "I had to get you somewhere safe. It was only a matter of time before they would strike again. So I took you to the Orphanage, to keep you safe, to keep you hidden."

Gabriel inhaled a deep breath. "But I was not safe. The headmaster was cruel. He tortured me."

"I," the Duke's jowls quivered. "I did not know. I am sorry."

"And if you had known?"

"I had to separate you and Vincent," Duke Lombard said, reaching out and clasping Gabriel's hand. "I had to keep you boys as safe as I could. The Orphanage was my only choice. It was the safest place until Owyn could come for you to join him in the Windstriker Militia."

Gabriel rocked back on his heels. He was beginning to understand. "And there was another purpose."

"Another purpose?" Gabriel remembered his inheritance then—the three broken shards of the Heart of the Dragon. "You had to separate the stone."

"That's right." He gave Gabriel's hand a weak squeeze, then let go. "Vincent had to keep the necklace, in order to survive. I gave you the broken shards. It was the only way to keep the Heart of the Dragon from being made whole. It was the only way to keep the Fortress of the Moon from falling into the wrong hands."

Gabriel sighed.

"But Cardinal Rominas," said Duke Lombard. "He learned of this."

Gabriel furrowed his brow, not understanding.

"The Cardinal seeks power, Gabriel, and he will stop at nothing to attain it." He shifted his weight to lean a little closer. "I devised a plan," he told him, "to have the sky city removed from the Four Winds. It would not do to have its power in the hands of a tyrant. So I had Vincent take this castle hostage and make two demands. One, the resignation of Cardinal Rominas. And two, the removal of King Rikard IV from a seat of power."

Gabriel was taken aback. "Why would you do that?"

"To lure the Cardinal and the Knight's Order," Duke Lombard answered. "They sought to capture Vincent and the Heart of the Dragon. So I gave them an opportunity."

"You are telling me the Highwinds hostage crisis was a ruse?"

"I am." Duke Lombard clutched his chest, face contorting momentarily. But the pain must have subsided because he eased his hand away and continued. "And by demanding the removal of King Rikard IV, I knew parliament would send their best windstriker to quietly deal with the incident."

Gabriel opened his mouth to speak, then snapped it shut, speechless.

"It was the only way to bring the Heart of the Dragon back together," said Duke Lombard. "To bring you boys back together. I told Vincent that when he took the castle, the gemstones would present themselves. And when they did, he should know that the man who has them is the one foretold to succeed him. That's when you showed up during the hostage crisis with the gemstones. So Vincent baited you to the Fortress of the Moon by kidnapping Patrick. His job was to prepare you, and the stones, for succession."

To prepare me. Gabriel remembered Vincent telling him the same. "But why draw the Knight's Order?" he asked. "It makes no sense."

"Captain Steele," the Duke said, "was destined to fulfill the prophecy. His presence was necessary."

"For Des'tok's sacrifice?"

"Yes, my son. For His sacrifice." Duke Lombard pointed a shaky hand toward the dark mountain wood table. "Open that drawer," he instructed. "There's a box inside, bring it here."

Gabriel opened the drawer and found the small wooden box . *So familiar*, he thought as he handed the box to his father. The Duke opened it, and Gabriel saw it was lined with black velvet. "Is that the box ..."

"... that held the Heart of the Dragon, yes." Duke Lombard reached inside. "It holds something else now." He pulled out a jewel-encrusted dagger—its hilt carved into the likeness of a serpentine dragon, its blade wrought of the same dragonglass metal of Vincent's dark armor. "This, my son, is the Blade of the Undying—a key to unlock the Army of Believers."

"The Army of Believers," Gabriel repeated as he took the dagger from his father and held it in his own hands. He turned the blade over, admiring its artistry and razor-sharp edge.

"Your journey will be perilous," Duke Lombard said. "But it is one you must make."

Gabriel nodded.

"There is a door," he told Gabriel, "beneath the sea. 'Tis magick-bound. No key shall open its lock ... save that blade you hold there in your hands. Take it to Maelstrom Island."

Gabriel was confused. "The island prison?"

"Aye," the Duke answered. "The island prison. Inside its walls and beneath its cells, the Army of Believers await the one foretold to release them from their chains. You will need their assistance to restore the lost Kingdom of Vehayne. But, I must warn you ..."

"Warn me of what?"

"Cardinal Rominas. He is dangerous." Duke Lombard grabbed his chest again, digging fingers deep into his clammy silken shirt. "He was the one who sent the Blind Brotherhood to kill you boys," he went on, grimacing. "He was the one who sent his puppet, Captain Steele, to acquire the Heart of the Dragon. He is the true threat, Gabriel. Don't you forget it."

"I–I won't."

"And one more thing." Duke Lombard's breathing was quickening, chest rising and falling in a rapid rhythm. "Your brother ..."

"Vincent?"

"No. You have another brother … Patrick."

Of course, Gabriel realized, *the boy is the Duke's son as well.* He nodded.

"Vincent used him to lure you, but also to keep him safe. Do you know what has become of him?"

Gabriel searched his memory. "He is under the care of a spy of parliament." he told the Duke. "Alivia's a friend. She will keep him safe."

"Good, see that he is kept safe. Patrick is so young."

"I will," Gabriel said. "I promise."

The Duke suddenly cried out in pain. He clutched his chest with both hands.

"Father!" Gabriel moved to help. "Are you okay?"

After a moment the pain subsided, and Duke Lombard looked at his son. "I am an old man, Gabriel, too old." Spittle glistened on his chin. "A curse of the Heart of the Dragon, I am afraid." He grunted again, this time throwing his head into the feather pillows behind him. "It would seem," he said through gritted teeth, "my time is nigh." Another cry sounded from his thin, blue lips, louder than before.

The chamber doors burst open …

… and Gabriel could do naught but stand beside his father's bed, and watch as the last of his life went out from those tired eyes.

"You!" the guard shouted. "What have you done?!"

It was then Gabriel realized he still held the jewel-encrusted dagger. He looked up at the guard.

"You murdering thief!" The guard charged closer, twirling his longspear in both hands.

I did not kill him, he wanted to say, but realized the guard wouldn't listen. He dashed for the balcony.

"Halt!" Gabriel heard the shout from behind—just as he jumped from the balcony and the guard's longspear soared overhead.

The wind whistled in his ears as he plummeted to the cobblestones a hundred feet below. Gabriel clenched his right hand into a fist, and shut his eyes. Then he opened his mind and called her name.

Shadowmere, the name whispered in his thoughts.

High above, grey clouds darted across a pale half-moon, whilst stars shone too dim to see clearly. Yet something dark broke through those high clouds, and dove, racing toward Castle Lombard. Gabriel opened his eyes …

... and was swept into the great wings of a massive byrd as black as the midnight sea. The dragon rose higher and higher, beating its dark, leathery wings till Castle Lombard dwindled to nothing more than a small anthill. When the dragon finally leveled off, the calming *whoop-whoosh, whoop-whoosh* of its flapping wings was all that filled Gabriel's ears. The chill air grew colder. The gentle rippling waters of Lake Blackwater passed slowly below as the two soared east.

Gabriel shifted his weight in the small hollow at the base of the dragon's neck. The jagged scales felt rough between his thighs. He took one last glance behind toward Castle Lombard, then brought his gaze to the dagger still in his grasp.

The Blade of the Undying, he thought. *Opens a door beneath Maelstrom Island—a door beneath the sea.*

No easy task, he knew. The prison housed the most vile of the kingdom's criminals and was heavily guarded from both ground and sea.

Gabriel sheathed the dagger in his swordbelt. Then he reached up and grabbed hold of a silver chain about his neck. He pulled on it, until a dark stone fell atop his golden breastplate.

The Heart of the Dragon pulsed in a dim, red glow.

Gabriel touched the stone with his right hand. An unusual scar now disfigured it—a fire breathing dragon with wings outstretched.

"Looks like I may need support," he told the byrd, and then banked Shadowmere north. To begin his story as a messenger to the kingdom, a Prophet of the Dragon.

The End

Continue reading Mark's stories. Check out Curse of the Terracotta Warriors: A Maddie Jones Mystery, Book 1!

Don't miss updates on new releases from Mark Douglas, Jr. Sign up for his mailing list at <u>www.Mark–DouglasJr.com</u> and receive a FREE Maddie Jones mystery!

If you enjoyed reading this book, I would sincerely appreciate it if you would give me a review! It only takes a few words, but it means so much. Thank you!

JOIN MARK'S NEWSLETTER

Want to be notified the minute Mark's next book is released? Sign up for his newsletter at www.Mark-DouglasJr.com to get cover reveals, exclusive content, and new release announcements. Plus, you'll receive a FREE Maddie Jones mystery for signing up!

ACKNOWLEDGMENTS

Writing a novel is no easy feat. And not one accomplished by the efforts of one man. *The Prophet of the Dragon* would not have been a reality without the support of a multitude of people—too many to name, but not too many to love. Nonetheless, I will try my best to name them all now. Thank you to ...

... all the readers of my early drafts: Hollind Douglas, Wayne Garrett, Ed Pipkin, Barbara Winters, Mike Gibson, Mike Ramsey, and the dozen or so members of the Panama City Writers Association and the Florida Writers Association. I kept writing because of your encouragement. I kept improving because of your criticism. If not for you, I would not have been prepared to handle the criticism of ...

... Bradley Woodrum. If not for his hard truths and crucial edits, I wouldn't have undertaken the brutal, but necessary, rewrites to make this the best story I could. Additionally, I'd also like to thank his father ...

... Rob Woodrum. If not for him, the cover of this book wouldn't be so stellar. And it really is stellar, isn't it? He made it easy for ...

... Pat Douglas, my brother and a fellow author, and my dad, Mark Douglas, Sr., who both gave me insight and direction as I used Rob's artwork to design the wrap of the book. Also, thank you to ...

... Mark Boss, a sage on publication. If not for him, this book would be a mess and nigh unreadable. Each of these individuals helped to shape *The Prophet of the Dragon*. Without them, this book would not exist. A similar book, perhaps, but not the book you are holding in your hands.

And, lastly, to my history students at Surfside Middle School. Over the past few years I told you all I'd mention you in my first novel. I keep my promises.

About the Author

Mark Douglas, Jr. finds inspiration from history and cranks it up to eleven. After graduating college, Mark went on to teach history to teenagers. Each day, the kids participated in a program called Drop Everything and Read. However, many of Mark's students hated reading, so he began reading aloud to them. Mark read Wednesday Wars, Treasure Island, and the Egypt Game. But the kids enjoyed Percy Jackson & the Olympians most. Several kids checked out the series from the library so they could read ahead.

Inspired, Mark embarked on his own storytelling journey. And a decade later, he's telling stories about the exploits of spunky teenage heroine Maddie Jones.

WANT MORE?

Love Mark's books? Join his mailing list at www.Mark–DouglasJr.com to be notified of new releases and giveaways! You can also hang out with him on Facebook, Instagram, Twitter, and Goodreads.

Want even more? Subscribe to Mark's YouTube channel or join him on TikTok to get insider information on his writing process, how he finds inspiration for his stories, and what it's like to be an author. He also creates fun games and challenges for his viewers.

Connect With Mark Online:
www.Mark–DouglasJr.com

Made in the USA
Columbia, SC
16 June 2025

59445034R00174